I0585375

# Profane Fire
## at the
## Altar of the Lord

# Profane Fire
# at the
# Altar of the Lord

*A novel*

## Dennis Maley

Jublio
Oklahoma City, OK

Copyright © 2018 by Dennis Maley
All rights reserved. Published 2018.
Printed in the United States of America

Jublio
Oklahoma City, OK
www.jubliobooks.com

*Editor: Kristin Thiel*
*Cover artist: Streetlight Graphics*
*Book Designer: Jennifer Omner*
Set in Blandford Woodland NF and Garamond Premier Pro

PUBLISHER'S CATALOGING-IN-PUBLICATION DATA
Names: Maley, Dennis.
Title: Profane fire at the altar of the Lord / Dennis Maley.
Description: Oklahoma City : Jublio, 2018.
Identifiers: LCCN 2017906097 | ISBN 978-0-9861158-4-4 (pbk.) |
  ISBN 978-0-9861158-5-1 (ePub ebook)
Subjects: LCSH: Europe—History—Fiction. | Deception—Fiction. |
  Messiah—Fiction. | Rome (Italy)—History—Siege, 1527—Fiction. |
  Historical fiction. | BISAC: FICTION / Historical. |
  FICTION / Humorous / General. | GSAFD: Historical fiction. |
  Humorous fiction.
Classification: LCC PS3613.A4354 P76 2018 (print) |
  LCC PS3613.A4354 (ebook) | DDC 813/.6—dc23.

Fire is never a gentle master.
—*Proverb*

# CHAPTER 1

Near Munchen, Bayern (Bavaria), *anno Domini* 1515

David had never faced a swindler as unprincipled as Beza. The devious impresario was a purse-thresher without equal. David idolized him.

"I pay two groats a day and I will make you famous," the burly showman crowed. His name was Beza. Grand, flamboyant, he could hold a legion of peasants in thrall. "You will be the most famous fool in Bayern."

The little man studied the face of the paunchy impresario, his leering grin, looking beyond his jowly features, deeper, into his mind. David often saw truth as something real, as if he were peering through a window. Beza's soul was open, nothing was hidden from the little man, all was revealed. The showman was eager to hire this dwarf David for his troupe of entertainers. Greed feasted in his heart. He had a single-minded lust for money. He was weak.

David waited, held his tongue, his patience learned alongside his father, long ago, near the fire. The snare was set. Beza was overeager, as ruttish as a bridegroom. *He will bargain against himself,* David thought.

Beza licked his lips and wrung his hands. The little man was silent. Now the showman turned away as if to reject any more bargaining, all the while his mind churned. This dwarf was special. He could read minds. The opportunity was too great. Beza twisted on his heel and punched his finger in David's nose. "No. Not you. You are the clever one. You will never be the fool. You want to earn. That's what you want. Yes. Then so be it. You will work on shares. Half for me. I will teach you to earn so you can make me rich."

*We will both be rich,* David told himself.

Beza was right about David Reuveni. The dwarf could never play the fool.

Beza's troupe of actors, jugglers and sword swallowers journeyed in colorful wagons over the rough and rutted roads of the German states, the heart of the ancient and decaying Holy Roman Empire, a confusion of fiefdoms, cantons and duchies reigned over by warlords, dukes, counts, landgraves and mongrel strongmen. Their travels took them from vulgar town to smoky village, over rushing streams and through dark forests teeming with wild boars, bison, stags, wolves, bears, and lions with no tails.

The troupe followed a regular, annual circuit. Each town feted the arrival of Beza's company with festivals. The locals clogged to the celebrations in square-toed wood or thick leather shoes, the men in hosen with bulging codpieces, the bare-armed frauen in linen smocks under fitted dresses that strained to contain copious breasts. The troupe performed theaters staged on rickety platforms that the locals erected on the edge of their towns. People came to see magicians, fire eaters, and dancing bears. But most wanted to lay eyes on the newest oddity, the dwarf that the showmaster Beza exhibited, a desert chieftain in flowing robes, a sheik of Araby. On holy days, he became a prince from a lost tribe of Israel.

Not a single German, whether peasant or freeman, churchman or noble, no one doubted the showman's claim as to the dwarf's heritage. David set himself to learning the *Oberdeutch* tongue. He trained himself in show skills. He juggled, he performed magic tricks using the cups and balls and sleight-of-hand. And when he dressed as a desert chieftain, he told fortunes and destinies.

He only had to pretend to be heavy of tongue. "The pin. I see... a woman?" Just as Beza couldn't hide his greed, the peasants and freemen were powerless to contain their private pain. They told him what they wanted to hear. A mother, a sister, a lost love. If the fortune David told them was fanciful enough, they paid extra. *Cabbageheads*, David thought.

He was scheming, shrewd, and caught every lie. No one could keep a secret from David Reuveni. In no time he made himself the best earner in the troupe. He gave Beza his share, and still his purse bulged.

After the plays, the German people lit candles, men, women, and children alike. Then they clomped their way back through the village gates and into town, singing hymns, shouting salutations to the magnificent troupe, thronging Beza, the dwarf in desert robes, and the other human oddities, who led them in a long, extravagant procession to the town's cathedral.

Beza strutted before the splashy pageant like a grandee, carrying a scroll closed with seals of lead. It was a document called a papal bull, and he bore it on a cloth of gold and velvet. All the priests and monks of the town, the *burghermeisters* and the town councilors, the teachers and the street urchins, the freemen and the peasants, even those who had stayed inside the gates went out with banners to meet Beza's spectacle.

Bells rang, church organs played, and the crowd, mobbing Beza, streamed into the town's cathedral. The entourage marched through high-vaulted naves lit by stained-glass windows that seemed to rise to the heavens, past statues of angels, saints, and *Judensau*, grotesque depictions of Jews taking carnal pleasure with swine. Beyond the nave was the apse where, under David's direction, the retainers erected a great red cross upon which, with much pomp and circumstance, Beza unfurled the banner of the Pope.

Then the selling and buying began.

Beza plumped down his bulk before the altar, atop a heavy money chest with iron straps and hinges. Behind him was a stack of indulgences—official church documents printed on parchment. Around him he exhibited his most venerated relics: the bones of saints preserved in silver and gold boxes, the body of an innocent baby killed by bloody King Herod, a feather plucked from the wing of St. Michael, a vial of milk from the breast of the Virgin Mary, and a shock of straw from the manger of Jesus.

Beza's hands flew, rolling the documents into scrolls, sealing them with wax, and collecting coins from the supplicants. No one ever unfurled the scrolls—as they were written in Latin, only the priests read them. From the night's haul, Beza would pay his troupe, himself and his expenses. The rest went on to Tetzel, the Dominican priest for whom Beza was chief lieutenant; then to bankers. The coins trickled up, all the way to the Pope in far-off Rome.

David's lips moved nearly as fast as Beza's hands. He beckoned them: "See ancient relics. Never before exhibited. Here for your pleasure. Buy an indulgence. Escape purgatory. Complete absolution!"

Beza smiled. His top moneymaker's skill grew stronger at every village.

The peasants scrambled to buy the indulgences for every mortal and venial sin imaginable: murder, adultery, burglary, blasphemy and false witness. Beza exalted his wares to every peasant, no matter how low, and he exacted even higher tariffs from freemen. The cost of an indulgence depended on the buyer's offense: five pfennigs for a peasant's incest, six if it were known.

To David, the German peasants were muttonheads, just as gullible as the Christian traders he'd met in his homeland. *Ignorance*, he often muttered under his breath. *How stupid can these peasants be?*

David Reuveni first stepped foot on the continent of Europe in the Republic of Venice, Bride of the Sea. The little man possessed a hundred carpets woven in Asia, and a few red stones. Venice was a republic and had no king. Neighboring states looked to a great religious leader, Pope Leo X, as their monarch. Italian city-states further to the south venerated the Pope but accepted the King and Queen from faraway Castile and Aragon as sovereign. David stared in open-mouthed awe at these strange customs of the Europeans and saw no obstacles to keep him from becoming as rich as a Sahib.

After a week in Venice, still clothed in his desert robes, David set his mind to acquiring common language. His desire knew no bounds. A fire burned in his gut to become rich and comfortable. That opportunity presented itself largely because, to his great good fortune, he had foretold the destiny of a priest soon after his arrival. He was a squat, black-robed cleric who had been eying David's goods.

"Your sins will be pardoned; your soul will fly from hell," the little man told the priest.

The cleric had a round face that made him look like the man in the moon, and owing to his impressive girth, he waddled like a goose. He was a gastronome of prodigious proportion and could fart at will. He often punctuated his oratory with great zephyr blasts from his backside. The rug peddler told him what he wanted to hear and the priest was deliriously happy. He bought all of David's carpets. The priest saw promise in David and his industrious nature.

The jovial Christian churchman was named Johann Tetzel and was fluent in David's native languages, Hebrew and Aramaic. Tetzel was a Dominican. Like all the members of the Blackfriars, he specialized in preaching. He lived in grandiose style in Venice but kept richly appointed apartments in many cities, having earned the right to live like a pontiff in service to both Pope and Empire as the Grand Inquisitor of Poland and the German States, places beyond the boundaries of the Pope's kingdom, north of the Alpine mountain range, in the realm of the Holy Roman Empire. But Tetzel loved Venice, and Venice is where his posterior took root. He refused to budge from La Serenissima, the Republic Most Serene, the City of Bridges, even if a cask of gunpowder exploded under his throne.

Tetzel's chief lieutenant was the freeman Beza. He was neither a priest nor in the clergy and was not a noble, but nevertheless, he had risen to the post of principal agent in Tetzel's organization. He was in charge of selling indulgences, and he wore out a lot of shoe leather. He was always on the road, and he went about his work as if he were killing rats.

The practice of issuing indulgences held the Roman Catholic Church in a stranglehold for three hundred years. In 1095, eager to beat back the advances of the followers of Mohammad, Pope Urban II promised complete and unlimited remission of all punishments—relief from the canonical penances—to any man who would serve in the military campaigns he organized. These were the crusades, Christian military ventures to Palestine that killed as many Jews as Turks and Arabs. Aragon and Castile, together known as España, had as recently as 1492 driven the Muslim invaders off the Iberian Peninsula—they called the Arabs "Moors"—and every Christian heart longed to restore Christian dominion to Jerusalem and the Holy Lands.

By the fourteenth century, popes were routinely heaping indulgences on the faithful in order to recruit their support for all sorts of Vatican-sponsored political and military maneuvers. Indulgences were granted to the religious orders as well—the black-capped Dominican preachers, the gray-capped Franciscans—which they could pass along as they saw fit to their members, or as rewards from the Order to the faithful.

The good friars and preachers bestowed indulgences on churches, hospitals, bridges, and collections of relics. Pilgrims received indulgences, and before long, clever lawyers found a way to give out indulgences to noble souls who were willing to cough up cash in lieu of participation in a pilgrimage or crusade. Dogma held that indulgences drew on a treasury of merit that had accumulated—somewhere in the firmament, the ether, or even farther above—out of the abundant sacrifice of Christ and the virtues and penances of the saints. The treasury was considered as boundless as Christ's love.

Credit belonged to Tetzel for the design of the indulgences that came next: indulgences for the dead.

Church doctrine said that indulgences applied only to sins committed by those still living. Tetzel argued that since purgatory was not located in heaven, it must logically follow that a soul detained in purgatory was enduring a worldly punishment. It was just a matter of classification.

Tetzel preached that contrition and confession were not the exclusive ways to shorten penance in purgatory, not if the sinner had an indulgence issued by the Pope. Therefore, preached Tetzel, and his words were trumpeted by Beza, his chief lieutenant—nothing more than an offering of money was required to purchase an indulgence which would free a loved one's soul from purgatory...an indulgence for the dead.

The Dominican also taught that an indulgence could apply to any given soul, to any sin, the mortal, unpardonable sins just as well as the venial, forgivable, worldly ones. Purchase of an indulgence by the most vile thief, murderer, or heretic resulted in an unfailing remission of sin, so said Tetzel. As he often told Beza, "Wenn die Münze im Kästlein klingt, die Seele in den Himmel springt." "As soon as a coin in the coffer rings, the soul from purgatory springs."

The Church never sanctioned Tetzel's teachings but neither did it disavow them. The leaders considered his sales pitch harmless puffery and rewarded him for roping in more followers. Pope Leo X promoted Tetzel to the role of Commissioner of Indulgences of the German Provinces for outstanding service to the Holy See. The peasants were overjoyed to accept Tetzel's assurances. As long as everyone agreed that the indulgence removed a mortal sin as well as its stain, for sinner and saint alike, everyone was happy. During Beza's visit, the local cathedral coffers always swelled with donations for the consecration of bells, chapels, books, and cemeteries.

And a veritable torrent of cash streamed to Rome, managed by a German banking family, the Fuggers. The treasuries of the Church overflowed, so much so that Leo demolished the Colosseum, which itself had been built nearly fifteen hundred years earlier by Titus, the emperor of Rome, using treasure looted from Jerusalem. Pope Leo X laid foundation stones for the grandest cathedral in all of Christendom, St. Peter's Basilica, to replace an ancient sanctuary over the grave of St. Peter. He earmarked proceeds from the sale of indulgences to its construction.

Tetzel's scholarship, logic and reason, lubricated by the free flow of cash, lifted the scales of blindness from the eyes of the Pope. He annexed purgatory to the domain of the Church. Beza's magnificence grew as more lost souls sprang from purgatory. The peasants paid Beza, Beza paid Tetzel, Tetzel paid the Fuggers, and the Fuggers paid the Pope.

Tetzel tendered payment in gold for the carpets. He asked David to help Beza, his chief lieutenant, transport a dozen of the rugs to another of the Dominican's homes in Verona.

"If the little man is worth his salt," Tetzel told Beza within David's hearing, "see if he can join you in the troupe. He might be a valuable asset in the indulgence trade."

David's heart jumped in his chest. In his rocky homeland, a man might work a lifetime and never earn the trust of his master, certainly not a great man like Tetzel. Fortune, he felt, was smiling on him in Christendom. In his dreams, he could not have envisioned a more advantageous situation. Yet he held fast to that rule he had learned from his father: never accept a man's first offer.

"I need a suit of proper clothing."

"Beza, if you let him go near a tailor, I'll have you flogged." Tetzel let fly a fart. "He's dressed the way I want him dressed."

So David wore desert robes. One overcast day, as David ushered a drab rabble of German peasants in an orderly line down the central aisle of the cathedral, ahead the penitent wife of a shoemaker dropped a five kreuzer coin in Beza's money chest. "One indulgence, please," she said. Beza thrust a parchment roll into her fist. She crossed her bosom with the document and then kissed it, pressed it again to her breast, and turned her grateful, tear-filled eyes to the firmament above.

David was about press the shoemaker's wife to hurry along, but as she turned, the poor soul was stricken by a fit of apoplexy. Her lifeless body hit the cold stone floor of the cathedral like a three-pound turd.

For once, even David was caught off guard. People shouted, one woman ran to the find the shoemaker. A curate scurried to tell the priest. David's eyes searched the nave of the cathedral for a place to hide. A place to hide his fear. Townspeople lugged her dead corpse away without ceremony. Beza, callus to the loss of a customer, continued selling indulgences.

*The man's an inspiration,* David told himself.

The priest met the shoemaker in the vestibule. His voice was stern. "The custom is to pay for a mass to be said for the salvation of the deceased," he instructed the widower.

"But she possessed an indulgence," the shoemaker said. "She still has it in hand."

That night, the bishop met with his council in secret. After deliberation, their decision was firm. "The shoemaker must pay for a mass for his wife's salvation," the council decreed. "The indulgence in her possession does not exempt her."

The cobbler refused. He complained to the burghers of the village, seeking relief from rigorous demands of the Church in the law of man. "I am her husband, and I did not authorize her purchase," he said. "If I must pay for a mass, I want my money back."

The bishop's council instructed a curate to keep an eye on the shoemaker. He reported back to them. "The husband has forsworn the mass. He's telling all the peasants in the town square." Thereupon, the bishop charged the shoemaker with contempt of religion. His curate took him into custody, flogged him soundly, and dragged him before a magistrate.

In due course, the shoemaker presented the indulgence into evidence, the one his wife had purchased, torn from her dead hand. "She bought it just before she drew her last breath," the widowed shoemaker plead through tears, his face caked with blood from the beating. "She died with it pressed to her lips. If a mass is necessary, then my poor wife was deceived by the Pope."

Against all expectations, the magistrate acquitted the shoemaker's charges. The law of man triumphed. Beza's sales tripled.

The night of the acquittal, David and a drunken Beza played at dice in a tavern, gambling with pious peasants and freemen alike, using indulgences as currency instead of the coin of the realm. The wenches that served beer to the little man were friendly and generous with their favors. Addled with drink, Beza neither noticed nor cared.

Farmers and burghers awoke the next morning with pounding skulls. They found their purses empty, slit open as if by a tiny blade. No one suspected the little man who secreted a dagger in his sash.

After the acquittal of the shoemaker, Beza could reach beyond the heavens. He often paid for merchandise with indulgences, the number of souls who thus sprang from purgatory varied depending on the amount of consideration supplied by the vendor. Even innkeepers and carriers accepted indulgences in exchange for services rendered, and they in turn offered them to their own purveyors when they settled accounts.

Then everything changed.

On All Saints Eve, 1517, in the German town of Wittenberg, a friar, Martin Luther, nailed a parchment to the door of Castle Church. He was a professor, but unlike most scholars of the Bible, Luther had actually read the New Testament in Hebrew and Greek. He was enraged that pious Christians were paying for gifts that God gave freely. His document outlined ninety-five reasons to renounce the power of indulgences.

Luther's parchment didn't flap quietly on that church door. Gutenberg's printing press let his supporters circulate three hundred thousand copies of his "theses" in the German states, where peasants were fast learning to read. His act of defiance struck the hearts of the German people as if it were a bolt of lightning. Popular opinion shifted. Beggars used Beza's indulgences to wipe their asses.

By the following spring, Tetzel's money machine had lurched to a halt. Beza and David found themselves, the troupe long ago scattered, riding a pair of ragged horses, alone on a lost and muddy road.

"How much farther?" David asked. He had allowed Beza to convince him that Portugal was the new place for them.

"Two leagues," Beza said. Two horizons farther.

Even as Beza stood in the saddle, he could only see a short distance into the dark forest. Dismounting, he told David, "I need to piss."

David dropped to the ground as well.

"Our prospects are bright in Portugal," Beza said. "The gold is abundant."

"We will buy many camels," David said. "I will teach you to ride."

Leaning on a forearm against his steed, Beza created a steaming puddle in the roadway that would rival that of a draft horse. With a healthy shake, Beza pushed his privates back into his codpiece. He stepped up and into his saddle and, without warning, snatched David's horse's rein into his beefy fist. He spurred his own horse to run and with a gregarious wave shouted back, "That's where you'll find me, little friend, Portugal. That is where the money is. Look me up if you get there."

Gobs of mud thrown from the hooves of the horses splattered David. One hand pulled his turban down to shield his face; the other still gripped his pizzle. He squinted from behind the loose fabric to see Beza disappear into the forest at the next hilltop. Beza was gone and with him, both horses.

A year earlier, David had been rich and comfortable. He had a strongbox full of gold and silver coins, and his purse was always full.

A moment ago, he had been lighthearted, afloat on a sea of promises of better days in Portugal. Now, he had even less to his name than when he escaped slavery in Arabia. He was on a forgotten road, his hopes dashed, his hand dripping piss. He was cold, hungry, alone, afraid. And ashamed of his fear—he should have anticipated that his mentor would bolt. Beza's shrewdness was what David had admired.

The pain of his failure with Beza was excruciating, ashamed that he was unable to prevent it. Even before his servitude, because of his stature, he had often been the object of scorn or ridicule. David had experienced this feeling before, the sense that he was disappearing, unconnected to the road, to the forest, to life. *Beza must love me, it cannot be the money.*

He trusted this lie he told himself, as barefaced and shameless as it was. He would never have bought the bargain "Beza loves me" if someone else was peddling it. He was fearful of the feelings that he knew would wash over him if he allowed himself to think about Beza's scorn, that his friend had forsaken him. He hid for a time in a copse of brush in the deep, black forest. The thicket shut out sunlight from every direction and calmed his disquieted mind. Solitude helped him think, helped him push down the fear.

He worshiped Beza. So he reasoned that Beza must have been driven to leave him behind by some force outside either man's control. He would will himself to have hope, hope that he could make his way to Portugal, hope that Beza would welcome him back, hope that together they could restore order. *I will go to Portugal and, together, Beza and I will again be in business.* He had no choice.

David was broke.

# CHAPTER 2

## Lisbon, Portugal

The woman's cries of pain could mean only one thing. Childbirth. It was the year 1500, *anno Domini*, and she was no longer in the flower of her youth, too old to be bearing her first child, especially one without a father, one she could scarcely support.

"Diogo, my sweet child," she said.

Her midwife told her, "People will be drawn to your son; he will be a great leader, a friend to all."

In her weary state, the woman couldn't tell. Was the midwife offering comfort? Or was she mocking her?

Diogo Pires and his mother lived in Lisbon, *Rainha do Mar*, the Queen of the Sea, a city that spills down a castle-topped hill, across an ancient Arabic quarter to the River Targus. Farther into the setting sun than even the capital cities of England or Ireland, Lisbon might have been the most exciting place on the face of the planet—colorful, vivid, vibrant, alive, and vital.

In this city of possibility, providence smiled on young Diogo Pires and his mother. She found a husband. Diogo's new stepfather was a bookseller named Costa. Publishing flourished in Lisbon. Sixty years before, Gutenberg, a German printer, had invented movable type. With his discovery, the age known as the Renaissance exploded as if it were a volcano. Literacy spread among the nobles and peasants alike, even in backward England, where *Le Morte d'Arthur,* an eight-volume history penned by an imprisoned knight, Sir Thomas Mallory, jumped off the booksellers' shelves. Books ceased to be luxuries. Art and science blossomed.

Costa cornered the Portuguese market on Latin and Greek editions of the New Testament, penned by a Dutchman named Erasmus.

"I fear I spend too freely," Señora Costa told her husband.

*"Estou-me nas tintas,"* Costa replied. "I'm in the inks. I'm rich. Your wish is law to me."

When the Señora engaged a tutor for her son, she believed that her midwife's prophesy was fulfilled. "My best and brightest," the teacher told his mother.

She embellished the teacher's praise when she boasted to other women at the market, "His tutor says he's the smartest in all of Portugal."

The "best and brightest" evaluation said more about his tutor's small number of students than Diogo's aptitude. But he was definitely a charming fellow. Lord above, the child grew to become a handsome thing. He approached manhood like a paladin, armed with a ready smile and an eagerness to show off his bright, snapping eyes and his curly black locks. Nimble and athletic, he moved in a "look at me" way that commanded attention of admirers and detractors as well.

Like many Jews, Diogo's parents converted to Christianity when Portugal expelled the last Jews and Muslims from the Iberian Peninsula in the decade before Diogo's birth. The Portuguese called them "Conversos" to be civil, but more often, by the epithet "Marrano." Never did a day pass when someone on the street did not call young Diogo "filthy Marrano" or "dirty Marrano." He was ten when he learned that "filthy Marrano" was two words.

He acted as though his mother were the true sun around which the world revolved. She bent to his will when he was attentive to her. She returned his love tenfold. She smothered him in affection, she doted on him, she overfed him. But she was overbearing, and demanded constant recognition for her boundless self-sacrifice. "Who bathed you when you fouled yourself?!"

A mere eight years before Diogo's birth, an Italian sea captain completed a voyage to "the Indies." He sailed under a Spanish flag, Portugal's rival, but his financial backer was Isaac Abravanel, an influential Jewish banker from Lisbon. The sailor was a Marrano from the Italian city of Genoa whose given name was Cristoforo Colombo.

Colombo thought his discovery had laid claim to the East Indies for Ferdinand, the King of Aragon, and Isabella, his wife, the Queen of Castile. Across the continent, people called the king "Ferdinand the Catholic" to avoid confusion. He was Ferdinand II in Aragon, Ferdinand III in Naples, and Ferdinand V in his capacity as King Consort to Isabella, a woman that was shrewd in a bargain. Terms of her pre-nuptial agreement mandated a co-regency with Ferdinand. Retaining divided thrones, their subjects called the shared dominion España.

The Spaniards called Colombo's discovery "the West Indies" since later ventures showed that Colombo had found neither India nor China. After the navigator's death, when Diogo was the tender age of six, Colombo's admirers Latinized his name into "Christophorus Columbus." How better to preserve a man's accomplishment than to give him a name in a dead language? Another Italian explorer, Giovanni Caboto, sailing for the scapegrace crown of England, could do no better than get his name altered to John Cabot in the under-bred English tongue.

Diogo acted in the street theaters when he could slip away from his post in the Ministry of Trade, a job he despised. He chaffed in his post, his influence was limited.

Portugal's obsession with exploration and maritime trade had begun with King Henry the Navigator, who never spent a day at sea.

Mamluk Turkmen had wrested control of Egypt and the Red Sea led by their warrior king, Timur the Lame, Tamerlane. In a class by himself, the campaigns of this man, the cruelest conqueror in recorded history, killed more than seventeen million of his enemies. After years of conflict between the rival Turkmen, the Ottomans wrested control of the trade route from the Mamluks. Any tyrant worth his salt would do what the Ottomans did next. They upped the tariffs, exacting outrageous duties from the European fortune seekers for access to the Suez, the shortest route to the spices of the Orient. The Red Sea was in a stranglehold. The extortion was particularly offensive to Portugal's good King Manuel, who, according to the Church of Rome, owned the eastern half of the earth. Portugal lost access.

Fortunately, with Manuel's backing, Vasco da Gama found a sea route to India around the southern tip of Africa. Along it, the Portuguese Ministry of Trade managed a network of trading posts and customhouses; encouraged the flow of duties, imposts, and merchandise from Asia to Lisbon; and facilitated trade and diplomatic alliances with China and the Persian Empire. Portugal, its monarch, Manuel, and his bankers grew fat on the import of spices, most notably black pepper.

Along with the voyages of discovery, Manuel generously sponsored many missionaries on their journeys to the new colonies. As each new bar of gold was stacked in the vaults of the exchequer, King Manuel became more pious.

The young king with the pointed black beard determined then to follow the lead of Ferdinand, king of Aragon, and Isabella, queen of Castile. They had expelled all the Jews and Muslims from Spain in 1492, shortly after taking the Jewish Abravanel up on his offer to finance Colombo.

Expulsion of Jews was not without precedent. Two hundred years earlier, after decreeing money-lending illegal, the English monarch, Edward I, Edward Longshanks, had expelled the Jews from Britain.

So it was not a fresh idea, but by all that is holy, it was such a corking good one on the merits alone. Peasants and nobles alike damned the Jews for causing poverty, disease, and religious apostasy. To hell with the Jews. Perhaps, Manuel thought, Ferdinand and Isabella would be favorably disposed to give King Manuel the hand of their oldest daughter, also named Isabella. As a proffer of his righteousness, he would expel the Jews, to flatter them, to do as they had done a few years earlier.

Manuel's decree ejected every Muslim from Portugal and stipulated expulsion for every Jew who refused to convert to Christianity. Departure by land was not an option. Any overland escape would allow the emigrants to remove too much in the way of goods. Jews and Muslims could only depart by sea, in ships specified by the king. Officials met twenty thousand Jews at the port of Lisbon, enough to sink the fleet. Clerics and soldiers sprinkled droves of the infidels with holy water and then, at the point of the sword, declared them Christian. They permitted no more than half the Jews to leave; those with babies had to hand them over to Portuguese to be raised as good Catholics.

Ferdinand and Isabella took proper notice of their neighbor's virtue. They consented to the marriage of their eldest daughter to the young Portuguese king, now popularly known as Manuel the Fortunate. Manuel's hope was that Ferdinand and the elder Isabella would soon meet their maker and leave open the door for unification of the crowns of Portugal, Aragon, and Castile. "Merger of the thrones is a laudable goal," Manuel said, and all his counselors agreed, so long, they hastened to add, as the nations joined under Manuel.

*De Espanha, nem bom vento nem bom casamento.* From Spain, neither good wind nor good marriage will come. Spanish wives were trouble. Indeed, one of the sisters, Catherine of Aragon, Queen Consort of England, had failed to produce an heir. Manuel the Fortunate's first wife was less fortunate. She died in childbirth, and Miguel, the child, died only days before his second birthday.

"A plan to unify the thrones of Portugal, Aragon, and Castile might still be workable," a counselor whispered to Manuel the Fortunate. "You need only to marry the next sister."

The key to unifying Portugal with the twin thrones of Aragon and Castile lay at the end of the path between a pair of ample thighs, deep in the womb of the second daughter, Joan. Unfortunately for Manuel the Fortunate, Joan's deceased husband had forever stained her name. He had often regaled his cronies with lewd stories of her peculiar episodes. He called her 'Joan the Mad.'

"You would have me wed Joan? The widow?" Manuel asked.

"Yes, Joan. A tender flower of feminine beauty. Marry her and sanctify your union by depositing some royal seed between her legs. How difficult can that be?"

"She's barmy as a loon!" Manuel shouted.

"That barmy widow's reproductive tract holds the prime claim to both thrones, Aragon and Castile, once Ferdinand and Isabella are dead," his counselors said.

"She's got a son. He inherits. He will be the heir."

"We have lawyers," the ministers argued.

"You rotten-faced shameless dogs. She has a son, and she's as nutty as a *cuenco de frutas*," Manuel said. "If she had her way, they would have stuffed her syphilitic husband and stood his cadaver in a corner." Indeed, Joan the Mad had refused to allow burial of her unfaithful husband after his sudden and unexpected run-in with the grim reaper during an outbreak of typhoid.

"Still, we have a strong case against the son." That was the larger problem. Manuel might unify the thrones but for what end? He had no assurance that he could pass the crown to his own heir.

"We will not hear another word of it," Manuel said, *pluralis majestatis*—the regal "we."

So Manuel rejected Joan and instead chose to share the sacrament of holy matrimony with Maria, his dead wife's younger sister. The coverture produced a masculine heir, but the affairs between

Portugal and its neighbor—España—were chilly once again because Joan the Mad had been rejected and had no husband.

Plans for a Portuguese union with Castile and Aragon collected dust on a forgotten shelf. The maritime expeditions of the Spanish and Portuguese easily eclipsed the puny efforts of the English, French, and Dutch. Their ships docked in harbors at the far corners of the earth. On the high seas, the two countries were head-to-head competitors. Violent clashes between Portuguese and Spanish merchantmen were becoming common.

To resolve the brewing conflicts between Spain and Portugal—no one wanted warfare on the high seas—the righteous king of Portugal eagerly agreed to a treaty urged on him by the Pope. Inked and plastered with lead seals, the diplomats laced the edges of the parchment with ribbons. The Church ceded the western half of the world to Manuel's in-laws, his antagonists, his neighbor Spain. Portugal received the eastern half of the earth.

None of the parties to the treaty had any reason to doubt the Church's worldly claim to all the earth—its lands, its seas, and the firmament above.

King Manuel was as giddy as a schoolgirl. He was positive that the treaty gave Portugal the better end of the bargain. His ultimate goal was not wealth or religious power but fame, immortality, and the key to everlasting life lay in the east.

"We have consulted all the natural philosophers and mathematicians," the king said, using the royal we. "They all agree that the Fountain of Youth is located in the Indies of the East. The real Indies, not those piteous islands stumbled upon by Cristoforo Colombo. Even court fools know that."

Diogo chaffed in his post in the Ministry; his influence was limited. He was never more than a midlevel functionary. Yet his mother credited all of Portugal's success to the efforts of her handsome son. "Think of the riches you are bringing to the Crown!" she crowed. "Think of the lost souls who are finding salvation at the cross!"

"That's all well and good, Mother," Diogo said. "But for all I care, let Aragon convert every heathen on the face of the earth. Let Castile fill its treasuries with gold. For my part, I will throw in my lot with King Manuel. He will be the most famous man on the face of the earth once he finds the Fountain of Youth. And I will be his champion."

"Fame? What does fame buy?"

"How can you say that?" her puzzled son asked. He could scarcely understand his mother's attitude. Diogo would never sacrifice himself for someone else's cause. Money could never satisfy his needs. *What prize could be greater,* Diogo thought, *than becoming the most famous man in Portugal? Or the earth?*

Because Diogo hated his job, he escaped as often as he could, usually to perform in street theaters. The handsome wife of the minister of trade, Diogo's boss, frequently attended those performances. Erelong it came to pass that none other than the minister himself discovered Diogo and his raven-haired wife in a compromising communion. She and Diogo were in the minister's cloakroom, the giggling lady with her bodice bunched at her waist, and he with his stockings at half-mast. She held the hem of her robes above her knee. Diogo, kissing her breast, had his arm squarely between her legs, his extremities obscured under the folds of her satin robe, when the minister burst in from the vestibule.

"My husband! My lord!" the startled lady cried.

"My Lord, your husband!" shouted Diogo. The minister's dagger seemed to spring from its sheath. Diogo felt the wall of the cloakroom at his back, the minister's shiny blade pressed into the flesh under his chin.

The minister rejected every reasonable explanation Diogo offered. Diogo froze in time as if he were a Greek sculpture.

An image raced across his mind, that of an ugly scar across his face. Disfigured! Such a fate was too horrible for the actor to imagine. Cold sweat ran down his back. His mind raced for a solution that would ease the chaos, some tactic to manipulate his situation, some way to feel safe. In that moment, the actor became a beggar. He pleaded for his life.

"My lord, please, spare me."

"Dress yourself, harlot," the minister scolded his wife, his voice rimmed with rage. "And ready your countenance to watch me let the blood of this filthy Marrano."

She burst into tears, bawling like a colicky baby, and throwing herself across her husband, she begged tearfully for his forgiveness.

Diogo felt the knife blade ease away from his neck, and without delay, he slipped under the minister's arm and bolted out of the vestibule and into the street, his elbows and knees pumping high to gain speed. He twisted to run backward so that he could look back at his path. He gulped, and his eyes opened wide. The cuckold was in hot pursuit. Worse than that, he was wielding a sword and gaining ground on the trespasser.

Diogo redoubled his stride and tried to breathe more deeply. He got a stitch in his side, and judged that the minister's efforts must be flagging as well. But his pursuer's footfalls grew louder. Diogo needed more than his role of interloper could give. He needed control. Diogo closed his eyes and allowed his mind to imagine a courier running from Marathon to Athens.

"Be with me, Pheidippides," he said, and in so doing, he caught a second wind. He sprinted over cobblestone streets, down twisting lanes, past warehouses and churches; he scrambled over red-tiled roofs and danced across the tops of walls and toward the river wharves lined with the merchant ships headed out to reap their fortune on the seven seas.

A line hung from a yardarm of a departing ship, out over the quay. Diogo grabbed the rope while running at full speed and then swung high, up and onto the gunwale of the ship, just as the little craft left the dock and rode away on the current of the river. Gripping the rigging for balance, he surveyed the busy quay with a broad grin.

Below him the florid minister bent double, gasping for air. The noonday sun glinted from the tip of his unsheathed sword.

The actor could now shed the runner Pheidippides. Diogo Pires, the triumphant actor, was once again in command. With a sweeping gesture, he took a final bow to the *estivadores* on the quay; then, rising, he waved a belaying pin in salute and fond farewell to his home and native land, shouting out the obvious to Portugal's minister of trade, "I won't be in on Monday!"

The little ship was a Portuguese caravel. The captain could crew the caravel with fewer than twenty men, but on this journey, he didn't even have the small number he needed. Lisbon had no idle hands. Since his ship was shorthanded, the captain eagerly signed on the late arrival, and Diogo found himself playing a new role, that of moon curser, hoping, along with his shipmates, to smuggle goods past the customhouses of the Mediterranean port cities under dark night skies.

The ship was adaptable to both sea and river travel. The work was strenuous. The actor had never toiled so hard at physical labor in all of his life. His skin looked broiled, and his hands were blistered raw.

The moon was bright in the sky as the captain sailed past Marseilles. Flags in the harbor warned of an outbreak of plague, so the captain sailed on. Reaching Tuscany, the caravel entered the Arno River to a port of call in Florence. He hoped to trade a small amount of black pepper for a large amount of wool.

Florence rivaled Lisbon in beauty, so Diogo jumped ship. He found himself in a center of European trade and finance and, until the Spanish and Portuguese started sacking up and carrying home the treasures amassed in their foreign conquests, it was Europe's wealthiest city, the birthplace of the Renaissance, the Athens of the Italian peninsula, and it was ruled by bankers, the *famiglia* de'

Medici, a Tuscan dynasty that founded Banco dei Medici—the Medici Bank—the largest and most prestigious banking house in Europe. The de' Medicis used a system of double-entry bookkeeping, so they never lost track of their accounts.

The members of de' Medici family were citizens, not monarchs, but as the wealthiest family in Europe, they assumed a place of power. The Banco dei Medici wielded fiscal and political clout that surpassed that of most sovereigns.

An order drafted on de' Medici accounts was as good as gold in every European capital. The family gave generous financial support to artists the caliber of da Vinci, Michelangelo, and Raphael. The monarchs of Europe were their most reliable borrowers and guaranteed their loans with their full faith, credit, and blood.

The Pope, Leo X, was a de' Medici. His chief diplomatic minister, a cardinal, Giulio di Giuliano, was also a de' Medici. Pity Giulio. He did not carry the corporate name because his parents never married. Assassins killed his father a month before Giulio's birth. Yet he was no bastard.

"Canon law allows the progeny of betrothed parents to be considered legitimate," declared Giulio's lawyers. This argument was all the more compelling because the brief was carried on behalf of *famiglia* de' Medici. Thus, the happy accident of his father's untimely death qualified Giulio to wear the robe of a Cardinal.

In his new home of Florence, Diogo met a political enemy of the de' Medicis, Niccolo Machiavelli. His patron, Soderini, had established a republic in Florence, but the aspirations of the republicans were dashed when the bankers, the de' Medici family, regained power after a brief hiatus.

No matter where he went, Machiavelli carried a notebook. "I can live without breathing," Machiavelli said, "but I must write." Diogo sensed that his new acquaintance cared more about showing others what he was working on, and thus had a kindred vanity. He charmed

Machiavelli into investing in a theater. "We will present some wicked comedies. The name Machiavelli will be known throughout Florence!" Diogo proclaimed to the writer.

The characters of Machiavelli's commedia dell'arte wore masks and played stock characters. The audiences flocked to the theater, temporary outside stages, to watch skits about the baggy-trousered Pantalone, a miserly Venetian merchant, but they cherished the masked Arlecchino. He was a black-faced, mischievous servant who delighted the crowd by punctuating his stage action with cartwheels and flips.

Diogo served as impresario, director, and principal actor. He usually played Arlecchino—the same character the French comedies called Harlequin—and armed himself with a club made of two slats. It made a loud but painless smacking noise when he hit the other players.

The exaggerated violence of the comedies never aimed to deliver an uplifting message, so of course, the audiences loved them. The size of the crowds was respectable, but when Diogo passed the hat for gratuities, the Florentines were strangely stingy, far less generous than the Portuguese.

After every performance, Machiavelli pressed Diogo for his share. "Don't be so selfish," he would scold.

"Your share? I should say!" Diogo raged. "I have made you famous! Who do you think you are?" But Machiavelli had a share of nothing because the theaters were unprofitable, and Diogo's vanity would never let him own up to the truth with the members of the troupe.

In short order, Diogo found himself escaping across a bridge over the Arno. Not far behind, in unflagging pursuit, Machiavelli's largest and meanest retainer brandished a red-hot poker.

"Tortured for my art!" Diogo told his supporting players. "I am too big for Florence! I shall depart this wretched place for Milan!"

Diogo's fortunes soured further in Milan. He had little influence with the Milanese and decided not to waste his time. *Pearls before swine.*

He hit bottom in Venice, the City of Canals. The mood of the Venetians was sour. They were in no frame of mind for street comedies. No wonder: just beyond the eastern horizon, across the Adriatic Sea, the Turks had advanced on and occupied the Baltic States, and were so close now that the Venetians sensed that they could almost look across the bay and into the Turkish latrines.

Fifty years earlier, with a well-trained and well-equipped army and navy, the Turks had captured the Eastern Roman Empire's capital, Constantinople, killed the last Byzantine emperor, Constantine XI, converted the grandest basilica in Christendom to a mosque, drove a stake through the heart of the ancient Roman Empire, and renamed the city Istanbul. In one brutal conquest after the other, steadily, one step at a time, they had expanded their control into the Balkans. The Turks were led by Sultan Mehmed II. Turks called him Mehmet el-Fatih, Mehmed the Conqueror! He was a follower of Mohammad who, with little opposition, had marched his armies into Europe's backyard. Now the Ottoman Empire stretched from the Balkans east to Turkey, then south, around the Levantine shore of the Mediterranean Sea, reclaiming half of the territories that the followers of Mohammad had once commanded before losing them to the Christian crusades. The Turks' grip on Palestine and Egypt choked off access to the Red Sea and denied passage to any merchant unwilling to pay an exorbitant tribute.

So Diogo's theaters in Venice played in empty piazzas. "The Venetians have no sense of humor," he told his company of unpaid artisans. *A talent such as mine cannot be appreciated here* was all Diogo thought as he swam across a canal to escape one particularly angry bunch of disappointed creditors. Pulling out of the filthy water, his mind was resolute. *I will take my talents to the Eternal City*, and in so saying, he shook his head like a wet dog. A grimy fog flew from his dazzling, onyx locks.

He worked his way to the Papal States, a loose confederation of Italian city-states in north-central Italy, ruled by Pope Leo X. Unlike most of the European states, Leo and the Church maintained a standing army. His soldiers fought and died as did the armies of the Christian monarchs, sometimes with them and sometimes opposed.

Diogo entered Rome by way of Ponte Milvio, a bridge constructed by Nero. He was unimpressed by face of the ancient city located on the Tiber River, inland at the central part of Italy's boot. Compared to Florence, Milan, and Venice, Rome was a dusty, backward, out-moded, and crumbling town, shrunken to one-twentieth of its size in the time of the Caesars. The dry climate, at least, pleased Diogo.

He had no interest in war or conquest. He hoped that Rome would be a place where art could be appreciated for art's sake, a place where he might gain authority in theater circles and shape the fame he so richly deserved.

It was Rome in *anno Domini* 1520. The actor could afford to have ideals, but little more.

Diogo was broke.

# CHAPTER 3

France, *anno Domini* 1520

Charles, the Duke of Bourbon, rode a massive warhorse onto the king's estate, the Chateau d'Amboise, on a spur of the Loire River, 150 miles southwest of Paris. The purpose of his journey, his advance letters had told the king, was to venerate the grave of Leonardo da Vinci, but that was pretense. The thirty-year-old hoped to secure an audience; he vowed to himself to recover some of his shattered dignity.

His steed was a pale, dappled gray stallion, one he had acquired in the north of France. The warhorse was impractical for travel, but Bourbon had lost most of his riding stock, seized by his creditors.

Across the charger's broad shoulder, Bourbon's retainers had draped blue velvet embroidered with the arms of the House of Bourbon: three golden *fleur de lis* bordered with red. Bourbon wore his finest day clothes too, an embroidered close-fit jacket covered by a matching robe that resembled the quilted garments worn under armor. His soft, flat-crowned cap was cocked jauntily to the left; a trio of feathers plucked from the tail of a pheasant careened to end behind his right shoulder. He dressed like a Florentine coxcomb, but his crisp beard, which fit perfectly within his high, open white collar, shaped the outline of a strong jaw. He had a stark, sturdy face and the piercing eyes of a warlord.

Bourbon stood in his saddle, shielding his eyes from the sun as he surveyed the tournament lawn. As he did, the sound of weapons clashing against one another fell upon his ear. A wave of emotions washed over the rider. Feelings swept him to another, faraway place, and he was inundated by horrific reminiscences of chaos and clangor, ecstatic days of conquest and glory, recollections of the best days of his life and hideous memories he couldn't erase: memories of war.

In September 1515, Swiss armies met the armies of Francis I, the king of France, outside Marignano, a war-ravaged village near Milan, in Lombardy. France's young king had one desire, and that was to seize Lombardy from the Swiss Confederacy—seize it back, in actuality, as the Swiss had stolen Lombardy from the French only a couple of years before.

The province of Lombardy was destined to have the boot of a foreign monarch on its neck, blessed as it was with fertile, militarily indefensible plains along the Po River. The broad land produced rich bounties of cereals, vegetables, fruit, vines, olives, cattle, pigs, and sheep. The river itself was an invaluable eastward thoroughfare to Venice and the Adriatic Sea. Milan, the principal city, was seductive, beautiful, alluring, and rich.

The loins of the boyish French king ached with carnal lust for the rich province.

At six feet tall, Francis was a head taller than any of his knights. He had sensuous brown eyes and thick lips. A pageboy haircut and a lack of facial hair exaggerated the size of his prodigious nose. His mother called him "my Caesar," but his subjects called him *le Roy Grand Nez*, "King Big Nose." The dreamy-eyed Francis was the most rapacious libertine in France, and his cousin Bourbon, five years older, was a close second.

The cousins devoted their days to poring over maps and topographies, moving figurines that represented armies and supply lines on maps the size of dinner tables. A night of drunken debauchery followed each day's planning session, and on the morrow, another day of preparation outlined schemes for the next adventure of the king. Some days they broke to play tennis or practice fencing. They sharpened their jousting skills in armor so heavy it took a dozen varlets to hoist the warriors onto their mounts.

It was during one of those play-acts five years earlier, when Bourbon was twenty-five and Francis twenty and in the first year of his monarchy, deep in the night, after a particularly grueling day of studying maps, tennis playing, fencing, jousting, and close-quarter debauching, that the intoxicated young king became seized with the notion that his life had no meaning if he failed to recover Lombardy from the Swiss Confederacy.

The enterprise was folly, and Bourbon spoke his mind. "Look at the map, cousin. Have you forgotten? The Alps!"

"Didn't Christ tell us the kingdom of heaven is like a merchant in search of fine pearls?" the king asked.

"Indeed he did."

"And on finding one pearl of great value, he sold all that he had to buy it?"

"To the death, then," the drunken Bourbon swore, and his fealty to the glory of the crown brought a smile to the countenance of his young cousin.

In due course, Bourbon increased taxes on his peasants in Auvergne, hocked all his worldly possessions to the banking houses of Paris, and began outfitting an army of infantry, archers, lancers, armored cavalry, and heavy artillery. Francis named him a general. Bourbon set engineers to finding a way to transport his division's armed men, provisions, and heavy, sledge-mounted cannon over the Alps.

The great prize was Milan. It was defended by the Swiss Guard and possibly even the armies of the Pope in Rome, all financed by the wealthy and powerful-beyond-measure de' Medici family.

Francis chose one division for himself and appointed Bourbon as general over another. Bourbon deserved the appointment, but rewards at the French Court rarely came because of accomplishment. Still, Bourbon had recruited the French soldiers himself and had personally paid a handsome retainer to a captain of a corps of German mercenaries.

Bourbon set engineers to finding a way to transport armed men, provisions, and heavy cannon over the Alps. Dazzled by the prospect of a share of the plunder, as well as an alliance with France that they hoped would rattle the Turks, the Republic of Venice begged to join the enterprise. France's treaty with the Turkman Suleiman remained a well-guarded secret.

With the mere threat that Venice might join the battle and assault from Lombardy's rear, Francis and Bourbon both believed that Milan was certain to capitulate.

But for a small standing army, the main divisions of France's force came in the form of peasant soldiers, led by a hodgepodge of rich and poor nobles, a picture of the agrarian French kingdom itself. Fiefdoms divvied up the greatest part of the realm. In exchange for their tenancy—their tenure, their titles—barons and lords, earls, dukes, and princes, peerage, so-called tenants-in-chief, every nobleman was obligated to supply knights to the monarch, as were bishops and abbots. The tenants-in-chief sublet shires to knights, and knights sublet farms to freeholders. At the bottom of the heap, held in check by shire reeves—sheriffs—were the peasants. They were bound to the land for the benefit of the knights as certainly as the sons and daughters of Adam, according to God's Word: "Because thou hast hearkened unto the voice of thy wife, and hast eaten of the tree, of which I commanded thee, saying, Thou shalt not eat of it: cursed is the ground for thy sake; in sorrow shalt thou eat of it all the days of thy life."

Every nobleman owed obeisance to the crown under the shire levy. The king had a right to summon the able-bodied: dukes with a thousand personal retainers, indigent aristocrats with noble bloodlines and borrowed swords. Heavily armed and saddle-sore cavalrymen rode into battle alongside poorly shod swordsmen, archers, and artillerymen, peasants who could only hope their valor would help them gain the status of a freeholder, a pension, or some concession from his lord.

Each manor equipped its lord with a retinue under the command of a knight. The brothers and sons of the knight fought in lighter plate armor and mail and on horseback armed with a crossbow or sword and lance. The knight himself rode a heavy charger and was clad in armor, *cap-a-pie,* head to toe, and armed to the teeth with lance and sword, a short sword and mace. He carried nothing but a small buckler shield for defense. Even his horse wore armor.

The battlefield was a place for noblemen to gain glory, an extension of the tournament lawn. Killing a yeoman never helped a knight gain magnificence. If he was victor in a just war (*jus in bello*), he captured as many knights as possible—therein was the glory—and he held them for ransom, leaving the pillage and plunder to his peasants. Only the English, the most uncivilized mongrels of Europe, set out to kill foot soldiers. They had never held chivalry in high esteem, and to them, widespread death in the ranks was an important objective of battle. Whether chivalry was respected or not, after the first charge, most battles collapsed into individual combats, the larger strategies and philosophies forgotten.

Sergeants among the foot soldiers fought with a broadsword behind larger shields, while the lesser-ranking fighters were archers, armed also with short swords. Spain was rich enough to outfit its infantrymen in armor. A French foot soldier was fortunate if he had a coat of mail.

A white cross on a field of blue adorned the sleeveless cotton mantle—the livery—of the members of Francis' standing army. Each earl and all the captains, knights, and foot soldiers in his retinue wore battledress adorned by the coat of arms of their lord. The colors, also displayed on shields, pennoncelles, pennons, banners, standards, guidons, gonfannons and streamers helped the sharp-eyed heralds who stood at the general's side, keeping score. Their job was to identify the individual fighting units and evaluate their contribution.

Each retinue also included camp boys to tend weapons and care for livestock, and older men to forage, cook and provide firewood. It was a cohesive unit of perhaps fifty members who were so suspicious of outsiders that they refused to fight in companies that included strangers. The problem of mistrust went all the way up the chain of command. A general commanded an internally divided army. The horse-mounted nobles were jealous of one another, could not be relied on to follow orders, and were in open contempt of the infantry.

The most important task for an army was the demolition of castles, which were built to project military power, not to provide refuge. The strategy was to lay siege and beat down the walls with artillery. Guns were awkward to deploy but given enough time, they reduced castle walls to rubble. A French cannon, "Mons Meg," fired a nineteen-and-a-half-inch ball that weighed 549 pounds.

To protect their castles, defenders sent out their own soldiers in force. When armies massed on opposite sides of a pitch, if events took their usual course, the soldiers waited patiently for their leaders to meet one another under flags of truce and negotiate a settlement. Both sides expected these showdowns to conclude with promises of compensation and a peace. No one wanted to attack first. Defenders held a huge advantage.

"We have the best artillery in Europe," Francis bragged. "We command seventy large bronze cannons and three hundred smaller pieces of ordnance."

"Our training is paying dividends, cousin," Bourbon reported. "Batteries can fire and reload four shots an hour."

"We must do better." The young king's loins ached for battle.

"And we will," Bourbon assured him.

"Try loading those guns with canisters of grapeshot, Bourbon.

Frenchmen were put on this earth to kill my enemies, not walls. Chivalry be damned until the Swiss are driven from Lombardy."

Bourbon yearned to lead men in a fiery cause. He was a ruler, appointed by the Almighty. If asked to lead an army to hell, dignity demanded that he measure the magnitude of his task and meet it, for his family, for France, for his king, and God.

In spite of his great wealth, Bourbon needed more manpower than he could muster in Auvergne if he were to slake his king's lust for Lombardy. He hired a company of mercenaries commanded by Fruendesburg, a grizzled old German whose face bore the scars of a hundred campaigns. He loved to brag that no man was his match in eating, drinking, fighting, or fornicating. His was a company of bloodthirsty German pikemen who eagerly fought for the highest bidder and were seldom out of work. He demanded payment in gold.

A century before, a nobleman never offered consideration in hand for services rendered by a peasant. But times change. Now the Crown had money for mercenaries, and it was better to be a mercenary than a peasant soldier. Capital in the hands of the peasants eroded the power of the shire levy. A cancer grew on feudalism.

It was the Swiss who elevated mercenary fighting to a profession. They called themselves the Swiss Guard. The Swiss Guardsmen were so cock-sure that they supplemented their income by train-ing German peasants in their methods. Fruendesburg's men called themselves *landsknechts*—men of the land—and they usually allied with their mentors, the Swiss, the men of the mountains.

Switzerland, a collection of largely German-speaking states called cantons, was a cornerstone nation-state in a larger confeder-acy that was popularly called the Holy Roman Empire. Its actual name was the Holy Roman Empire of the German Nation, a name that rolled off the tongue in the German language as Heiliges Romisches Reich Deutscher Nation. Although confederated for mutual support and defense, each canton guarded its independence.

Protected by a treacherous rim of mountains, the Swiss captains and their men-at-arms brimmed over with confidence. The Swiss cantons fielded the most powerful military force in Europe. Only the armored infantry of Spain had been able to stand against them.

The Swiss Guard shunned the guns that were beginning to show up in battle. They reinvented and deployed themselves in an ancient formation called a phalanx. Columns of pikemen marched forward, thirty men across the front, supported by ranks 150 men deep. Each man armed himself with a pike. These were eighteen-foot-long wooden shafts, cleverly tapered to avoid bending under the weight of a three-foot iron point on the business end. They carried a short sword on their left hip and a dagger on their right, but those who guarded the company flags, the double-pay men, the *doppelsoldners*, wielded a cumbersome, two-handed broadsword, fifty inches in length with a foot-long handle. With the pikes, the reinvented ancient Greek phalanx had great success in neutralizing armored cavalry, which had for years held sway on the field of battle.

Locked arm-in-arm, the phalanx marched forward, accompanied by fife and horn music and the beat of drums. Shields helped protect them from heavy sheath arrows launched from the bows of their rivals, and upon engaging the enemy, they could inflict great injury on the opponent merely by their superior reach. In defense to oncoming cavalry, the phalanx shifted into a hedgehog. The first rank supported the butt end of their pike in the ground behind them and presented a low wall of deadly points to a horseman. The second rank backed the butt under their foot and raised the point slightly. The third rank held their pikes at waist level and the fourth rank, at head level. As long as the formation held, the phalanx negated the killing advantage once held by mounted horsemen.

The mercenaries lived like lords, tough and jovial, indulging every vice. A day that was not spent fighting was frittered away with wine, women, and song, "Wein, Weib und Gesang." Theirs was a life of drunken revelry, the abandonment of all morality, allegiance, or duty to any cause other than either their company or debauchery. A life of wild abandon was a great improvement over the grinding toil, sorrow, and shame that feudalism settled on a peasant, even if the freedom from the soil lasted only a few short weeks.

In the countryside, the sheriffs considered that if a peasant wore anything other than olive drab or dirty brown, their clothing was an outrage to decency or, worse, a sign of resistance. In defiance, the Swiss mercenaries took to wearing flamboyant garb. The ostentatious colors of the mercenaries' clothing had practical benefit. On a field of battle, a soldier dressed in garish garments was a Swiss soldier's ally. He wore either a hip-length doublet, a jacket with no collar, and stockings to the knee. Vertical stripes of blue, gold, green, red, and orange covered his sleeves and breeches. The bands of the material gathered at the knees and elbows. The Swiss Guardsmen wore tight-fitting sheaths on their forearms and knee-high stockings on their legs and covered their pates with wide-brimmed, feather-festooned floppy hats.

The German choices in costume made the Swiss Guard look like rag pickers. The style of the landsknechts ran to multicolored stripes, puffed and cut, with overblown doublets above and high-waisted, two-layered hosen below. The inner layer of the hosen fit tight from the knee to above the navel. The second layer showed through vertical slashes in the top. Garters gripped the unslashed sheath that covered the shin. Their hats were wide platters made from wool, affixed to each pikeman's head by a *schlappe*, a close-fitting cap that extended below the ears, with a line of slashing around the crown. Feathers were optional but preferred. Most men covered their genitals with obscenely large leather codpieces, embroidered and festooned with jewelry. Fruendesburg never had a shortage of eager recruits.

The showy dress so outraged decency that it required a waiver from Europe's gloomiest monarch, Emperor Maximilian, the latest royal in the Habsburg dynasty, whose own life was mired in despair.

He never smiled, possibly because of melancholy, but a physical deformity contributed. His lower jaw jutted out so far beyond his lip that he could scarcely chew his food, that condition because of the Habsburg family's centuries-old practice of marriage between siblings. Unwilling to share his sadness, Maximilian decreed that the sheriffs were to extend lenience to the mercenaries in the choice of costume. "Their life is so short and bleak that great clothes are one of their few pleasures," the dour monarch said. "I'm not going to bereave them of it."

In attack, both the Swiss and German phalanxes looked for all the world like manic rainbow-painted porcupines.

The young cousins entered Lombardy from an Alpine passage with no roads. Bourbon's engineers blasted a path of sorts through the high passes, and the army hauled dozens of heavy cannons into Lombardy undetected. No army since Hannibal's had succeeded in crossing the Alps. The Swiss were allied with the Pope, and the audacity of Bourbon's military exploit caught Prospero Colonna, commander of the army of the Pope, unprepared.

The French troops and their mercenaries were dead on their feet after the brutal crossing. As they massed against the Swiss in Lombardy, each side tallied its potential losses. Neither liked the outlook. Under white flags, the Swiss nobles negotiated a treaty that provided that they would surrender Lombardy to Francis in exchange for two wagons loaded with gold. Each canton bargained separately for an annual pension.

The armies of the Pope struck their colors and left the conflict. Swiss commanders led twelve thousand fighting men back to their cantons.

But peculiar to the Swiss, major decisions were reserved for a prickly council of captains. Each captain decided whether his company would continue the campaign or retreat. Some twenty thousand of the Swiss Guard and their captains, hungry for French spoils, rejected the treaty.

Two divisions chose to defy the nobles and defend Lombardy and Milan, the gem in its crown. They determined to conceal their intention to stand their ground and repel the French invaders.

The main body of the weary French army camped several miles distant at Santa Brigida waiting for reinforcement by a division of foot soldiers and cavalry from its ally, the Republic of Venice. The remaining body of Swiss tarried in Milan. Abiding their expected retreat of the Swiss, Bourbon, leading the division that would have formed the French front line, the vanguard—the avant-garde—bivouacked close by on the plain at Marignano.

In his tent near Santa Brigida, King Francis savored what he thought was a bloodless conquest of Lombardy. The day before had been his twenty-first birthday, and the monarch strutted around his tent, his treaty clutched in his hand. He was trying on a new suit of armor—German made, a birthday gift from his mother. The heat was oppressive even midmorning. He looked forward to the cool of the evening and refused to believe the rumor that was circulating in his camp that some Swiss captains had rejected the treaty that he had so carefully negotiated with the Swiss nobles and the Church.

He did, however, believe a late-morning dispatch delivered by a boyhood friend. The courier had raced since sunrise to tell his sovereign that three Swiss phalanx divisions, each with seven thousand men, were in an advance on Marignano. The attack caught Francis completely flat-footed.

"Sound the alarm!" he shouted at his lieutenants. Soon, the high-pitched voice of French trumpets roused the king's division to action.

The Swiss Guard had hoped to surprise the French. They marched forward without drumbeat, horn, or fife. But clouds of dust kicked up by the ranks of Swiss betrayed their movement. And so alerted, Bourbon quickly mustered the division under his command and formed an avant-garde, hoping to protect the right flank of the king's division, whose arrival he expected at any time. He sent dispatches to the king recommending he stage his division to the left and somewhat farther back than the avant-guard. Bourbon also sent instructions for the Duke of Alençon's division to form a rearguard.

Each of the French divisions had ten thousand men in a combined force of foot soldiers, archers, horse soldiers, crossbowmen, and heavy gunnery units. Bourbon wished he had the unit of lancers that were under his king's command. They were the foremost horse soldiers in Europe.

Bourbon massed a battery of seventy field guns in his front center. He stationed the landsknechts beside the artillery to guard the battery. On each flank of the front, brigades of foot soldiers alternated with brigades of archers.

Standing in his saddle, Bourbon could see the Swiss advance—three divisions of multihued, densely massed phalanxes of pikemen. Behind them were lesser units of infantry and archers. The Swiss had no artillery or cavalry.

The pitch that separated the armies was a rice field broken by ditches and canals, a terrain that was flat and treeless, one that favored Bourbon's avant-guard, standing in defense.

As the Swiss came in range, Bourbon deployed his archers. With each French longbowman launching twelve unaimed shots in a minute, their heavy, mail-piercing sheaf arrows rained down on the Swiss, but protected by shields held overhead, the phalanx continued to lurch forward. Flag signals sent on Bourbon's orders directed his horsemen to meet the oncoming Swiss, in the hopes of breaking open the phalanx that was now advancing at a trot. His goal was to create confusion and panic in the opponent and cause the Swiss to retreat. Armored horsemen would make the battlefield a scene of carnage if the enemy's infantry and archers lost the protection of the phalanxes of pikemen. Heavy cavalry could butcher unprotected Swiss infantrymen at will. The nobles had trained a lifetime to slay their foemen from the top of a horse; indeed, it was much easier to kill from horseback than it was in hand-to-hand battle at eye level. An armored knight riding a half-ton warhorse was impregnable; he could kill at will once defenders were in disarray.

The Swiss swatted the light cavalry away as if the horsemen were so many horseflies. Bourbon's cavalry gave way. No nobleman wanted to be run through on a Swiss pike, from breast to back, as had Sir Mordred on the point of King Arthur's spear.

Bourbon was baffled. His gun batteries stood silent in the din. He dispatched one of his staff officers to find out why grapeshot had not already mowed big holes in the oncoming Swiss lines. Anxious for intelligence on the matter, Bourbon paced, eagerly alert for a break in formation of the oncoming phalanxes, for any sign of the Swiss phalanx losing cohesion. Only when the formation broke would he redeploy the horse soldiers. His heavy cavalry would rout the Swiss. Fast cavalry from the rearguard would overtake and slaughter them in their flight.

To Bourbon's dismay, the Swiss phalanxes remained intact, even as they lost forward momentum at a mud-choked ditch. French archers took up their short bows and harassed the flanks of the phalanx with their lighter flight arrows. But regaining strength, the Swiss phalanx slammed into the French lines of artillery.

The Swiss called their ground strategy a forlorn hope, a technique that had proven its value in numerous past actions. The commanders expected most members of the first wave of fighters to suffer mortal wounds or die. But who knew what Providence would allow? Perhaps a few soldiers would survive long enough to seize a foothold. More realistically, the first offensive merely bettered the prospect of a second assault, if the second wave could time their attack to arrive while the defenders were reloading their guns. And if the second surge met any success, if they could withstand the shortbow armed skirmishers harassing their flank, the pikemen might overrun the French batteries, where they would try to turn the captured French cannon on their owners.

The first wave of the attack succeeded beyond the wildest dreams of the Swiss commanders. Inexplicably, the French guns had remained silent. The gaudy Swiss drove the garish landsknecht defenders back and captured fifteen of the big bronze guns from the French.

"The speed of the surprise Swiss advance has rendered the French artillery fire useless." Bourbon's courier refused to look him in the eye.

"I will run you through if you don't tell me the truth," Bourbon told him.

"The gunners have no gunpowder."

"No gunpowder? Any shot?"

"None."

"Why in the name of Christ not?"

"Why would they transport gunpowder and shot to Marignano, a city with no walls?"

"Rotting away with the rearguard," Bourbon cried. "My artillery is as useless as teats on a boar."

A sheepherder farting through a twelve-spoked wheel would have presented the Swiss phalanx with a more formidable obstacle than the empty French cannons. Thank the heavens, without gunpowder, the guns were useless to the Swiss as well.

Bourbon shrewdly held back his cavalry until the Swiss were fighting hand-to-hand with his landsknechts. On his signal, he led the cavalry, swooping into the flank of the Swiss from the French right.

Bourbon's charge succeeded in arresting the advance of the Swiss suicide mission. And as if on cue, high-toned trumpets sang out across the battlefield. They signaled the arrival of the king's division. The infantry lagged behind, but cavalry, led by their armored king, attacked the flank of the Swiss from the left. Routed, the phalanx broke ranks. Francis and his cavalry joined with Bourbon's horsemen to slaughter the Swiss foot soldiers and archers as they fled back to the loathsome ditches of the plain. The pursuers retreated only after they faced the main body of the Swiss.

The battle ebbed and flowed as if it were a frenzied ocean tide. A fresh phalanx advanced on the French. Slowly, as gunpowder arrived, the gun batteries came to life and opened up on the phalanx. The Gaulish guns ripped foul paths of death and destruction through the Swiss ranks, and soon heavy, acrid billows of smoke shrouded the battlefield. Vision was impossible. Maddened with lust for the blood of this audacious enemy, Francis and his flag led thirty blind charges into the smoky forest of Swiss pikes, returning to the rear only to recover from exhaustion. Men on both sides butchered one another as if their enemies were shoat pigs.

An unhorsed knight crawled on his hands and knees through one muddy ditch after another until shouts of "France! France!" led him back to the safety of his own lines.

Francis led repeated desperate cavalry charges across the blackened pitch. Each time, he met stiff resistance from a Swiss phalanx and lost more of his horse soldiers.

Time and again, the French threw back the Swiss offensives. The Swiss seemed to erupt out of banks of dust stirred up by shuffling feet and nose-stinging smoke from the red-hot guns. The warriors on both sides were blind past fifty feet in any direction. The legion of landsknechts blunted the Swiss onslaughts and, driving them away, pursued the Swiss as they retreated yet again. Not until the darkest hours of the night did the fighting stop. Exhausted men fell to sleep on the foul battlefield alongside the bodies of their enemies and brothers in arms.

But where was Alençon's rearguard? Where were the Venetians who had been so eager to ally with the French?

A windless nighttime seeped onto the plain of Marignano and with it a chill, reeking air. The battlefield was now shadows, clouded in dust and smoke from the smoldering wreckage, shrouded in grief. Vapors arose like ghosts from the wretched, open guts of the garishly clad dead and dying souls who littered the plain and joined the dark air into a bitter, choking fog, heavy with the pungent smell of spent black powder and the mordant odor of sweat, urine, and gore.

Lying against the wheel of a French gun, Francis pleaded for water. "I'm at death's doorstep!" he cried, so great was his thirst. In the dark, a trumpeter filled the king's helmet with water from a nearby ditch. The monarch gulped down the offering, then spewed it out violently. The swill was more mud and blood than water.

The French reassembled their scattered artillery batteries under the cover of darkness. At dawn, the battle began again. Encouraged by the events of the first attack on the preceding day, the Swiss lowered pikes and charged the French guns. This time Bourbon's artillery battery was ready. As if it were the scythe of the grim reaper, the grapeshot from massed cannon fire gouged deep valleys of death through the Swiss ranks. The lines of the Swiss vanguard became a bloody abattoir. Still the mountain men pressed forward, trying valiantly to push the French and their landsknechts back.

But the artillery was too much for the Swiss. Bourbon led another cavalry charge against their flank, and the Swiss gave ground. And with the arrival of Venetian forces in support of the French, the Swiss Guard withdrew. The French were too exhausted to harry the retreat. They searched for their wounded on the stinking battlefield.

Bourbon savored the victory, musing with his aides about the plunder he expected to seize from the conquest of Lombardy. Thousands of bodies rotted on the plain at Marignano.

In the days and weeks that followed, the peasants of Marignano prayed for the onset of cold weather as they stripped valuables from the putrefying flesh of seventeen thousand resplendently dressed cadavers. Some twelve thousand of them were Swiss. Again, smoke choked the rice fields, this time from burning heaps of corpses. The funeral pyres signaled the *fin de siècle*, the closing of an era.

Gone was the age of the sword. Under Bourbon, Marignano ushered in the age of the gun.

Following his victory, while still on the battlefield, King Francis asked his brother-in-law, the Duke of Alençon, to knight him in the old style. He wanted to be a chevalier whose only duty was to his lord, who happened in this case to be himself. Knighthood was an orgasm of hubris by the king. "Is his legacy not rich enough?" Bourbon stormed.

"He desires the glory," an aide answered.

"What sort of fool tries to brighten a rainbow with a taper?"

Worse yet, the arrogant Alençon was undeserving; his division had never advanced one step from the rear. Nonetheless, he complied with the wish of his sovereign.

The Duke of Bourbon could scarcely bear the scorn. He was insulted by this attack on his honor. Bourbon had engineered the harrowing crossing of the Alps. Bourbon's division had formed the avant-garde. Bourbon's army had turned the tide of battle. Bourbon's strategy had won the day. He, above any other, deserved the honor of knighting his lord.

Bourbon was eleven when his elder brother died and he inherited the family's feudal domain in Auvergne, a rural and sparsely populated province in south-central France. At age fifteen, he married his cousin Suzanne, the Duchess of Bourbon. She held tentative ownership of all the family property as its heir-general. His standing was heir-male, the first male in the Bourbon family line of succession. Once they joined in holy matrimony, her status as heir-general of the family upgraded him to the rank of duke, the Duke of Bourbon. Her estates, his bloodline—and gender—made him the wealthiest man in France. He bore himself with dignity; honor and pride were paramount to Bourbon. He was polite but not kind.

It was a heady time for the adventurous Bourbon, and the world was his oyster. His young cousin, Francis I, was the king of France, having ascended to the throne in 1515 after the death of his father, Louis XII. King Louis had passed from this world, dead from over-exertion brought on, the tongue-waggers claimed, by his energetic 15-year-old bride, the sister of Henry VIII of England.

His king wielded arbitrary power, and he was all the more power-ful because he used his power in the most arbitrary ways possible. Tomorrow might hold either punishment or reward for anyone at his court, so the principal occupation for the courtiers and throne-sniffers was speculation and gossip. Today's friend might find himself a rival in a fortnight.

"I spend my days spying on friends and my nights gathering gossip about the scandals of my enemies," Bourbon joked. "Every noble is afraid of his shadow. The king's court at d'Amboise is like a pen of sheep: three ewes in season and two unwilling rams."

Only five years apart in age, Bourbon and Francis were two peas in a pod, both narcissistic and each the embodiment of France. They were both war-obsessed and continually sought ways that France might dominate its neighboring countries. Francis lusted for Navarre, a smallish coastal province to the south, beyond the Pyrenees, claimed by the monarchs of Spain. He dreamed of a conquest of Flanders to the north, and the Low Countries beyond. In the east, he coveted the city of Milan, a pearl of great price, the capital of Lombardy, a border province beyond the Alps that had changed hands so many times the locals never knew whether they were French, Italian, or Swiss.

Francis's archenemy was England and its king, Henry VIII.

In 1154, after returning from the Second Crusade, Eleanor of Aqui-taine had her marriage to the French king, Louis the Fat, annulled on the ground of consanguinity within the fourth degree. She left for England and married Henry II, her cousin of the third degree. Control of Aquitaine shifted. France annexed the region in 1453 at the end of the Hundred Years' War, and since that time, the wine merchants of London and Southampton had yearned for the wines from the vineyards of Aquitaine and its port city, Bordeaux.

Henry VIII coveted Aquitaine, but England was at a huge disad-vantage to take it back. A hundred years before, Henry V had taken Aquitaine by defeating the French at Agincourt, but in the after-math, the English could not preserve his gains. It was foolhardy for anyone to propose mounting a military campaign across the English Channel.

Both Henry and Francis were drunk with desire for a land beyond his reach, protected by a military obstacle.

Other European states held Bourbon, Francis, and their fierce, war-like attitudes in check. France lacked European allies. Desperate for an alliance, Francis even aligned himself by treaty with Suleiman the Magnificent and his Ottoman Turks, an odd alliance by any standard. The Turks had no desire to control or influence Flanders and the Low Countries, not at any rate in Suleiman's lifetime, and had no interest in defending France from England.

While corpses still smoldered on the plain of Marignano, still squiffy on his conquest, Francis ordered a medal struck to honor what he called "the battle of giants." It bore the modest phrase "I have vanquished those whom only Caesar vanquished."

The Swiss Cardinal of Sion and his mercenaries had taken refuge in the strategic castle, *Castello Sforzesco*, in Milan. With the assistance of Pope Leo X, at a meeting attended by Leonardo da Vinci, Francis negotiated an eternal peace between France and the Swiss Confederacy. Though bested, the Swiss promised to renounce all claim to Lombardy upon receipt of four hundred thousand ounces of English crown gold, roughly fifty wagonloads of silver. The Cardinal of Sion received thirty thousand ducats, about 250 pounds of gold.

Soon, Zwingli, a chaplain in the Swiss Guard who survived Marignano, took to the street to decry mercenary service and to renounce the high clergy of the Church in Rome. The Swiss Guard took part of Zwingli's advice and never again went into battle, though they did hold on to one lucrative contract. The Swiss Guard continued to serve as the Pope's private bodyguard.

Bourbon stared at the train of treasure-laden wagons as it streamed north out of Milan. It was he who should have the honor of knighting the king; instead he reaped nothing but the king's scorn. Adding to the injury, the wagon train, filled with the plunder of Lombardy, should be, by all that was holy, headed to Auvergne. He was the victor, he deserved the honor. His king was letting the vanquished Swiss cart away a trove that the custom of warfare said belonged to Bourbon: his silver, his gold, his compensation and reimbursement. By rights, it belonged to him and the House of Bourbon. He alone had taken the king's fight to the Swiss.

His obedience meant nothing to Francis; his fealty was as filthy rags. By a capricious, quicksilver decision, one his arrogance would never let him reconsider, his cousin was letting Switzerland gather in to itself the accumulated wealth of generations of the Bourbon dynasty.

Rage stirred in Bourbon's breast. He was delirious with distress. The loss of treasure was bitter, but it was his monarch's disdain that was a burden too great to bear. "What of my investment, cousin?" he demanded.

"What of it?" the king answered.

"The army, the cannon, the mercenaries, the food, uniforms, mine! All mine...all gone..."

"What am I, foie gras? This battle cost me plenty!"

"Plunder is the sacred right of war."

"I'm not going to allow you and your mercenary rabble to plunder Lombardy. It is mine. Don't mention this again."

Francis influenced the aging da Vinci to relocate to Paris, one of Europe's largest but most squalid and flyblown cities. Still hot with pride, he hoped to improve Paris, make it into a cultural capital, and perhaps to move his court there. Together, he and da Vinci transported a large quantity of objets d'art to the Louvre Palace, enough to start a museum.

As Bourbon's reward, the young *Roi-Chevalier*, Knight-King, elevated him to the position of Constable of France. This was no mean post—as constable, Bourbon held one of the five most power-ful offices in the land. He was marshal of all the French armies. Francis also installed Bourbon as governor of Milan. Peppercorns. Neither post offered him an opportunity to rebuild the wealth of the Bourbon family. He supposed that every whisper or wink at court had to do with the indignity he suffered at the hand of the king he still served.

Now, as he rode his massive gray warhorse onto the tournament lawn at Chateau d'Amboise, Bourbon was angry and weary. His wife, Suzanne, the Duchess of Bourbon, had refused to thrive after the loss of their son, who died at age six months, their one and only child after sixteen years of marriage. She died giving birth to stillborn twins shortly after her husband's arrival home from war. His last five years had been spent in constant conflict with angry creditors, all seeking opportunities to satisfy their claims, to no purpose. He had squandered his wife's wealth in service to a crown that had stripped him of dignity. He was a laughingstock at court. He was thirty.

Bourbon was broke.

# CHAPTER 4

*All of Rome seems to have soiled its breeches. What a garbage dump,* Diogo thought as he walked through the decaying, small, backwater town. Rome's money tree had withered and died after a short but exciting life. Once brimming with gold from the sale of indulgences, the Church now had no cash flowing into its coffers. From atop the Vatican Hill to the northwest, beyond the west-to-south bend of the Tiber River, the skeleton of an undressed St. Peter's Basilica hovered over the moldering city like a hungry vulture. The once-loyal tradesmen found work where pay was more reliable.

The city was much smaller than Venice, Naples, Milan, Florence or Lisbon. Its population could not have exceeded 50,000 citizens. The climate was pleasant enough, but the city itself was miserable and inadequate, depressing and drab. The buildings were crumbling right before his eyes. Even the language of the Italians was falling apart. The citizens spoke in a pidgin tongue that cobbled together German, Tuscan, Florentine, and Venetian dialects.

The city was literally built on death—dank catacombs below every building were packed with the bones of ancient saints and sinners. The gloom seemed to have seeped up and infected the still living, who looked, in their dress, as good as dead. *Dreary*, he told himself, looking at the Romish citizens. Diogo was forced to adopt the monotonous dingy greens and browns, a dark sleeveless jacket over a collarless undershirt. The sumptuary laws outlawed the bright clothing Diogo loved, but poofy sleeves, rolled collars, and showy headwear, like those in Portugal, if sported in public, were punishable by hard labor in Rome.

Only the landsknechts and Swiss Guard were exempt. Other than the outlandish garb of the mercenaries, the only color to brighten the streets were the swatches of yellow cloth pinned over the breast on the waistcoats of the Jews, their yellow flap-hats, and the yellow scarves of their women.

The only subject that seemed to titillate the citizens of Rome was the vendetta against Martin Luther. Tetzel had nearly gone into convulsions over Luther's 95 theses, and had launched a blitzkrieg of correspondence in the Germanies, Austria and Poland to discredit the monk.

No sooner had Tetzel leveled his barrage on Luther than, out of nowhere, accusations against Tetzel himself arose. Tetzel? Immoral? Perish the thought! His detractors claimed Tetzel had committed frauds and embezzlements too numerous to count. As if a dam had broken, a torrent of charges flooded over the corpulent monk from every quarter.

Tetzel retired to Leipzig, broken in spirit and health. Defending his honor would be futile in any case. He was guilty of every charge, guilty as sin, and he had no way to get his hands on money. The peasantry in the German states had embraced Luther's ideas almost overnight. Tetzel would have found it easier to sell a stone to a Turk than an indulgence to a German.

Diogo arrived in Rome at the right time. Pope Leo had threatened Luther with excommunication, and in Rome, that was a prelude to a sought-after public execution that would draw an audience of thousands from the richest city-states on the Italian Peninsula. The trial promised to create scores of jobs, as more servants of the court would be needed, so Diogo, along with many others, haunted the halls and lobbies of the Vatican. Dozens of well dressed, well spoken, and well mannered job-seekers tried every means possible—threats, intimidations, bribes and extortions—to get past the stalwart halberd-armed Swiss Guards who protected the Pope. By hook or by crook, they risked life and limb for the opportunity to plead for an appointment. As long as a man had skills in foreign languages and did not behave or smell like a fisherman or farmer, he could be useful in whatever matters came before the Holy See, particularly those that furthered the Pope's ambition to kill Luther.

Diogo persisted and received the promise of an appointment as a bailiff. He rubbed his hands together with glee. Agents contracted for every vacant apartment in Rome, to serve the crush of diplomats, their wives and pretty daughters who would attend a momentous trial for excommunication. Diogo saw the inside of more than one of those apartments, through the gauze of thrown petticoats, and that was before he even officially assumed the role of bailiff. Then the wheels of justice ground to a halt suddenly, unexpectedly, in January 1519. Maximilian, the morbid, melancholy emperor of the Holy Roman Empire, who never went anywhere without his coffin in tow, accomplished the totally unexpected. He died. Plans for the greatest excommunication in a millennium went on hold and with them, the promise of Diogo's appointment.

The throne, the post of emperor of the Holy Roman Empire—der Heiliges Romisches Reich Deutscher Nation—was to be filled by an individual chosen by an electoral college of nobles. But Maximilian had seen no reason to leave his succession to a caprice as whimsical as an election. A year before, the Fugger family had loaned him one million guldens, fifteen wagons full of gold. He used the cash to bribe the electors. He wanted them to settle on a candidate of his own choosing. Now, with the bribes distributed to the virtuous electors, he spent the last year of his life blissfully planning his death. It seemed as if he had worried himself into an early grave, terrified of having no more worries to feed his insomnia.

Now the Imperial throne was empty. One question remained. Would the German electors stay bribed? Christendom forgot about Martin Luther.

Maximilian's final choice had been his grandson, Charles. Philip, Charles's father, had gone to meet his maker years earlier. Once, even as Philip's widow mourned, the disconsolate Maximilian had hastily offered the Imperial throne to the vain Henry VIII of England. But now, Charles was approaching adulthood, Charles brought with him a resume: he would become the king of Spain on the death of his maternal grandfather, Ferdinand. Poor Aunt Catherine of Aragon. Succession to the Spanish throne passed her by because of her gender. She would have to be satisfied with being queen of England, Europe's most vulgar throne.

Charles was intolerant, illiterate, and young enough to know everything. He had been raised in Flanders by handlers because of his mother's madness. Retainers whispered in his ear daily that he was Christ's vicar on earth. He believed them. During Lent, he whipped himself bloody.

Emperor, the Imperial Highness—the name of the title alone had a supernatural attraction to every nobleman in Christendom, a plum well worth the fight. To Charles, the throne was the zenith of all earthly grandeur and the means to turn the minds of the sinful European monarchs to the narrow path of righteousness.

Another name was thrust into consideration, that of Francis I, the young king of France. Many of the paladins of the Imperial Court held the war-obsessed Francis in high esteem and threw their support to him, hoping that he, like Charlemagne, would bring a war on the Turks and put an end to the threat that the Turks might regain control of Europe. Francis would revive the crusades, free Jerusalem, and recover the Holy Sepulcher from the infidels.

France's treaty with the Turks remained secret as Francis's retainers fought for his appointment.

"The Imperial Crown is not hereditary," they plead, "and Germany doesn't need a nineteen-year-old boy!" They hoped that the electors would overlook the fact that Francis was only twenty-five. "The empire needs a prince with tried judgment and proven talents. Francis will unite France, Lombardy, and Germany. Europe will come together as one to make a war on the Mohammadans!"

Francis was universally unpopular among the electors for his strutting arrogance, and he sensed defeat. He needed a more pragmatic track. He would make the stew more savory, he would resort to that time-honored rhetorical stratagem, bribery. And drunken banquets festooned with courtesans. His payoffs totaled four hundred thousand crowns.

This was not Diogo's first trip to the fair. He needed a job, preferably one that paid generously and demanded no exertion. Charm would disguise his dubious qualifications. He sought employment in the cause of winning the Imperial crown. The eventual winner of was no consequence to Diogo. He hoped for a long, drawn-out selection process not only to maintain employment but to open more opportunities with the needful wives and daughters of ministers to the court. *I will stir their dull roots with the spring rain of my passion,* he told himself.

One court peacock pranced with a loftier gait than all the others. He was Thomas Wolsey, an English cardinal with folds of skin around his neck that looked as flabby as a sailor's foreskin. As a younger man, in the post of the King's almoner, an office responsible for giving money to the poor, Wolsey diverted huge sums of money to his own purse. Now he was Lord Chancellor, chief adviser to his king, Henry VIII, and wealthier than most of the lords. Wolsey's king held claim to the throne—he owned some smallish estates in Austria, and Wolsey carried his king's brief. Pope Leo even favored Henry.

Diogo followed Wolsey's every move at a distance. That wasn't difficult, as Wolsey stood out in a crowd. His housedress was a black ankle-length cassock robe with scarlet piping, buttons, and sash. A cross hung from a long chain around his neck, and when he went outdoors, he donned a wide-brimmed scarlet hat. For public prayer he wore his choir dress, a violet floor-length cassock under a white lace rochet overshirt that almost reached the hem of the cassock, with sleeves that gathered at the wrist. Over that, he wore a red cape with a train, a cappa magna, and a short ermine overcape.

Diogo stole into Wolsey's toilet, pretended to be the son of an exiled nobleman, and pitched his talents.

Wolsey had his doubts about this charming character's story. His own resume was larded with lies. "I am but the son of a butcher from Ipswich," he often said within his court. But in truth, his father had been a wealthy cloth merchant. But he saw himself in this intruder in his toilet. He might be suitable to his wiles.

Wolsey offered employment. "I need an enterprising agent to snoop around. See if you can get a sense of just how much money the French are spending on bribes."

Within a week, Diogo had information to report. "Four hundred thousand crowns, Eminence," he whispered into his patron's ear. "All paid by King Francis himself."

"Are you certain?" Wolsey demanded. "Four hundred thousand is the sum he paid the Swiss. I don't believe in coincidence."

"Maybe it's his lucky number."

"Don't be a fool."

"The girl with the apple blossom checks," he said, and Wolsey nodded knowingly. Early in his career, he had gained Henry's favor by offering his young prince Henry certain attractions, pleasures, and disorders at his residence that so outraged decency that no royal would have ventured to indulge in them at his own palace. The edict that priests should observe celibacy had never taken a firm hold over England's clergy in general, certainly not with Wolsey in particular. The cardinal once lived in a marriage-like relationship with a woman from Yarmouth. She bore him two children, but as his career advanced, he sent the children to foster homes and arranged an advantageous marriage for the woman, sweetened by a dowry. "She told me herself," Diogo explained.

"And she knew because...?"

Diogo filled Wolsey's cup with wine. "Pillow talk, Eminence. She rutted with Francis long before me."

"Bollocks."

Diogo and Wolsey enjoyed one another's company, despite the fact that Wolsey was thirty years older. "I will be the grandest man in Christendom."

One evening, his tongue lubricated by wine, Diogo told Wolsey a popular story about a Roman lady of substance whose husband had snubbed her carnal needs. One day, Pietro, her husband, came home unexpectedly, and in mortal fear, she hid her boy of the moment under the hencoop. When an ass stepped on the fingers of the lady's gallant, he cried out in pain.

"Would that fire might fall from heaven and burn all women, brood of iniquity that you are," Pietro said.

"Consider that I am a woman like other women, with the like craving. You have denied me gratification, and it is no blame to me that I seek it elsewhere. At least I do thee so much honor as not for-gather with stable-boys or scurvy knaves."

"Go then," said Pietro, "get us some supper. I will arrange this affair so that you shall have no more cause of complaint."

Wolsey loved the story and begged for a second telling. The next night, Wolsey insisted that Diogo bring a cortigiana to Wolsey's apartments. She was a well-educated and independent woman of free morals, and together, the three of them played out the story of Pietro and his sex-starved wife. Diogo hid under Wolsey's bed since no hencoop was available. The first night, Wolsey played Pietro and altered the ending slightly. He had sexual intercourse with the cortigiana while Diogo looked on. The next night, Wolsey reversed the roles. The older man played the part of the boy, but this time, the storyline had changed. In this version, the husband caught the couple in the offense, *in flagrante delicto*. Diogo, in the role of Pietro, had carnal relations with the cortigiana while Wolsey watched.

As much as Diogo was happy for the intercourse, he found he enjoyed having a friend in Wolsey and realized the exploits were as much about maintaining that bond as satisfying any carnal urge. But Wolsey seemed focused on the latter.

Wolsey was endlessly resourceful in adding new twists and turns to the script. Often he dressed as a woman and asked for spankings. On occasion, he gossiped about certain reputable clerics and political leaders who had a predilection to couple with other men in the Italian fashion. Diogo regaled the cardinal with stories about such acts that he had seen occur between shipmates.

Wolsey began bringing up the subject of same-sex relations daily. Disquieted now by such chatter, the actor sought to change the subject. "The things you have the power to imagine will in no time fall within your taste and mores, Eminence. I want no part of it for myself." He feared that coupling with a man would foster rumors or ridicule when what he wanted was to be the object of adoration.

Fearful that Wolsey's tentacles might draw him into wrongdoing, he sometimes arrived at Wolsey's apartment by himself. "The cortigianas all have prior engagements," he lied. "I expect the condition to persist."

"You're too miserly. How much did you offer?"

"The action in bribes from Charles and Francis sets the price at a level you can't afford."

"I see."

"Your king has the virtue, but not enough gold to match the enticements of his rivals."

Wolsey had to agree. The Pope was sick to his heart when Henry pulled out of the race. Wolsey returned to England.

Henry's withdrawal left the Pope a choice between two bad outcomes. But the bright line for Leo was that no good could come to famiglia de' Medici from adding to Charles' strength. Charles was king of Spain and the southern Italian states, and now he wanted the empire? No sovereign in his right mind wanted such a neighbor, not one as strong as Charles would be. In the privacy of his apartments, the Pope railed at the suggestion of Charles gaining the crown. "Hasn't the Church given Spain half the earth?!" he roared. "When is enough enough?"

He harbored resentment for Francis as well. Only four years before, the French monarch had driven the Church and it's his influence out of Lombardy. But it appeared that Francis would win the day. The Church would lose considerable power and prestige if it failed to support the eventual winner, so the Pope had no choice but to shift his support to the king of France. Francis was the lesser of two evils. "Charles is too young," the Pope told the ambassadors in his court.

Pope Leo's retainers began a whispering campaign. They told the German electors, "Charles has only been at the Spanish court for two years." To the nobles: "Francis will crush the insane cult that is building around this monk, Martin Luther." To the landgraves of Germany, they said, "Francis will surely reinstate Tetzel."

Then news came to the court that Tetzel had been found dead. A life of frequent and flagrant debauchery had finally caught up with the indulgent seller of indulgences. Not a single eye shed a tear. The Pope's argument to the German states rang hollow.

Some electors had not been bought and were yet undecided. German tradition held to an unspoken creed not to elect someone who was already a major monarch. The idea of a French Emperor was repugnant. No one liked Francis.

So electors pushed forward the name of the most popular man in Germany, Luther's friend, Frederick of Saxony. His election would end any chance of a prosecution of Luther's heresy. Pope Leo took a stand against Frederick. The heresy of Luther must be prosecuted. It looked for a time as if storm clouds were brewing in the northern sky. But to everyone's surprise, Frederick bowed out. "The Turk is at our gate," Frederick said. "Charles is our natural defender."

Frederick's statement alone was enough to settle the matter for the German electors. They would oppose the Pope. So it was that Francis's campaign of bribery was derailed, and Pope Leo had to withdraw his objection. Charles took the day, June 28, 1519. An enormous amount of graft had greased the skids of his election, but Charles owed the crown to one honest man, Frederick. He traveled from Spain to Bologna and was crowned emperor in October.

Francis fumed over his loss. Pope Leo was beside himself with anger and disgust. Trapped in a lurch, caught supporting the losing candidate. By custom, the Pope was to have the glory of placing the crown of state on the head of the Elected, but in his wrath, he refused to make the journey to Bologna, a mere 250 miles to the north. Charles took the affront personally and was blistering mad at the insult. He publicly berated the Holy See's ambassador, Giulio, the bastard nephew, over the wound. It was a dressing down that the diplomat would not soon forget.

Charles had little time for petty grievances. Maximilian had not prepared the young emperor to face the most stubborn problems that faced the empire. He had no treaty with England and only the begrudging support of Pope Leo. Bribery had served the will of God but had planted the seed of enmity in the dark heart of Francis. The German states were approaching a state of revolt because of this mad monk, Martin Luther. And at the western end of his realm, in another peasant uprising, communeros had seized Castile, the heart of Spain.

Not a single king in Christendom would support Luther, but neither was a single king allied with the empire. While Charles's fondest dream was one of Luther's body burning at a stake and, with it, the heresy of the German peasants crushed, the fulfillment of that dream would just have to wait until he could resolve his problems in Castile.

Succession in the Empire now settled, the demand for foppish connivers in Rome plummeted. Diogo was again unemployed.

# CHAPTER 5

The back street was barely wide enough for a cart. Pieces of garbage stuck to the walls of the homes and shops and sent long stains streaming down the plaster crusts. The feces of horses, dogs, pigs, and humans seeped away down a greasy central ditch. A dingy vapor hugged the ground, coating the street's stone surface with a pungent dankness.

"Stay away. Leave me alone. Sanctuary. Help!" Slipping and sliding, David Reuveni fled down the narrow passageway, his ponytail of greasy hair flagging behind. Its length and dark color matched his scraggly beard. Although he was strong and surprisingly agile for a dwarf, behind him, a bigger man was in pursuit. He closed the distance with each stride.

The man overtook David and snared him by his collar. "Got you, runt."

He dragged David, squirming and floundering, down one grubby pathway after another. Some bystanders looked away, and some watched without shame, but no one did anything to help David before the men reached the building that was their destination.

David slumped onto the rough bench as the big man directed him. His eyes darted around the room, assessing his situation. His captor was the constable of Treviso, an inferior office held by a coarse man that deplored magic. David had avoided him for a week by hiding under a bridge. His dreams for Portugal seemed far away. Every day brought a new struggle for existence. David examined his colorful waistcoat, searching for any signs of torn fabric. The constable's handling had been unnecessarily rough. Nothing good could come from capture by this beast.

David's outer garment was a pourpoint, a long-sleeved, fitted shirt of sturdy fabric that ended at his waist. He scraped a gob of mud from it and then rubbed the dirty spot that remained back and forth between his fists but his efforts were fruitless. Nothing dried in Treviso, a delta town in the marshes of the Republic of Venice. David's efforts only smeared the stain. He frowned. His pourpoint was so much more difficult to keep clean than his desert robes had been.

A seamstress had created the frontpiece of this showman's jacket by patching circles, diamonds, and lozenges of red, green, yellow, and blue fabrics, David's design. He also wore a high, stiff white collar. His linen undershirt bunched at his neck and cuffs, where cords gathered it. Dense stockings matched the color and design of the pourpoint. A belt anchored all the garments to his waist, along with a codpiece, a padded leather flap, which served as a fly. The toes of his shoes upturned; the shoes were held in place by tiny chains around his calves.

David rubbed the spot harder, irritated with his misfortune, his detention, glaring at the dreary constable, a dolt draped in a colorless doublet smock and drab stockings.

*Degenerate,* David thought. *Cabbagehead.* He could not believe this was happening. *Not again.*

Soon enough, the constable, the head of Treviso, was rousing David from his seat. He led him across the street. Stopping at a low door, he kicked David in the buttocks, and the little man tumbled into a dark room. To David's consternation, the degenerate shackled his ankles. He drove rivets into the hinges to lock him to a wooden dock at a rail. The prisoner looked around and could only see shadows.

Once his eyes had adjusted to the gloom, he found he was in a chamber that was as smoky as it was foul-smelling. An overhead rack of lethargic candles struggled to illuminate the room. Another couple of tapers burned on a crude desk at the far end. Several men were in the room, and they were all talking in loud tones. Order only came to the room when a bailiff yelled, "Quiet!" All the men quit talking and found seats. An older man entered the chamber—the magistrate, David guessed; he took a seat behind the candlelit table. David stood on his toes, a move barely allowed by his chains, to afford himself a better line of sight to the magistrate.

Ahead of the bar sat four well-dressed gentlemen, local lawyers. A guard flanked David on either side. Another ten men or so roosted in the gallery. *Courthouse cronies. Just like every courtroom I have ever seen.*

A bailiff reported, "Your Grace, this gypsy was caught performing black magic."

His body trembling, David said, "Your Grace, it's not black magic. Lucifer has no hand in my exhibition. It's merely a trick." From a purse held under his belt, David produced three polished cups and one little red ball. Lining the cups upside down on the bar, he demonstrated his sleight of hand.

"Merely a trick." David demonstrated again. "It amuses the peasants. It is not black magic. It is just a prank, Your Grace. See?" David demonstrated again, slowly this time. He turned his palm to the magistrate to show him that the missing ball clasped under his thumb. "See?"

A murmur belched from the gallery. The black-robed magistrate rearranged his backside in the seat, crossed his arms, and rolled out his lower lip to assist in his contemplation.

He mumbled back and forth with himself, over and under his breath. "Amusing," he blustered. Then, wrenching his neck, he searched the back corners of the chamber. "Where are the clerics? Surely some churchman wants to weigh in on this matter." The magistrate rolled a jaundiced eye around the gallery. The room answered his query with a sustained silence.

With some relief, the magistrate settled on his ruling by himself. "You are probably right. It's not black magic." He cleared his throat. "The charge is reduced to swindling by a gypsy. Constable, dispossess the prisoner of his belongings, give him twenty lashes, and escort him to the outskirts of town."

"Aarrgghh." David's voice seemed to emanate from his bowel. The punishment was ridiculously severe. He struggled against his bindings. "Not again. I won't have this." David's chains rattled as he yanked at his constraints.

A genteel voice broke in. "Your Grace." Having gained the attention of everyone in the chamber, an older man stood up from among the lawyers seated in front of the bar. His attire was dark and conservative, with a black overcloak draped across his shoulders. "Your Grace, as a friend of the court, I pray forbearance to advise the court that there is no evidence that this prisoner is a gypsy, other than the fashion of his attire." A guffawing series of laughs broke out from the other lawyers.

Another member of the bar shouted, "Then he must be a Jew." More laughing. "In either case, he's a dog."

David whined. "Your Grace, Your Mercy. I am begging. I am pleading. I am not a gypsy. And I am not a Jew."

The magistrate stood as if to aggrandize his ruling. "There's one way to tell for sure." He stretched out his arm and pointed at the prisoner. "Guard. Remove the prisoner's lower garments."

The guards manhandled David and stripped away his stockings. A few small coins fell out of his codpiece. All the gallery, the lawyers, the guards and the magistrate, roared in laughter. David's circumcised manhood gave eloquent evidence in rebuttal. The lack of a turtle-necked penis put the lie to his testimony.

"Liar. Liar. Your lie is revealed." The magistrate's voice was low and bitter with anger. "What do you have to say for yourself?"

David struggled against his shackles again. His resentment was building. He did not think he would gain much sympathy with the court by explaining that he had surrendered his foreskin to the Islamic faith of his father. "I am Hebrew, indeed, Your Grace," he said.

"A Jew then."

"I'm not a Jew."

"Gypsy."

"No. No. I am a Hebrew, but not of the tribe of Judah. I was born"— and now unreal words began to tumble off his tongue. What he said was totally false and told as effortlessly as if he were telling a German peasant his destiny. "I was born to the tribe of Reuben."

Abraham begat Isaac and Isaac begat Jacob. Jacob was also called Israel. These men are the patriarchs of the Children of Israel.

Jacob fathered eleven sons by two wives and two servant girls. The oldest son was Reuben. Reuben convinced his resentful brothers to spare the life of a younger, flamboyant half-brother, Joseph, whom the brothers sold into slavery. Reuben later lost his birthright because he slept with his father's concubine, the mother of two of his half-brothers.

Israel's family founded a nation of twelve tribes, with ten tribes named for a son of Israel, and two tribes named for sons of Joseph. After a four-hundred-year sojourn as slaves, Moses led the tribes out of Egypt. During the consecration of a tabernacle in the desert, his indolent nephews obtained coals from their hearth, profane fire, rather than from the altar-fire as commanded. "And there went out fire from the Lord, and devoured them, and they died before the Lord."

After wandering in the desert for forty years, the Children of Israel muscled their way into Canaan, Palestine, which sat astride a busy trade route that connected Babylon (Iraq) and Egypt. When the

Israelis were not at war with nomadic desert tribes from the eastern wilderness, or the sea-faring neighbors who occupied the shore of the Mediterranean Sea, they fought with one another. Ten tribes grouped into a northern kingdom known as Israel while the southern kingdom of two tribes was called Judah. Macabre stories of intrigue, treachery, assassination and fratricide are chronicled in the annals of the Kings of Judah and Israel.

Invaders from Assyria (Syria) captured the lands of the ten tribes after years of bitter fighting for control of the trade route. Not eager to fight for this troubled ground again, the Assyrians deported every Israelite they could get their hands on. Then Babylon destroyed Assyria. After more battles, Babylon laid waste to Judah's capital city of Jerusalem and her cherished Temple. Babylon finished what the Assyrians had started: they killed or deported the remnants of the Tribes to Babylon.

Babylon soon fell to Persia (Iran). Eager for another rich city to be built in his realm, King Cyrus of Persia returned two tribes, the southern tribes, to Jerusalem. This remnant of Judah came to be known as "Jews." The northern ten tribes of Israel had completely disappeared from the face of the earth. The Tribe of Reuben was one of them.

"What? What kind of—What are you saying? No, quiet. Do not say another word. The tribe of Reuben disappeared many years ago, two millenniums ago. You mock me. You mock this court. You, you, you mock—This is heresy. This is blasphemy!"

David's teeth clenched. His temples pounded. His face burned red. The rubes had never reacted this way. With each passing moment, he grew more unwilling to suffer the pain and humiliation these cretins planned to dish out to him. "Your Grace, I am the youngest brother of Joseph ibn Reuveni, the Hebrew king of the tribe of Reuben. King Joseph is a proud king of a proud tribe of Hebrew warriors, a tribe of thousands. All well armed and well trained. I am on a mission from King Joseph himself." David gained every inch of stature he could muster. "I am my brother's emissary to the doge of Venice."

A collective gasp erupted from the bar and gallery.

"Then what are you doing here? Swindling the ignorant peasants of this district?"

"I was captured by the gypsies. I was their captive. Their prisoner. Their slave. Had it not been for my small size, they would have killed me. The gypsies killed all my guards, every last man, and stole my horses and all my servants and all my treasures. Treasures, gifts from my brother to the doge of Venice. The gypsies pressed me into service, into slavery, and they stole the doge's treasure."

The first lawyer addressed the magistrate. "Pray, your worship, allow me to speak for the prisoner."

David had no choice. He and the magistrate both nodded acquiescence.

"The prisoner may be a heretic or a blasphemer. But consider the possibility that he is telling the truth. Perhaps he is a diplomatic emissary. He was indeed carrying unfamiliar coinage." He stretched himself to fullness. "I submit that the gravity of this matter exceeds your jurisdiction, Your Grace. You can lay on sanctions for his manner of dress if you choose to do so. This cloak of many colors is a clear violation. Our sumptuary law prohibits colorful clothing such as the prisoner wears on his wretched little body. Punish him for that. But then send him to Venice. Let Venice decide if he is guilty of the crime of heresy."

"Well," mumbled the magistrate, "this counsel has some merit. Perhaps you are correct."

David bit at the rivets in the cuffs that confined him to the bar. He did not want Venice, he wanted freedom. Perhaps he could get away. His activity drew the magistrate's attention.

"Be still, you dog." the magistrate ordered. Turning to the lawyer, he asked, "What of the possessions of the prisoner? What was this you were saying about unfamiliar coinage? Are these coins silver? Gold?"

The constable responded, "Just a small purse, Your Honor, some rings, and some stones sewn into his belt." He omitted to mention David's dagger that was now under his own sash..

"Good. That is good. Then on the matter of the prisoner's costume, the court finds a violation of the sumptuary law. The prisoner will be dispossessed of these coins, rings, and the stones in his belt—"

The lawyer stepped forward with urgency and interrupted, "Your Worship. On the matter of—"

"Sit down, Counsel. The court directs payment of fees to prisoner's counsel in the sum of the value of the prisoner's coin that is lying on the floor." A frown stretched across the lawyer's face as he stooped to pick up his earnings. The other lawyers and the gallery guffawed, and for their trouble, the lawyer cocked his middle finger in their direction.

"Constable. Have the prisoner beaten. Give him twenty-five good lashes. Detain him in your jail, and at your earliest convenience, escort him to the Council in Venice on a charge of heresy. Further this court sayeth not on this matter. Bailiff. Let us keep moving. We will be here all morning. What is the next case?"

David grew faint; he crumpled into his bindings. He could not focus his vision. Fearful of Venice and dreading the whip, his legs lost their strength.

Through his stupor, a voice told him, "Come on, you little bastard, let's get this over with." The constable prodded David back to his office, then out a rear door and into a stable yard. He was jolted out of his daze by the alkaline smell of the muck underfoot and the damp coolness of the air. Strong hands ripped David's pourpoint and undershirt away. Passersby laughed at his lumpy, shortened body. The constable bound each wrist with a length of hemp cordage. He threaded the tail of each rope through a ring imbedded in the wall and then cinched up the bindings to expose David's bare back.

David gritted his teeth and tightened every muscle to knots. Beza had exhibited him as a prince scores of times. No one ever accused

Beza of heresy. His mind raced frantically to fight off his fear of the whipping the constable was preparing to inflict on him. *When this is over,* he thought, *I am going to Portugal. To escape this wretched ignorance. And I will find Beza, and we will be in business, and I will be rich again.*

The constable's grunt as he unleashed the scourge sounded like an oink. With each biting slap, pain jolted through David's body, grossly out of proportion to the song of the whip. *Concentrate,* David told himself. *This too will pass.* A second slap and his knees buckled. *People will look up to me.* The next slap burned like fire. *This will not happen in Portugal.* Slap. A dark turbulence clouded David's eyes.

David woke from his faint face down on a pallet of hay. Alone, he worked his bonds till daylight, but made no progress toward escape. Soon after first light, a guard fetched him.

Along a swampy road David slogged along behind the constable, who rode a cadaverous, dingy horse. With every step, David's linen undershirt scraped across his tender back.

"Could we lay aside for a few minutes' rest, Constable? I'm not sure I can go on."

"No, we need to keep the pace. I want to return home tomorrow evening."

David could go no further. He stumbled, got up, walked a few steps, then stumbled and splashed to the muddy roadway again. The constable dismounted with a grunt and boosted David into the saddle. A couple of cold, slippery miles further down the road, the constable led David and his horse into the town of Mestre. They boarded a barge and crossed a lagoon to Venice, the city of islands in the sea. David considered jumping overboard but put aside that thought. He might be killed in Venice, but probably not today. Perish the thought of a cold, watery grave.

Disembarking the barge, the constable of Treviso strained to flatten his abdomen. Under his belt, he had been carrying a floppy yellow hat, an open flap made from a square of fabric. As he pressed the hat down over David's head, the little man squirmed to remove it.

"It's called a *bareta*. Wear it, Jew."

"I'm not a Jew," David said. Everywhere he looked, on the quay, on the buildings, and customhouses beyond, the winged lion of St. Mark looked back at him.

Seven hundred years before, martyred for having refused paganism, Theodore of Amasea, a Byzantine Christian, a dragonslayer, was chosen to be Venice's patron saint. The puny saint was a constant source of embarrassment to Justinian Partecipacius, the doge of Venice at that time. How could such an emerging mercantile powerhouse revere such an undistinguished saint? Venice needed a saint it could be proud of, and one that was a Roman Catholic, not Eastern Orthodox. A more prestigious saint was needed, perhaps a martyr. St. Theodore the dragon-slayer would have to go.

To remedy the situation, the doge financed an expedition by two merchants, Tribunus and Rusticus, to find a first-class saint for Venice to venerate, to replace its paltry dragon-slayer. They landed by sea in Egypt, claiming a storm blew them off course. Providence revealed to them that the Caliph of Alexandria was planning to destroy the local Christian church and with it, its relics. The remains of St. Mark the Evangelist, the author of one of the four gospels of the Christian bible, lay interred in a crypt hidden by monks under the cathedral altar. His bones represented one of the greatest treasures in Christendom.

With the aid of monks, the merchants removed the skeleton of the saint from the crypt, secreted the bones in their robes, and then to hide the pilfering, replaced the missing body with the remains of St. Claudia. On board ship, the merchants covered the bones of the saint with the carcasses of pigs to stop Muslim guards from searching the place that hid the contraband relics.

During the journey back to Venice, the merchants experienced a series of miracles. The voyage was miraculously quick, the more so considering they had laid over in Istria, where the relics saved a skeptic from demon possession. Nearing home, St. Mark himself quelled a savage storm. As a final miracle of the escapade, the doge promised to build a church in Venice, which became the basilica of St. Mark. In time, the location of the most important bones in Christendom was forgotten. Two hundred years later, during construction of the basilica, the saint himself extended an arm from a pillar to reveal the location of his remains. Venice was indeed Mark's home.

The constable took David over bridges and across rancid canals and into a courthouse. He threw his prisoner into a dank holding cell. As he tumbled across the floor, the dwarf shouted at the constable, "If you cross my sight again, you're a dead man." His threat was for the ears of the three other peasants who occupied the cell. For good measure, David reached inside his pourpoint as if he were concealing a weapon there. "Any man foolish enough to touch me has drawn his last breath," he told them, his voice muted but intense. The eyes of the other inmates searched the dwarf, from the top of his yellow *bareta* to the curled-back toes of his shoes. He had nothing they wanted.

He leaned back against the clammy cell wall opposite the barred door. His lashes throbbed. Everything in Venice smelled like a wet dog. Cold and soggy and nasty.

"He's mad," one muttered, "a mad Jew." Perhaps they feared that lunacy could pass from one person to the next like the Black Death. He opened his eyes wide and grinned at them. They backed away as if in mortal fear of his madness. David had an entire wall to himself.

Sitting with his raw back to the musty, moldy stone, David tried to plan for what would happen next. They would first take him to a courtroom, and in his defense to the charge of heresy, he would tell his tribe of Reuben story. He was in Venice only because he had told it. Those words would not go away. *The tribe of Reuben, indeed.*

Perhaps a demon had put Beza's words on his tongue. He had

almost forgotten the prince-of-Israel gag. He was as shocked as the feeblewits in Treviso when those words spilled out across his lips.

The story had actually increased his punishment. Damn the rotten luck, it should have been far too outlandish for any rational person to believe. But he was stuck with it, he would have to tell it to the Venetians. For all their sophistication, Venetians were still Christian, and to David, chances were good that a any Christian was a muttonhead.

So far his cellmates had not molested him.

*I can fool these sapheads just long enough to gain release,* he thought. The story he had told the court in Treviso had been believed dozens of times in Germany, and after all, as lies go, it was nothing. *Portugal awaits me. I will make my fortune back, tenfold. I only hope that Beza has left a few crumbs on the table.*

Alone, surrounded by stone. He remembered a time when he hid himself in a rocky crevice. The darkness and quiet comforted his spirit. He thought then about the journey that had brought him to this dungeon.

# CHAPTER 6

With the end of Henry's campaign for Emperor, England was free of the grinding burden of its foreign alliances. A season of romantic love settled over the English countryside. Thomas Wyatt penned a poem entitled "Whoso List to Hunt," about the object of his desire, his erstwhile lover, Anne Boleyn. He longed to chase after her again, as one might pursue a deer, or hind, but alas, she had also aroused an iniquitous lust in the loins of their sovereign, King Henry. Thus, Wyatt plead with his sweetheart, *noli me tangere*, touch me not, as conquest of the prey might prove lethal to the hunter.

> Whoso list to hunt, I know where is an hind,
> But as for me, hélas, I may no more.
> The vain travail hath wearied me so sore,
> I am of them that farthest cometh behind.
> Yet may I by no means my wearied mind
> Draw from the deer, but as she fleeth afore
> Fainting I follow. I leave off therefore,
> Sithens in a net I seek to hold the wind.
> Who list her hunt, I put him out of doubt,
> As well as I may spend his time in vain.

And graven with diamonds in letters plain
There is written, her fair neck round about:
Noli me tangere, for Caesar's I am,
And wild for to hold, though I seem tame.

In interludes between his toilsome endeavors to produce an heir to protect England, Henry set himself to the authorship of a book. He wrote in Latin, since the English language was barbaric vomit unfit for the written word. *Assertio Septum Sacramentorum* (Defence of the Seven Sacraments) set out a strong defense of marriage and heaped scorn on Martin Luther. The Pope promised a ten-year indulgence to anyone who would read it.

With the Pope's endorsement, the book flew from the shelves of booksellers, and of course, the success proved to the swollen-headed King Henry that his writing skills exceeded those of Wyatt. To further magnify Henry's literary talent, Pope Leo gave the virtuous King of England the title "Fidei Defensor."

On receiving notification of his award, Henry was jubilant. "The Pope," he roared out to his court, "has just named me Defender of the Faith!"

The King's fool replied, "Ho! Ho! Good King Harry, let you and me defend one another, but take my word for it, let the faith alone to defend itself!"

Henry ignored the warning of his fool and changed his royal label. His action was not without precedent. When he took the throne, he instructed his court to refer to him as "Your Majesty," No more the runty "Your Grace," as had been the custom. Hereafter his formal title was "Henry the Eighth, by the Grace of God, King of England and France, Defender of the Faith, and Lord of Ireland." But the words of Henry's fool echoed in the shouts of Luther's followers in the German hinterlands, and by the communeros in Castile. Fools and peasants seemed to have been receiving communion from the chalice of truth.

During the long, dark winter months, Francis fumed and schemed. He obsessed, hoping to find the most futile and destructive way to settle accounts with his opponent Charles. He pored over his maps and imagined a French advantage in the other territories he coveted, Navarre in Spain and the Low Countries to his north.

Francis set his lawyers to digging for precedent, and they did not let him down. "Charles's dominion over these lands is forfeit," a jowly lawyer told him.

"The trespasser! The interloper! The intruder! I knew it!" The young king jumped to his feet, ecstatic. "What did I know?"

"Are you sitting down, majesty?"

"Are you blind?"

"The line of Charles's succession...Ahem." The lawyer paused to clear a sticky wad of phlegm from his throat. "His succession...has come through, of all things"—the lawyer's voice dropped an octave, and the flabby wattle of skin at his throat jiggled like a flap of cold chicken skin—"a woman!"

"And?"

"Under Salic law, women cannot inherit a throne or fief, majesty," the lawyer explained.

"What's Salic law?"

"It's complicated. It's ancient. Some would argue archaic..."

"No true Frenchman would have the temerity to besmirch Salic Law. Archaic, eh? I'll have their heads on a pike!"

Francis was eager for a fight, any fight, Salic law just gave him a convenient imprimatur. He would seize a couple of territories from the empire while Charles was busy tending to his peasant revolts in Castile. Little more than a lark. He would snatch Navarre, a Spanish province to the south, icing on the cake, an easy and delicious way to retaliate. He would snatch it out from under Charles's fat Austrian Habsburg nose. And following that, he would take the Low Countries as well, Charles's boyhood home in the north, a lazy and decadent land, where slothful nobles squandered days at a time clubbing a leather ball around the grassy wastelands near the churning, weather-ravaged sea.

Lombardy was at peace and under no threat from her immediate neighbors, so Bourbon, its governor, traveled home to Châtellerault to attend to his ailing wife. She had remained childless for the first sixteen years of their marriage. But then she bore a son, a male heir, destined to be the Duke of Bourbon. He died suddenly at the age of six months. Suzanne, the Duchess of Bourbon, refused to thrive after the loss. She died giving birth to stillborn twins shortly after her husband's arrival.

As spring warmed itself into summer, the world-weary and financially embarrassed Bourbon stood tall in the saddle of his giant Percheron stud. He had buried his wife and children, and then ridden hard for an audience with his king. At every step of the journey, the grief brought on by the loss of his wife only deepened, regretting now every day of their frequent partings that service to crown and country demanded. He was despondent too over the loss of an heir and the grand estates of the Bourbon dynasty. He was unable to take nourishment on the two-day journey from Châtellerault to the Chateau d'Amboise, southwest of Paris, where clangor from the tournament lawn inundated him with the horrific memories of warfare, all the crueler because of the dishonor shown him by his king.

He carried with him a letter that his agents had intercepted, one he hoped that might open opportunities to recover his family's fortune.

A large group of lackeys attended the king, as always. An unending number of courtesans decorated the lawn and porches of a nearby pavilion. Their dresses lay over the top of farthingales, hooped structures the French called a *"vertudagins."* The hoops helped guard virtue, it was supposed. Silly idea, really, the courtesans who attended the king had no intention of guarding anyone's virtue, least of all their own.

The point of the monarch's lance repeatedly missed his target, a dummy topped by a melon painted with the crowned likeness of Charles, his mortal enemy, the Emperor of the Holy Roman Empire.

Bourbon's warhorse clomped onto the field just as Francis missed the target again. He could not remember the last time he had laughed, but he could scarcely disguise his mirth when Francis shouted at the melon, "Emperor Charles, see if your bribes will save you now. The crown belongs to me! Pretender!"

"Show him no mercy, King Francis!" Bourbon shouted.

On the next pass, Francis's lance found its target. With a great sound, *SQUAAATT*, the melon exploded into a red fog.

Francis reigned in his great warhorse, a huge black charger. He spun the mighty steed in a wheeling turn and lifted his visor so that he could see the remains of the melon. "Death is the only mercy Charles will receive from my hand!" he shouted, holding his lance high overhead, victoriously.

An attendant secured another painted melon on the dummy, but Francis dismounted. His armor clattered with each step. At the entry to the pavilion, Bourbon bent to a knee and kissed the ring of his monarch. The canopy covered a table that sported foods, fruits, wine, weapons, and maps.

"Someday, cousin," the king said to Bourbon, "I'll see the head of that Hun Charles on my lance." He scorned the Hapsburgs, whose roots were Austrian.

"May the lord allow me serve you that day, Majesty," Bourbon said, bowing. Deference to his king was as bitter as hops on his tongue.

The king was gloomy and cross with his understrappers as they helped him remove his armor. The breastplate was stuck.

"Perhaps if you lifted your arms, cousin."

The king snapped back, "Shouldn't you be somewhere killing my enemies?"

Bourbon was accustomed to deflecting Francis's ill-tempered outbursts. He pulled a document from a satchel. "My agents intercepted a letter, Majesty," he said, clearing his throat. "A Christian king writes it. From the east. He calls himself Prester John." Focused on the document, Bourbon did not see that Francis's eyes were rolling and that he was shaking his head.

"Cousin."

"He's as wealthy as three Indias...Inheritor of the magi...Rivers filled with gold...A fountain of youth, the tower of Babel, giants, centaurs, amazons...Pebbles that cure blindness!"

"How droll."

"He can see anywhere by looking through a magic mirror," Bourbon went on. "He possesses the body of Saint Thomas."

"And where is this kingdom?" the king said, allowing his eyelids to droop.

"East of Persia, south of Sahara and Abyssinia. It is a bit unclear, I admit. But Prester John wants Christian kings to make a war on the Turks. He on the east, his allies on the west."

"Let's see that," Francis demanded.

Bourbon turned over the parchment scroll with a self-satisfied smile.

"Ha! Prester John, indeed." Francis crumpled the scroll into a wad and pretended to wipe his backside with the letter, then hurled it at Bourbon. "Cousin, you're a ninnyhammer."

"I paid a great price for this." Bourbon struggled to escape yet another indignity from his king. His stomach churned as if it were overfilled with resentment.

"This drivel turned up when Louis XI was king. And a dozen times before that."

"Francis. No." Sickening bile churned in Bourbon stomach. Every sou was dear to him. "It can't be."

"It can be and it is. It's a fake. A fraud. Sell it to the Portuguese. Or the Spanish," he snarled. "Those fools believe this tripe."

"Then I say drink. Drink to the death of Emperor Charles!" The crestfallen Bourbon saluted Francis with a goblet, and both men guzzled. Each man a warrior, neither took his eye off the other.

The letter might be a fake, but Bourbon's quest to recover his family fortune was undeterred. "Imagine the feast we will have when the Hun is dead," Bourbon said, wiping his chin on his sleeve. "Wine will flow like water. It will eclipse the feast we enjoyed after my conquest—our conquest—of Milan."

"Cousin, we weary of your talk of Milan," the young king said. "Can't you gossip about debauching virgins?"

"My expenses remain unreimbursed," Bourbon plead.

"You should have plundered Lombardy when you had the chance."

"Plunder *your* province? We had a treaty! They laid down their arms!" Bourbon lacked the courage to remind his sovereign that it was on the king's orders that Lombardy had escaped the pillaging that ordinarily followed a military defeat.

"Bourbon, my dear cousin, the crown expects initiative from the supreme commander of the French armies."

Bourbon could scarcely restrain the pent up anger and resentment that sharpened Bourbon's tongue. "My bankers demand repayment. Twenty-five thousand German mercenaries don't fight for chicken-feed." Even as the words left his tongue, Bourbon's sensed his body was clothed in a weary pall.

"Damn the Germans."

Bile choked his throat as Bourbon fell to his knees. "I need a hundred thousand livres."

"Get up from there, Constable," Francis demanded. "Emperor Charles grows strong while you allow my army to dawdle in Lombardy."

"I should be leading the armies in the low countries," Bourbon sputtered, rising to his feet. "Instead, you gave the task to Alençon. Your limp-wristed brother-in-law! That job belongs to me! How can I ever hope to recover?"

"You won't," said the king. "Not by malingering around Châtellerault."

"I went to Châtellerault to bury my wife." Then with a quiver in his voice, he told his monarch, "I pledged our family estates. I haven't a sou to my name."

"*Your* estates? That is rich. Your wife left no heirs. In the opinion of the treasury, your deceased wife's lands escheat to the crown. They were never yours to pledge."

As sickly smile widened across the face of the big-nosed king, the soldier felt his hand grip the handle of his sword.

The king unrolled a map of Western Europe on the table, redirecting Bourbon's attention. "France has greater concerns than a few manure-encrusted little estates in Auvergne. The empire has armies of Austrians and Germans in the Low Countries to our north. And to the south, just across the Pyrenees, Spain crouches like a lion. All serve Charles, the prince of bribery."

"Cousin, I have no income to wage further wars."

"And I do? I spent a king's ransom to win that crown."

"Much of that was my money…"

"Are you the only one with bankers?"

"I can't sustain a fight in Lombardy. I don't have the treasure to fight in the Low Countries." Bourbon hung his head. "It's impossible."

"Women love you."

"My wife isn't yet cold in the ground."

"Odd. Your agents extend offers as we speak."

Bourbon turned his toe in the ground. "Rich women have spurned every overture that my agents have advanced. Everyone knows my finances. Because of you, I'm a laughingstock."

"The crown could influence an advantageous union." The king's smile grew even more bent and sickly.

Perhaps the king was offering a port for refuge from the storm. "All I ask for is relief from my creditors."

"Then the woman of your dreams awaits you," said the king. He drank again from his goblet. "Queen Louisa. Madame de Savoie."

Bourbon gagged involuntarily. "You jest!"

"You couldn't hope for a better advantage."

"She's your mother. My aunt!" he told the king, as if he did not know. "Plus, she must be fifty years old!"

"A flower of delicate beauty. Her proximity in blood might rescue your wife's lands..."

"She's the worst woman in the country!"

The king slammed his wine goblet down onto the map table. "It is my pleasure!" he shouted.

"Not for all the wealth in Christendom!" Bourbon shouted back.

"You would betray your king?"

"Cousin..."

"My ministers assure me that she'd pay a handsome price..."

"I have no interest in her dowry," Bourbon interrupted.

"A handsome price for your estates, Bourbon. For treason, your estates would be forfeit."

"If I committed treason."

"If you committed treason, which I am satisfied that you will not." The king turned his back on the general of all his armies. "Kindly gather the divisions that are quartered in Lombardy, Constable, and join me in the Low Countries without delay. You are dismissed."

His mocking king had stripped the Duke of all his dignity. Enmity smoldered in his heart. Bourbon was bereft of even an ounce of the honor he once held so sacred.

In the Low Countries, Swiss mercenaries filled the French lines. Many fought against Francis at Marignano. German landsknechts were in Charles's employ, as he was now emperor over the German states.

Both sides had soldiers armed with the new hook guns, a weapon called an arquebus, carried into conflict by units called arquebusiers.

Their weapon was a smoothbore hand cannon fired by a matchlock device mounted on the side of the gun. A clip held a serpentine, a short length of smoldering rope above a pan of black powder. When the arquebusier eased back the trigger device, the ember on the end of the serpentine lowered into a pan filled with black powder. The flash carried fire into the chamber of the gun where it ignited a charge, which in turn, propelled a ball of lead and a cloud of thick smoke hurtling from the muzzle of the gun. No two guns were alike. A hook added to the butt of the gun allowed the arquebusier to steady the weapon against his chest, shoulder or hip. The arquebus was the first handheld weapon that could penetrate heavy armor, as long as the target was at close range. The shooter could reload and fire eight shots per hour.

The arquebusier units promised to deliver their side a great advantage, as long as it did not rain. Francis was eager to test a tactic his lieutenants bandied around that suggested the arquebusiers fire in volleys to increase casualties.

As word came to Pope Leo that the French armies were massing near Navarre and in the north, threatening the Low Countries, he sent an urgent dispatch to Cardinal Wolsey, asking him to mediate. "The emperor loves me not," Francis told Wolsey in a meeting attended by Charles's ambassador. "I do not love him, even more than before, and I am determined to be his enemy."

The French renewed an alliance with Venice, promising the Venetians that France would break faith with the no-longer-secret treaty with the Turks. Aware of France's pattern of treachery, Venice could only hope that France would return Venice's allegiance, should the Mohammadans advance against the City of Canals. A friendly open port at Venice was beneficial to France, so long as Francis held the Po Valley and Lombardy.

The defenseless provinces of the Low Countries were sure to be lost without strong assistance from other nations. Charles unconditionally opposed Francis's aggression on both fronts, north and south. Navarre was his, and he would lose face if he failed to defend it. But he had his German peasants and the Castilian communeros to worry about. His armies were undermanned in every province. He needed allies.

The Pope, who months before had abandoned Francis's campaign to defeat Charles, again switched allegiances. "My enemy's enemy is my friend," Francis said, happily accepting treaty with the Pope. Francis would have given Martin Luther weapons if the mad monk had promised to raise an army or, for that matter, even a pitchfork against Charles.

While pretending to be an honest arbitrator, Wolsey had his jaw at the Imperial ear. "King Henry's defeat in seeking the Imperial throne is a still-bleeding wound," Wolsey whispered. "But nonetheless, he might be persuaded..."

"If the king of England sides with me," Charles promised Wolsey, "you shall be elected Pope at the death of Leo."

*He has been reading my correspondence,* Wolsey thought. His lifelong dream—for the taking!—the papal tiara, and it was almost within his grasp. But first, Wolsey had some heavy lifting to do with his king.

He told Henry, "You are the king of France, the true king." He whispered this slogan in Henry's ear time and again, playing on an article of faith to the Tudors that they were the just heirs to the throne of France. "This war will prepare your rightful throne."

So it was that in Calais, Wolsey signed a secret accord between England and the empire. It provided, in the first part, that Henry would withdraw the offer of the hand of his daughter, the five-year-old Mary, to the three-year-old dauphin of France, Francis's heir apparent. She would marry Charles instead. In the second part, Henry would issue an order to destroy the French navy and invade France, as French corsairs had been harassing Spanish shipping in the

New World. And in the third part, the empire agreed to pay Henry a pension in the annual sum of forty thousand marks, a wagon and a half full of silver, every year for life. Charles's promise to make Wolsey Pope would have to remain unwritten.

The Diet, or Reichstag, a general assembly of German nobles, was meeting in Worms. The Diet was presided over by the new Emperor, who was itching to get back to Castile to quell the peasant revolt. On his orders, the Diet issued an edict that declared Luther to be a heretic and banned the reading or possession of his writings. It also promised a reward for his capture. Luther escaped arrest, hid out in Wartburg castle, and to help endure his dull existence there, he began work on a translation of the Bible into German.

Pope Leo, born Giovanni di Lorenzo de' Medici...so much of his life had been disordered, a chaotic fusion of construction and demolition, light and dark, tragedy and comedy, good and evil. He began wearing his hair in a tonsure at the early age of seven. His family arranged his ordination as a cardinal-deacon while he still had baby teeth. At sixteen, he voted in the conclave to elect a Pope, even though he had never entered a priestly order. His dead cousin needed a replacement. When elected Pope, Leo was thirty-seven. Two days later, he received his priestly ordination, and after another two days, he was consecrated as bishop. The two-day wait served to preserve decency – no one wanted to make a farce of his accession. After a third two-day wait, the tiara of the Pope was placed on his head.

Leo had enjoyed many same-sex relationships prior to his ordination, but remained chaste while serving as Pope. He took pleasure in spending his autumns in the country. He would leave his papal robes in Rome, and if that were not enough of a scandal, he even wore boots, amusing himself with hawking, hunting stag, and fishing.

In the autumn of 1521, after an exciting and energetic year, the pontiff was in the country with a large entourage of musicians, actors, and artists when he received intelligence that his army had recaptured Milan. His generals had exercised initiative and sprung a surprise attack on Lombardy while France was engaged in Navarre and the Low Countries. Venice had sat this battle out, fearful of leaving its own city-state unguarded while the Turks were at the door. As his courtiers and officers rejoiced in the hour of his greatest victory, discharging their hook guns into the night sky, Leo paced the floor of his bedchamber, unable to sleep.

He returned to Rome, fatigued and inexplicably disconsolate. He had scarcely reached the Vatican when he suddenly fell ill. "Pray for me," he plead to his attendants. The pontiff fell to the floor and without time to receive the holy sacrament, died in the prime of his life. He was forty-five.

Crowds of angry Romans vilified the procession that carried the Pope's remains to his grave. The faithful would never forgive Pope Leo for dying without receiving the sacrament, the last rites, nor would they soon forget that he had left a mountain of unpaid debts. "You gained your pontificate like a fox," shouted one angry Roman. "You held it like a lion. You left it like a dog."

A few days later, before news of the Pope's death had reached far-away Lisbon, King Manuel, aged fifty-two, went to meet his maker. Gone was a father who had taken the hand of a woman betrothed to his son. Now John III was King of Portugal, Diogo's homeland. He was nineteen.

His first year as emperor could hardly have been worse for Charles. Efforts to hold the Low Countries against Francis's advance had hamstrung his progress in subduing the rebellion in Castile. The rudderless, corrupt Church was now in alliance with France, his mortal enemy. Charles exiled the lawyers that had counseled him to give so dearly to secure England's allegiance—he packed them off to stations in the New World. The English sea captains were happy to attack the French corsairs on the high sea without encouragement from the empire, so he stood to gain nothing from his promise to marry this sickly five-year-old English girl. He was stuck with his pledge to support Wolsey for Pope. The emperor's one success had been that charges had been brought against the mad monk Martin Luther, but the heretic priest had only become more beloved by the peasants for having evaded capture.

The emperor took leave of the German states to attend to the peasant uprising in Castile.

# CHAPTER 7

In David's beginning, he feared a dark spirit that he thought lived concealed in the folds of his mother's tent. Showing fear brought his father's reproach. So David was both fearful and ashamed of being afraid.

From birth, he had short, stubby, camel-teat fingers and stunted arms and legs. Dwarfism beset his body.

He demanded the respect of half-brothers and half-sisters. He did not realize that always in the background was his father, hissing at them to "make room for the little one." Their pretended adoration was really jealousy.

He was wise beyond his years and a shrewd leader among his siblings. Passing traders who mistook him for a child did so at their own peril. His dark, knifelike eyes struck fear into the hearts of any soul that was foolish enough to cross him.

His father pitched his black goat hair shelters on rocky, windswept mountain slopes, above a small village in the Afghani province of Parwan. A larger town on the plain beyond was Bagram, an important stop on the Silk Road, which sat in the junction of two river valleys. Further on, to the east, following the river, the Silk Road picked its way upward, alongside the rocky banks of the churning white-water, on to Jalalabad, Peshawar, and through the Khyber Pass, then Islamabad, and India beyond. The people in Bagram cursed the river. They longed for a wide, slow moving stream, one that would bring trade to Bagram and, with it, wealth and education from the Indus valley to the land of the Afghanis. Their prayers went unanswered. The waters here ran in torrents.

The local tribesmen were Pashtun. An ancient proverb gave voice to their creed. "I against my brothers; my brothers and I against my cousins; my brothers, my cousins, and I against the world." They led lives as wild and turbulent as the rivers that roared down from the snowcapped peaks.

Like all his tribesmen, the boy dressed in trousers that tied at the waist with a string. A loose-fitting shirt fell to his knee, and over the shirt, he wore a vest. His turban was made of long cotton strips that left his forehead exposed, so he could touch it during prayer. One end dangled over his shoulder—he used it to wipe his face. The turban protected his head from heat and cold, thick leather sandals protected his feet from sharp rocks, and a curved blade tucked under his vest protected him from everything else. Many other tribes and peoples with diverse languages, manners of dress, and customs filled the land. Most were far more brutish than the Pashtun.

The little boy's father owned many sheep and goats and had taken many Muslim and Hindu women as wives. The Muslim women wore baggy black trousers, long shirts belted with sashes, and lengths of cotton cloth over their heads. Over their clothing, they often wore a burqa, a veil that covered them from head to below the knees, loose enough for the little boy to hide behind when his father disapproved of his youthful pranks. To please their husband, the Hindus dressed in silk dresses, but during the day, they donned baggy trousers that were narrow at the ankle and, over that, long embroidered tunics. They worshiped many gods, daubed red paint on their foreheads, and smelled of curry. One of them taught the little boy to be attentive to a man's face, his dress, his language, and religion. She taught him to read minds.

The little boy was quick with strange languages and often engaged travelers on the Silk Road. He told them their fortunes, often in their native tongue. His performance easily convinced the superstitious traders that he knew more about them than they knew about themselves. The most gullible traders, the pale-skinned ones that traced the figure of a cross on their chests, hailed from a land that had produced Alexander, beyond the horizon, even further west than Turkey.

He learned that he could invent the messages that he delivered to the unwary traders. He could even demand gold in payment, if he persuaded the traders that the messages came to him from distant loved ones. The little boy bit each coin to test the metal they gave him in compensation. If he received a coin his tooth could not indent, he promised the offender that the destiny would change, and he threatened the donor with a fiery grave and eternal torment.

The boy's extended family revered those who were the best storytellers. One of the Afghani wives told tales of a great migration of Copts, the race of the Pharaohs. She claimed that when the prophet Moses got the better of the infidels at the Red Sea, many of the Copts fled Egypt and settled in the mountainous region, there to become the Pashtuns.

His Pashtun mother was Muslim, but her explanation of their origins was quite different. She held to a common Pashtun belief that people called the Bani Israel—the Children of Israel—took refuge in this rocky land, having set out from the west at a time the northern tribes of Israel dispersed.

His father was the best storyteller of them all. His windy yarns held the little boy in rapt attention late into the night, long after the camel-sheep-and-goat-dung fire tended by the lesser wives had burned down to embers. The best stories were about Daoud Roubani, the greatest folk hero of the Pashtun tribesmen, greater even than Alexander.

In his twelfth year, his father performed his little son's circumcision. In the days following, the little one asked his father to tell the heroic Daoud Roubani stories again and again. When an older cousin crowded the little boy away from his father's side, his place of honor, near the fire, the cousin endured the stinging rebuke of the tongue of the patriarch, and counted himself fortunate to escape the edge of his uncle's sword.

His long barren mother died, and in the same year, a flash flood swept his father away as he sought to retrieve a lamb from the torrent.

The jealous brothers now scolded and ridiculed him, chiding him for failing to saving their father from the flood.

He hated the awareness of grief, of guilt. He had no protector now. He was afraid. His body shivered involuntarily as he hid in a cleft of rock in an escarpment above his father's tents. He was without sanctuary. His siblings would not defend him. He was not his father's oldest son, and given that his mother's ancestry was in the Bani Israeli tradition—people who were not violent and loved peace—he had no hope of seeing the next sunrise if he fought for a share of his father's wealth. His destiny was foreseeable. His half-brothers would capture him, bind him with heavy cords, and beat him nearly to death. He would do the same to them if he had a chance. With any luck, his brothers would kill him or trade him for a dog.

His greatest fear was that they would sell him into bacha bazi. Many powerful Afghanis owned young boys. They dressed them as women and trained them to sing and dance for their kin. The audience devoured the youngsters with lustful eyes, and their most ardent admirers forced them to submit to sexual relations.

As nightfall approached, he clambered down the ridge and entered the camp. He made no effort to resist capture and did his best to endure the whipping that followed. He watched as a neighboring chieftain offered a great price for a younger half-brother with fair features. The price was reasonable. The buyer hauled the beautiful pre-pubescent half-brother away in the night.

But the little one had a predominant, piglet's nose, dense lips, a heavy brow, and coarse features. He was ugly, and his uninviting looks foreclosed any chance that his fate would be bacha bazi, Allah be praised.

It came to pass that his half-brothers sold him away for a few silver coins, to Muslim traders on the Silk Road, who carted him off like so much hashish or a block of salt, off to the west, toward the setting sun.

They journeyed in a camel caravan across mountain ranges and down to Herat, where the plain pushed the mountains away to the horizon. Here, Persian traders purchased the little boy for a few more pieces of silver and carried him away to Susa, a city on the Persian Gulf.

Never before had the little boy seen a sea.

Again, his captors sold him away, this time to a Bedouin who offered a great price.

Still robed in his Pashtun clothes, the little boy suffered greatly under the burning rays of the desert sun. The captive studied his master, who did not seem to be bothered by the heat, from head to toe. A high, tight collar gripped his neck while cords girded long, triangular sleeves. Under the shirt, he wore a short skirt, and over it a striped robe, open down the front and tightened at his waist by a belt, and over that, he wore another robe, striped and without sleeves. Folded over his head he wore a richly decorated triangle of fabric held in place by a strap of camel wool.

The Bedouin women wore necklaces, rings, anklets, and bracelets that displayed family wealth. Some bore symbols to avert the evil eye while others contained verses of the Koran to ward off scorpion stings. The anklets and bracelets were hollow and filled with noise-making stones. The women's faces were unveiled, but they hid their hair with dark coverings. Their robes were similar to that of the men but less belted, more open.

The Bedouin men wore no jewelry. Tied to the chieftain's belt was a purse that contained a handful of golden coins and a few shiny red stones, and always present, fastened to his left side, inside an ornately decorated sheath cinched tightly under his sash, he carried a khanjar, a stubby, curved knife. It was always within the reach of the Bedouin. But more important, to the boy's mind, it was within the reach of the captive as well.

The Bedouin band trekked into Arabia. The women pitched tents with other Bedouins, near Riyadh, but the man who had purchased him pushed on, ten days to the west, to Medina. Most Bedouins would not trek across the wilderness alone, but this striped-robed creature had invested so heavily in his human freight that his solitary trip across the desert was worth the risk. Except for some baskets of dates, his only cargo was the little boy. He hoped the prize might bring a big price from an oasis caliph—dwarves brought good luck—as an oddity, or perhaps a fool. A healthy sum would allow the Bedouin to buy gemstones in the markets of Medina.

Medina did not produce a satisfactory offer for the little boy. The Bedouin sold his dates and headed south to Mecca, alone but for his dwarf and his camels. The trek was arduous but the little boy had good reason to fear what fate held in store for him at the end of the journey.

The sun was high in the sky, and its heat was unbearable when, without warning, the little boy slipped from the saddle of the camel, and like so much dung, flopped down on the burning desert sand. He cried in anguish, then fell as silent as a corpse. The trader, at the sound of the shout, pulled back on the looped rein that led to a small wooden peg in his own camel's nose. With a barking command, he told the beast to stop. A soft tug to the side directed the animal to return to the pile of rags in the desert. On another voice command, the camel knelt, and the Bedouin dismounted. He tested the bindings of the dwarf's saddle. They were firm.

He leaned over the heap of rags lying on the desert floor, and as he did, the little boy threw a fistful of sand in his face. As quick as a cobra, the little one was on top of the camel driver's chest, his rump in the face of his captor. His swift hands found the hilt of the khanjar. Unsheathing the knife, he stabbed down into the inner thigh of the Bedouin. A great volume of the Bedouin's lifeblood spurted out and soaked into the floor of the wilderness to become one with the dust of colorless desert. The Bedouin's grip relaxed. The captive's task was over as abruptly as it had begun. The Bedouin was dead.

The little boy was careful to hide the dead man along the side of a low, rocky hill. He partially covered the carcass with stones to disguise the heap from the eyes of men. The odor of death was certain to disclose its location to the marauding scavengers and wild dogs of the wilderness. In a day, not a scrap of flesh remaining to putrefy, bones would be scattered widely by beasts of the wilderness. He kept the camel driver's knife and the purse that contained golden coins and red stones.

Near nightfall, the little boy drove six camels into an oasis called Khaibar. The camels found the way. They knew the exact whereabouts of the closest source for the water they needed to quench a deep thirst born on a long trek across the desert. He arrived in Khaibar in his twelfth year, the year, he would later discover, that the pale-skinned Europeans, the ones who traced the figure of a cross on their chests, reckoned to be the year 1500 *anno domini*, fifteen hundred years after the beginning of the Christian era.

Nine hundred years earlier, Mohammad and his followers attacked a fortified village of Jews who were living in the oasis of Khaibar. One night before the siege, the future revealed itself to Safiyya, a Jewess, in a dream. She saw a moon fall into her lap. When she told her husband of her vision, he blackened her eye with a slap. "That is because you desire for Mohammad!" he chastised her.

The attackers could not hold the siege forever; they needed water from the oasis. From his sickbed outside the oasis, Mohammad's nephew Ali arose to bear the banner of the Prophet. He met a Jewish chieftain in single combat. On his second blow, Ali cleaved straight through the helmet of the Jew, splitting his skull to his teeth. In the battle that followed, having lost his shield, Ali defended himself with a door from a wall, and then threw the door down as a bridge across a chasm that guarded the citadel. Conquest was certain. The Jews of Khaibar surrendered. The door was so heavy that it took eight men to replace it on its hinges.

While the conquerors searched Khaibar for the treasure of the Jews, the prophet himself inquired about Saffiyya's black eye. She told him that her husband had hit her. The husband denied it. He also foreswore knowledge of Khaibar's treasure. Seeing thorough his deceit, Mohammad had him followed. After he was spotted near a ruin, an excavation revealed part of the treasure. Interrogated and tortured, the husband refused to break, even after Mohammad's men drove a torch into his chest. As he gasped for breath, Mohammad handed him over to a warrior who had lost his brother in the battle for Khaibar. His captor beheaded him in revenge. Mohammad took the widow, Safiyya, as a wife.

The Jews continued to live in the oasis, able to practice their faith. The prophet protected them from outside aggression on the condition that they give up half of their treasure and half of their future income to the Muslims.

"Lion of God." Victory in Khaibar greatly raised the status of Mohammad among his followers. Seeing his power, the Bedouin tribesmen swore allegiance and converted to Islam. Not in Khaibar, but afterwards, Islamic law required the imposition of tribute from conquered non-Muslims as well as confiscation of their lands. The booty he plundered and the weapons he captured strengthened his army. Within eighteen months, Mohammad conquered Mecca.

A remnant of the Jewish settlement survived in the oasis at Khaibar that the dwarf boy and his camels approached.

Young boys of Khaibar helped the little one water the beasts. As it was in his homeland, hospitality to strangers was expected and freely given. He recognized a few of their words—they used an Aramaic dialect that had similarity to one his mother had sometimes used. They all wore long cotton robes over skirts. Some wrapped their heads in knotted scarves while others covered their heads with cotton panel held in place by a rope circlet.

Once his camels had consumed their fill of water, he was able to understand that the boys wanted to know his name. Thrusting his chest forward, he lied. "Daoud Roubani," he told them.

"David Reuveni. He's a Jew," one boy said to the others. The name "David" marked him as a Jew. The Muslim boys, those with the cotton caps held by ropes, walked away.

From this time, David Reuveni was the name of the little one. One boy gestured for him to follow and he did.

He was welcomed into a community of Jews that prospered in this desert oasis. Jews fed him and gave him new clothing. He might have continued his journey, but warm food and a comfortable bed convinced him that it was to his advantage to stay. He evaluated his possessions. He had the red stones, some gold coins, a dagger and six camels. He sold his freight and the camels and found steady work in the synagogue. While serving the rabbis as a valet, he learned enough Hebrew to read the Torah, the Prophets, and the Books of Wisdom.

David's Hebrew and Aramaic improved. He practiced with the writings of the rabbis—the Talmud—but he devoured the narratives in their holiest books, like the story of David and Goliath. He also loved the story about the pharaoh's army drowning. He imagined that it took place in the sea that grew out of the desert beyond the mountains west of Khaibar. His fantasy was closer to the truth than he might have imagined. As he soaked up the language, he also absorbed the literature and customs of the Jews in much the same way that the desert sand had taken up the blood of the Bedouin the young boy had killed.

Strangers often arrived in Khaibar. The newcomers were Jews fleeing faraway lands, some from Aragon and Castile, also called Spain, but most were from Portugal. The Jews from the Iberian Peninsula fled to North Africa, Turkey, Palestine and Arabia. The only Jews permitted to stay in their home countries were those who converted to Christianity. David listened to their lamentations and their tearful prayers to the God whose name was not to be spoken.

"Of all the nations in the world, the most powerful are Spain and Portugal," a rabbi newly arrived from Portugal told David. His name was Abraham ben Eliezer Halevi.

"I've met a few Christians," David said. As a boy, he and his brothers had mocked the foolishness and gullibility of the Western traders.

"Spain lays claim to the western half of the world, and Portugal the eastern half. And their claims sanctioned by the holiest man in Christendom, the Pope, who sits on a throne in Rome."

"Rome, yes." Traders talked about Rome, a faraway city that had ascended to become the most powerful nation in the world after the death of Alexander, whose name still demanded respect in the Afghani mountains. David was not surprised to learn that Rome was the seat of a great religion.

Halvei told him that Rome no longer dominated. Only a scrap of ancient Rome remained. The remnant had taken to calling itself the Holy Roman Empire. It was sprawled across a vast north country, lands guarded in the night sky by the stars that formed the figure of the great bear. A small population of Jews also peopled the empire.

For a time, David studied to become a teacher under Halevi. His mentor spent the rest of his time writing manifestos which calculated the end of days and interpreted contemporary events as heralding a time of redemption for the Jews. By his own admission, he believed in the unknowable. He called his latest work "The Epistle on the Secret of Redemption." In it, he outlined plans to disrupt trade. He hoped for a Portuguese intervention at the port of Jeddah or, better yet, a European invasion of Arabia. Halevi said that the destruction of Jeddah's fortifications would be the final sign of the end of days. He slaved night and day to reproduce his newest epistle on parchment and delivered many copies to the towns and cities in Arabia.

As David approached the age of twenty, the lands in the north began to occupy his dreams. By all accounts, this country was a place rich with grass, timber, game, life-giving blankets of winter snows, and in the summertime, fish in its gentle streams. *A rich land populated by muttonheads,* he thought. He was tired of the freezing desert nights. He was tired of being a Jew; the daily rituals they observed were a nuisance. They served no valid purpose. He was tired of the rigorous dietary laws. The rabbis had reverence and respect, but they were poor. Only a fool would want to be poor in Khaibar. It must be the worst place on earth. The land in the north beckoned the little man who wanted more.

Halevi issued an offer to any man seeking adventure. He would pay a generous sum to any fortune hunter who was brave enough to carry his most recent epistle to Jews in the Italian states. David's friends chattered that only a madman would take the offer. But David jumped at the chance. "This Europe sounds like a place where a man can get his fill of warm food, where he can sleep in warm beds, and where he can tussle plump, muttonheaded ladies till the wee hours of the morning," David told his friends. "Europe is the ideal place, and it is in Christendom that I will make my fortune."

So it was that David bound up the rabbi's epistle, all his gold coins and precious red stones in a leather pouch, slid the Bedouin's khanjar under his sash, and bid farewell to his friends in Khaibar. He pushed north and west, beyond a range of mountains, to a city on the Red Sea, Jeddah.

Halevi's prophecy had broad circulation. When the Portuguese arrived in Jeddah, he predicted destruction of the city and its towers, the end of days. The imam of Khaibar hated the rabbi and railed against all seafarers from the west. "The Portuguese are butchers who kneel before idols!"

Possession of the rabbi's letter was a curse to David. He would be greeted with scorn in Jeddah if the citizens knew he carried it. So, on his arrival, he burned the letter and claimed to be a descendant of Mohammad. The women of Jeddah, covered head to toe in veils, rubbed his feet with oil. He purchased local garments for himself from traders in the market, suited for ventilation and protection from the sun, but decorated at the neck and borders with the silk. He also bought a turban.

He showed the villagers his red stones and told them that he had removed them from the prophet's tomb. He had no shame in telling the bold lie because the truth was not uncovered. But the inhabitants of this village by the sea did not sit him in an honored place near the fire, as custom demanded, and he cursed them.

A fishing boat sailed him across the Red Sea to Nubia. In Cochin, he found more Jews. They told stories about men with black skins, some of them Jews, who lived in Nubia. *Black skins? Preposterous*, David thought. Whether they were fools or liars, it made little difference. David claimed to be an emissary from a large Jewish kingdom in the faraway east, a kingdom, he told them, that had been built by the lost Hebrew tribes that the rabbis had told him about in Khaibar. The Jews ministered to him as if he were a prince, but because of the Mamluks Sultanate, Cochin was no place for a Jewish emissary.

The Mamluks gripped Egypt in a stranglehold. They were a blue-eyed, bloodthirsty gang of ex-slaves that had a testy relationship with the Ottoman Turks. They prided themselves in horsemanship and reveled in their history. Their cavalry had driven both the Mongol hordes and the crusading Christians out of Palestine. The Mamluks took no interest in governance of the lands they possessed. They maintained control by assassination.

David wanted no part of the Mamluks. His quest was to find a rich land filled with muttonheads not a society ruled by miscreants.

The Jews of Cochin encouraged David to move on. Purchasing passage with their gifts, David traveled north, up the Nile River in a felucca, a single-masted river craft with a triangular sail. The boat was heavily laden with grain and sailed directly through the heart of deadly Mamluk country. The boat's captain slipped his cargo past Cairo under the cover of night. Anytime was a good time to avoid a Mamluk. David hid low among the sacks of grain as they glided past on the whispering water of the Nile River.

The felucca docked in Alexandria, where David purchased passage on a cargo ship headed across an inland ocean, to the Christian north. It was laden with colorful rugs crafted from goat hair.

Their captain headed to the city of Venice, farther west than Greece, where his rugs might have great value. Even in Greece, controlled by Ottoman Turks, suspicion attached to anything Egyptian. The mariners traveled around the Peloponnesian peninsula, into the Adriatic Sea, and well off the coast of Dalmatia, toward Venice. Nearing the harbor, the ship's captain was careless in an attempt to relieve David of his gold coins. His body, drained of blood from a deep gash across his throat, went over the ship's gunwales and into the wine dark sea outside the Venetian lagoon, there to feed the fishes of the deep.

Once on dry land, David surrendered a few gold coins to the first mate along with the little ship. He kept the cargo for himself. He was dressed in desert robes that hid his purse, red stones, and knife. He wore a turban. Even with that added height, he was no taller than the youngest of the boys who were wrestling his cargo of rugs out of the ship's hold and onto the quay.

In his cell, David told himself with resolve, *Venice was no obstacle to me then, and it will be no obstacle to me now.*

# CHAPTER 8

Wolsey disembarked a barge on the River Thames, having just returned home from France. While still on the landing, he received news of Pope Leo's death. Word of his passing raced across the docks and into London as if it were the Black Death.

Wolsey partied as if it were 1499. No revelry was too extreme, no debauchery too flagrant. He gave no quarter in his efforts to put the devil back into hell with every wench in London.

His agents rushed to Rome with strict instructions. "Represent to the cardinals," the bleary-eyed Wolsey told them, "that by choosing a partisan of Charles or Francis, they risk incurring the enmity of one or the other. And if they choose some feeble Italian priest, the Church can only yield to Charles, or Francis, whichever becomes stronger. Luther threatens the papacy. There is only one means. It is to choose me. Now, go and exert yourself." It was the best he could do on such short notice. England had more virgins to debauch, and Wolsey had so little time. The papacy was within his grasp. Almost.

The conclave opened in the Vatican during Christmastide, December 27, and Wolsey's name was promptly proposed. The cardinals received his nomination as if his name had spilled out of a chamber pot and into the aisle of a crowded chapel. Then began the objections of his opposition. "He is too young." He was two years old when Leo was born. Some said, "He is too firm." Others said, "He will fix the papacy in England and not Rome." Wolsey's nomination failed to garner twenty votes.

Another faction would have elected the next de' Medici in line, Cardinal Giulio di Giuliano, Leo's bastard nephew, who was long on experience, having served Leo as his minister of diplomacy. But the cardinals lacked the stomach to elect another de' Medici.

In desperation, they voted for Adrian. Born in the Netherlands, he was Charles of Spain's long-time tutor. He brought experience to the table as well, hard lessons learned in a couple of stints as Inquisitor General in Spain. Yet he had never been to Rome and was so ignorant of affairs that he wrote ahead to secure assistance. He worried that he would be unable to find suitable lodging.

Wolsey boiled with rage. Charles had done nothing to further his nomination; worse yet, he had advanced the name of his own tutor. The promise the emperor had whispered in Wolsey's ear was trumpery. The very thought. Plans for revenge consumed Wolsey. He refused to pay the tailors who had already crafted his papal wardrobe.

Charles correctly anticipated Wolsey's despair. He dashed off a message. "The new Pope is old and sickly. He cannot hold office long. He has arrived in Rome attended only by his female cook. You shall soon make your entrance there surrounded by all your grandeur. I beg you, Eminence, take great care of your health."

To add some certainty to his position, Wolsey made secret approaches to his monarch's enemy, Francis, and waited for the death of Adrian.

Far to the east, in Istanbul, Suleiman kept an alert eye for advantage in the west. The Turk's spies reported to him that armies of the papal states had advanced toward Lombardy. He concluded that the maneuvering of Leo's armies left Venice far more vulnerable to assault from the sea.

Suleiman was twenty-seven. He had been sultan of the Ottoman

Empire for less than a year, but he was wise, careful not to overreach. Christians had machines to measure hours, days, and years, but Suleiman had time.

Tall and wiry, Suleiman was obsessed with Alexander the Great and his vision of building a world empire that would encompass the East and the West. The Mediterranean would be his own in due course, and it would be around the great inland sea that he would establish his own Islamic caliphate.

The Knights of St. John, also called the Knights Hospitallers, a remnant of the once-powerful Knights Templar, had occupied the Island of Rhodes for three hundred years earlier after losing their crusader stronghold in Palestine. Rhodes bellied up to the southern coast of Turkey and gave the Hospitallers an easy base for harassing Turkish shipping in the eastern Mediterranean. The presence of the knights just off the southern coast was a major obstacle to Ottoman expansion to the west.

The fortress at the largest city, Rhodes, was formidable. The castle had no moat. Slanting walls, designed to deflect artillery barrages, had recently replaced old battlement parapets. A heavy iron chain now blocked the harbor entrance. In ancient times, a statue of immense proportions straddled that same outlet to the sea.

An invasion force of four hundred Turkish ships arrived outside the harbor of Rhodes. Suleiman commanded an army of one hundred thousand infantrymen that stormed the unguarded beaches on either side of the island. Artillery moved ashore without opposition.

The Turkish ships blockaded the harbor. Pirates under the command of a red-bearded Turk, Barbarossa, aided their action. Suleiman's ground artillery batteries bombarded the town. Infantry attacked daily, and because the castle had no moat to protect it, the Turks set miners to the task of digging a tunnel underneath the fortifications. After five weeks the shaft was complete. At the back of the tunnel, the miners had chipped out and shored up a large, high-ceilinged chamber. They filled the void with dry timber and dead pigs and set the room ablaze. The fat from the pigs fed the heat of the fire and quickly reduced to ashes the wood shoring that had supported the ceiling of the chamber. Inside the inferno, two Turkish gunpowder mines exploded, and in the bastion-wall above, a twelve-yard section crumbled into a pile. The Turks assaulted the breach, but still, English and German Hospitallers held the gap for three days.

An angry Suleiman sentenced his brother-in-law, a general, to death for failing to take the city, but eventually spared his life.

An experienced siege engineer took control of the endeavor, but it was still in stalemate after two months. The Turks were growing demoralized by their fatalities and the diseases that infected their camps.

Suleiman offered the citizens of Rhodes a peace, their lives, and food on the condition that they surrender. If compelled to take the city by force, they promised only slavery or death.

The Hospitallers accepted terms, and agreed to leave the island in twelve days. They took all the weapons, valuables, and religious icons and relics they could carry. They marched to the harbor, with banners flying, drums beating, and in full battle armor. At the harbor quay, they boarded fifty ships and sailed to Crete, a possession of Venice, and with them three thousand civilians.

Luther completed his translation of the New Testament into German. A visiting professor from Oxford, William Tyndale, was impressed. He gathered texts in the ancient languages and set about to translate the Bible into English.

In faraway Spain, a single ship, the *Victoria*, crippled into port at Sanlúcar de Barrameda, on Spain's southern Atlantic coast. It was manned by eighteen men who had circumnavigated the Earth, and the only ship to return out of five that had departed Seville with 237 able-bodied seamen three years earlier.

It was September. Every waking moment, Bourbon fretted over the loss of his estates. He should be leading men in fiery battle, in a just cause, instead he parleyed with angry creditors. It was the clangor of wild war that he desired. Justice had played no role in the battles he'd fought for his own king or his creditors. Moral weight was desirable but not required. He was born to fight.

He should have been in Lombardy for harvest, but instead he arranged a secret meeting with his enemies. He did not return to his post in Milan, he slipped away, disguised as a peasant, and journeyed north, to the Low Countries.

Emperor Charles was with his armies in Flanders. The emperor always felt at home there, and it was a convenient place for his court to gorge themselves on bread, biefstuk, eels, and herring. Cardinal Wolsey and a delegation of other lickspittles to the English king were also in Flanders to take advantage of the emperor's largesse.

As Bourbon rode into town, a bell pealed. The townspeople in the roads and lanes put down what they were doing and scurried ahead of Bourbon in the direction of a town square.

Tied to a post in the middle of the square, a freeman struggled against bonds. He had a cord of firewood stacked below his feet. As Bourbon stood aside, townspeople stacked books up around the man who was bound to the pole. The stack grew until it was under the chin of the burgher.

The townspeople were shouting at the poor offender and at one another.

"He is damned."

"Lead him to hellfire." A torch ignited the pile of books.

"Who is this man?" Bourbon asked.

"A follower of Luther," a beggar told him. "A bookseller."

As the flames of fire slowly consumed the wretched flesh of the doomed bookseller, Bourbon squeezed his way through the throng, away from the jeering crowd, and toward a palace gate.

Inside the palace, Bourbon withdrew a dagger from under his peasant's cloak. As a peasant, he might have to fight his way past an angry gang of job seekers. Inside, in a sumptuous hall lined with rich tapestries, a bailiff announced his name to the court, and Bourbon cringed. So much for secrecy.

An army of German and English officers, sycophants, yea-sayers, counts and viscounts, crawlers and understrappers attended Emperor Charles. Wolsey sat to the right of the emperor, and a plumpish lady sat to his left. Bourbon rightly deduced that she must be Charles's mother, Joan the Mad. Sausages packed her cheeks. She looked like a chipmunk.

"Great Emperor," Bourbon said, bowing low before the monarch. "I am Charles de Bourbon, the Constable of France." He bowed again, more deeply this time, and then said, "Great Emperor. I am your humble servant."

"What do you want?" Charles asked. He was a man of few words.

"To serve you, Your Majesty." Bourbon's mouth knew what he wanted before his brain did. He had not hated his king until this moment. He could contain his wrath no longer.

"Germany is full of French traitors."

"He stripped me of my estates."

"That seems like a proper way to reward intrigue." The emperor looked out the window.

"I have not plotted against the knave. I declined the hand of his wretched mother."

"You seek favor. What compensation can you offer the Empire?"

"I'm financially embarrassed, Majesty. I can only offer my obeisance."

"Perhaps a military commission?"

Bourbon rose to the offer. "I'll enlist every French traitor in the German states, if it pleases Your Majesty."

"What if it means killing Frenchmen?"

"For a chance to see my sword at Francis's neck? Yes."

"And a husband for my devoted mother?"

As a butler removed a tray of sweetbreads from beside Joan, she snatched up a teapot and brained the poor valet over the head.

Bourbon's mind raced. "A husband handpicked from my most loyal captains," he said.

The emperor laughed, and in another moment, all the ass-kissers in the hall did too.

"She's mad," the emperor said. "No one wants her."

"Don't say that!" Joan shouted. As servants rushed to calm her agitation, Bourbon noticed that several members of her entourage had black eyes and facial bruises. The Queen Mother kicked one on the shin. With a high, hard reverse elbow, she under-chinned another. The poor bastard writhed on the floor, too addled to regain his feet.

"Madness is a blessing in a mad world, Majesty."

"Come the spring, a great army will invade Burgundy from the east. Our urgent prayer is that we be joined by England on the west. We are readying now for war. We won't be satisfied until Paris falls."

His was not a cause for justice, but Bourbon vaulted into the breach. "How can I serve?"

"You know this villain king. You know his generals."

"I'll recruit lancers. Arquebusiers!"

"Information is more valuable to me. Remain in your post and report to me."

"And my compensation?"

"To hell with Bourbon and his compensation. What about Henry?" Wolsey roared out. "What portion are you willing leave for England?"

"Henry shall recover his lands in Aquitaine and Normandy. Enough?" the emperor asked.

"My king will take the offer under advisement," said the Englishman.

"And Auvergne will be restored to Bourbon..."

"I've grown fond of Lombardy as well, Highness."

"Good enough. Auvergne and Lombardy. Excepting Henry's share, whatever that might be, and yours, the rest is mine."

A sick chill slithered down Bourbon's spine. Treason should not be this easy. France would never reward a spy so richly. But with his betrayal came hope. He had the promise of recovery of his ancestral lands, but more important, with this emperor, his dignity could be restored. Heedless to risk, he bowed deeply. "Great Emperor."

"Anticipate his movements. Keep me informed. Bring him to me on his knees." The emperor rose and strolled out of the court, his mother on his arm, followed by his gang of yes-men and bootlickers.

Wolsey's black heart rejoiced in the sight of another man's fall. He hid a gloating smile.

# CHAPTER 9

Cardinal Wolsey might have offered his right hand to Charles, but behind the scenes, with Henry's blessing, he had secretly reached out to Francis with his left. Henry and Wolsey both feared a victory for the empire. If the pious Charles were to defeat France, he could easily interpret the outcome as the Lord's will and seek a universal monarchy over Europe for himself. So Wolsey went to work laying the groundwork for the aftermath of what was certain to be Francis's loss. Once France was defeated, England would end its treaty with the empire and make an alliance with the weakened France. Wolsey told his enemy Francis as much in surreptitious correspondence. "We can forge an indissoluble peace by land and sea between France and England," the letters said.

The buds had not yet emerged on the sour cherry tree in Wolsey's garden when he received a secret message from Bourbon. He implored Wolsey to tell Henry "If the king of England will enter France immediately by way of Normandy, I will give him leave to pluck out both my eyes if he is not master of Paris before All-Saints."

Bourbon's promise was bold and unsolicited. "A vow like this can only gain him honor," said Wolsey, the master of treachery and deceit. "What fool would make a pledge for anything other than money or power? Bourbon is not to be trusted."

Bourbon was naive to think that England would risk an ounce of treasure to win all of France. Henry had no male heir. Why would he advance the boundaries of the kingdom for some other man's son? Even the re-conquest of Aquitaine needed to play a subservient role to that of producing an heir.

Wolsey was in the game for himself and the clergy that did his bidding. He reasoned that a successful campaign on the continent would not produce an ounce of gain for his interest and he had no desire to lift a finger to raise money for an expensive expedition to take Paris. Henry was preoccupied with chasing his Saint Peter around the Tower of London day and night, too busy to even take notice that Wolsey was looting the treasury to build Hampton Court, a palace fit for a king, a private residence for himself.

The thought that England would have any interest in helping Bourbon recover his ancestral estates was laughable to Wolsey, but if he could string Bourbon along, he would. First, the cardinal demanded evidence that the message came from Bourbon's pen, and when he did receive such assurances, he demanded conditions. The general's treasonous message never made its way to Henry. England wavered. The English delayed the invasion that Bourbon hoped would restore his honor and his estates.

June was in the air. Imperial armies stormed France's northern borders from Flanders. They advanced without resistance. First, they razed Ardres, then Mouzon, and continued to Tournai, where they put the city to siege. The token resistance at Tournai delayed Charles's advance and gave Francis time to gather an army to defend the assault.

On the whole, the incursion went poorly for the Imperial army. By the time autumn fell upon the land, the French army appeared out of nowhere in the north. Francis first encountered the main Imperial army, commanded by Charles himself, camped near Valenciennes.

The French commanders advocated caution, all but Bourbon.

"Don't listen to these cowards, cousin," Bourbon shouted, drawing his sword. "The prize is ours, the time is at hand. For France."

Time passed at a snail's pace while Bourbon waited for his king's eyes to rise from the map table to meet his own. His expression was without affect.

"Their counsel is wise, Bourbon. The situation demands prudence." The king's decision was firm. He had no use for Bourbon's opinion.

The king's hesitation allowed Charles time to retreat, in disarray, but without penalty. France did not harass the retreating Imperial forces as they fled to Flanders and found an ally in the bad weather. Heavy rainfall muddied the roads. Had he changed his mind, pursuit was now impossible. His infantrymen would return to the dust someday, but because of the mud in Flanders, it would not be this day.

Wolsey had journeyed to the continent to observe. He cared neither a jot nor a tittle that the empire was fighting without the support of England. He was indifferent to any cause other than his own. He had visited the front and seen for himself how the armies of his enemies were confounded in the mud. His hoped-for sponsor Charles had survived, and he returned to London with a smile on his face.

The papal tiara would be his. He had no other desire. His schemes had yielded a fruit that was sweet to his tongue. He would be reading the mass at the Vatican in short order. Wolsey would be Pope, and with the holy vestments on his shoulder, he would crush out sacrilege. Henry's first marriage would be null and void if he desired it to be. The tiara was his just reward for the high crimes and misdemeanors he had committed in his holy cause, a heavenly war on heresy.

Bourbon entered Bruges dressed as a merchant, under the cover of darkness. He was ushered into chambers occupied by Emperor Charles.

"The peasants and freemen have had it with Francis. So too with the nobles. The half of them that are not yet dead. Or broke. It's as if he's trying to kill us all."

"And what do you propose?" Charles asked.

Frustration with Charles was growing in his belly. Francis was never so witless to an opportunity. "Isn't it obvious? I'll start a rebellion. I'll overthrow the king."

"What's stopping you?"

"I need money. The peasants will not fight for turnips. With the right funds, I can even enlist a couple of divisions of German mercenaries."

"Wait until Henry joins the battle..."

Indignation swelled in Bourbon's heart, anger boiled the blood in his veins. "Am I to share victory with Henry?" he asked. "I have assumed enormous risk by spying on Frances and I will willingly lead a division of men into hell for the glory of killing him." The humiliation that Francis had heaped on him after his triumph at Marignano was all too fresh. He muttered under his breath, "Why bother with anything? What's the point?" He turned on his heel and pushed aside the guards at the door.

As Bourbon inspected his troops in the Lombardy countryside, he received a dispatch. In it, Francis summoned him to Lyon. Bourbon returned first to Milan, overcome with a sense of foreboding. He found a train of wagons outside the door of his home. Dozens of peasants were loading wagons with his furnishings, even the paintings of his children. He stole closer and found parchments posted on walls and posts that announced that control of the army was now under Bonnivet, and that the king had placed a bounty on the head of the Duke of Bourbon. Francis had discovered his plot with the emperor. He no longer owned a stick of furniture or an ounce of respect. He knew now that his days in France were numbered.

Bourbon returned to his camp, feigned illness, and under the cover of night, fled to Flanders.

When he learned of Bourbon's defection, Francis stormed his palace with his sword drawn. He ordered the execution of as many of Bourbon's associates as could be captured.

"I'll give you a division of Spanish regulars," the emperor told Bourbon. "And a like number of German peasants and mercenaries. The army is yours."

"Have the English joined?" Bourbon asked. His question went unanswered.

As the winds of autumn swept the fallen leaves into the hedgerows, the French situation suddenly deteriorated. Intelligence officers returning from the continent convinced Henry of the hopelessness of Francis's position. In November, eager to align himself with the putative victor, Henry signed the alliance Bourbon had been urging on Wolsey. Finally, England was aligned with the Pope and Charles, and against Francis. The parties agreed to coordinate their movements.

Under Bourbon's command, the Imperial army maneuvered to the east, then south toward Lombardy. Francis had reinforced Milan with Swiss mercenaries, who had signed on with the promise that Bourbon would provide for their pay. Now, because of Bourbon's truancy, the Swiss had no hope of payment other than by delivering a crushing defeat to the Imperial army.

In September 1523, the Lord on High heard and answered Wolsey's prayers. Adrian died. The cardinal was overjoyed. Adrian, the man of Flanders, had never been popular with the Roman citizens. They celebrated the death of the erstwhile Inquisitor and joked about erecting a statue to venerate his inept physician.

Before the last grape went to the presses in the fall, before the frost had settled on the autumn flowers of Lombardy, the death of Doge Antonio Grimani brought Andrea Gritti into office as the doge of the Republic of Venice. He quickly began negotiations with the emperor and removed the Republic of Venice from its alliance with France.

With Venice no longer at war with the emperor, the French situation had entirely collapsed. Francis had no ally among the Christian kings.

The conflict on the continent meant nothing to Wolsey, not even for its amusement value. He ignored any news of progress. He was champing at the bit to occupy the papal throne. With Adrian's soul in purgatory, Wolsey's genius would finally have Europe for its stage. No more tiny, grotty England. His head spun with plans. He would destroy heresy in Europe and the British Islands, mend the schism with the Greeks, defeat the Turks, and plant the Christian cross again in Constantinople and Jerusalem.

But another man was in the wings who again had his zucchetto set for the papacy. It was Giulio de' Medici, Leo's bastard nephew, who had served the Church so well as minister of diplomacy.

Office seekers and their ambassadors stormed to Rome and besieged the College of Cardinals.

Charles abandoned his promise to assist Wolsey because of a muddy rut somewhere in Flanders. Paris should have fallen to Charles, but England had loitered. Wolsey was the face of England's cowardice. Wolsey had pissed on the leg of the empire, and it was now Emperor Charles's desire to return the favor. "Paris was Wolsey's failure. He is a traitor. Not to be trusted," Charles shouted to his court. The emperor had more confidence in Bourbon, a proven traitor, than he had in Wolsey, his supposed ally.

Notwithstanding the private promises he'd made to Wolsey just two short years before, Charles threw his Imperial weight behind Giulio's candidacy. Treachery was best left to kings, not cardinals and ministers.

At irregular intervals, dark puffs of smoke belched into the sky from a chimney over the Sistine Chapel, the building on Vatican Hill that housed the conclave. The debate among the cardinals was endless and aimless, making little progress toward the selection of a successor to the throne of the Holy See.

Crowds collected outside the meeting hall shouting, "No foreign Pope." The papacy was a station for the elite churchmen, the cardinals from Rome. Even the peasants were wary of outsiders.

On the forty-ninth day, a puff of white smoke appeared, and the crowds cheered. Giulio took the name of Clement VII at his ordination. Wintertime had passed.

Wolsey's stinging rebuke at the hand of the cardinals was more than a great man should have to bear. And privy to Wolsey's lust for the papal tiara, the egotistical King Henry savored the opportunity to mock one of his ministers. Wolsey couldn't face ridicule in front of the bishops and peers. He stormed the halls of Hampton Court, raging at the paintings on the walls.

So Wolsey lied. He told Henry that Clement's election was what he wanted all along. In the darkest recess of his coal-black heart, he was not angry with Clement at all, but his entire being was afire with hatred for Charles.

Wolsey went further to disguise his wrath. He sent a congratulatory greeting to the new Pope, which Clement received with gladness. He had every reason to covet a strong friendship with England and sent Henry a golden rose. In addition, feeling pangs of contrition for jumping ahead of Wolsey, he wisely slid a golden ring from his own finger and sent it to the English cardinal. An accompanying note read, *"I am sorry that I cannot present it to His Eminence in person."* He also invented a new office and conferred it on Wolsey: "Legate for Life," but the cardinal was not content.

With the coming of spring, Emperor Charles suspected Wolsey's enmity. His spies repeatedly confirmed the emperor's intuition. He knew that Wolsey's hatred had no bounds, and he had no way of guessing when and how the Cardinal would spring from hiding, like a snake in the grass, to exact his revenge. Charles dispatched ambassadors to England to appease him. His agents whispered in Wolsey's ear, "Henry is the rightful king of France, and the emperor will undertake to win his kingdom for him." But the promise of a conquest to magnify his monarch's glory only darkened Wolsey's black demeanor. Henry could go to hell as far as Wolsey was concerned. Wolsey was only interested in glory for himself.

With the arrival of the hazy days of summer and with Bourbon in command, Spanish regulars, in service to the empire, invaded southern France. They advanced from Spain, entering over the rugged Pyrenees Mountains.

Acting in concert with Bourbon's attack, a massive English army crossed the channel and advanced into French territory by way of Calais. Wolsey was with the army and sent a communiqué to Henry. In it, he included a map that traced the route recommended by Bourbon. The road led straight to the king's residence, the Louvre Palace, on the banks of the Seine. "Mezieres will fall; afterwards there is only Rheims," Wolsey's dispatch told his king. "And thus your grace will very easily reach Paris, the Lord be praised."

The Flemish division of the Imperial army also attacked France from the north.

The French were unable to defend three fronts. The English advance left death and destruction in its wake. The countryside was devastated. Henry's army bivouacked in an unsheltered camp only fifty miles from Paris, a stoppage they attributed to the poor roads. The allied commanders doubted the explanation. The French had given no resistance to the English advance.

In July, Bourbon's force, eleven thousand men campaigning east along the southern French coast, looped north, crossed the Alps, then turned back west to invade French Provence from Italy. His artillery joined his rear at Monaco, arriving by sea. Provence offered little resistance to Bourbon's well-trained and disciplined army. The regulars advanced outfitted with arquebuses, lances, halberds, and swords. The Spanish foot soldiers wore striped, close fitting hose, calf-high Moorish boots of red Moroccan leather, red tunics and mail shirts. Sergeants and officers wore iron breastplates and vibrant blues, and all wore helmets. If appearances could kill...

Bourbon's Spanish-Imperial forces easily captured and sacked most of the smaller towns. The northern division under Charles's command tarried. Bourbon advanced on Lyons, a risky maneuver, as he had no reason to expect support from the locals. But for Bourbon, an army that was not on the advance was worthless. He needed conquest.

Bourbon's spies told him that Francis and his beleaguered army were mustering themselves only sixty-five miles away. They were inland, at the City of the Popes, Avignon. Francis was stalled with the difficult chores of exacting duties from the local peasants, taxing the clergy, collecting subsidies from the cities, and forcing nobles to take out loans at the point of a sword.

With winter fast approaching, Bourbon pressed for an assault on Marseilles, but his Spanish lieutenants recoiled before the danger. "One last conquest before winter," he assured them, "and we will control Provence." Over a chorus of objections, he unleashed his army on Marseilles, the last stronghold in Provence that remained in French hands. "We will storm Marseilles," he told his commanders. "Damn the supply lines. The navy will give the Spanish army all the support they needed to drive the French garrison into the sea."

The port town had prepared for its defense, so Bourbon's forces laid siege. The French garrison at Marseilles managed to repair breaches in the walls and protect themselves with earthworks. The agile French naval fleet, quartered in Marseilles, held against the lumbering Spanish galleons, which Bourbon had supposed were superior. With no supply from land or sea, Bourbon's situation threatened to turn dire.

In far off England, Henry still had no male heir, only one daughter, Mary, betrothed to Charles. His agents reported from the front lines that the Imperial armies of his intended son-in-law, allied with him against France, had failed to deliver support his offensive on Paris.

The Tower of London could scarcely contain the tirades of the English king. His primary objective in sending his armies to the continent was to reclaim Aquitaine, yet his army was foundered on the road to Paris. It was that mud that was foremost in his mind, the mud that had handed the English King Henry V a victory on St. Crispin's Day, a mere century ago. At Agincourt, an English invasion had met an overwhelming force of Frenchmen. Led onto the battlefield by cavalry, the French wallowed in mud, unable to maneuver. The sky rained heavy sheath arrows on their ranks, launched by the longbows of the English archers. The English tallied French losses at eleven thousand lives. They put their own death toll at one hundred, and the minstrels sang "A Song on the Victory at Agincourt":

> Owre kynge went forth to Normandy,
> With grace and myyt of chivalry;
> The God for hym wrouyt marvelously,
> Wherefore Englonde may calle, and cry
> Deo gratias, Deo gratias Anglia redde pro victoria
>
> Ther dukys, and erlys, lorde and barone,
> Were take, and slayne, and that wel sone,
> And some were ledde in to Lundone
> With joye, and merthe, and grete renone
> Deo gratias, Deo gratias Anglia redde pro victoria

Noe gratious God he save owre kynge,
His peple, and all his wel wyllynge,
Gef him gode lyfe, and gode endynge,
That we with merth mowe savely syng
Deo gratias, Deo gratias Anglia redde pro victoria

Paris was large; siege was impractical. Conquest would require an assault and was likely to succeed. But Henry had to consider the possibility of setback, which would mean the English armies would have to retreat, and retreat meant a desperate, ruinous, hopeless crossing of the English Channel, every step harried by the French. A loss of armies and treasure on that scale would doubtless so weaken his crown that he would be unable to defend it against any challenge, either from alien interests or from enemies homegrown. If Henry gambled his kingdom on a victory in Paris, what would he profit? Triumph in Paris would not guarantee him Aquitaine, and if events soured, he stood to lose his kingdom. And why? Because Charles, his future son-in-law, had been unable to support his assault on Paris. And mud.

It was a devastating prospect. Wolsey framed the question in the starkest terms, "You have a choice, Majesty. Will it be abattoir or boudoir?" Would Henry lead his army to Paris? Or would he pay heed to kingdom and serve God with his pizzle? On All-Saints Eve, the English, unwilling to risk an attack on the French capital, turned away from Paris and returned to Calais.

With dark clouds of winter gathering on the northern horizon, and stuck at Marseilles, Bourbon had to examine his options. Support from Charles had not materialized, support he had promised his commanders. His breeding told him to press the attack, but his brains told him that the only army getting closer to Marseilles was one with bad intentions, the French army, which was under Francis's command.

Fear drove Bourbon to order a humiliating retreat. His Spanish regulars struggled across the bitterly cold Alps, toward the Italian states. After a summer and fall of campaigning, even the handsome Spanish-Imperial army was ill clothed, ill provided, and ill shod. Francis dogged their retreat.

Bourbon held out little hope of capturing the garrison in Milan before the French army arrived. Worse yet, the city was suffering an outbreak of the plague. With Francis approaching, Bourbon's retreat took him on past Milan.

Again, Bourbon was shamed by his cousin. He was shamed by the emperor he served. He determined to hold at Pavia.

# CHAPTER 10

After David spent three days and three nights in the dungeon, jailers half dragged him to a cramped antechamber and, after an hour, forced him into a grand hall. At one end, a three-judge panel sat in black robes behind a long table. The room reached upward to a high, vaulted ceiling. Tall windows lined the walls, so stained with grime, inside and out, that no sunlight managed to wander its way down to the floor. Guards had locked David into a dock ahead of the bar that divided the chamber. The smell of soot and perspiration that filled the courtroom was an improvement over the cell. *It's better than piss and vomit,* David thought.

A dozen or more lawyers lounged in seats in front of him, and behind him, shouts and catcalls rolled over him from a gallery full of rowdy courthouse hangers-on.

The constable stepped forward to offer his testimony to the tribunal, and as he did, a bailiff shouted out, "Your Honors, this prisoner has been referred from Treviso under arrest on a warrant for heresy." A bundle of official-looking papers passed from the constable to the bailiff, who handed it to a clerk seated in front of the panel.

Afraid he might show his fear, David tested his chains. Secure. *I would give anything to be back under that bridge.* He tried to calm himself by recalling earlier days with Beza when the cabbageheads believed his little exaggerations. He spoke up, out of turn.

"Sirs, I thank you for your patience under these difficult conditions." His eyes roamed around the room, and he sneered at the noisy gallery in disgust. "I would ask for quiet," he shouted. He could not hear his own voice and his words did not penetrate the din. Then he found himself pounding the dock with his fists and yelling, "Quiet."

No one was more surprised than David was when the chamber fell still.

He bowed as deeply as his chains permitted and continued. "Peace on you and on the day of your birth, and on the day you die, and on the day you are raised to life. Sirs, I am David Reuveni, an emissary from Joseph ibn Reuveni, king of the Hebrew tribe of Reuben. I am here, respectfully, to request an audience with the prefect of this district." David bowed again, his face pressed into his knees.

The brow of one of the judges darkened. He snapped his fingers at a clerk. The clerk turned and handed the warrant to the confused judge. He snatched up the papers. The words spoken by the little man in the dock had no connection to the charges announced by the bailiff.

"This is a warrant, you gypsy fool. You are bound up here on charges of heresy. This is not your lucky day, my little friend."

"It is your lucky day, your Honor," David replied. The words spilled from his mouth. It was easier than telling a destiny. "I'm not a gypsy. Tell your grandchildren you met a prince this day."

The gallery seemed to inhale as one.

"Enough. Heretic. What do you have to say in your defense?"

"I am David Reuveni, your grace. I am Hebrew, but not a Hebrew from the tribe of Judah. I am a Hebrew. Born to the tribe of Reuben."

The cat was out of the bag. A whisper arose in the gallery. A wall of blank faces stared at David. No one in the gallery had ever heard of the tribe of Reuben, but to a man, all the onlookers were eager for a story. They perched on the edge of their seats. The gallery might be with him, *so I will give them more than what they came to see*, he thought.

"Your grace, I am a prince of the tribe of Reuben, the youngest brother of Joseph ibn Reuveni, the Hebrew king of the tribe of Reuben." His arms and hands animated his story and his chains clanked on the dock. "King Joseph's army has thousands of brave, well-armed and well-trained warriors. And I am my brother's emissary to the doge of Venice."

The gallery inhaled deeply, collectively. Not another sound issued from the listeners as David continued his recital.

"I was captured by the gypsies and held as a slave." David held his palms up and looked to the heavens. "Thank the Lord God for my small size." His gaze returned to the judges. "The gypsies would have killed me otherwise." And now the little man's voice rose, shouting to the stunned gallery. "They killed all my guard and stole my horses and also the gifts I was bearing from my brother to the doge. The gypsies stole the doge's treasure. And if that is not enough, they stole the gifts I had for the Holy Father. Yes, the gypsies even stole from the Pope." The gallery remained silent.

*The Pope? Yes, that is good. I should have thought of that before.*

The lawyers at the bar sat dumbfounded.

"And finally, your grace, let me answer this false charge by saying it is no heresy for an adherent to the Hebrew law, the law of Moses, a son of Abraham, Isaac, and Jacob—well, your grace, simply put, one has to be a Christian to be a heretic."

The courtroom erupted in shouts. "Blasphemer! Heretic!"

The judges were the first to regain composure. All three shouted and banged gavels "Quiet. Quiet. Bailiff."

With peace restored, the first judge asked, "What is this story again? What is your defense?"

David had expected a challenge to his ruse before now. He drew a great breath, and holding his chained, clenched right fist to his chest, thrust his chin skyward. "I am David Reuveni, prince of the tribe of Reuben, the youngest brother of Joseph ibn Reuveni, may the mention of his name be a blessing, the Hebrew king of the tribe of Reuben. I am my brother's emissary to the doge, sent on a diplomatic mission from King Joseph to ally with the Holy See...for...an enterprise that I am not at liberty to reveal."

"Say it," one judge growled.

"For...for...for a Jewish crusade against the filthy Turkish infidels."

His voice echoed in the chamber. Most of the onlookers froze in shock for a long moment. Someone shouted, "Blasphemer!" and the gallery exploded in a chaos of outrage. Amid the cacophony, the judges conferred.

A black-robed priest stepped forward out of the gallery, and the noise subsided. He wore a faux smile that matched his tone. "Your grace, might I remind the tribunal that in matters connected with the worship of God, the Vatican has sovereignty."

"That cannot be," David shouted.

A judge, one with a great shock of gray hair, spoke back to the priest, over the noise. "Your advice is noted, Father. We have heard it frequently enough before. But the secular courts adjudicate the charge of heresy in the Republic of Venice. Venice does not recognize the Vatican's supremacy in such matters."

The priest cast a withering stare on the older judge as he left the courtroom.

The judges conferred, and the older judge again addressed the chamber. "This tribunal finds itself in agreement with the prisoner. How can one be apostate if he has never accepted the faith? So as a matter of law, a Hebrew cannot be a heretic. Whether the prisoner is from the Hebrew tribe of Judah, or the Hebrew tribe of Reuben, it matters not. His tribe is not relevant." More papers rustled as the din from the gallery wanted.

Continuing now, the older judge said, "We are troubled, however, by the prisoner's claim of agency as respects said tribe or tribes unknown, even those not known to exist." The gallery reacted, some loudly voicing support of David, others shaking furious fists at the tribunal.

"Your grace." David spoke with great authority in his voice. "With greatest respects, my urgent prayer is simply that this court permits me to continue my mission. On a not-too-distant date, I hope to seek an audience with the Holy Father in Rome. I have no wish other than to see my king allied with your republic and the Church. A holy war to crush those filthy infidel Turks once and for all. And to this end, I petition for your forbearance."

Slamming down a gavel, the second judge bellowed, "You are on your own, sir. Guard. Release the prisoner."

The bailiff pulled rivets from the fetters that secured David in the dock. They clattered to the floor.

The bailiff freed David without protest from the gallery. His story had not fallen apart, but it had enlarged with the chewing, as if it were a cheap cut of mutton. In that moment, David might have imagined a riddle about his own destiny. *Freed from my bonds, am I shackled to my lies?* An inferior man would so wonder, but David did not.

As he left court, a group of Jews swarmed David. He easily identified them as Jews by the yellow badges on their cloaks and the yellow flap hats, such as the one he wore. They crushed on him as if the sight of him, or touching the hem of his garments, was a blessing. They came from everywhere as the news arrived. A Jew had been acquitted on charges of heresy. Was he a Jew or was he not? What was certain was that he was not Christian, and that was remarkable enough. The pack swallowed up the diminutive David.

David had spent a good fifteen years trying to get inside large, preoccupied crowds. Every man, woman, and child was trying to engage three others in animated discussion about David and his mission. No one listened to his neighbor; full purses hung from sashes like ripe apples. He had no knife. *My angelic little knife. Someday I will make that bastard constable pay for his sins.*

David dried his lips with a lateral swipe of his stubby fingers, and concerned that the swarming Jews might trample him, he grabbed the cloak of an old man with a long, full beard, obviously a leader. "Rabbi. I am in need of a physician."

"Come with me," the old man told him.

David clutched the tail of the bearded man's robe. Otherwise, he would lose himself in the crush, disappear, as the yellow-hatted Jews swarmed him and the elder. His eyes darted about, seeking an escape route, a place to hide. But no way to slip away clean presented itself. He was headed for yet another trial, this next one called at his own request. He sighed inwardly at his strange misfortune.

Servants ushered David into the kitchen of a great house. It was the home of Simon Meshulam, a banker and Jewish leader.

He gorged himself on a hearty soup of herbed chicken and rice served with a heel of bread. He had not eaten this well for months. His head sagged so low over his bowl that his chin dipped into the broth each time he opened his mouth. One arm curled around the dish as if to protect it from theft.

Five rabbis observed his every movement, eager to interrogate him. When a plump young housemaid offered to dress the wounds on his back, he removed his shirt and pourpoint. The salve was soothing; her hands were gentle. After she finished, he arose from the table to warm his buttocks at the hearth.

His mind churned. If things had gone according to plan, he would have been out of sight by now. But the tribe of Reuben story had drawn the gathering of Jews outside the court as if it were a talisman.

Providence had intervened and filled his belly with the first warm food he had eaten in weeks. The balm applied by the pretty maid had soothed the sting of the whip. *If this is what it means to be a Hebrew, I can be Hebrew easily enough.* Anyone who knew his name was David, even without seeing a *bareta* on his head, instantly knew that he was not Christian. For a moment, he considered sharing the truth with the rabbis, but that moment quickly passed. *I will keep the Jews in the dark. They won't believe this story long. I must have a plan of escape.*

He rubbed his flanks before the flame and then ate another bowl of soup. As he did, his eyes searched the faces of the five rabbis sitting across the table. Before the indulgence business had turned into a steaming pile of cow manure, he had prided himself on his ability to read minds. But he knew he would need to call on every bit of his experience to avoid discovery by this gang of educated and inquisitive rabbis. Unlike the Christian peasants, these men were not half-wits.

He stopped eating when his skin stretched across his stomach like the head of a drum. "Not another spoonful, please." He groaned as he put his pourpoint back on. It was too tight now for comfort.

The elder rabbi spoke. The same man had led David out of the crowd. "We hunger to hear word of the tribe of Reuben and King Joseph. Tell us everything."

"Where should I start?" David asked. His eyes searched the faces of the rabbis for clues. *What is it that they want to hear?*

"Where is your homeland?"

"Arabia, Rabbi. Arabia."

"East of the River Jordan?"

"Yes."

"In Gilead?"

"Of course. Where else would it be?"

"And the priesthood. What of the priesthood?"

David selected the most expressive face from among the rabbis, the youngest man, and concentrated on the mouth. The lips revealed an ancient name to David, hinting sounds to his practiced eye, letter-by-letter, just as surely as if they had been written down on parchment.

"Z—zzzaaaa—Zadok. Zadok is the priest of Reuben. The chief priest."

The rabbis grabbed one another's hands and confirmed, "Yes. Zadok. Zadok." It was the name they wanted to hear. Tears of joy filled their eyes.

A younger rabbi took up the inquiry. "Tell us about the king and his armies."

David rose and walked to the fire, every moved followed by the eyes of the rabbis. He rubbed his hands together. "Well, uh, King Joseph commands an army..."

"A cavalry? Horses? Camels? Asses?"

"Certainly."

Another rabbi interrupted, "How large?"

"King Joseph warned me to be very cautious about revealing..."

"You are among friends, Prince David. Tell us, we implore you. We are starved to hear. Are there as many as ten thousand? Twenty-five thousand?"

*The Jews have no army at all and all they want to know about is the size of the army.* David took a long look around the room. He noticed that the larder was full. He did not answer quickly. He had learned long ago the value of silence. It added weight to his words when he told a dupe what he wanted to hear. "Conservatively," he answered.

The rabbis muttered among themselves. "Twenty-five thousand... twenty-five thousand. And an infantry?"

"Sure."

"Fifty thousand?"

David looked over his shoulder, installed a somber face, and dipped an eyelid, almost imperceptibly.

The rabbis interpreted the gesture as a "yes." "Fifty thousand then. Five divisions..."

The expressions on the faces measured the fervor of the rabbis for David. They must have knots in their stomachs. His expression serious, David told them, "You shall meet King Joseph, every one of you, in Jerusalem. Next year. Next year, Jerusalem."

The eldest rabbi closed his eyes. "Prince David, people will call you Messiah if this dream is fulfilled."

"I...I know you are saying that from the heart, Rabbi, but that is not such a good thing for you to say aloud." *The man has lost his mind.* "I am just a minor prince from a minor tribe of Israel. I'm not even a warrior."

The rabbi looked to the heavens. Tears the size of horse turds flowed down the rabbi's wrinkled cheeks. "O Jerusalem. The Temple."

"Rabbi, there's a considerable amount of work. And money. Money is a problem. I am an indigent in this alien land."

"Meshulam will feed you. Meshulam will clothe you. Jews will see to your every need."

"This kindness is greatly appreciated, Rabbi. I can't remember the last time I warmed my buttocks at a hearth or had a meal so warm and wonderful."

The rabbis cried and patted the little man on the shoulder. David flinched; the flesh on his back was still sore from the manhandling he had suffered in Treviso.

"You will speak at the synagogue tomorrow evening."

David was confident that the rabbis believed his story. He avoided the further inquiry of his host, the sad-eyed Meshulam, by telling the banker his destiny. "You may fool the others. But it has been given to me to see, Meshulam, and I see that you are a believer in the occult, the unknowable. You are a mystic in your own right." Those who practiced the occult were largely shunned everywhere in Christendom, but David's insight was true, and because if it, Meshulam treated the little man with great reverence and generous hospitality.

Meshulam was tall and wore his beard short, and when he entered his home, he replaced his *bareta* with a skullcap. He treasured an audience for his own voice. David did not worry that Meshulam could discover any of his secrets because once he drank a glass of wine, he never stopped talking. He talked about the courts the Jews had organized for themselves after arriving from Spain and Portugal, how they imposed taxes on themselves to support education and a synagogue. "Twenty years ago," Meshulam told him, "the Venetian Council began to fret over the immigration of Jews. Their worries grew into fear."

"The Jews are no threat."

"An offended brother or sister is harder to win than a fortified city. And the gentiles construct walls. So what if a rabbi ties *tzitzit* according to an ordinance? Where is the harm in this?"

"There is none."

"Such practices upset the Council, the Christian Council that is; they hate the occult. Now the Christians spread rumors of Jewish inhumanities. Of Jews roaming at night along the lanes and canals of Venice, stealing children. Stealing babies for their blood, using the blood of innocents in ritual sacrifice. The very thought."

"And because of it, now all Jews must reside in the same quarter, the Corte de Case. Walls. They think we were all born in treachery. 'The Christ killers' they say. They believe these venal lies about the blood of babies, the blood libel."

Meshulam left his villa in the afternoon, and David took the opportunity to assess the objets d'art in his host's study. The candlestick—was it gold or merely gilded? How easy would it be to conceal in his clothing?

When Meshulam returned, David realized he had given himself no avenue of retreat from the private room. The shame of a thief is in getting caught, and David didn't want to feel fear or disgrace again. He concealed himself behind a heavy drape. As he heard the sounds of more than one person settling on chairs, he chanced a peek. Meshulam and one other.

His host brought a well dressed man, a nobleman, into the study. "Now tell me about Agostino."

"He's a good boy," the nobleman said. "He does well in his studies. He will do well. He is a sweet boy. He knows his role."

"I have seen Agostino many times. He dresses right. Displays the right manners."

"He pays homage to the right people," the aristocrat said.

"Yes, he will find a good match for marriage. Then what?" Meshulam asked. "Sailor?"

"I wouldn't have him take to the sea for all the pepper in India. He wants the cavalry. Please, Signor Meshulam, we serve the same God. Pray lend me enough for a retinue for Agostino. I need the money."

"A retinue. For Agostino. Hmmm." Meshulam rubbed his chin. "For a retinue you would pledge it all? All your treasure pledged to the House of Abravanel? What if he has no talent for war?"

"Then I will buy his way into the clergy. Please, Signor Meshulam. My son serves the same God as you. He will be a general someday. Or a bishop. A cardinal. He can repay, with interest."

Meshulam dribbled a small amount of wine into his own glass and filled his guest's cup to the brim. To the little man stealing glances from behind the drape, the decanter appeared to have value. His host placed it on a low table that bore a jade statue that might be too heavy to carry away. Stemware might be easier and safer to purloin.

Meshulam bragged about his relationship with the owner of his banking house, his principal, a Florentine banker named Samuel Abravanel, and assured the aristocrat that his loans would be approved. "Abravanel is the king of the Jews," Meshulam boasted.

David sat on the edge of his bed. He did not like the idea of having to speak to a group at the synagogue. He could easily disgrace himself. Every muscle in his body tensed with anxiety; he was more wide awake now than he had ever been. He remembered days of defiance in his youth and the pain of his mother's gentle rebuke when he lied to her. He fought a desire to crawl under the bed; instead he laid back and pulled the blankets over his head, rolled over to his side and cuffed his pillow, hoping for sleep, to no avail.

And what of Meshulam. He thought about feeding a greater destiny to his host, some shrouded, dark vision of the future. He decided he would tell the banker that he would be the lender of money that would be used in a crusade on Jeddah. David snorted. *He would believe that. This occultist. This believer in the unknowable.* Meshulam. With his wealth and power and a firm belief in a madcap destiny, the little man would have all protection he needed in Venice.

David had the luxury of time. The food was warm, and so was the bed. He told himself to relax, to recover from his wounds and regather his strength.

*I will just quote the prophets.* The scripture would come easily enough. In Khaibar, he had committed long passages of the wisdom of the prophets to memory. *Wisdom is what anyone would expect from a prince, certainly.* The Jews wanted to hear lies; that was the price of his ransom. A bargain. He would lay his cock-and-bull tribe of Reuben story on thick, as Beza had shown him. He was certain that if he told the Jews a satisfying story, it would be several days before anyone became curious. That was plenty of time for him to regather his strength. Only then would he escape soggy Venice and its waterlogged Christians. He could disappear at a time of his own choosing. His host wouldn't miss the baubles that David planned to take with him. Until he was nourished and strong, he only needed words to speak at the synagogue.

# CHAPTER 11

The synagogue was a beautiful and ornate structure, built by the best architects and craftsmen using only the finest materials. Although it was smaller than the cathedrals where he had sold indulgences, it rivaled any David had seen in richness. An inner aisle divided a large central room. Men sat on one side and women on the other, and it was bursting with worshipful Jews of all ages, all facing the east.

At the eastern end of the hall, four massive stone pillars stood on the corners of a raised platform, a *bimah*, a covered portico inside the synagogue. In the middle of the pillars sat a table and a desk. Behind the *bimah* was a cabinet that housed the Torah scrolls and a lavishly veiled ark with doors. The chamber had no statuary, no depictions of men or beasts, nothing to match the *Judensau* so prominent in the cathedrals. Artwork and tapestries, an ornate chair, and a large, seven-branched candlestick decorated the *hekhal*, the front of the sanctuary. The ceiling arched high and dark, beyond the reach of the dim light from oil lamps. Below, *baretas* were not in evidence. Yarmulke skullcaps covered the backs of the men's heads.

The most honored seats were taken by men in *stolas*, long silk mantles girdled under the breast and embroidered with gold. But for these elders, people dressed in the manner of the Italians. Every man was busy reciting prayers and blessings, and each covered his shoulders with a *tallit*, a fringed shawl. Some were silk and others wool, but they all hung far enough down over the chest to obscure the yellow badge each man wore on his street robe or cloak. A tassel—*tzitzit*—hung from each corner of the shawl.

News of David's exoneration had blazed like fire through the Jewish community. Every Jew in Venice was either inside or outside the synagogue. They gathered as if they had come to see street theater.

David wore a new robe that Meshulam purchased for him. It was a long cotton shirt and a robe of striped silk that hung from shoulder to toe. He also had wound his head with a white scarf. Now washed and trimmed, his hair fell well short of his shoulders, was combed back and full. His clean-shaven face revealed his dusky complexion. With the exception of a yellow badge, he looked for all the world like a magician from east of Eden.

He stood in an alcove until introduced by a rabbi, then, marshaling his courage, he clambered up into the *bimah* at the head of the congregation. Firmly ensconced in the middle of the front row, robed in a black silk *stola*, more resplendent than all the others, sat Meshulam, his host.

"An Ishmaelite," said a voice that carried over the whispers of the congregation. The speaker thought David was an Arab.

When the crowd was quiet, David began. "I am David Reuveni, an emissary from Joseph ibn Reuveni, king of the Hebrew tribe of Reuben."

A collective "ahh" arose from the congregation. All the Jews, men and women alike, had read from the Torah, even the children had heard the rabbis tell them stories about the history of the Jews in general and the tribe of Reuben in particular.

"I am Hebrew, but not a Hebrew from the tribe of Judah. I am a Hebrew, born to the tribe of Reuben."

The congregation buzzed in crosstalk. Did they believe? David did not know.

"I am David, the son of King Solomon; may the memory of the righteous be for a blessing. And my brother is King Joseph, who is older than I, and who sits on the throne of his kingdom beyond the wilderness of Arabia. My brother rules over thirty myriads of the tribe of Gad and of the tribe of Reuben and of the half-tribe of Manasseh. I have journeyed here from before the king, my brother, his counselors, and his seventy Elders."

David gathered his breath, and his voice grew louder, now booming in the hall.

"I am David, a prince of the tribe of Reuben, the youngest brother of Joseph ibn Reuveni, the Hebrew king of the tribe of Reuben. King Joseph's army has thousands of brave, well-armed and well-trained warriors. And I am my brother's emissary." David's voice carried beyond the platform and into the farthest reaches of the synagogue.

Total silence blanketed the congregation. A *tzitzit* dropping from a shawl would have made more noise than all the people who had crowded into the hall. Every soul sat upright on his bench, open-eyed and alert. *Do they believe?*

"I was captured by the gypsies and held as a slave. They killed all my guards and stole my horses." Not a sound issued from the assembly. It seemed to David as if no one in the congregation was breathing. *Do they believe?* "I was sent by my brother to organize a Jewish crusade against the vile Turkish infidels." *They want more, I need to give them more.* "I am here to lead the Jews out of exile."

In the hinterlands of the Germanies, Beza's words frequently had the Christian peasants jumping up from their benches as if shot from a cannon. He had witnessed women fainting, their hands clasped to their breasts. He had seen men bite knuckles, shake fists to the heavens, and shout threats to exterminate the Turkish infidels. Not so with the Jews of Venice. Here, close to what promised to be the front lines of conflict with the Turks, the Jews, those who he was calling upon to unleash the dogs of war, chose instead to sit on their hands. All but Meshulam, who stood, eyes cast heavenward, "Enter into his gates with thanksgiving," he plead, "and into his courts with praise, be thankful unto him, and bless his name."

"The Lord God says you are my sons, children of the living God," David shouted. "And in those days, the people of Judah and Israel will unite." And pointing at Meshulam, said, "And have one leader. They will return from exile together. What a day that will be."

David was plucking every string that his second sight told him bound the collective heart of the Jews together. The audience squirmed in their seats, agitated, as if unnerved, David supposed. *They got a good show,* David thought. *Beza could not have done better.*

No one spoke a word, aside from Meshulam, who standing, roared out ecstatically, in a booming voice, "Emanuel. Hosanna." And then, tears welling in his eyes, "Next year, in Jerusalem."

Then the whispers started again. The only word David could pick out was *"Messiah."*

David was glad to have given a good account of himself at the synagogue but was relieved to be in his bedchamber, hidden as it were, soothed by the aloneness of the room. No one could see that he was frightened. A susurrus filtered through a window from a nearby waterway. *I will sleep like a baby.* He had secreted a decanter of wine in his room, and he drank the remaining portion, enough to dampen his fear that his lies would be discovered, that he would be beaten again, or worse, carted off be burned at the stake on the *auto-da-fé*. He drowned those fears with wine but still a restful sleep eluded him.

Tonight his mind was haunted with the word the Jews had whispered at the synagogue. *"Messiah."* He tossed fitfully, thinking about *Messiah* and trying to think about anything but *Messiah*. Each time he slipped into slumber, a different vignette played out in his dreams, and each of them ended horribly. A daughter stepped out of a mist in his dream. Escaping the fog, she became bloody. When she whispered, *"Messiah,"* he startled awake. Next, a tree changed form, and in it, a branch became a man nailed to the trunk.

He sat up in shock. That is what *Messiah* meant to his Christian friends, Tetzel and Beza. It meant this Jesus fellow, the Christian redeemer, a hideous dying figure nailed to a crude wooden cross.

The word *Messiah* conveyed a different essence to the rabbis in Khaibar, and he supposed it was so for the rabbis of Venice too. To them, *Messiah* could refer to a king, or a priest, or even a sword or shield, something anointed with oil, even the jawbone of an ass, a thing rendered holy by an anointing. *Messiah* also carried an underlying meaning, the thing that kings and priests and swords and shields were symbols of, restoration—restoration of the ancient kingdom of its most revered warrior king, King David. Even the name "David" that he had taken might remind a Jew of his inborn yearnings, a return to the everlasting hills of Judea, a regathering of the exiles, and a restoration of the Temple. This was the meaning of the whisperings of the Jews at the synagogue, a prayer to the heavens for someone to lead them back to their homeland.

Half-awake, he imagined what the Venetian Jews would do if Elijah himself appeared in a piazza to announce the coming of a warrior king. Someone even greater perhaps than Moses or King David, someone who might come to redeem Israel from exile, whom all the people of the world would follow, and who would establish an ideal homeland for the Jews. *This Messiah business is why I must escape. How long would it take the Venetians to burn a Jewish Messiah at the stake?*

A lighted candle stood in a brass holder on a low stand alongside his bed. As he gazed into the flickering flame, he was pleased on one account. The Venetian authorities had shrugged and sent him on his way. It was the Jews who had believed his story.

The Venetian Jews were sheltering him with care in much the same way as the Jews in Khaibar. *Jews,* he thought. *Khaibar.* Days that he had shut in his heart for so many years, memories that he had almost forgotten. *Khaibar would be a delightful place to be on this evening,* he thought. He missed his friends and the rabbis of Khaibar and wished that he could see them again. Someday. *Should I steal away tonight? No. I need some time to recuperate,* he told himself again, rearranging the blankets and testing the comfort of his mattress. He rolled from side to side. *The food is warm. The bed is warm.*

Even though his story was frail, he was safe. He had learned long ago that the lie that was the most difficult to detect was the one the mark told himself. The rabbis let him know what they wanted to hear, and they had swallowed his story as if they were a school of mullets. They put the hook in their own jaws. He had provided the framework of a fanciful story with nothing but a nod. It was the rabbis who were responsible for the richness of its details, not David. He could only shake his head in disbelief at their gullibility, but so long as Meshulam and the religious leaders backed him, he should have no reason to fear that the laymen of the Jewish community would fail to buy into the bargain as well.

He pushed away any thought of regret, back into the darkest recess of his wits. *Regret is for tosspots.* David turned onto one side and punched his pillow. *Quit fretting. Sleep will never come.* He thought about the two men that he had killed, about stolen purses, too many to count, and about the virgins he had debauched with degenerates of the highest order. He felt no remorse for his deeds.

Beyond the table alongside his bed, a sooty smudge twisted to the ceiling above the candleholder. Patches of darkness played across the damp wall when the flame danced in David's breath.

Shadows on the wall. He remembered his dread of a monstrous beast whose strong breath seemed to come from behind the heavy folds of fabric opposite his mother's hearth. He remembered too the comfort that settled on him when he ran from fear and hid behind his mother's robe. He considered slipping away into the night. The bed was warm and soft. He jammed his mind with memories of his better times, the heady days he had spent with Beza, and soon, his mind drifted away, yielding his bruised and exhausted body to a fitful slumber.

He awoke from another dream in the middle of the night. In it he reveled with plump barmaids, Tetzel and Beza, and a thousand other muttonheads. Awake, his body hurt; his heart felt miserable. He fell asleep, fitfully, again.

Toward morning, his image of himself appeared in another dream, covered over in yellow badges and a floppy yellow hat. He and a long-bearded rabbi were chessmen on a gigantic board. They joined forces against a cleric in rich vestments. David was a pawn, but he could move in all directions and press the attack as if he were a queen. All seemed lost for the cleric until the rabbi spoke up to challenge one of David's moves. "You cannot do that. You're nothing but a pawn," the rabbi said. Just then, David startled awake.

David knew that if the rabbis discovered that he was not a prince, then they would turn him over to the authorities, they would do it for their own protection. *The princelings of Venice would never believe that this tribe of Reuben story had taken in the Jews.*

He rose before the sun was in the sky, unrefreshed by sleep, still shaken by his fearful dreams, and resolved to be more careful with his words.

# CHAPTER 12

Meshulam secured an audience for the little man with the doge, and told him so at breakfast.

"He is wise if he listens to the counsel of wise men, such as you," David said. "But gypsies stole all the gifts I brought for him."

"It is your audience, not mine," Meshulam said. "Quite a powerful man, the doge. Very highly esteemed. But if he does my bidding, it is because of Abravanel. Samuel Abravanel can buy and sell the doge of Venice."

David did not expect much to come of his audience. The doge would assume David was trying to cadge some benefit from the citizens of the republic and dismiss him with a brusque "no" and a sharp kick in the rear. *But I must remember to ask him for something; I'm sure everyone asks for something, and if I do not he will be suspicious,* David thought. *He will give me the boot, and I will do my little disappearing act.*

A week later, David was unafraid as he walked across a grand piazza. One night alone, while drinking what seemed like a cask of wine, he thought about the tribunal, the rabbis and Meshulam. All of them had believed him. He was in truth from a place beyond Arabia. He had only lied about the identity of his father, that he was a chieftain not a prince. Who among these Christian dummkopfs would know the difference if it jumped up and bit him. He told himself that his story was strong, ironclad, unassailable, and he believed it. His sleep had improved. He quit scheming to escape. The schemer could spot a lie a league away, but he fell for his own falsehood as easily as anyone else.

David looked up at the doge's palace. He stumbled repeatedly, tripping on the hem of his robe as he craned his neck to count the floors above. *This building must have five levels—no, six*, David thought. *These Venetians have built the tallest building in the world in a swamp.*

Shining nearly white, the color of washed-out ashes, the doge's palace faced south, overlooking Venice's Grand Canal. Wide columns adorned with ornate filigree embellished the lower level. Fancy capitals topped delicate pediments on the second level. The arches created arcades behind the façade. A latticework of diagonal concentric squares emerged from shades of stone as the palace reached higher. David measured the building against his memory. He had seen it from beyond the lagoon when he first arrived in Europe so many years before, almost in another lifetime.

Across the piazza, a magnificent many-domed cathedral adjoined the palace. The exterior of the basilica had three levels. Round-arched portals were at ground level, these separated by marble columns. Sculptures in bas-relief stood astride a central door. On a second level, statues of saints and warriors commanded the piazza. Statues of four horses stood on a high balcony, and in the middle of the façade, the winged lion that symbolized the venerated saint held a book open to the square.

This was the basilica of Saint Mark and the piazza dedicated to him. People and merchandise filled the public place. Every banner, insignia and emblem in the piazza exhibited the image of the winged lion.

He tiptoed through a tall doorway into a long marble corridor leading to the doge's administrative office. Chairs choked the gallery, each seat occupied by a well-dressed job seeker. Petitioners—"suitors,"

Meshulam had called them. Each carried a brief for some suit, job, or project he was urging the doge to support.

The sunlight seeped through tall windows on one side of the corridor as if it lacked spirit. Dull tapestries covered the walls. Damask upholstered some chairs; velvet overlaid others. Traces of inlaid gold ornamented still others. Even though he had lived most of his life in a glorified ditch, David noticed the shabby woebegone elegance of the palace. Few items of furniture matched. The moldering furnishings scandalized the doge's palace, the once-rich fabrics showed threadbare and tattered. Years of foreign entanglements had exhausted the Republic's coffers. The palace was like its Republic, graceful and crumbling as if it had been washed by alternate waves of prosperity and denial.

David crawled up on an empty chair as far away as possible from a guarded double door, near the entrance to the long corridor. He seated himself, holding his *bareta* in his lap as if it were a bird's nest. A perfect place to go unnoticed.

After a brief wait, the tall double doors at the far end of the corridor opened. Every suitor sprung to his feet and shouted his petition to the doorman at the top of his lungs. "Me next!" The tempest of waving fistfuls of paper frightened David.

"David Reuveni!" the doorman shouted over the throng. After a long pause, again: "David Reuveni. David Reuveni."

"Here I am! Here I am!" David yelled out. He fought his way through and under the gaggle of suitors.

The doorman bowed and held the door open wide, signaling David to enter the doge's administrative office. A considerable grumbling undertone arose among the offended suitors. A Jew, a dwarf, and out of turn.

David stood in front of a table, his yellow *bareta* in hand; the doge sat behind. Around them, artists and craftsmen swarmed the office in a busy reconstruction project. The doge was Andrea Gritti, a nobleman who was new to the post. He was the chief administrative officer of Venice, chosen by a council of noblemen. Gritti was bogged down in the most urgent task that a new appointee to high government office must face, remodeling his office. Decorators and carpenters crawled all over and around the doge's office, stirring buckets that exuded pasty smells, seemingly indifferent to the efforts of the doge to engage in his work.

Gritti had no desire to preside over Venice's funeral, which he and his friends were certain would occur if they lost control of the city to their political enemies at home. Its foes beyond the lagoon were legion. The Turks had a ravenous appetite to reclaim all the lands surrounding the Mediterranean and subjugate the Christian nations. Nearby, across the Adriatic, the Turkish army gathered the strength and resolve to invade. The Venetians had as much to fear by surrendering their sovereignty to the Pope, or the empire, or the French or Spanish.

The doge leaned forward. He looked down and, seeing nothing, looked further down. The doge got plenty of practice looking down his nose, but he was not used to having to drop his chin to do it.

David never felt as small as he did today, but it was time to perform. "I prostrate myself at the feet of you, gracious lord, my sun, the sun from the sky, seven times and seven times, on my back and on my stomach I greet you, great lord, and beseech you on behalf of my brother..."

"Well, now, seven times seven. How droll," the doge interrupted. "David Reuveni, is it? We have heard your name repeatedly." A smirk smeared across the face of the doge. "A prince, I am told. A prince of the tribe of what, the tribe of Reuben?"

"Yes, Eminence. Reuben, a tribe of Israel."

The doge slouched back in his chair and extended a flaccid arm in David's direction. David took his hand and bowed. The doge's hand was as cold and limp as a dead eel.

"Of Israel, of course. Israel. Please, refer to me as Excellency. Or Magnificence."

David nodded in assent. "Excellency it is. I greet you, Your Excellency, and beseech you..."

"The Jews of Venice have seen to your comfort?"

"Yes, Eminence. Excellency. Simon Meshulam has been more than generous."

"Generous. Yes. Good." The doge paused and looked at David from head to toe. "Your arrival here in Venice has caused a stir in some quarters, sir."

"Any inconvenience to Your Excellency, doge...Ahem. I am the dirt at your feet and the groom of your horses..."

The doge shook his head, then tilted it back and looked again at David. "No, in fact we are overwhelmed with the religious fervor your visit seems to have fostered among the Jews." A wry smile twisted the corners of his mouth. He was lying. David could read this man's mind as if it were an open book. His mind was imagining the construction of roads, bridges, a bridge for David Reuveni to cross to leave Venice.

"My intention, Excellency, was to stay in Venice only so long as necessary to recover from my wounds. But Meshulam has been so generous. He has a deep yearning..."

"Your wounds?"

"My wounds, Excellency, yes. I was captured by the gypsies. They killed my guard, stole my horses and the treasure I was taking to the Holy Father. Some gifts were for you, of course, Excellency, but they took every gift. Stolen, everything. Every bit of tribute. They held me a slave for ten years. I escaped only days ago. And then I was whipped to within an inch of my life in Treviso."

"The local constabularies can be a little heavy-handed sometimes," said the doge. "They might have been somewhat taken aback by this discussion of a crusade."

"I was careful not to reveal my true purpose to the magistrate in Treviso, Excellency. My brother has so many enemies..."

"That purpose—I am profoundly interested in your true purpose, as you say. I have reports that you discussed a crusade. So, please feel free to reveal this so-called true purpose to me, Prince Reuveni."

David's temples pounded. His hands trembled. *Here it comes,* he thought. *The doubter. There's always one in the crowd.* "Excellency, I have no purpose in mind other than to follow your gracious counsel and assistance. I freely admit that I may have let the word spill out that it might be desirable for the tribe of Reuben to make a treaty with your State..."

"There was mention of an alliance with the Pope."

"Yes, Excellency." A salty drop of perspiration stung each lash mark as it trickled down David's back. Outwitting peasants was one thing, they were powerless to seek reprisal. He rubbed his slick palms together to dry them. "We Reuvenis don't know much about the politics of the Church, but I must tell you that there has been counsel at King Joseph's court to the effect that it would be advisable to enter a treaty with the Church for the purpose of making, and I'll be blunt, yes, making a crusade on the infidels. It is obvious to the generals in Arabia that it would be difficult for the Turks to fight Venice and the Church and the empire in Greece and Macedonia, while at the same time fight the tribe of Reuben in Arabia. A treaty with the tribe of Reuben, the Church and Venice, Excellency, this would be a treaty of obvious advantage to Venice."

A chill, seeming to emanate from the doge, settled on the room. *He's not believing it,* David thought.

At that moment, a ladder fell, crashing across the desk separating David and the doge. As the doge startled backward, a leg of his chair snagged on some imperfection on the floor. He and his chair alike tipped over and disappeared to David's low line of sight behind the desk.

The doge shouted an impiety as he gathered himself from behind the table. His pleated, circular white collar skewed sideways; his face flushed crimson. As he stood up from the floor, he relocated his chair to its proper orientation and cleared his throat. His voice searched for tranquility. He was stripped of his mask of greatness by the fall. "Come. Let us take a walk, sir."

Together they strolled slowly and silently behind the arched façade of the palace. Through the vaulted colonnade he had seen from the street, David looked out over the lagoon, the city, and its canals. Everywhere in sight, tradesmen and construction workers swarmed partially completed buildings. Venice was a city in rebirth.

With collar askew and still goosey from the accident, the doge seemed to have lost interest in verifying David's story.

"The Christian world has been under attack from these godless Mohammadans for five hundred years. Now it's Suleiman." He spit out his enemy's name, one that raised such wretched bile in his mouth. "Nothing would make every man in Christendom more pleased than to see the Mohammadans turned back."

They walked the length of the arcade before the doge broke the silence. "Venice doesn't survive by treaty." Again, the colonnade was quiet. He waved his hand at the panorama. "None of this is possible when Venice is at war. Every time we join with others in a treaty of peace, we no more than turn around, and suddenly we're thrust into another war."

The doge turned back, and David followed. They retraced their route, back to the doge's office, without a word. Finally, the doge said, "Venice must stay isolated."

David stooped forward with his hands gripped behind his back as the doge continued. "These filthy Turks are menacing Venice, and the threat grows worse each year. For five hundred years, we have fought them. Beaten them back time after time with crusades. Christian kings have driven them out of Spain. Out of Italy. But the tide is turning against us. By the heavens, man, the Island of Rhodes fell to the Turks only two years ago. And the Jews...I have reports..."

"What about them?" David asked.

"This whispering. Messiah. Meshulam. We don't want them getting ideas. Oh, forget I mentioned Meshulam. The Jews are fanatics, all of them."

*He's afraid of what I've given the Jews and he needs Meshulam's money,* David thought. They walked another few steps before David spoke. "I have the gift of second sight. I have seen your destiny. The problem lies in Paris. France will destroy Venice so they can march on the Turks."

Blood drained from Gritti's face. "France would never..." he said, knowing full well that France would.

"The treacheries of the French are as the stars in the night sky," David said.

The doge stopped, turned, and looked out west over the bustling square of Saint Mark. "Venice has bloodthirsty allies and bloodthirsty enemies. It is clear to me now. Venice cannot crusade against the Turks, even if ten Tribes of Israel fought at their back in Arabia."

Every muscle in David's body exhilarated. *He is taking my advice.* Suddenly, the thought of living a life of ease in Venice sounded worthy. He had to restrain himself to keep from dancing, but he assumed his saddest frown and rubbed his chin. It was time to make his request. *If I were counsel to the highest officer in the republic, what would I ask for? A pension.* "My orders from Joseph are flexible enough to permit me to establish my embassy here, in Venice. To help establish a bulwark here, Excellency. Just imagine the glory that will be heaped on us when we repel the invaders."

"I don't think so. The Turks are strong. Suleiman won't leave two stones standing."

"The Republic of Venice could provide me a pension..." *This idea gets more savory with each bite,* David thought.

"I have a better idea. Venice will finance your passage out of Venice."

"But my embassy, Magnificence." David could scarcely contain his glee.

"Your wounds will heal more quickly on your journey to Rome."

The elation drained from David's body in a heartbeat. "That certainly might be true, Excellency. Rome can wait a few months...or years...with a small pension..."

"Your journey cannot wait. You must share your vision of our destiny with the Pope. So it is done, then. Prince Reuveni, return here in three days. We will provide you with an armed guard to make your journey safe and serve you with letters of introduction to the Court of Saint Peter in the Vatican and a generous sum of ducats to make your departure speedy."

"It might take years to get an audience."

The more this suitor talked, the more the doge pushed him toward the door. "Yes. Venice will provide you a letter of credit to draw upon until you secure that audience. To your good fortune, sir."

The doge turned and walked away.

"By your leave, then, Your Excellency." David bowed deeply, and when he raised his eyes, the doge of Venice was nowhere to be seen.

An escort led David away from the offices of the doge. After a moment's reflection, he was swept up in a wave of joy. He could drop his escape plans. He'd be accompanied out of Venice by an armed guard. This new prospect was a great opportunity. He disliked the dank air of the City of Water, the City of Bridges...a city of too much water and too few bridges. The idea of traveling farther south met with his approval—and with an armed guard! It was too delicious. *No one in Christendom will ever be clever enough to detect the truth,* David told himself. It was easy to believe because he wanted to believe. *I will go to Rome, fair enough, but just for a time, until I find a way to Portugal. As long as Venice keeps up a steady supply of ducats...*

David met five of Meshulam's retainers outside the palace. "What is it? What did the doge want, Prince Reuveni?"

David shook his head, refusing to explain until he returned to the Jewish quarter. He figured it would be a tragic loss if he failed to exploit the enthusiasm of Meshulam for these last few days of hospitality. What fool would pass up a soft bed and warm food?

The little brigade of Meshulam's men slithered over and past the canals of the city as if it were quicksilver, with David caught up among them, unable to see that they were headed straightaway for the synagogue. Once safe in the vestibule, David could no longer turn away their inquiries. He had no choice but to answer questions for the swarm of rabbis who now encircled him.

"He wants me to go to Rome."

"Rome? Why?" the oldest rabbi asked.

"To have an audience with the Pope."

The rabbi tugged at his beard. "A Jew? An audience with the Pope?"

"He's sending me with letters of introduction. With an armed guard."

The rabbi shook his head. "He'll change his mind. In a few weeks, why he will..."

"I leave for Rome in the next few days," David interrupted. "My sojourn in Venice is over." He had nothing to gain by telling the Jews that the doge had a knotted sphincter over Meshulam's religious fervor.

"We will send the good news to our friends in Rome. To Samuel Abravanel. He will know what to do. The word will go by sea."

"*Ya basta mi nombre ke es Abravanel*," the youngest rabbi said, and the others nodded in agreement. "Abravanel will know what to do. You will need a horse."

The synagogue gave David the reins to a grayish nag, a poor example of horseflesh, and gave him a purse containing twenty ducats, where he also secreted a letter of introduction from Meshulam to Abravanel.

Before the week was out, David departed Venice on a muddy road bound for Rome. The air was chilled and promised an early winter. An armed guard—a captain on horseback and ten foot soldiers—accompanied the robed emissary. Venetian flags topped the halberds carried by the soldiers. The captain of the guard allowed David to wear a turban. He supposed it was an advantage to keep it secret that he was in transit with a man who might be a Jew.

The passage to the Eternal City followed the ancient Roman roads, curling west from Venice a day's ride, then south across the fertile lowlands of the Po River delta. The column advanced slowly in these marshy areas. David and the guard forded small streams and boarded ferry barges to cross the major streams in the delta. On the fifth day, the travelers reached Bologna.

From Bologna, the road took up away from the delta, into foothills first, and then on higher ground, crossed the rocky Apennines, where David passed up his best opportunities to flee. Why run away? The beds in the inns along the way were warm and the food pleasing to his palate.

The road took them to Florence—Firenze—the birthplace of an awakening that had overtaken Christendom, and the richest city David had ever seen. Florence easily surpassed Venice in beauty. The ancient highland road was dry and made the going easy. Out of Florence, David and his guard followed a road that led back in a southeasterly direction, across the upland then down the Tiber River valley to Rome.

David chortled to himself during his days and nights on the road to Rome. The fact that he was not a prince was immaterial. Neither the Venetian rabbis nor the doge, the most sophisticated gentile that he had ever met, had detected a single hole in his story. David reminded himself often, *My story is perfect.*

Once, he might have thought about slipping into Rome to disappear. But stealing away now held little attraction to David. *Venice will supply the ducats, and the Pope will have in Prince David his most conscientious and unsuccessful job seeker.*

The Jews in Rome would know to expect him, his arrival would be foretold by messages arriving from sea traders, dispatched by

Meshulam. *The best chance of taking advantage of my circumstance in Rome will be in telling my story to every Jew, gentile, and feeblewit I run into.*

The road from Venice to Bologna to Florence to Rome traveled a busy trade route, so David and the guard rested in comfortable beds every night. The difficult trek from Venice spanned three hundred miles. It took twelve days and guided the little man and his entourage into a beautifully dry and temperate climate.

# CHAPTER 13

It was mid-October. Francis marched his army down the Rhône River Valley, crossed the Alps, and advanced on Milan, hot on the heels of Bourbon's retreating Spanish-Imperial army. His force included more than forty thousand men. Bourbon and his army were exhausted and poorly provisioned after abandoning the siege of Marseilles, and as weather conditions worsened, they were unfit to put up anything more than a token defense. Bourbon posted skirmishers in his wake that slowed Francis's advance, but the French brushed them aside with relative ease.

Bourbon's bedraggled Imperial army was unfit for a fight, and his Spanish lieutenants were frantic to avoid engagement. Arriving in Milan, they found a city that had been devastated by a recent epidemic of plague. Bourbon ordered the sixteen thousand men who sought to garrison there to withdraw farther, to Lodi, twenty-five miles to the southeast. He saw no advantage in leaving fighting men to die of disease, and even less the military need to defend Milan.

Summer-like days still kissed the cheek of Lombardy, and with no armed resistance, the French forces marched into Milan. Francis immediately installed a governor. With a month or two of autumn weather left, Francis certainly had enough time for one last conquest. He rolled out his maps and pointed at a town twenty-five miles due south of Milan, Pavia. His spies told him that that Bourbon was encamped near Pavia, and his senior commanders counseled caution.

Francis ignored them. "I took your advice at Valenciennes. 'Caution,' you told me, and I hesitated. I should have listened to Bourbon. If it weren't for you, my enemy Charles would be pushing up daisies in Flanders." Soon the French troops were on the advance, determined to seize a garrison that defended the little town of Pavia.

Francis arrived in the vicinity of Pavia in the last days of October. He stationed his command inside Mirabello, a huge rock-walled hunting preserve that fanned out north of the town. A tributary to the River Ticino split Mirabello in the middle, north to south.

Bourbon had convinced nine thousand mercenaries to stay on with him as he moved them into Pavia for winter quarters. He melted down gold plates that he had confiscated from the cathedral in Milan for their pay. The citizens of Pavia collected chunks of broken marble to throw at the French. They had no other defense.

Skirmishing and French artillery bombardments marked the initial conflict for Pavia. The Imperial garrison and the towns-people of Pavia dug ditches and piled the borrow into earthen walls. Bourbon placed light artillery, arquebusiers and archers in positions that allowed his soldiers to sweep the ditches with shot should the French breach the wall.

In early December, a Spanish force landed near Genoa, eighty miles to the south. Their orders were to come to the aid of Bour-bon's Imperial garrison at Pavia, where they would winter. With the unexpected arrival of a few French men-of-war, the Spanish galleons turned tail and abandoned support for the infantry. Without a navy to support their rear, the Spanish troops surrendered. The stars were in alignment for Francis. Bourbon and the occupiers of Pavia had little hope.

Rains fell as Christmastide approached. The French breached Pavia's east and west walls and attacked the city from both directions. The earthworks proved their worth. Pavia threw back three assaults.

Covered with hoarfrost, the bodies of hundreds of Frenchmen poured out their life's blood into the quaggy trenches below the earthen fortifications of Pavia.

Francis pondered his next move. Soggy soil and increasingly cold weather hindered the assault at every step. The ground on the city's south side was the only place dry enough to transport cannon, but Francis's artillery was fast running out of gunpowder. He ordered his engineers to dam the Ticino River north of Pavia. A dry riverbed would offer access to Pavia from the south. Even though the dam succeeded in lowering the water level before Francis launched another attack, a series of storms flooded the river and destroyed the dam works.

Francis was loathe to retreat to Milan. He had an overwhelming force and advantage in ordnance and supply. Siege was a last-ditch tactic. Francis would need to abandon the classical deployment of his companies in defensible positions and completely surround the refuge so that he could deny Pavia any reinforcement or communication with the outside and, all the while, guard his own rear against attack from relieving forces. Such a large concentration of men made foraging impossible and contributed to camp diseases. Nevertheless, Francis determined to reduce the city by siege and let the defenders starve.

Francis felt confident in his position in the walled hunting preserve north of Pavia, so much so that he agreed to assist the Church in the conquest of Naples. He secretly dispatched a small portion of his force to aid the Pope, who was an ally of his enemy. The French position further weakened when at the same time, nearly five thousand Swiss mercenaries returned to their cantons in order to defend their homes. Winter was in the mountains over the northern horizon and German landsknechts were marauding in the unprotected cantons.

In spite of Francis's efforts to blockade the town, Bourbon managed to reinforce the garrison at Pavia throughout the winter. Francis and the bulk of his company remained encamped inside the walls of the Mirabello hunting preserve. Skirmishing and sallies by the garrison continued through the month of February. The French lost lines of communication between Pavia and Milan.

In late February, Bourbon had a decision to make. His supplies were in a state of desperate shortage. His spies reported to him that the French forces were far more numerous than his own.

What was left of his honor hung over him like dirty rags. He needed to save face, so he lied to his lieutenants, "If we can demoralize the French, we can make a safe withdrawal." His lieutenants nodded acquiescence. They had no other options. Bourbon would launch an attack on Mirabello.

As evening fell, Imperial troops snuck out of Pavia and began a northward march outside the eastern wall of Mirabello. At the same time, the Imperial artillery began its routine bombardment of the French siege lines, some four hundred yards beyond the walls.

Under the cover of a pitch-black night and a driving rainfall, Imperial engineers arrived at the northern barrier of the Mirabello preserve. They breached the wall before dawn broke, and three thousand arquebusiers entered the park, pressing southward through a dense forest. Their orders were specific and fanciful. Capture Francis. Spies had informed them that Francis had stationed his headquarters in a castle at the center of the preserve. Behind them, Imperial light cavalry entered the breach and rushed south into the park.

Soon, skirmishes littered the park. Swiss pikemen, fighting for Francis, countered the assault and overran a battery of Spanish artillery that the gunners had dragged into the park through the breach. A couple of miles to the south, undetected, the arquebusiers emerged from woods near a castle. They swiftly seized the stronghold. Francis was not there. Behind them, in the original breach, a full-scale infantry battle had developed.

A third battalion of Imperial cavalry had pressed westward from the breach and stumbled upon a clearing where Francis and his entourage had pitched their tents. Francis awoke to thunderous artillery barrages. His lieutenants told him the French were firing back at the Spanish lines. But the sound of conflict was earsplitting, not far off.

Francis quickly mustered a cavalry attack. His force easily outnumbered the Imperial cavalry, but he soon discovered that the charge pulled his horsemen away from the mass of French infantry that he thought was his vanguard.

But a mauled infantry was behind him, and he was unaware. The French army was broken and routed, and the massacre was on. The French foot soldiers fled the winter battlefield, leaving the bodies of ten thousand of their fellow warriors to feed the worms, the flesh eaters in the hunting preserve. The Imperial army, ignorant that the real purpose of their advance was to decoy and mask a safe retreat, lost five hundred men.

Imperial pikemen and arquebusiers descended on Francis's detached cavalry from all sides. The French horse soldiers, unable to maneuver in the choking forest, surrounded and unhorsed, fell victim to the butchery of Bourbon's foot soldiers. His horse killed from under him, the French king fought on. Detachments sent out from the infantry to assist Francis met only slaughter at the hand of Imperial landsknechts. Remnants of the Swiss mercenary units tried to flee across the river. They suffered massive casualties in retreat.

The French rearguard, under the Duke of Alençon, took no part in the battle. As soon as the duke learned of the desperate assault on the park, he quickly retreated to Milan. By nine o'clock in the morning, the battle was over.

Bourbon and his staff rode into the forest and to a clearing where a clutch of exultant soldiers had congregated. Inside their circle, unhorsed, yet defiant, Francis faced the swords, pikes, and arquebusiers of the gang of soldiers. Ice clung to every beard; each man's face dripped blood and sweat. The mouths of the frenzied Imperial foot soldiers frothed with bloodlust as if they were a pack of wolves.

"Don't harm him," Bourbon shouted at them. The rabble screamed back at him in protest. The morning's conquest had not sated their appetite for blood. Bourbon unsheathed his sword. "Not a hair on his head. Take him to my camp."

As the rabble hoisted him on their shoulders, Bourbon told his once-king, "You'll be in the tower before nightfall, cousin." Then he freed his soldiers to plunder the dead and dying. "Divide his purse among you. Whatever else you find is yours."

Surveying the camp of the defeated French army, Bourbon found the treasonous letters from Cardinal Wolsey that Francis had secreted in a strongbox in his tent.

Bourbon took Francis to the fortress of Pizzighettone and held him prisoner until Charles arrived. Behind bars in Lombardy, the land he most coveted, the vanquished king wrote to his mother, "To inform you of how the rest of my ill-fortune is proceeding, all is lost to me save honor and life, which is safe."

At Pizzighettone, a brisk guard escorted Francis into the court of the emperor and his horde of understrappers. Bourbon was at his side.

"An interesting year for you, Francis?" the emperor asked.

"Your terms are fair. I accede."

The emperor nodded approval.

The settlement might have been fair as between the monarchs but not to Bourbon. His claims against France were still unsatisfied. "And my ancestral estates in Auvergne?" he demanded. "And Lombardy?"

"They are yours," Francis said. "I relinquish my claim."

"What about my pension?"

"It is restored to you."

"And a hundred thousand livres."

"As soon as humanly possible, cousin."

"I must have assurances."

The emperor was aghast. "He's the king of France, Bourbon. There's no need to humiliate him."

"He's a lying bastard, Your Majesty!" Bourbon stormed. "His treachery has no bounds. He will plunder my estates. He probably already has."

"You served him once."

"Yes. I served a heel-biting dog."

"What do you expect? He would not pay you when you won Milan for him. Now you want to be paid for taking it away?"

Bourbon's blood boiled in rage, and he feared his life was forfeit if he answered.

The emperor continued. "A nobleman has nothing if he has no honor. Who leads my army?"

It was no time to be bashful. "I need money to pay your army, Majesty," Bourbon said. "I demand it."

"Greedy peasants. Lutherans."

"It's not just the peasants. The Spaniards go unpaid as well. They have all lost patience."

"My army threatens overthrow? How dare you leave them unattended?"

"They demand their wages, Majesty."

"Fear will make them follow you. Make them understand. Take leave of Pizzighettone or face my wrath."

The Imperial victory was complete but Charles was angry. At home the peasants were insubordinate. The capitulation of the Spanish navy and infantry miffed and bewildered him. Now Bourbon's triumph had put the lie to Wolsey's exaggerated reports. The French were nowhere near as powerful as the cardinal had assured him. The English armies that he had expected never arrived to reinforce Pavia.

"Henry should have moved heaven and earth to be here. He's an impudent knave, if there ever was one," Charles said. "He even frittered away the opportunity to seize Paris. Where were the English?"

The answer was that Paris was still in French hands because of Wolsey's treachery. The evidence was in the letter Bourbon carried inside his tunic, the letter written by Wolsey that he had discovered at Pavia. It laid bare the fact that Henry could easily have taken Paris himself—it was his obligation to do so, and it was an obligation he neglected. The contribution of Henry to the assault on France had been magnificently trivial. Henry, the English king, Charles's uncle, Charles's future father-in-law, could no longer be viewed as anything other than an enemy of the Empire. But Bourbon decided to keep his mouth shut, to keep his powder dry.

He saw in the letter an opportunity to blackmail Wolsey. If he disclosed the letters to Charles immediately, he would gain nothing. The letters spoke the truth, and Bourbon, as would any noble, would spare no cost to conceal the truth.

Pavia's fall should have brought a season of tranquility. Instead, it dashed any prospect for peace. "Where were the English?" was a refrain that echoed in every marble hall in Christendom. Imperial agents pressed Wolsey for an answer. The cardinal raged in faux anger at the inquiry of the emissaries, pounded on the table with his fists, and threw a goblet at them as they fled his chambers.

The chattering class counted the empire's victory to be a tremendous loss for Cardinal Wolsey. He grew more hated by the day without help from Bourbon. The value of the letters Bourbon withheld became chaffy. They atrophied. They were worthless. So he turned the diplomatic letters over to his monarch in secrecy.

Charles's countenance burned crimson. He pressed his face close to Bourbon's. "Now England is my enemy. I had two enemies before this victory, and today I still have two enemies. Another triumph like Pavia and the empire will be doomed."

Charles' closest advisers chuckled into their sleeves. England had not even set foot on the pitch, yet it was a bigger loser than France. Never again would any sovereign trust Wolsey; his counsel had the value of a rusty sou.

Charles now had every reason to withhold the crown of France from Henry, now his sworn enemy because of the behind-the-back treachery. He abandoned his plan to assist England in any large-scale annexation in France or Aquitaine.

Wolsey was also on a slippery slope with his own monarch. Before Pavia, he had assured Henry that, if the empire won, Charles would make good on his promise to restore the French crown to Henry. "Your Majesty's contribution to the war will be a sound investment," he had assured Henry.

The king reluctantly accepted Wolsey's counsel. With Wolsey urging him forward at every step, Henry had spent money as if it were water, as if there was no tomorrow; he spent the inheritance of his hoped-for children, he squandered the birthright of any grand-children, and still he did not have Aquitaine. Henry's chance of gaining all of France now faded to a miniscule order of probability. The grand plans that lay stinking on the maggoty dung pile had Wolsey's fingerprints all over them.

"You must produce a male heir, Majesty," Wolsey told his king. Henry should have charged the cardinal with treason, but in this matter of an heir, Wolsey was right.

"Catherine is too old to conceive a prince for the English throne," Henry answered.

"Aristotle says, 'if their hearts be not united in love, how should their seed unite to cause conception? If persons perform not that act with all the heat and ardor that nature requires, they may as well let it alone, and expect to have children without it; for frigidity and cold-ness never produces conception."

Because his wife was too old, and because his heat and ardor was on the wane, if he were to produce an heir, he needed cunning. Wolsey lasted. No one could replace Wolsey.

Francis' mother, the regent Louise, ruling as monarch during his absence, paid the mercenaries who had been in French service from her own treasury, those that had kept her country secure from invasion. Her son remained in captivity. She would not surrender Burgundy and other annexed territories in return for his release.

# CHAPTER 14

The warm, dry climate of Rome appealed to David; it was such an improvement over the clammy perpetual wetness of Venice. A low brick wall designed to keep out beggars, lepers, thieves and the plague surrounded the city. It had no value in defense. Open sewers ran down Rome's streets and byways. And the Tiber River—it was a pestilential, infectious stream. The locals blamed the river for the widespread bad-air sickness indigenous to Rome.

The city of Rome disappointed every one of David's expectations. Rome was fortified by low, crumbling walls. It tumbled up, over, and down hills and was much smaller than he would ever have imagined. The citizens lived in brick buildings and grottoes. Above and below ground, they lodged in rooms with no kitchens to protect against fire. They purchased food in the markets and ate it in the streets. *The Eternal City, ha,* David thought. *An eternal trash heap. Surely, some cynic gave the city that name.*

Seven hundred years earlier, Saracens conquered Sicily. They were Syrian Arabs, and their advance had conquered every coast—north, south, east and west—of the Mediterranean Sea. They built cities on the Iberian Peninsula and held dominion over Aragon, Castile, and Portugal. After establishing a foothold on the Italian peninsula, a large naval force moved north, having sailed from Campania and farther south down the coast. The Saracens made their way to Rome by sea as the Roman militia retreated behind the Roman walls.

The Saracen's expeditionary force had stumbled over the richest city in Christendom. The many sacred sites and opulent basilicas were easy plunder, sitting outside the Aurelian walls, and filled to overflowing with rich liturgical vessels and jeweled reliquaries. The walls were insubstantial but just enough to turn away a second attack three years later. Rome was never again threatened by infidels, but for seven hundred years, the West had lived in holy terror of the followers of Mohammad from the East. Christendom launched nine crusades in the four hundred years after 1095. In accomplishing the stated goal of reclaiming the Holy Land for Christianity, the crusades were a failure, but they did succeed in driving the Saracens and the Turkish Mohammadans out of Europe and back to their homelands. The Mediterranean Sea was no longer Lake Mohammad.

Only two thousand Jews lived in Rome, but as in Venice, all the Roman Jews wore the yellow badge on their garments. The men wore the yellow *bareta* and the women covered their heads with a yellow scarf. Though few in numbers, they were easy to spot. David had not put on Western garments since Venice. Although he always dressed in desert robes now, he suffered the indignity of a yellow badge sewn over his heart.

David's guard found lodging at an inn on the edge of the Jewish quarter. The captain inhaled deeply. "Agreeable enough," he grumbled. Aromas from the kitchen promised a far better fare than the guard could expect in a gentile inn.

The eye of the inn's proprietor shifted back and forth from David to the guard. "What is your business in Rome?"

"I am David Reuveni, prince of the tribe of Reuben. I am here as an emissary from my king to the Pope, and I have business with Samuel Abravanel."

The innkeeper rolled his eyes and considered turning the sojourners away, but the size of the guard promised him a lucrative piece of business. He turned to the captain and demanded, "And you?"

"What the little man says is true. We need rooms for this guard for some time."

The proprietor of the inn relayed David's story to his wife, then his baker, his meat purveyor, and a candlestick maker around the corner. Word of David's arrival circulated straightway throughout the Jewish community, and the attentive Jews associated David with the messages received a few days earlier from the Venetian Jews. In no time, lips whispered to Samuel Abravanel, "The emissary has arrived." Every Jew with ears to hear knew some version of David's story—every Jew with a tongue to wag bickered over facts of David's arrival with his neighbor.

David sold his mangy horse, and since the poor nag was no longer around to put the lie to David's exaggerations, descriptions of its beauty circulated. People argued, "The horse was far more magnificent than you have described. It looked like Pegasus."

Or, "It was a colt and whiter than snow."

Outside the inn, across the avenue, David spotted a tall woman in a tug of war. The jaw of a growling dog cinched on the hem of her robe. A laughing group of young Jewish boys urged the mongrel on.

She was older than the boys, thirty perhaps, but an apparition of loveliness. Her dark robe opened over a pale dress. The gown's high waistline hoisted below the lady's breasts. The valiant effort of the bodice to flatten her ample bosom failed. She wore tall platform shoes to keep her feet above the filth in the uneven avenue, but they added to the difficulty of her duel with the beast. She bent at the waist, grabbed her robe, and tugged repeatedly against the dog. Every yank on the robe nearly bounced her bosom out of her garments.

David ran over to assist. "Shoo. Shoo. Get that cur out of here."

One of the boys grabbed the dog up in his arms, and then all the boys stared at David. At first, startled by any show of boldness from a man of such short stature, they encircled him with puffed chests and jutted jaws.

"Who do you think you are?" one surly youth demanded.

"He's the one. He's the one they say is Messiah!" another answered, pulling back. In moments, the street toughs that had threatened to thrash the impudent dwarf melted away.

David grabbed the lady by the hand. His eyes devoured the magnificently beautiful lady. He was smitten, tongue-tied. He knew he would give anything in the world if only this lady would like him.

"Aren't you supposed to say something like 'my compliments, madam?'" She giggled.

David nodded, still unable to speak.

"Try saying, 'My name is David Reuveni.' Isn't that your name?"

"Yes. David. David Reuveni."

"Such a pleasure to make your acquaintance, David. My name is Bilhah."

"I am stunned by your beauty, madam."

Bilhah pulled a fan from her sleeve and hid her face, coyly, batting her dark eyes. Bilhah had a large nose. A patch in the shape of a half-moon on her cheek disguised a pockmark. David thought his heart might leap from his chest. "Come. Follow me," she told him.

With David in tow, Bilhah led him to a magnificent mansion, an old Roman domus. A crested sign at the door read, *"Abravanel."*

"Come in," she said.

"You live here?" he asked, and she nodded.

David and his lady friend entered a courtyard inside the exterior wall that obviously served the owners as a reception for their guests. "The atrium," she told him. It had no windows, only alcoves in the wall, and was open to the sky. Doors opened to vestibules for the cloaks of visitors and rooms that its master must use for business. An elaborate staircase climbed up to a second story.

The lovely lady led David down a corridor. She bent at the waist so that her tall, twisting hairdo would not snag her black hair in the low ceiling. Rooms opened onto the passage. Inside one was a clavichord, seven-stringed lira de braccio, and a trombone. The walls were clad in dark red and subdued green tapestries, and farther along, many paintings hung from the walls in a chamber filled with vases full of cut flowers.

The walkway opened to a second courtyard at the rear of the residence. It was pleasant and surrounded by plantings of flowers, herbs, and shrubs. David supposed this space was the center of the Abravanel household. Housemaids curtsied away when Bilhah entered. He noticed how her stomach protruded fashionably, exaggerated by the waistline of her gown. This apparition of loveliness was not someone in service to the House of Abravanel.

"Please. You are welcome to come in," she told him. David was puzzled. *Could she be a daughter?*

Bilhah dismissed the retainers and then found a comfortable chair for her guest. "Please. David, be seated. The master will be here shortly."

*Then she is not a daughter*, David thought. The Abravanel home made Meshulam's parlor look like a wasteyard. The walls of the courtyards were dressed stone, laid in courses. One door of the courtyard opened to a kitchen and, on the opposite side, a dining room. Above, behind a balcony, the house had many small sleeping rooms. David found himself peering into a library where many books were stored in cabinets around the wall, and beyond those, a windowed room filled with sunlight.

Bilhah turned to leave by the hall. David's heart boomed like a kettledrum in his chest. This vision of loveliness had made the last five minutes of his life such bliss.

"Will I see you again?" David asked her.

"Oh yes. I'm going to make you tell me everything about yourself."

As she left, David's host, a man nearing fifty, appeared. Samuel Abravanel's head was as bald as a pig's bladder, and his jaw sprouted the brushiest white beard David had ever seen. It trailed to his waist. That was just what was physically distinct about him. The way he made his living was just as unique.

Canon law prohibited Christians from charging interest on a loan—even a 1 percent interest rate was considered usury—but canon law had no meaning to Jews like Abravanel.

The de' Medici family of bankers was Christian but had no difficulty circumventing the rules even when the Pope was a de' Medici. They deflected criticism by lending in florins (Florence) and demanding repayment in ducats (Venice), in pounds (English), or in livres (France). Hundreds of types of coins circulated in every corner of the Christian world, and it took an expert moneychanger to know their relative value.

The de' Medicis often took goods or discounts on goods in compensation from merchants. The merchant bankers also used bills of exchange to facilitate long-distant credit for their trading customers— they took commissions—and letters of credit for travelers that needed access to cash without the risk of carrying it on their person.

Abravanel had not found it necessary to be so crafty. Like the de' Medicis, he took commissions and discounts, but he also charged interest. His honesty was above reproach. Every banker in Christendom knew the maxim "Ya basta mi nombre ke es Abravanel"—"It is sufficient that my name is Abravanel."

"We have heard your story, Prince Reuveni, and wish to assist you in your charge. Let your burden be our burden." Gripping David by the hand, Abravanel bent in a gracious, practiced bow.

As a prince of the tribe of Reuben, David could not have hoped to be greeted by a better man than Abravanel, the so-called king of the Jews. "Please, call me Samuel. You'll find the beds here more to your liking than a thin straw pallet in some rowdy inn."

His father, Isaac, had served Ferdinand and Isabella as finance minister at the Spanish court. Horror-stricken that the monarchs planned to expel the Jews, Isaac offered the co-regents a tremendous sum of gold, and for a moment, the regents balked. Just then, Torquemada, Spain's Grand Inquisitor, burst into the chamber and, brandishing a crucifix held high overhead, shouted, "Behold the Savior!" He then pointed a bony finger at Isaac and said, "This wicked Judas would sell our Lord for thirty pieces of silver. If you approve this deed, then sell Him for a great sum." The royal couple immediately signed the decree for expulsion, and in the months that followed, their finance minister resigned his post and led the Jewish exiles out of Spain and Portugal, leaving behind his eldest son, who converted to Christianity.

Isaac's youngest son, Samuel, studied the Talmud in Turkey, and then took residence in Naples. He worked in banking and amassed a great personal fortune. He owned mansions in all the principal cities on the Italian peninsula. He was a patron of Jewish learning, generous to a fault, a philosopher and political leader who always promoted the welfare of the Jews.

After Isaac's death, his contemporaries referred to his youngest son as the king of the Jews, as he followed in his father's footsteps. His generosity extended to even the small day-to-day matters; for example, the servants dined with the Abravanel family.

David learned all this while he himself dined with them that night, with his arm crooked around a plate filled with minted mutton. He stuffed himself on the fruits that graced the table—pears, grapes, apples, peaches, and figs.

Samuel's wife, Benvenida, was a woman of culture and grace who brought a large dowry to her marriage and who was devoted to the charities of her husband. She fasted every day, ransomed captives, and was widely known for charitable generosity toward all who sought her aid. She was Samuel's first cousin. Her marriage to the most prominent Jewish leader in the world, together with her own piety, made Benvenida the most influential woman in the Italian states.

Benvenida's imposing grandeur overshadowed Bilhah's sublime

beauty at the dinner table. Of the seven children at the table, four boys and three girls, the youngest, Benjamin, David noticed, addressed Bilhah as Mother and Abravanel as Father.

Abravanel's inquiries of David were predictable.

"Where is your homeland?"

"Arabia, east of the River Jordan in Gilead."

"Your king is Joseph?"

"Correct."

"And the chief priest?"

"Zadok."

His host smiled with obvious glee and shook his fists in front of his face. "And the army?"

"When I departed, there was a cavalry of twenty-five thousand and an infantry of fifty thousand. But that was ten years ago."

The friendly questioning continued late into the evening until finally, exhausted, David said, "Sir, I am indigent."

Abravanel was quick to respond. "This is a concern that you need not worry about. I will see that your needs are met. You will be well fed and clothed. You are the brother of a king."

Bilhah ushered David into a little room that David thought must serve as a parlor for the servants. They spent a blissfully happy few moments discussing the weather, but too soon, Benvenida joined them.

Multiple wives and many children were evidence of his own father's greatness. He put them on display, much like Beza with his oddities and relics. But bowing to the custom of the Christians, Abravanel had taken only one woman as his wife. Bilhah had given him a son and their relationship was without shame. Still, he sensed a tension between the women that gave him an opportunity.

"Calm your worries, great lady," he told her. "Can I tell you your destiny?"

She nodded. "Yes."

"The Lord God hears your affliction. You yielded your handmaid to your husband, but no wrong is upon you. She shall be cut off from you, and you will not be despised in her eyes."

The worry lines around Benvenida's eyes disappeared. She was raptured with David, and promised to put her carriage at his disposal. She extracted a promise from Bilhah that she would accompany David on an exploration of the Eternal City. David was pleased.

David paced the princely room his host provided him. His muscles twitched excitedly, and he desired wine. He sensed that his story was drawing him into a whirlpool, disappearing, so he secreted himself in a wardrobe for an hour. The tension passed. He felt as if he were lying on a cloud when he finally slipped between the silky sheets embroidered with an *"A."* He slept fitfully. He dreamed of being unmasked, uncovered, that he was naked, with a dread unspoken. The waking David ignored the warning from his dreams that the story might not be safe.

Every day for a fortnight, David and Bilhah prowled the riones of Rome together. Brick walls and heavy gates set the neighborhoods of the Eternal City apart, sectioning the city like an orange.

Benvenida insisted that David and Bilhah share their days together. Her carriage was comfortable and at their disposal. She bought a gown for her husband's mistress, one with a plunging neckline, loaned her jewelry, and presented her with the services of her hairdresser.

"She's always been leery of me. So distant and reserved," Bilhah told him. "Since you told her how her future will unfold, much has changed. All she talks about is the prince and his mission."

Abravanel's mistress smiled when she strolled with the little man. David never sensed that she was ill at ease with his stature. She was gracious and never spoke of the great man unless David asked. David read her thoughts. He saw in her thoughts that she embraced an infant but not Abravanel. She did not love the son's father.

David met with groups of Jews at the synagogue—Rome only permitted one—where he proclaimed his mission. Every Jew in Rome knew his name and his avowed mission, and not a single voice rose to oppose him.

Erelong the day arrived when David was compelled to proclaim his story to the Christians. If he delayed longer, he would arouse the suspicion of Abravanel. He would cross the Tiber River and enter the walled rione atop the Vatican Hill northwest of the city. The bare bones of the unfinished basilica stood over Vatican City as if it were a grim reaper.

With one of Abravanel's retainers as a guide, and dressed like an Arab chieftain, he marched through a tall gate and up a long avenue to the Vatican Palace to seek an appointment for an audience with the Pope. His story was solid. David had no waking fear that his fraud would be detected, having convinced his imagination. *My audience is with an ignorant bunch of gentiles. I will tell my story and ask this Pope to sweeten my pension.*

"There's no necessity of pressing this matter forward," David urged the priest who served as the engagement secretary for the Pope. "Listen, I'll just come back in two or three months. Thank you and good day."

"Not so fast," the secretary told him. "The matters discussed by the doge are weighty. We will make time." He set David's audience well ahead in the Pope's calendar.

David found the great lady was cutting flowers in the courtyard. "I know so little of this Pope," he told her.

"What would a woman know?" Benvenida said. "Gossip is so unbecoming."

"You know his name is Clement."

"Clement the Seventh. He has only been Pope a few months. Fifty or thereabouts. He is a nephew of Old Pope Leo."

David's nose was in a flower. "Clement is a de' Medici." His intense eyes compelled Benvenida to tell him more.

"But of course. He was Leo's chief diplomat. Very elegant. Courteous. Sophisticated."

David saw that Benvenida was less than forthcoming. She knew much more than she had revealed. So he told her something he knew was untrue. "And a fortune almost as grand as the Abravanels."

"Oh my no. The treasure of the de' Medici's far exceeds that of the Abravanels," she said, eager to demonstrate her superior knowledge. "He has a grand fortune. He seems more interested in the de' Medici family than the Church and he has no use for these German reformers. My father said he is cautious. My husband calls him indecisive. What would a woman know? That's just what I've heard."

"What else does your husband say?"

She clipped a long stem with a graceful hand. "Clement wouldn't be Pope if it weren't for the de' Medici family, and he wouldn't be a de' Medici if it weren't for the Church."

David wrinkled his brow. "I don't understand."

The great lady snipped a few more stems. Things David needed to flow were pouring out of her mouth like a river. "His parents weren't married. The Church legitimized him anyway. So he would not be a de' Medici if it were not for the Church. And it is the de' Medici family that picks the Pope. Always. Almost." Snip. Another flower for her basket.

David was pleased.

On the appointed day of his audience with the Pope, ushers escorted David through a succession of tall, double doors. Finally, David found himself in a long corridor. At the foot of the marble gallery was a massive staircase.

Agitated suitors sat on either side of the corridor, poised to plunder the Holy See. The number in their rank made the collection of applicants at the doge's palace look piffling in comparison. *Not a one smart enough to carry my turban*, David thought.

David strode to the head of the line as if he were a warrior marching into Sheol. The angry murmuring of the suitors uplifted his spirits.

A priest posted at the end of the gallery immediately positioned David on a particular spot on the marble floor, and then led him up the staircase, wide enough to accommodate a dozen men standing abreast. The sweeping curve of granite steps was supported by columns of white marble. Leaded, stained-glass windows admitted little light from a wide piazza outside the walls. Corridors richly decorated with tapestries and paintings led away from the top of the staircase.

David's escort led him into a gigantic hall with a mosaic marble floor. It was a long, broad, barrel-vaulted chamber with a carved cornice supporting a richly gilded and coffered ceiling. The walls were clad in red damask which reduced the light from outside to nothing. A massive chandelier hanging from the middle illuminated the hall, even the alcoves, where David imagined one might secret himself. Decorations and frescoes, broken on the side by doors, graced the walls. At the rear, opposite the entrance, two dozen Swiss Guardsmen, armed with halberds, flanked a large wooden chair that sat under an ivory crucifix. By the measure of the rest of the hall, the seat itself was relatively unadorned. Its occupant was dressed in a long, white robe, a red satin stole wrapped over his shoulders, and a red skullcap covered his head. He was clean-shaven and his fingers displayed several golden rings.

In a sonorous, deep, and mellow voice, David's escort announced his entrance. "Holy Father, David Reuveni, prince of the tribe of Reuben." The priest bowed deeply, and like him, David genuflected. Then he coughed, choked by the powerful incense burning in the court. He spoke, almost inaudibly. "Holy Father."

"Welcome, my son."

David bowed again, as if to delay meeting the eyes of the Holy Father. And again. David cleared his throat and began anew: "Your Holy Majesty." His voice was bold and resonated in the great hall. "May your hand be lifted to the nations and set up to the people. May the nations bring your sons in their bosom, and your daughters carried on their shoulders. May kings be your guardians and their princesses your nurses. The Nations bow down to you with their faces to the earth and lick the dust of your feet. I am David Reuveni, prince of the Hebrew tribe of Reuben, the youngest brother of Joseph ibn Reuveni, the Hebrew king of the tribe of Reuben. I am my brother's emissary to you, Pope Clement. I am on a diplomatic mission from King Joseph; may the memory of the righteous be for a blessing. My mission is to ally with the Church for a Hebrew crusade against the Turkish infidels. I began my journey ten long years ago, but alas, I was captured by gypsies. They seized and killed all my guard. All my horses stolen. And the vast treasure of jewels my brother sent as a gift to Your Holiness was stolen by the gypsies as well." The air was thick with incense. David coughed as he filled his lungs with air.

"Come with me, my son," said the Pope. "It is the time of day for my walk."

The Pope led David and his entourage onto an elevated colonnade outside the hall. David and the Pope strolled side by side, leading an uninvited two dozen or so men who followed three steps back. To David, the barren, unfinished structure of the Cathedral of St. Peter menaced the Romish riones that lay below it on the east shore of the Tiber River. Its empty framework dominated the view from the porch of the Vatican palace.

The sunlight brought out a luster of the floor-length, long-sleeved, white satin robes clothing the Pope. David guessed that some of the members of the entourage were emissaries from kingdoms in the Church's realm. They wore varied costumes. Some, distinguished by their bright red or purple robes and caps, were obviously priests. Still others wore black pourpoints and cloaks, probably lawyers, diplomats, or military advisers. Two of these wore yellow badges.

"My people have told me a great deal about you, Prince Reuveni," said the Pope. David bowed again, uncertain of his etiquette. He assumed that bowing too much was preferable to bowing too little. "Your homeland, sir. Tell me about your homeland."

"King Joseph pitches his tents in Arabia, Holiness. East of the River Jordan. In Gilead. King Joseph pastures his horses, asses, camels, cattle, sheep, and goats on the slopes above the Sambatyon, a stream that flows into the Euphrates River."

"Gilead. Yes, yes, that is right, Gilead. Tell us something of the king and his armies. How large is King Joseph's army?"

"Your Eminence of course knows that Hebrew law regards a numbering of the tribe as a very great sin." *He will believe better if he thinks he squeezed me to tell.*

"Of course, but you certainly have some estimates in mind. You can give us some idea of the composition of the armies of your king."

David shrugged and rattled off his inventions: a cavalry of twenty-five thousand, asses and camels, fifty thousand footsoldiers, distributed across Arabia. The Pope's silence was unendurable. David feared that the whispering noise of his sweat being absorbed into his undergarments might shatter the Pope's silent concentration.

"In King Joseph's army, all positions of leadership are held by veterans," David prattled. "The leaders are elected by councils of veterans. King Joseph doesn't believe that armies should be led by princes and their relatives."

"Very wise. Very wise indeed." The Pope winced.

*The Pope owes his papacy to family connections*, David reminded himself, wishing he could kick himself for the error.

David kept at the pontiff's side. The Pope pinched his lips between his fingers and walked forward a few paces. "I must admit that our military advisers have frequently mourned the inability—well, that there's a certain military advantage to the idea of engagement of the Turks on both an east and a west front."

David judged that it was best to remain silent unless he was asked a question.

"I wonder what a good Crusade...Well, the petty jealousies and infighting among these kings is enough to drive one to insanity. Hmmm. I'd like very much to believe your story, David Reuveni."

"I wish you could meet my brother, Holiness."

The Pope's countenance clouded over again. He seemed lost in thought.

*He does not believe it.* The nothingness of the silence on the porch loosened David's tongue.

"Holiness, you may be interested in some of King Joseph's honorary titles. The people call him King Joseph, the Scourge of Mushki, Afflictor of Tabal, and Balm of Gilead. I predict that you shall meet King Joseph in Jerusalem, Holiness."

The Pope abruptly stopped walking. Members of the entourage bumped into the pontiff.

"Yes, yes. Very good. Is it not enough that the Turks are threatening Venice? And these German peasants." The Pope walked again, shaking his head. "These maddening, interminable squabbles among the kings...Spain and Portugal are at one another's necks, attacking merchant shipping on the high seas. And Emperor Charles goes unhinged at the notion of any civility between the Church and France." The Pope stopped, and again, his entourage bumped into him.

The Pope turned to David; his countenance was stern. "We are hearing reports now that peasants are in revolt in some of the German States and in Spain." The Pope shook his head. "I simply am at a loss. Cesena?"

One of the Pope's principal understrappers, a cardinal, stepped forward. "Yes, Eminence."

"What is your counsel, Cesena?"

"My counsel, Eminence, is to advance strongly with caution.

There is no need to rush. The correct course, the true course, will be revealed. But in the meantime, we should not lose sight of the fact that the authenticity of this Reuveni fellow is not fully established. My counsel is to first secure proof of his kinship."

"But how?"

"One of the kings must vouch for this man's authenticity."

The Pope turned to face his entourage. "Which of your kings is willing to vouch for David Reuveni? Which among them will guarantee to me that he is indeed a prince of the tribe of Reuben?"

One man stepped forward. He was dressed in a black robe—not one of the priests. "King Carlos of Spain has his doubts about this Reuveni fellow, Holiness."

Another non-cleric stepped forward. "Likewise, Eminence, Charles the Fifth, emperor of the Holy Roman Empire, reserves judgment on the authenticity of this Reuveni." The remaining members of the entourage tittered.

"Pope Clement, I've been a slave for ten years and even I know Carlos and Charles are the same person," David said.

"Yes, Prince Reuveni," the Pope said. And to the diplomats, "Spare us the silliness, sirs."

"A thousand pardons, Eminence, but the German states, the problems of Austria, the proximity to the Turks, the threat of the infidel..."

Annoyed now, the Pope said, "Now, help me remember, sir. The German states have initiated how many crusades on the infidels? Have they ever even participated? And the defenses of the papal states. What provision have the Germanies made for the protection of the papal states from the infidels? Or protection from the peasant hordes your monarch is falling all over himself to appease?" The German diplomat hung his head and slipped back into the scurry of emissaries. A third diplomat stepped forward.

"Holy Father, King John of Portugal will vouch for the authenticity of David Reuveni."

*Portugal? Portugal! Beza.*

"David Reuveni is a legitimate prince of the tribe of Reuben," the diplomat continued. "You can be assured. He is indeed the brother of Joseph ibn Reuveni, king of the Hebrew tribe of Reuben."

*The song is sweet to my ears,* David thought, *but even Beza could not have plucked this string.*

"Portugal?" the Pope snapped. "Sir, Portugal has a rather minor role to play, it seems. The Turks do not threaten Portugal. Does King John consider this true simply because Spain considers it false?"

"We are threatened by the Turks daily. The coast of Arabia on the south, our routes to India. The Turks and the tribe of Reuben reside in King John's realm. In his half of the world."

The Pope continued his stroll, rubbing his chin, unconvinced.

"King John is an acknowledged expert on Palestine and Far Eastern affairs, Eminence," the Portuguese ambassador said, scurrying to get to the Pope's side. "The Turk has cut us off at the Red Sea. Cut us off from our half of the world."

As the Pope hesitated, an anxious David felt his flesh begin to crawl. He looked for a place to hide. The porch offered no refuge. Welts raised on his stomach.

Finally, the Pope motioned for his aide. "Cesena." The two stepped aside and exchanged hushed words. David turned his toe into the stone surface of the terrace. His stockings dripped with perspiration. He sensed a puddle of sweat inside his codpiece.

After several minutes of deliberation, the Pope motioned for Cesena to return to the entourage.

A purposeful tone overtook the voice of the Pope. "Excellent. Then since King John has such faith in this fellow David Reuveni, we are glad to hear King's John offer to finance the crusade as well. We will send David Reuveni to Portugal to help plan."

David closed his eyes and inhaled. *My story is foolproof. No one can doubt me now. The Pope believes. It must be true.* Bowing deeply, he declared with great authority to the pontiff and his entourage, "All is proceeding as I have foreseen."

Benvenida came to his room that night. She gave him a Turkish gown of gold and asked him to wear it in Portugal, "For my sake," she said. She also gave him a silk banner that she had commissioned to carry before him. Both sides carried the Ten Commandments written in gold.

She sensed that the little man was overwrought with events and sought to give him comfort. She sang and danced before him with a tambourine.

> Sing to the Lord, for he has triumphed gloriously
> Horse and rider he has thrown into the sea.

David slept fitfully. His dreams were filled with images of a serpent devouring the genitals of the Pope's counselor, Cesena.

# CHAPTER 15

David confirmed the final details of his passage to Portugal at the Vatican palace. He received letters of introduction to the court of King John as well as a packet of banking papers from Abravanel. They were drawn to allow David access to funds from the Abravanel bank his brother ran in Portugal.

David wanted gold, but he got paper. He thought back at how he and Beza had used indulgences as money and shook his head in amazement. Paper. If he had ever doubted that the Christians were muttonheads, the idea that they would accept paper as money set his mind right.

David sat on his bedside and thought again about the lies. What difference did it make to these Roman Jews if he were born in Spain or Arabia? It only made a difference insofar as it concerned a hot meal, as well as a few clothes and a warm place to bed down. Up until now. Now the lies embraced his shoulder, guiding and beguiling him to Portugal, the court of King John, and Beza.

He had no remorse about lying to the Pope and the Christians. *Lying indeed. Lying? Indeed.* The Pope's entourage of advisers served no purpose other than to follow him around and lie to him. David sensed that the Pope did sincerely want all the kings to quit squabbling. And he wanted to crush the infidels. So David's lies yielded the Church a degree of hope. *The lies are good for the Pope. Christians. The devil to them. They deserve one another.*

As to his lies to the Jews, David thought, *I have never seen Jewish people so happy, so animated. So filled with the hope of a regathering.* They zealously praised their Lord in the piazzas and in the synagogue. Jewish ladies sang songs while strolling to the market.

A few little lies had given the Jews promise. What prophet before him could claim to have given the people a gift of such great price? *The Jews need someone to help them lift the yoke of the Christians,* he thought. *Perhaps I...* he stopped. *"Messiah"* was a thought too absurd to consider.

But lying to this lovely creature Bilhah—David lied to her for a different purpose. He was no novice with the fairer sex. When he worked for Beza, he had taken his pleasure with women of easy virtue, but none of them had ever returned any interest in anything but his money or his indulgences. *Maybe this one just likes me. No harm in that. What woman entertains an interest in an unimportant little man?* Besides, despite being a Jewess, Bilhah needed Abravanel. She surely stood to lose her patron's affection if she discovered the truth and failed to reveal it. David reasoned that his lies protected her. *The lies were for Bilhah. For her own good. Like the other Jews. For their own good.*

A week later, David boarded a handsome little ship that was bound for Lisbon, far to the west from Rome, beyond the Pillars of Hercules. Flags embroidered with the Star of David painted the wind. Benvenida's banner flapped from the top of the mainmast as well. David had once hoped for nothing more than to disappear in Rome. Now, below him, the Jews of Rome crowded the docks, all displaying the scurrilous yellow star on their breasts or a yellow scarf or hat. They thronged his departure, all rejoicing. And why not? To them, the little man with the audience at the Holy See was a legitimate prince of one of the lost tribes of Israel.

David found Abravanel and his wife in the mob, with the beautiful Bilhah at their side. The king of the Jews, his wife, and his mistress all had tears in their eyes. The prince of a brother tribe was bound away on a voyage to faraway Portugal, the first step on a blessed journey that Jews and Christians alike prayed would ransom the captives and return the Jews to Jerusalem. Every son of Abraham longed for burial in the land of the patriarchs.

Even if the prince was unsuccessful in eradicating the plague of Mohammad from the face of the earth, at least he would drive the Turks out of Europe and back to their rocky mountainous home.

David was saddened, but he would not weep. He could not cry for himself or for the suffering of the Jews. He might cry for lost love, for this Jewess Bilhah, but not for her people. He could cry but was powerless to stay in Rome. A venomous bile rose in his throat, and he gained bravery. He must remember Beza. He held power over the dreams of the Romish Jews but knew he must summon the capacity to hold them in contempt. *The Jews are not my problem,* he told himself.

David raised his arms high overhead, and as he did, the crowd hushed to a whisper. He knew that once he was in Portugal, he would find Beza and never again set eyes on the Eternal City. But with a shout, he lied again. He told them, "I'll be back."

The crowd wanted more. "David." they shouted, "Don't leave. Come back."

Under his breath, the little man said, "Fools. Who do they think I am?"

In that same moment, the crowd took up a low but intense chant. "Messiah. Messiah. Messiah."

David waved his *bareta* in farewell, and the ship slipped into the river's current. "Arrivederci, you morons," David muttered. Nothing he could have shouted to them would have been able to overcome their plaintive cry: "Messiah. Messiah."

As the little ship shrank away from the quay, some of the Jews cheered and others sang songs. The hosannas to the Messiah collided with praises glorifying Prince David.

The last face that he could see belonged to his beautiful Bilhah. His brave resolve was nearly shattered as he read her lips, sobbing, "My little prince."

At the stern of the little ship, a dark, curly-headed deckhand took it all in. Under his breath, he muttered to himself, "This is a man I shall get to know."

The vessel was a caravel, a small, sleek craft with two masts and a bowsprit. The foremast and mainmast carried large triangular canvases known as lateen sails. A short, square sail flew from the bowsprit.

The little ship's keel measured just forty feet. At amidships, from rail to rail, the deck was only fifteen feet wide. Beneath the ship's deck, sailors stooped—the low bulkhead overhead bumped the heads of the careless. The captain's cabin sat above deck. Its door was so low even David crawled on all fours to enter. Unlit and jammed with fifty tons of iron implements and Venetian glass, the below-decks hold also berthed the sailors. The little caravel was fully laden with merchandise, a crew of ten men, and its one passenger.

David welcomed the company of the ship's captain, a Greek named Poulous.

"David, come on. Come with me. It's suppertime."

"If I have no other engagements, then I will."

"Ha. Would you refuse my dining table for a duke? A king?"

"You've changed my mind. Lead the way, Captain Poulous."

David and the captain squatted on the main deck along with the sailors and the cook. They dined on pasta and cheese, the staple diet at sea. Most of the sailors spoke Italian or Portuguese. Except for an Arab—his mates called him "the Moor"—David could not identify the nationality of the others. The cobbled-together crew seemed to care nothing of the ethnicity of their shipmates or their passenger and spoke among themselves in a stream of pidgin profanity. The sound of wooden spoons scraping melted cheese from tin plates almost drowned out the creaking of the timbers and the wind whistling in the rigging.

On the evening of the first day out to sea, David failed to find sleep. He went fore to watch the water break off the bow. The night was pleasant, and he had only taken a few sips from the bottle of wine he brought with him.

One of the deckhands stood on the rail, holding onto the rigging with one hand, looking out over the spent sunset and the wine-dark sea. He wore loose-fitting trousers and a blousy long-sleeved linen shirt. David smiled when he heard the sailor's voice and turned aside to listen, taken in by the resonant voice and theatrical delivery. He pushed the cork back into the neck of his bottle of wine.

> Be silent, then, my lyre
> We sing 'fore lords in vain
> I will leave the minstrels' choir
> And roam a Jew again.

The verse was unfamiliar to the little man, but it pleased his spirit. "A poet, I see."

The surprised lyricist turned back in the direction of the voice that spoke to him, spraying piss all over the deck. While standing on the rail, the deckhand had been relieving himself. The little man's eyes surveyed the seafarer. He was young, of average height and weight, ridiculously handsome, and clean-shaven. Thick, curly locks of black hair framed his dark complexion.

"What is it that you want, little man?" An edge of anger burned in the sailor's voice. "Can't a fellow piss in peace?"

David ignored the anger of the deckhand. "Marrano. You're the one they call Marrano."

The deckhand jumped down from the rail to the deck and gripped David by the neck with one strong hand. "I may have to bite my tongue when these deckhands call me Marrano, but I'll be damned if I have to listen to that from you, runt."

"Please. Excuse me. A thousand apologies. What have I said? How have I wronged you, sir?" David's hand found the handle of the short dagger that he had acquired in Rome and now kept secreted in his sash.

The deckhand's grip eased. "Ha-ha. I am only acting. *Marrano* means 'swine' in Portuguese." He waved his robust arms and gestured with his hands as he talked. "That's what they call Christian Jews in Portugal. Pig." The deckhand spat out the epithet. "Marrano."

David's grip on his dagger loosened. "How delightful. I thought Marrano was your name. You can see, I don't speak Portuguese."

"Diogo Pires, at your service, little man."

Old habits sent David's mind exploring. Nothing in Diogo's manner or bearing spoke "deckhand." *This is a man with a hidden past. Perhaps he can be valuable to me. I need to gain his allegiance.*

"Look, Diogo, I like being called 'little man' about as much as you like being called 'swine.' I am David. Please, call me David," as he thrust out his chest. "I am David Reuveni, brother of the king of the tribe of Reuben."

"I know who you are. I was in Rome. I heard what the Jews were whispering." Diogo turned to peer over his shoulder. Looking back at David, he scowled. "I heard the Jews whisper, 'Prince David the Messiah.'"

"That's not a claim that I have made, I will assure you."

"It does not look like you have done much to stop the whispering..."

David tipped back to bottle of wine to his lips and took a long drink. "It makes them happy. They want me to be their champion. I'm not sure I can fill that shoe."

"Actors are always in demand."

*This aloof deckhand is as stubborn as a camel,* David thought. "Let me give you some advice, Diogo. I've learned that when you are little, some cabbagehead always stands between you and the fire." Another ounce of wine disappeared down the gullet of the little man.

"What does that mean?"

"I'm talking about being cold and wet for the last twenty years. Since this whispering started, I found out how nice a warm, dry bed is. I had almost forgotten. And nice warm suppers. And sultry, plump ladies. Those things are good. So I am in no hurry to return to performing with the cups and balls. I'm sick to death of hiding from constables in grubby wet villages every night. Now I stand close to the fire. I like it, and you won't see me trading my nice warm things because a few lamebrains are whispering."

Diogo's stone-faced glare slowly softened. He and Diogo circled the mast from opposite sides as if it were a Maypole. Each scrutinized the other from head to toe. David placed the back of his palm to his own forehead, then grabbed Diogo's hand and rubbed it.

"Soft hands. You are no deckhand. What are you running from?"

"I am a deckhand."

"No one can keep a secret from me. What's your trade, Diogo the runaway poetry-reciting deckhand?"

"What is it to you? Who said I was on the run?"

"Every move, every gesture shouts it. I don't have to read your thoughts. You are on the run. Don't deny it."

Diogo threw back his head as if to shake out his long tresses. He puffed out his chest. "Ha-ha. All right. I'm an actor too."

"Actor? An artist. How fantastic. You are Portuguese?"

"Yes. And I'll tell you my story if you tell me yours."

"Exquisite. Let's hear it."

David and Diogo sat side by side against the ship's mast.

"Have another swig," Diogo said.

David drank deeply. He rubbed his hands together as he swallowed.

Anytime was a good time to listen to a tale, even one that he expected to be varnished with lies and inflated with embellishments, especially one told by an actor. Embroidery would only make the actor's saga more enjoyable to the ear.

Diogo described his departure from Portugal. He brushed aside the details of his assignation with the minister's wife in the vestibule. "Exiled. For a minor political dispute at the ministry." He added a few comical anecdotes about the Italian theater. "Theater is tricky. Bankers have taken over the theater. A man's thespian talents have no currency. Most of the characters are clowns, and I'm just too good-looking." Diogo rubbed his dimpled chin. "My cross to bear."

He told about his engagement with Cardinal Wolsey.

"He's important?" David asked.

"He's the next Pope. Everyone knows that. And I, alone among his most trusted advisers, convinced him to withdraw his king's name." He hinted that he had to flee because his role with Wolsey put him at risk of physical harm.

"I have seen your destiny, Diogo, and your blood will go unspilled," David told the actor.

"I will remember that." After another rant about theater, he looked David straight in the eye and said, "Now you."

*The first liar doesn't have a chance*, as Beza had always said, so Diogo's saga seemed tame compared to his own. But lubricated by the liquid courage of the wine that so satisfied his palate, David's tongue felt compelled to flap. "You're right when you say that the theater is tricky business, but it is much worse for me." He told about selling rugs to Tetzel and his years as a player in Beza's troupe. He could not hold that part back as the deckhand was a showman too, a kindred spirit. Diogo was a good listener. He laughed at David's jokes. *I do not know why I am telling this*, David thought. David told him more than made good sense. His head was spinning. He told Diogo that he was not a prince.

"Have another drink," Diogo told him, his eyes the size of Dutch guilders. David complied.

"So now I'm off to Portugal to organize a crusade. Until I find Beza. What about you? What are your plans?"

"I am off to Lisbon and who knows where after that. If the political climate has changed, I might return to the foreign ministry. I am not sure. Perhaps I will go to the New World, if Providence allows."

"I'm in need of a manservant. I have no facility with this Portuguese language. Warm beds, warm food and plump ladies. I'm offering."

"Plump ladies implies more than one."

"The last time I wanted two was before I had one."

David and Diogo looked at one another without expression. David closed his eyes slowly and then managed to get them open halfway before conceding to the wine and the rolling of the boat. He tipped over on his side.

"Manservant. Retainer. Interpreter. Surrogate. Disciple." A broad smile broke over Diogo's face. "Yes, I think I will like this role. I will proclaim you as messiah in Lisbon."

A sobering chill might have run down David's back, but since he had passed out on the deck, dead drunk, it did not.

The little bark sought to take on fresh water at a port called Marseilles, but warships turned them away. "Blockaded," Poulous told the crew. "C'est la vie. We'll take water further on."

While underway to their destination, David engaged Diogo in conversation almost every night. It had served him well to learn what he could about the doge and the Pope before meeting with them. He feared breaking the pattern—maybe he was superstitious—but he wanted to know more before meeting the man who was king of Portugal and half the non-Christian world. He also was hungry for more knowledge about Portugal.

"My family came to the faith at the point of a sword. So maybe I am not quite as religious as the peasants. But maybe that's because I can read and write. I do not know. All I know is that when the Inquisition needs a heretic, they come looking for Marranos first."

David sat on the deck, his back against the ship's side planks while Diogo walked back and forth.

"This Inquisition business. It's horrible in the Germanies," David agreed.

"Those Roman Jews seem to have forgotten about the Inquisition. They were going crazy with 'Messiah,'" Diogo said.

"It doesn't mean what you think it means."

"What else can it mean? It is Jesus. Jesus of Nazareth, the Son of God. You know. The Messiah. It's his title."

David stared with a blank expression at Diogo.

"Surely you know, David," Diogo said. "God as man? Man as God? The Holy Trinity? God? Jesus? Mary?"

"These ridiculous beliefs set my flesh to crawling," David said. He leaned back and twisted from side to side, letting the rough timbers scratch at his skin.

"I might break out laughing if I see Christ killers wailing for the Messiah," Diogo said.

"Christ killers?"

"Jews."

David looked at Diogo, he with the easy, effortless smile. "I thought the Romans killed the Christ," David said.

Diogo shrugged.

"You must never laugh, Diogo. We will both be dead," David warned.

Diogo told his patron about the manners and morals of Portuguese Jews, how those who remained had converted, and their way of life. "They have remission of sin now, so they are not as grim as the Jews of Venice or Rome." David thought it was odd that Diogo viewed the

Roman Jews as strict. In his estimation, the Italian Jews were lax in their observance of religious law, at least in comparison with the Jews of Khaibar, or the German states. Compared to the Northerners, the Italian Jews acted like a mob of drunken sailors.

The voyage to Lisbon took eighteen days. It steered a course generally within sight of land, west through the Mediterranean, past the Rock of Gibraltar, and out into the Great Ocean Sea. Once on the untamed ocean, the ship hugged the coast of the Iberian Peninsula, as it turned north leading to Lisbon, the capital city of the greatest seafaring power in the world.

Two days out from Lisbon, the little vessel easily slipped past a Spanish galleon. It seemed as if Neptune's trident held the large ship nailed to the bottom of the ocean. The caravel lacked the tremendous cargo space of the galleon, but the big ship had no prospect of matching the caravel for speed and the ability to sail into the prevailing wind.

Diogo exchanged his work garments for a pourpoint as the caravel sailed into Lisbon. The Portuguese had no sumptuary laws to punish colorful clothing like those of the staid Italians, so in preparation for his arrival, Diogo slit the sleeves of his pourpoint with a knife, lengthwise from just below the shoulder to the elbow. Through each slit, he pulled a handful of his linen undershirt. His handiwork created puffy white pillows of fabric around his upper arm, otherwise sleeved in the customary colorless Italian manner. The fashion looked quite dashing to David.

David was gladdened to hear that since no Jews lived in Portugal, Lisbon would not require him to display the yellow badge.

# CHAPTER 16

As the caravel drew into Lisbon's port, the estivadores working the wharf took anxious notice of the banners flying from the ship's mainmast. The well-dressed merchants did too. Diogo and David spotted an agitated group who were waving their arms and shouting.

The little man was eager to find a bath and a warm, dry bed, and so was Diogo. Jumping atop the gunwales, Diogo cried out in Portuguese to the crowd of merchants on the quay. "Shalom. Brother Marranos. Shalom."

A young man stepped forward out of the pack. "Shalom. May I be of service?"

"Yes, brother. Thank you. My patron and I seek lodging," Diogo said as he and David disembarked the little ship.

The young man sneered at David. "I doubt that any of the establishments in this quarter have rooms for a Jew. Maybe a Marrano. I am Tomas Costello."

Diogo grabbed Tomas's hanging right hand and, shaking it warmly, said, "I am Diogo Pires, agent for David Reuveni, this dwarf here, who is on a diplomatic mission. He is nuncio for the Pope to the court of King John."

Tomas looked over the dwarf, from the top of his turban to the bottom of his sandals. Hearing his name spoken, David nodded and extended his hand to Tomas. As they shook hands, Diogo engaged some boys to see to the baggage. Then Tomas guided David and Diogo in a direction leading away from the wharf.

Tomas glared at Diogo. "I'm afraid you jest with me, sir."

"Why?"

"King John? Really."

"Not at all," Diogo said. "You didn't notice the Jewish flags flying on our ship? How many Jews travel in such comfort as we obviously have?"

"The Jews have left Portugal."

"You're looking at a Jew with a manservant. Does that not tell you something?" Diogo's voice grew louder, his palms raised higher to the sky with each question, and his head slung lower and more forward.

"It's not so unusual..." Tomas disputed. Tomas would argue with a tree stump.

"All right. Then how many Jews do you know with letters plenipotentiary from the Pope himself?" Diogo propounded the question loud enough for anyone on the dock to hear.

Diogo reached into a deep leather pouch hanging from a strap over his shoulder and pulled out a rolled document. Lead and wax seals littered the parchment. Red and purple ribbons laced up and down through the papers along each edge. Tomas scanned it, and his face reddened. "My apologies, sirs."

"No apology needed. And I apologize to you if my answers seemed to rebuke. But we are here to organize a crusade. With the assistance of King John, of course."

"You have an audience with King John?"

"Certainly."

"Christ."

Sensing excitement in Tomas's bustle, David shouted, "Abravanel. Abravanel." He knew nothing of the language but he knew where he wanted to go.

"Sí. Abravanel," Tomas answered. Tomas ignored Diogo's request to help find an inn. Instead, he steered David and Diogo on a straight uphill course. Diogo bore the golden banner that Benvenida Abravanel had given David before his master, high on a pole. All roads in Lisbon, whether in, out or around the city, led unerringly to the Castelo de Sao Jorge, a fortified citadel perched on a rock outcropping on a high hill overlooking the city. As their trek took them higher, the homes became more elegant. They stopped at an iron gate outside a graceful home. A signpost bore a plaque that read *"Abravanel."*

"Señor Abravanel. Come meet these visitors." Tomas yelled as he pounded on the front door of a grand townhouse.

A manservant answered the door, and Tomas continued to pound at the portal and shout "Señor Abravanel. Señor Abravanel," between loud exchanges with the doorman.

The gentleman of the house finally emerged. He looked in many ways like his younger brother, the Roman banker. However, he wore his beard closely clipped. He wore no skullcap, neither did his breast display a yellow star. Diogo stood back as Tomas recounted his meeting and conversation with the arriving dignitaries. Tomas's excitement hindered Diogo's struggle to present his master to Isaac Abravanel.

Surveying the letter of credit and documents Diogo handed over, the merchant's legs wobbled. He and Tomas stood toe to toe, wildly waving their arms and yelling at one another. Then unsteadily, the gentleman turned to his household servants and ordered them to arrange for private sleeping quarters for David, a bath, and a bed for Diogo with the servants.

David emerged from a soothing soak to the aroma of food. "Anything but pasta," he prayed.

A servant ushered him into a dining room with the merchant and his large family. The Portuguese Abravanel, Isaac, son of Isaac, had converted to Christianity, so these Abravanels did not observe the strict dietary laws of the Roman Jews. Since David never pretended to observe Jewish dietary laws, he was eager to enjoy the cheeses served alongside strongly peppered meats.

Abravanel offered a prayer of thanksgiving in Hebrew. David wolfed down the food stacked in front of him by the servants, his arm curled instinctively around his plate. His cheeks bulged. He answered the questions directed his way with a brisk nod.

The merchant's cook served a round red fruit that was unfamiliar to David. The acidity of the orb startled David's tongue. The children of the house laughed as David screwed up his face at the first bite.

"Pommes dei Moor," one of the older Abravanel daughters explained. She spoke quite loud and succinctly, as if David was deaf.

David thought he might understand some of the words. The girl's face looked like an angel. *A fifteen-year-old angel*, he guessed.

She looked directly at him and smiled, repeating, "Pommes dei Moor."

"Pommes d'amor. Sí. Pommes d'amor." David blushed deeply.

The evening meal finished and the table cleared, Abravanel opened his home to several men, important merchants, and one other man. No one could keep a secret from David Reuveni, and David surmised that this singular man was the most *non grata* of all *persona* in Portugal. The others called him "Rabbi." The merchants were Conversos, or Marranos in the vernacular, one and all. Like Diogo's mother, they had all come to the cross at the point of a sword. But the elders, many of them, held onto vestiges of their earlier beliefs. David could only imagine how difficult it had been for the rabbi to remain in hiding.

All the guests peppered David with a fusillade of questions. "Diogo. Diogo," he shouted. He could not understand a word they uttered.

Finally, a servant fetched Diogo up from the servants' quarters, and soon he replaced David as the center of attention. All the Conversos chattered at the same time, barraging Diogo with questions. Diogo told anyone who would listen about the gossip among the Jews of Rome. "They believe he is the Messiah."

Because of David's planned audience with King John, the rabbi asked Diogo, "Would your master consent to speak at the synagogue—pardon me—the community center, tomorrow evening?"

Diogo quickly agreed. "Surely. Tomorrow. Of course." He did not seek the approval of his master.

Abravanel turned the statues of saints that stood on his chimneypiece so that they faced the wall.

Late that night in David's room, Diogo eagerly broke the news of the scheduled speaking engagement at the synagogue on the following evening. To Diogo's surprise, David was sanguine. "We are going to have to do this sooner or later."

David's thoughts focused on the attention that the older Abravanel daughter had paid to him. The sensation of being an object of temptation to a pretty member of the fairer sex was perhaps more keen for him than it might be for a man of regular height. He babbled out his story to his servant.

"And then she looked straight at me with those dark, love-starved eyes and said 'Pommes d'amor.' It was so delicious, Diogo. Not the fruit. Just her saying it. Her words were so delicious. And hungry. For me. She thinks I'm wonderful."

"What? Say it again."

"Pommes d'amor. Pommes d'amor. A lot of these Portuguese words sound like Italian words. But even without that, I could tell, she was melting inside. 'Love apples,' she called them. Fires of passion were raging in me. If she said another word, I would have turned into a wild beast. I'm telling you, Diogo, I almost took her right there."

Diogo began laughing uncontrollably. "You foolish little man. She was not saying, 'Love apples.' She was saying, 'Spanish apples. Pommes dei *Moor*.'"

"You weren't there. You would not know. Besides, *Moor* doesn't mean 'Spanish.'"

"It does to the Portuguese. They call me 'Marrano' because it means 'pig.' And they call the Spanish 'Moors' because they had carnal knowledge of the daughters of the Mohammadans. You are so stupid."

David's dusky complexion turned as red as the pommes dei Moor. Diogo's derision was too cruel. He would not be mocked. His hand reached for the dagger in his sash. "Listen, Diogo, enough with the 'stupid' and 'foolish.' Unless you want to tell your Saint Peter how you had your throat slit by a stupid foolish dwarf."

Diogo overcame his laughter as he watched the little man's hand withdraw the knife from his belt. Whether delivered by a giant or a dwarf, a deep cut might go septic. Diogo did not intend to try to win an argument with a tough runt who was skillful with a knife. A jagged scar on his beautiful face would be worse than death.

"David. I did not mean it. I don't know what I was thinking."

David leveled a cold stare at Diogo.

"David, I'm sorry."

Many unfamiliar faces sat in the audience at the ornately decorated, exceptionally well-crafted, solidly built house of worship. A few years ago, it had been a synagogue. The leaders wore rich vestments, finer by far than those of the priests at the court of the Pope. A central aisle separated the women from the men.

David was ill at ease about speaking in this place. It would be difficult to address real people through an interpreter, people he had little fondness for, these hidden Jews, people who kept their Jewish traditions all the while professing a Christian faith. In Rome, the Jews, whom David had respected, were misfits, adrift outside the feudal system, oddly emancipated by their stubborn refusal to surrender their beliefs. They accepted every day as a manifestation of loving-kindness of their God. He did not hold the Conversos of Lisbon in such high esteem. In manner and culture, they were indistinguishable from the Jews of Rome, but the Conversos had little opportunity to achieve higher station. In giving up their Jewish identity, they became nothing more than freemen.

Perhaps he saw something in the Conversos that annoyed him about Diogo. David was beginning see that his manservant held only the most superficial religious beliefs. In fact, neither he nor Diogo would put his life on the line for an article of faith, but the carefree indifference that he found so objectionable in Diogo was something he refused to recognize in himself. *I will never be keen on these crypto-Jews,* he told himself, *and they will never have the affection of my heart like the Jews of Rome,* the Jews that he forgot and abandoned in Rome.

He would tell these Portuguese Conversos that he was a prince, and he would tell himself again that they had no way to detect his fraud.

Diogo was eager to use his stage skills again. It had been a long time since he had an audience, and his body thrilled as if he were in the pursuit of sexual pleasure.

David began one phrase at a time, and Diogo translated. "I am David, the son of King Solomon—may the memory of the righteous be for a blessing—and my brother is King Joseph, who is older than I and who sits on the throne of his kingdom in the wilderness of Arabia. My brother rules over thirty myriads of the tribe of Gad and of the tribe of Reuben and of the half-tribe of Manasseh. I have journeyed from before the king, my brother, his counselors, and his seventy elders."

Hearing Diogo's translation, the Conversos squirmed, sitting forward in their seats.

"I am not a Jew. I am David Reuveni, prince of the Hebrew tribe of Reuben, the youngest brother of Joseph ibn Reuveni, the Hebrew king of the tribe of Reuben. I am my brother's emissary. I am on a diplomatic mission from King Joseph. My journey began ten long years ago. My mission is to ally with Portugal and the Church for a Jewish crusade against the Turkish infidels."

David gave voice to a Hebrew poem, and in turn, Diogo gave its meaning in Portuguese. "I have commanded that Israel be sifted by the other nations as grain is sifted in a sieve, yet not one true kernel will be lost. The Turks say, 'God will not touch us,' but I tell you that they will die by the sword."

Diogo's acting skills came to the forefront. His translation together with his physical presence magnetized the audience. He sparkled with charisma. Tensions mounted. His movements attracted every eye, even those clouded by age. The crowd sat spellbound upon hearing Diogo give voice to this ancient song, one that the non-spiritual Conversos had once learned, but since forgotten, except in their deepest memories.

Hearing his recitation of David's words, and to the great astonishment of Diogo, the staid and conservative Portuguese Conversos exulted, shouting to the heavens. The Marranos lost control. It was not so uncommon for peasants to fall into raptures at festivals, or at holy places, or when viewing splinters from the cross, or jawbones of saints, or withered penises of martyrs. But neither David nor Diogo had expected an outward showing of the Marrano's passion.

"This is too easy," Diogo whispered to David. "I've never seen anything like this."

While Diogo preached, David's eye settled on a wide-eyed young man seated close to the front. The youth touched his hair and his breast. David read him out of habit. The youth was fantasizing about wearing a soldier's helmet and tunic. As Diogo told the congregation, "God will not touch us, but they will die by the sword," the shoulders of the youthful Jew jerked backward and forward. His body language told David that the boy imagined himself at the most intense part of the battle, in the final hour of the final conflict, swinging a sword. Once, twice, three times a make-believe two-handed broadsword swung around the head of the fantasist until, before him on the ground, in his mind's eye, the mutilated bodies of three Turks lay, oozing life into the dust of the battleground.

As the rapture of all the Conversos grew, David could not help but notice that Diogo strayed around the room urging, "Messiah, Messiah," under his breath. Soon, a few of the congregation repeated, "Messiah," in a longing chant. The little man did not want to claim this mantle, but held his tongue. He would not reproach his manservant who had such power to cast a spell.

Diogo arranged for agents to deliver letters from the Pope to the court of King John, high above Lisbon in the Castelo de Sao Jorge. The communication advised the court of David's arrival. Less than a week passed before the crown acknowledged the letter. Aides in the prime minister's office fixed a date for an audience with the king.

David stewed over the mental notes he kept, everything he knew about King John III, the Portuguese king. John was two years younger than Diogo, twenty-two years of age, erudite and cultured. The first wife chosen for him had been Eleanor of Austria, four years his senior. But as John still mourned the loss of his mother, Eleanor's hand and heart was stolen by his widowed father, Manuel. Their marriage wounded young John's tender spirit. He drowned his disappointment in godliness; his chroniclers called him John the Pious.

King John reigned in his third year. A patron of Renaissance culture, other nations held his court in high esteem for its astute politicians. The king was young and generally trusted the advice of his cabinet of ministers.

Like all the Portuguese, Diogo smugly believed that Portugal had outdone Spain in a 1494 treaty under which the Roman Catholic Church gave Africa and India to Portugal. Spain's efforts to locate the Fountain of Youth in the New World had born no fruit. Portugal won the Indies and Cathay, and had even swindled Spain out of Brazil, which now was yielding up a rich bounty of treasure that by itself outstripped all the New World plunder that was streaming into Spain.

"All they think about at the Court of King John is spoils from the territories. Nothing else," Diogo told David.

David intended to lie to King John, lies that were supported by the plenipotentiary letters from the Pope, lies he had no remorse for telling the Conversos. They were Christian, but under their fingernails, they were Jews, and they hewed to the ancient law that instructed Jews to feed and shelter strangers in their land. So the lies did nothing other than help the Conversos in Portugal obey their ancient law. *What is the harm in that?* Diogo had told him that he had never before seen the stodgy Portuguese Conversos so enthusiastic, so spirited, and so fervent in their faith. *The lies are good for the Conversos*, David told himself. *Perhaps it is me that should be annoyed, by Christ. These Conversos do not appreciate me enough.*

Diogo had not found his mother so he and David walked to the Alfama one sunny afternoon. David asked his manservant, "Diogo, does it bother you that the story we have hold the Conversos is not entirely truthful?"

"It is a matter of no consequence to me whether I lie to them or not," Diogo answered. "These Conversos are so arrogant."

"Lie? I prefer to think of it as something that is mostly true. Many of them seem to be Jews."

"Whatever they are, they are no better than the Christians who call us 'Marranos.' Jews, ha. Only a fool would look back on the scriptures and history and deny Christ's obvious divinity. All the time they call themselves God's chosen people. If the disdainful bastards want to be Jews, they don't deserve better."

"Diogo, not so loud," David cautioned.

Diogo moderated his tone. "Look, David, everybody lies. Even my mother lied to me. In the theater, I never got a job without lying to the impresario. And no impresario ever staged a play unless he lied to the actors. Men lie to their wives, lords lie to their kings, and kings lie to one another. It is the way of the world."

"This is an illiberal view."

"David, it's you who told the lies, not me. All I did was carry water. I am doing the will of my master—I just follow orders. I only interpret his words. What man would condemn a servant for doing the bidding of his master?"

David and Diogo followed down narrow pathways to the oldest quarter in Lisbon, the location of his stepfather's bookstore, a mare's nest of steep, tangled lanes that dated to a time when the Moors dominated Portugal, where fishwives squabbled, where laundry hung from overhead lines, and where pots of garbage flung from above splattered to the uneven cobblestones below. Horseshoe arches opened into tiny squares adorned with decorative tile work, much as David had seen in Khaibar.

The Alfama smelled of fish and sweat. The bookstore was gone. Diogo was saddened when a baker remembered that Costa and his wife had perished in a fire. Life was precarious.

They continued to the shop of a tailor had attended the synagogue of the Conversos; moved by David's words, he generously offered to outfit David and Diogo in new apparel at his shop in the Moorish quarter.

Master and servant skirted a street theater in one of the larger plazas. "The craft of the players was better in my day," Diogo said.

One character wore a king's crown, and a clown knocked it from his head. The tiara rolled to Diogo's feet. He picked it up and placed it on David's head.

"Lord Grand Inquisitioner," Diogo shouted. "The Marranos are getting pushy. It's up to you to keep them in line." In a grand stage manner, he grabbed his chin as if he were deep in thought and then, with his face brightening, thrust an index finger into the sky, shouting, "I'll burn a moneylender. I'll roast a merchant."

He put the crown on his own head and, with a booming bass voice, said "No. I need the moneylenders. On second thought, I'll find some scruffy vagabonds."

An angry street urchin knocked the crown to the ground, and when the crowd applauded, Diogo returned the crown to the actor on stage. He and David walked on.

"You have a strange sense of humor," the little man told him.

"These Marranos would not give us the time of day if it weren't for the Inquisition."

The tailor offered David a selection of pourpoints and stockings. David chose instead to outfit himself with two more long shirts and another robe. Diogo chose garments sewn in the fancy Portuguese fashion: more frills, more collars, and more embroidery. To David's chagrin, the tailor sewed a Star of David on his robe, but those he provided to Diogo did not bear the stain of the yellow badge.

While the tailor worked with David, Diogo roamed about the tailor's shop. After the transaction was consummated, the master had to pry his servant loose from the friendly chatting seamstresses in the rear of the shop.

Pleased to be clothed in the new garments, strutting like peafowl, the wandering adventurers climbed the steep lane on their return to the house of Isaac Abravanel. In the alleyway behind the home of their host, they came upon a short, domed oven.

"For baking the matzo," Diogo told David.

"I knew that," David said.

Diogo stuffed the firebox full of their tattered old clothing, but before he could retrieve an ember from the kitchen, a maid redeemed the rags from a fiery fate.

# CHAPTER 17

With his victory over France so utter and complete, Emperor Charles repaired to Spain. The Spanish nobles had initially given the rebels a great deal of support, but the peasant's rebellion had taken on a distinctly antifeudal edge that the monarch steadily quashed. Now that the peasants were subdued, Charles needed to walk back some of the concessions he'd made to the Spanish rabble in the way of lower taxes and such nonsense. He also thought it best to appease the citizens by returning some Spaniards to appointive offices. Practically every one of Charles's boyhood friends from the Netherlands had some sort of sinecure in Castile or Aragon, and the indignity of service in petty and inferior offices was grievous to the passionate Castilians of society's upper crust.

With scores of corrupt Dutch officeholders needing to be removed from office and replaced with a new batch of corrupt Spanish functionaries, important judicial functions to restore, and the Lutheran heresy festering in the German states, Charles delegated authority to raise taxes to the general assembly, the Cortes that had formed during the rebellion. The trappings of monarchy could drive a man to peevishness. He would let the Cortes take the blame.

He listened to his advisers who suggested that an elite group of nobles, called the Order of the Golden Fleece, would be a good ally when the time was right to restore the Church in the German states. The order had only fifty members, but every single one enjoyed unfettered power in his own realm. The emperor needed a carrot to entice the sovereign members of the order to join in the effort to cleanse Germany, and he offered them authority over all disputes between knights as well as the punishments or admonitions that secular law levied on offenders. The order pledged their allegiance, and the bargain was sealed.

By embracing the Order of the Golden Fleece, Charles won the loyalty of one of its most powerful members, the king of Hungary and Bohemia, who by happy coincidence was a brother-in-law to his own brother Ferdinand. Charles's family, the Habsburgs, held hereditary estates in Austria and Slovenia, so Charles charged the twenty-three-year-old Ferdinand with the government of those lands, installed him as grand master of the Order of the Golden Fleece, and sent him packing, not to Austria or Slovenia, over which Charles had just appointed him, but to Frankfort, the crucible of the Lutheran conflict. Charles was getting good at this emperor business.

Ferdinand received strict instructions from Charles. "Return the German states to an acceptable pattern and practice of Church customs—return the liturgy and maintain it as it had been before," his older brother instructed. In the emperor's name, Ferdinand was to call upon the Reichstag, the general assembly of German nobles and strongmen, to punish anyone who refused to carry out the so-called Edict of Worms.

In its particulars, four years earlier, at a city named Worms, Pope Leo and Charles V had charged Martin Luther with the crime of *lese majesté*—high treason—for teaching iniquities and preaching false doctrines against the faith and the Holy Roman and Universal Church. Condemned to share his guilt was any party who would buy, sell, or read one of Luther's books, and punishable by "confiscation and loss of body and belongings and all goods, fixed and movable, half of which will go to the Lord, and the other half to the accusers and denouncers." The fine print detailed other penalties.

The heresies that Ferdinand found in the German states exceeded his worst fears. Luther's followers filled the German general assembly—the Reichstag, also known as the Diet. Most of the nobles were adherents too, and with them, half the clergy. Freemen and peasants all followed Luther.

The members of the Diet, the government ministers, the nobles, and the clergy all greeted Ferdinand with uplifted heads and cheerful faces. The churchmen preached daily in the corridors of the royal palace—the halls overflowed with immense crowds of peasants from the city and surrounding countryside.

On All-Saint's Eve, the first fasting day following his arrival, Ferdinand witnessed varlets carrying trays loaded to overflowing with dishes of meat and game. The servants delivered the banquets to tables in the apartments occupied by priests. Worse yet, the attendants delivered the food openly, to be eaten on a day set aside for abstinence. The next day, the feast day following, Ferdinand attended a mass celebrated in a church that was empty, except for Ferdinand and his entourage.

Everywhere, the government ministers, the knights and their grooms zealously extolled the word of God. They embroidered the sleeves of their right arm with the inscription "V. D. M. I. A." which meant "The word of the Lord endures forever." They inscribed the cipher on the heraldic shields at the doorposts of the nobles as well. The lawgivers had even taken the extraordinary step of forbidding the drunkenness and debauchery that generally went along with the assembly of a German Diet.

"All heretics, one and all," Ferdinand said. He decided to conceal the most extreme instructions his brother had charged him with. The Diet was in open rebellion. Perhaps in a few days he would reveal his mission. He would throw them a bone, ask the Diet to adopt a resolution, something a bit milder, a law that would forbid civil authorities from meddling in laws that would restrict abuses of the clergy.

His request fell on deaf ears; indeed, the Diet spoke out freely against the Pope and the bishops. "The priests would do better to marry than to keep women of ill fame in their houses," they said. "Every man should have the choice to worship, take the Lord's Supper, or have his children baptized in German or Latin, as he sees fit." And intruding further on the domain of the clerics, the Diet agreed that it would henceforth restrict the Church to interpretation of scripture, not law. And it didn't stop there. The Diet demanded that henceforth, when the Church did interpret scripture, it could not cite theological commentaries as precedent.

Still in hiding, Luther published another book, this one laced with sarcastic verses and unflattering engravings that pilloried the Pope and his cardinals. Comments below each figure were in German and Latin and mocked the clergy with biting ditties like "we can fast and pray the harder, with an overflowing larder." He called England's King Henry a pig, a dolt, and a liar. The book sold like Pfannkuchen and seized the hearts of the citizens.

Luther's derisive little book was the final straw for the Romish clergy. Adherents to the Church gathered around Ferdinand. They plead with him not to spare the smallest measure of cunning or bribery. Was he going to enforce the Edict of Worms or was he not? Running out of options, Ferdinand published Charles's decree. He was to cleanse Germany of its heresies. The sword drawn in Spain was eager to taste blood in the German States.

William Tyndale was an Englishman who was overwhelmed with annoyances.

As an outspoken chaplain and tutor in the house of a noble patron, he frequently clashed with the learned clergymen in South Gloucestershire. One bishop told Tyndale, "We had better be without God's laws than the Pope's." Tyndale responded, "I defy the Pope, and all his laws, and if God spares my life, ere many years, I will cause the boy that drives the plow to know more of the scriptures than thou dost."

Looking over his shoulder, the wary Tyndale packed his belongings and was off to the continent with ten pounds of silver, enough to provide for the necessities of life while he translated the Bible to English. He landed in Hamburg. Four years later his text was ready, but Tyndale's purse was empty. He was unable to pay his assistant, his debts, or move to another city. He ordered three thousand copies of his New Testament from a printer in Cologne, the expense guaranteed by English booksellers.

The Church discovered the clandestine printing just as the tenth page was thrown off. Tyndale fled to Worms, Germany, a hotbed of the Lutheran revolt, taking with him so much of the Testament as had thus far been printed. He went into hiding.

Soon Tyndale had the first five books of the Old Testament off the press and bound. Even though he was beyond the influence of the Pope, his life was in danger. England's Good King, in mortal fear that the Lutheran heresy would bring the English peasants to revolt, wanted Tyndale to burn.

It was a raw winter's day in Antwerp when Tyndale boxed his Old Testaments and booked passage to England. The sea was churning, whipped by bitter winds. He wrapped his manuscript in an oiled cloth for protection from the sea spray. He held it close to his bosom. A well-wishing friend urged him not to hide it. "The captain will take you for a thief."

As the tempest raged, the captain ordered his passengers below-decks. "We'll stay in sight of shore."

Beyond the harbor, the wind and waves of the dark sea battered the little bark. She pitched up as the massive swells hit her bow and then lurched down, skidding into troughs between the walls of water. Shortly, the captain lost the bow to a gust of wind; the ship turned sideways to the waves, took on water and could no longer ride. Torrents broke over the rails and swept below-decks. A sailor's voice shrieked over the gale, "We're being driven ashore." The passengers and crew scrambled to abandon ship. Still Tyndale clutched his manuscript, even as a swell washed him overboard.

The face of a fisherman's wife hovered over him when he awoke. "My bundle. Where is it?" The Leviathan, the gatekeeper of hell, had swallowed up all of his Old Testament books. The deep had consumed his precious manuscript.

Tyndale was despondent. No one could replace his text. No one but Tyndale.

By 1525, two editions of his Testament were in print, and by 1526, the books had crossed the English Channel by way of Antwerp and Rotterdam. Tyndale's Bible had the English clerics in a tizzy. "Today they attack the cardinal; tomorrow they will attack the king."

Tyndale wrote the book for the king of England. Every learned man in England read it, every man but Henry VIII. The rector of All Hallows Church, on Honey Lane near Cheapside, concealed the unsold books. The rector sold them secretly to the younger doctors and students at Oxford and Cambridge. "Honey out of the rock," the wags said.

One student, Roper, having read the Testament, received the truth. "The ears of God are always open to hear us all, saint and sinner," he told his father-in-law, Thomas More, a powerful minister and close ally of King Henry. "Would you assist me in procuring, from the king, who is very fond of you, a license to preach from the Gospels?"

Mustering his contempt, More lambasted the young student. He quenched the fiery questions in the young man's heart and replaced them with fear. Roper returned to his studies, broken but obedient to the established order.

The printers struggled to meet the demand for Tyndale's New Testaments. Thomas More sent his agent Packington to the continent to buy up every book, eager to see them destroyed. The merchant had even more books to sell than before. "You promised me that you would buy them all," Packington shouted at the shopkeeper.

"They have printed more since," the merchant told him, "and will so long as they have letters, stamps, and dies. My lord, you had better buy all the type too, so you shall be sure."

"And so forward went the bargain," said Edward Halle, "the bishop had the books, Packington had the thanks, and Tyndale had the money." Wayward to his will, Thomas More's money financed the production of Tyndale's Bible.

Meanwhile, a low-level priest, a devout curate named Smith, unwilling to live the boisterous and unruly life that most of the clergy reveled in, having found his rector's servant girl to be a discreet and pious person, openly took her to wife. "God has declared marriage lawful for all men, and accordingly it is permitted to the priests," he told his rector.

In a showing of his noble heart, Charles released the king of France from his prison in Seville. Francis and his entourage repaired to his homeland. Before Francis and his company reached the valley of the River Rhone, he threatened a deputy who disputed Francis's opinion that the battle of Pavia had been fought to a stalemate. In Burgundy, he decided that no battle had taken place, and by the time he entered Paris, he was ready to renounce the treaty with Charles. His commitment to abandon Auvergne and Lombardy to Bourbon was forgotten and along with it, his promise to deliver one hundred livres and a pension to his cousin.

Bourbon's claim on the spoils of Pavia had disappeared like a wisp of smoke on the wind. With his hopes of regaining his ancestral estates dashed, he made his way to Spain, to the emperor's palace in Seville.

A dozen job seekers held ears to the door of the hall where Charles held court. They could hear the angry exchange between the emperor and his general.

"You let him take pleasure with me as if I were a tethered goat. I have no ability to pay your Spaniards and the German mercenaries. I'm a prisoner in Lombardy, not a commander."

The words of the taciturn Charles remained unheard beyond the door.

Moments later, a dozen hangers-on spilled to the ground when Bourbon exploded from the hall. He ripped a parchment document as he stormed through the doorway. He shredded it to bug bites and hurled it at the job seekers.

Joan the Mad burst out of the court's doorway, chasing after Bourbon on a dead run. "Catch him. My Frenchie," she shouted. "He's mine."

Armed guards restrained the mother of the king of half of the world. Bourbon doubled his stride and ran from the palace. He didn't stop until he had reached the streets.

Camp in Lombardy was a mess. Rowdy Spanish infantrymen brawled. When a sergeant barked out orders for the soldiers to come to attention, his men mobbed him and stripped him of his clothes. Released, he ran for his life. He dove into a latrine ditch when an arquebusier-bearing soldier behind him fired a blast into the sky.

One of the Spanish lieutenants sat on the ground. Tears the size of horse turds streamed down his rosy cheeks. "It's us they'll attack next, General Bourbon. Their anger grows with each day." He was a young noble and relied on a family allowance for his maintenance. Affairs of the camp were not what he had in mind when he accepted his commission.

"I've sold every jewel," Bourbon told them, pausing his pacing. "Every tapestry. Every stick of furniture. The emperor has deceived me."

One of the German officers, Fruendesburg, spoke next. "My landsknechts are plundering the countryside. Is that what the emperor wants?"

"Thank God for the Spaniards," Bourbon said, hoping to curry the favor of their officers. "They know how to observe discipline."

"Until this morning," said a Spanish captain. He withdrew a document from his bodice.

"An indulgence. Ha-ha." The German snorted. "I have not seen one of these in years."

"Keep reading. The Pope offers absolution to anyone who kills a Spaniard."

Bourbon read the document and was incredulous. "It says Moor. It does not say Spaniards."

"That's right. The Pope calls the Spaniards Moors. And I don't know which inflames the foot soldiers more, putting a bounty on their heads or calling them Moors."

"The hypocrite. The Pope himself has an illegitimate son who is as black as ink," Bourbon said.

"Tell the foot soldiers. If the Germans mutiny, the Spaniards will follow," the Spaniard told him. "They are ready to fight for the offense."

"Damn them. Kings, Popes, emperors. Damn them all to hell's fire."

"Our larders are empty, General Bourbon."

"Can we do nothing to put down the unrest in the ranks?" Bourbon asked.

"We have issued standing orders," Fruendesburg told him.

Bourbon pulled back the flap of canvas that served as the door to his tent. He paused before entering. Soldiers danced around campfires on the plain below. When he spoke, not facing Fruendesburg, his voice was flat. "Damn them all to hell. Send your lieutenants among the men. Arm them well. Secure provisions for the officers from the rabble."

# CHAPTER 18

At the appointed time of the audience with King John, David and Diogo marched past the predictable swarm of suitors lining the vestibule outside the king's court. Diogo was absorbed in his role, and to capture as much majesty as the event would allow, he carried before his master, on a pole, the ancient silk banner with Ten Commandments written in gold that Benvenida Abravanel had given David. And as she had requested, he wore a robe of Turkish gold.

The resplendent hall outside King John's court seemed to mock the dreary interiors of Rome and Venice. Vivid tapestries and opulent chairs lined the wall opposite tall windows. Sunlight poured through the openings above a mezzanine. It illuminated the dazzling colors of the hall and the clothing worn by the suitors who occupied it. As a Marrano, Diogo expected scornful stares. The court suitors directed odious remarks at the little man and his manservant. "A dwarf," some said. "A Jew and a Marrano."

A large double door opened as if by magic. The portal stretched upward, perhaps two stories high.

"David Reuveni, prince of the tribe of Reuben." The doorman announced David in booming tones. David and Diogo stepped forward. Piquant incense masked the smell of humankind in the king's court.

David bowed deeply. "I fall at the feet of my lord. Your Majesty." Diogo stepped forward and interpreted, bowing himself. Sitting on a jeweled throne, King John acknowledged the emissaries with a nod. He seemed even younger than David anticipated, and delicate, almost effeminate.

As he had in Rome, David spoke in the Roman dialect. "Your Royal Highness, I am David Reuveni, prince of the Hebrew tribe of Reuben, your servant, the dirt at your feet and the ground you tread on, the chair you sit on and the footstool at your feet, the brother of Joseph ibn Reuveni, the Hebrew king of the tribe of Reuben. I am my brother's emissary to Pope Clement, who has in turn sent me on this diplomatic mission. I am here to discuss an alliance that the Church has made with the tribe of Reuben for a Crusade against the filthy Turkish infidels." When David finished, Diogo again interpreted. His manner of speaking had a practiced refinement and seemed exquisite to his master.

An aide to the king responded, and Diogo interpreted for David. "They welcome your arrival and look forward to forging an alliance with King Joseph." Both David and Diogo bowed low.

*No man can discover that I am not a prince,* David told himself. Again, no voice spoke to oppose him, neither the king of Portugal nor any subject in his court offered to question the story, only the voices in his dreams were defiant. "Tell him we need money."

But King John spoke before Diogo could interpret, and in that moment, a dozen gleaming blades were drawn and pressed at the throats of David and Diogo.

"Voce conhece o Preste João das Indias?" King John inquired of one of his secretaries, who nodded and in turn inquired of Diogo in Portuguese.

Concerned, Diogo said to David, "They want to know what you know of a Prester John." Diogo's eyes were opened wide when he turned to David. He clenched his teeth and shook his head to cue an answer of "no." But the little man had read the heart of the John. The young king was imagining himself on a quest, a stranger in a strange land, an archangel, sharing grace with the heathen. The master needed no signals from his servant to let him know to bite his tongue.

David shrugged, pursed his lips, and returned the "no" gesture, careful as he shook his head to avoid the blade under his chin. "Nothing. I've never heard this name. Perhaps my brother knows him." With great relief, Diogo communicated David's answer to the king and his court.

Another question flew at Diogo, and he interpreted. Drops of sweat rolled down his cheeks and onto the steel of a sword. "If your homeland is Arabia, how is it you've never heard of Prester John?"

*Why did I say no? I could have said anything.* "I...my home is...it's in a...a remote part of Arabia." David's imagination raced. "A river entirely circles my homeland. The Sambatyon. It is too wild to cross."

Diogo relayed the answer, and it elicited another query from the king. Diogo's voice quivered: "You crossed."

His mind raced for an answer. A sword was still at his neck. He remembered then the fanciful tales of Daoud Roubani, an ancient hero in his homeland, stories his father shared near the fire. "The river changes direction once every thousand years. The river stood still. I crossed. With my horses and guard." Diogo translated, and as he finished, David thought, *To perdition with this king.* "Now tell him that the mistreatment of the Marranos must end. My king demands it. And gold."

King John hung on every word Diogo spoke and then motioned to one of his chief rumpswabs, a man whose face hid under the hood of a priestly black robe.

"It's Selaya," Diogo moaned. "Holy Mother of God. We are dead. This man is Nuno Selaya. He is Portugal's Grand Inquisitor."

David looked beyond his servant's face. Mortal fear. David saw that he was frightened, consumed with images of a fiery death on the *auto-de-fé.*

The inquisitor motioned to a page. The errand boy briskly passed the aide a parchment, which he rolled out on a table before the king. Selaya snapped his fingers, and the swords returned to their scabbards. David and Diogo gulped air.

"Remind them that my king demands gold," David said. "Tell it, I said." Sweating profusely, consumed in his role, Diogo translated his master's demand. Selaya gritted his teeth.

King John signed the parchment with the flourish of a quill and sat back on his throne. The aide melted a large gob of wax onto the document and then impressed it with a heavy seal. Finally, the aide read the newly signed document aloud.

Diogo's eyes opened wide, and his mouth dropped open. He bowed deeply, a second and third time, urging the bewildered David to bow as well, and then, grabbing his master by the collar, pushed and shoved him out of the court.

In the gallery outside the massive doors, David asked, "What is it? What is it?"

"The king. He's just signed a proclamation."

"So what?"

"It prohibits the Inquisition from taking any action against Jews or Marranos. Perhaps you are the Messiah. You will never convince the Marranos that you are not. Not now."

David and Diogo met a throng of happy Conversos on the street outside the palace. The news of the proclamation had by unknown means escaped the palace before David and Diogo. And the entire crowd credited David as if he had written the proclamation himself. Everyone sang, shouted, and danced in circles, holding hands. The celebration carried on past midnight in the old Jewish quarter, high above the river, where most of the Conversos lived.

It was too unreal, and David began to sense a growing apprehension for what he did not know or understand in this land where he could not speak the language. The enigma of the king's inquiry about this John character gave David a fright that large quantities of wine were unable to ease. And too, when the word *Messiah* was spoken near him, the hair of his flesh bristled as if the shadow of a spirit was on his face. This night, it happened too many times to count.

That night, he hid in a wardrobe in his room.

Because of the celebration, David was unable to speak privately with Diogo until the next day. Because of a poor night's sleep, David bones ached as if he had been hit by a runaway wagon. After noon, David caught Diogo malingering with the maids of the house in the servants' quarters, and beckoned him outside with his index finger.

"Come, Diogo, let us walk," David said, his head pounding. "You need to tell me what in the world was that Prince John business all about?"

Diogo's laugh eased his anxiety. "Prester John. Have you never heard of Prester John?"

"No. That is why I am asking. Are you going to tell me?"

"It's a long, long story." Diogo kicked at a stone imbedded in the footpath.

"I'm ready."

"Well, three or four hundred years ago, a letter circulated in all the capitals of Europe. A priest-king of a huge Christian kingdom in the East supposedly wrote it. The writer said the kingdom was larger and wealthier than three Indias. Prester John was what the author called himself in the letter. He claimed to be the inheritor of the throne of the three Magi who visited Jesus at the time of his birth."

David smiled. "And these dullards believed it. There's more?"

"Much. The kingdom of Prester John had rivers filled with gold, a fountain of youth, ruins of the Tower of Babel, giants, centaurs, Amazons—and there were pebbles that gave off light, cured blindness, and allowed people to become invisible. All kinds of great nonsense." As the story grew more preposterous, the gyration of Diogo's arms grew in amplitude. "And our king believes it. Every word."

"No wonder these boneheads are so excited." The pair rounded a corner. The footpath led dizzily uphill, so David sat on a curb.

"There was no crime in this kingdom," Diogo continued. "Prester John could see anywhere he wanted through a magic mirror. And he possessed the body of St. Thomas."

"This Prester John makes my story sound absolutely unpretentious." David patted the curb beside him and Diogo seated himself. "It's laughable."

"What worried me so much yesterday," Diogo said, "was that this Prester John letter said he wanted to ally with the Church to make a war on infidels and barbarians. He wanted to fight infidels on one front and the Church fight on a second front. The same drum you were beating in Rome."

"So where is this kingdom supposed to be?"

"It's somewhere either east of Persia or south of the Sahara Desert. Or Abyssinia. It depends on who tells it. David, these Portuguese really believe they are going to find this king. That is what this discovery business is all about. They want to find Prester John and his fountain of youth. Every time they find a new river, they call it the Western Nile. They think it's going to lead them to Prester John and riches beyond measure."

"Diogo, I'd be dead right now if it weren't for you...if you had not managed to tell me 'no.' I don't know what I would do without you." David stood and embraced Diogo. "I wish you were my brother."

"You nearly pulled a knife on me a few days ago, David, remember? Besides, bad things happen to Jews who are brothers. Did you ever hear about Cain and Abel? Or Jacob and Esau?"

David was contrite. "I'm sorry, Diogo."

Disdain darkened the face of his servant.

*I'll never apologize to him again,* the master thought.

The thankfulness of the Conversos knew no bounds. They all believed that David had brokered the king's proclamation and the end to Jewish persecution. Even without the urging of Diogo, many people in the Converso community were speaking with one another in unguarded tones, pronouncing aloud that David was the Messiah.

Following the audience with King John and his proclamation, the excited Marranos started calling their community hall a synagogue again. The open naiveté of the people reminded David of his days in the north, dazzling the rubes with the cups and balls as he sized them up as marks. He had little respect for the Conversos and knew that he would have no sense of remorse for anything he told them. *It is time to see some benefit for me in this. Time to make these mongrels pay.*

Before the congregation again, David told Diogo what to say, and Diogo translated. It was an ancient song, forgotten by many of the Portuguese, yet hauntingly familiar. "Thus says the Lord God: 'I will rebuild the city of David which is now lying in ruins, and return it to its former glory, and Israel will possess what is left of Edom, and of all the nations that belong to Me.'"

Diogo sensed the tension of the congregation and pushed himself to even greater theatricality in his delivery.

*These Portuguese Conversos are worse than the Romans,* David thought. *And fleece them I will, as they are more deserving.* A few in the crowd restarted the longing chant. "Messiah, Messiah."

*The time is right.*

The emissary selected a spirit-filled patriarch with a bulging purse who sat along the aisle. He handed the old man the *bareta* that he had carried with him from Rome. The elder removed coins from his purse, deposited them in the hat and passed it along to the others. *Far easier than cutting a purse,* David thought. *And safer.*

David spoke in the synagogue on the following week. "This is God's message to the Turks: 'Disaster is roaring down on you from the desert, and the groaning of all the nations you have enslaved will end. Quick, grab your shields and prepare for battle. You are being attacked.'" Once more, the magnetism of Diogo's delivery whipped the big crowd into a delirium. David passed his *bareta* again, and when it returned, it overflowed with gold and silver coins.

*More in one night than I could make with Beza in a month. How can this sit well with the rabbis?* David thought. While secreting his bulging purse in a closet, he pulled a blanket and pillow in behind himself. After a time, his tension subsided and he drifted into a dream-filled, shallow sleep. Over and over, he imagined a falling rain of gold and silver coins. He lost another night's sleep.

In the following weeks, David departed his lodgings at the home of Señor Abravanel and rented an apartment nearby, high on the slopes of the city's central hill, in the Jewish quarter. The offerings he collected from the Marranos, together with his pension from Rome, also allowed him to also hire a room for Diogo in the Alfama. In no time, Diogo installed two plump ladies from the tailor shop nearby as mistresses for them. As in Rome, many Lisbon Conversos maintained mistresses in the gentile quarters of the city.

And he hired an agent to search for Beza.

King John's mood was generous. Love was in the air.

Even as plans for war on the Turks progressed, intense negotiations had forged two marital unions. Emperor Charles had given his sister in marriage to King John, and in turn, John gave the hand of his sister Isabella to Charles.

The news was as bitter as gall to Princess Mary of England, Henry's only heir. She, who at the age of five had rejected the three-year-old dauphin of France in favor of a betrothal to Charles, found herself, now, at the age of eight, rejected herself. The king of England had sowed the wind, and it was his only heir that reaped the whirlwind.

King John chose to neglect reports from his agents that complained that the Conversos were returning to their Jewish roots. The Grand Inquisitor, Selaya, hid this matter in his heart.

# CHAPTER 19

King John deliberated often with his secretaries and ministers concerning armament of the tribe of Reuben. David and Diogo even met with King John himself. Elaborate schemes were scribbled by his military advisers on ornamented maps drawn by the world's foremost cartographers. King John spoke to Diogo, who consulted David.

The planning bogged down often in frustration over the difficulty of language. David boldly insisted that the point of attack should be Jeddah; the ministers thought strategies that were boldly proclaimed must have merit. Almost monthly, returning seafarers presented maps with new discoveries about the world. The king, roaring with frustration, he tore up his old maps and formed new plans.

David gave much of his money to Abravanel's banking house. His account was credited monthly by an allowance provided by the Church. It was difficult for him to overcome his suspicious nature, but many merchants accepted the Abravanel bank notes in lieu of the coin of the realm in much the same way as indulgences had been treated as money before Luther. Isaac Abravanel liked David and he was tolerant when David dropped by the banking house, almost daily, to check on his deposit.

Isaac Abravanel had expanded his family's banking interests by knowing everybody and their business. Like Meshulam in Venice, he spoke several languages. Always eager for news from the European capitals, Isaac haunted the wharves of Lisbon whenever a new ship entered port. News about conflict in Lombardy arrived often; Abravanel always listened closely. War was good business.

Selaya, the pudgy Portuguese Inquisitor General, frightened David. He sensed that the Inquisitor was lurking in the shadows at every audience he had with the king. David channeled his discussions with Isaac to the Inquisitor from Badajoz.

According to Isaac, Selaya was in his sixties, a priest, a lawyer, and deeply religious. The Inquisitor was absolutely loyal to the task of ridding Portugal of heretics; David found Selaya mild mannered, considerate, and grimly solicitous.

"I suppose the proclamation was written by his hand," Isaac told David.

"Surely not the Inquisitor General...?" David asked. "He must hate Jews."

"The Inquisitors are after heretics, not Jews," Isaac explained. "They are lawyers first, and they are worn out from years of pursuing heretics out in the country. It is too hot in summer and too cold in winter, and the country inns are lousy with fleas. Selaya is not such a bad sort. A few thieves confess heresy to him every day. His Inquisition has been more lenient in its punishments than the courts."

David's agent reported back that he had located Beza, far to the north, in Braga, incarcerated in a debtor's prison. David's account with Abravanel held more money now than he had ever possessed before. He could buy Beza's freedom. But if he were free, David knew that Beza would demand a share of David's treasure.

David remembered how Beza had left him on the road, on foot. Now he was honest with himself. The wound of Beza's departure had been festering for four years; today it was as raw as the stripes he had received in Treviso. *Beza is good at his craft, but not better than Diogo. I do not need Beza,* David told himself. *Beza is nothing to me now.*

He told the agent to forget Beza. *I must be more careful about the people I do business with.* He instructed the agent to make discrete inquiries about Diogo's background.

The agent returned empty handed. "He once held a prominent office at the bursary. Other than that, nobody. Nothing. I can't find out anything about him."

"All the signals tell me that his mother was a prostitute," David said.

A week later, the agent told David, "You have a miraculous gift, David. About Diogo's mother, she is deceased, but your vision was true."

On another day, with Easter approaching, David and Diogo were in the king's war room. A sideboard sagged under massive trays that themselves were spilling over with spiced meats and cheeses. David and Diogo loaded their plates. The little man stood on a chair and was in the process of spearing a morsel of meat when the Grand Inquisitor, Selaya, oozed to his side.

"Sorry we can't offer your master any matzoh," Selaya told him. "The blood of martyrs is out of season."

David looked to Diogo for a translation, and Diogo shook his head. "Forget it," he said. "He's mocking you. The blood libel."

Selaya leaned over and speared a chunk of beef on a skiver and said to David, "Sad thing, being a Jew. Unlike you, I know I have the promise of eternal life. Our Lord Jesus saves my soul."

Diogo interpreted, and David nodded. "He knows I'm a Hebrew, not a Jew, right?"

"Who knows..."

David seated himself with a plateful of food and found that he had attracted the attention of a housedog. David gave him bit of roast goose.

Selaya was not finished. Now flourishing his impaled morsel of beef with a lordly gesture, he lifted his eyes to the heavens and to his own aggrandizement proclaimed to the angels, "Just as sure as this morsel of meat is going into my mouth, I know I'm redeemed."

In that moment, the meat slipped from the Inquisitor's fork, rebounded from the side of the tray, and skidded across the table just beyond the grand man's reach. Setting aside his soliloquy on the promise of eternal reward, Selaya stabbed after the greasy lump, which was now rolling off the edge of the table and onto the marble floor.

The housedog's ears perked up, and David told him, "Sic!" As the morsel fell from the firmament, the dog darted. He saw a heaven-sent gift, and he regarded it as his just reward. In reflex, and as if miraculously transfigured, Selaya dove in a headlong attempt to retrieve the unctuous morsel of flesh as it disappeared beyond, below and under the sideboard.

David laughed. He imagined Selaya and the curly-haired beast in a philosophical disputation under the loaded sideboard, the dog arguing for the proposition that faith without works is dead, with Selaya taking up the contrary proposition, that faith alone was enough.

Moments later, a purple-jowled Selaya gathered his bulk from underneath the sideboard, producing as he did a considerable swallowing noise, *"gawl-ulp!"* And taking two brisk steps in David's direction, he growled, "You'll live to regret that, little man. The suspension of the Inquisition isn't set in stone." Leaving the war room in a huff, he snarled at the guard, "Destroy that beast."

David may not have understood the words, but he read the Inquisitor's thoughts. Death and destruction. He reached into his purse and withdrew some coins. "Give these to the guard," he told Diogo, "and tell him that we will carry out this task."

"Redeemed from the wrath of the Inquisition." The little man roughed the shaggy ears of his new pet. The dog was longer than tall, with a solid, muscular body, a tightly curled black coat, and webbed toes. He and Diogo were on the way to show the dog to his mistress. Their journey took them near Abravanel's home.

The dog barked at a wisp of smoke that curled out of the cramped and cluttered alleyway behind the mansion. Clothing slouched from clotheslines that crisscrossed the passageway. Behind Abravanel's kitchen, a cook was removing matzoh from his short, brick-domed oven. Just then, Isaac stepped out of a door and into the alley. As if he'd frozen in stride, he stared at the oven, seemingly transfixed.

"Just a moment," David said. "Watch this. What's happening here?"

Without warning, Isaac raised a heavy cane over his head and smashed the handle down on the matzoh oven. Again and again, he struck the oven with the head of his cane as if it were wielding a sledgehammer. Dodging a spray of brick fragments, the cook screamed out, "Master!" and ran inside. The sound of screaming women's voices spilled out of the back door and into the alleyway.

Isaac's vigor grew with each blow. Cracks appeared between the bricks. He smote the oven again, redoubling his blows until the oven shattered into a thousand pieces. Then, breathlessly, and shaking a defiant fist into the sky, he yelled out, *"L'Shanah Ha-ba-ah bi-Yerushalayim!"* A joyful smile lit his face as he kicked at the remains of the oven to scatter them across the stone path. Isaac left no brick standing on another.

Beads of sweat broke out on David's forehead. He blew into his hands and rubbed them together. He was freezing. Diogo could see his fear as he had no place to hide.

"What in God's name was that?" Diogo asked.

"He said, 'Next year in Jerusalem,'" David answered. Abravanel's shout was in Hebrew, the prayer of a Jew, not one of a Christian.

Diogo shrugged.

*No good can come of this,* David thought. He tugged at the leash of the dog and hurried away.

One warm spring day, David hired a carriage, and Diogo drove his patron and their mistresses to the country for a holiday, dog and all. Diogo found a shaded spot upriver where the air smelled sweet.

David was doing his best to polish off a bottle of wine as he sat on a blanket in the shade of a willow. As he and the afternoon dissolved in haze, the exuberant little dog repeatedly jumped into the river to retrieve sticks thrown by the girls. The air turned into fog when the animal shook water out of his coat.

"David," one of the girls laughed. "This beast is crazy."

David neither understood nor cared. "I've seen others like him at the wharf," Diogo said. "The fishermen say these dogs will chase fish into a net."

"What do they call him?"

"*Cao de agua*," Diogo answered. He turned to David by habit and said, "Water dog," but David was too distracted to listen.

He was trying to focus his bleary eyes on a barge. Five brown-robed, hooded monks stood on the deck of the large, flat-bottomed boat. They had with them a man who was bound hand and foot. *Is he a Converso?* I think so, but the wine and the sun. David wiped at his moist and groggy eyes. But then an image overpowered him, one that no man would wish to see. The monks unceremoniously pushed this lost soul into the river. His fettered body disappeared below the roiling water, into the unbound stream. Not even a ripple marked his entryway to the underworld.

David rubbed his eyes in disbelief. He had no desire to assist the victim. He was only certain that he should not have seen what he thought he saw. His companions were still playing with the dog. "We need to go," he told the others. He was afraid of the images that would haunt his dreams. "Get the dog."

Diogo reached for the dog's collar. The dog nipped back and jumped to guard David.

"Is this what you think of me?" the servant asked. A trickle of blood ran down his finger.

David could only stare at Diogo. He felt his mind go fuzzy again. He finished his bottle of wine in one long last guzzle and slumped into the lap of his lady friend.

The next day, unaware of the murder that David had witnessed, Diogo reproached his master. "Two giggling girls, a drunken dwarf, and a stinking wet dog. How much do you think I can tolerate? Disgraceful."

David distracted his thoughts by keeping himself and Diogo busy with the work of the Lord while waiting for more audiences with King John and his ministers. David continued to speak, and the congregations grew larger and more zealous. David was well along the way of convincing himself that the improving the lot of the Conversos was due to his own efforts.

He watched a rabbi with a wide smile rub his hands together. Any concern that the rabbis would be jealous of David taking gifts had melted away. Giving to the synagogue increased greatly when David and Diogo taught.

He worried that it was too easy; the little man's suspicions and fears remained guarded. He drank too much wine. Some nights he hid in his closet to ease his tension. His dreams were tormented. On many days, he suffered from an unmerciful, stabbing pain in his back.

"The Lord God said, 'In those days, the people of Judah and Israel will unite and have one leader.' They will return from exile together. What a day that will be!" Again, a vessel returned, filled to the brim with contributions; the congregation offered praises in Portuguese "Come, Emmanuel!" "Next year, in Jerusalem!"

That evening, Diogo asked David, "Do you realize how many of these Conversos believe that you are the Messiah? And do you realize that these rabbis have got Marranos renouncing Christ and converting back to Judaism? Not just a few, David. Many are converting."

David did not answer. He was almost finished with a bottle of wine and could barely hold his head up. David took a deep breath and the room began to spin. He stumbled onto a bed and passed out. His dog curled up for a nap at his feet.

Diogo was happy to see him drift away. He wanted to read. Was someone watching them? Diogo felt a chill. He built a fire.

Once the fire was burning well, he turned to face the room. He startled backward, almost tripping into the fireplace. He was standing nose to nose with Selaya.

"Selaya, Eminence. Welcome." The wheyfaced Inquisitor disturbed him. He should not be able to enter so silently.

Selaya surveyed the room. His lip curled into a snarl. "Hardly fitting rooms for a prince."

"Would you like a chair?"

Selaya strolled around the room as if in slow motion, implying that nothing missed the eye of the Inquisitor. Diogo's question went unanswered. The dog bared his teeth and growled.

"I ordered that beast destroyed."

Selaya lit a candle in the fireplace, snatched a book from the mantle, and then pulled up a chair by the fire. "Commentaries?" He drummed his fingers in an ominous rat-tat-tat on the cover.

"No. Plays. It belongs to me."

Slowly, carefully, Selaya tore a leaf from Diogo's book. He dropped it in the fire. A sick smile smeared his face as the page burst into flame. He repeated the exercise again and eftsoons; a chill crawled up Diogo's spine with each page. He was powerless to object. Half the volume was gone.

"The little man hears us?" he asked.

"Not a word, Eminence."

"How humiliating. A Christian in service to a Jew."

"He is Hebrew, a great man."

"The king is blind. He doesn't see this man for what he is."

"I see what you are saying. Perhaps there's employment for me in your service."

Selaya shrugged. "They say rabbis hold ceremonies to mock communion wafers."

"I've not seen this blasphemy."

"Pity you're not more alert. No. There is no place for you in my service. God forbid a prohibited book turn up here." Selaya rose to his feet, ponderously, then departed the apartment without a word.

Diogo followed Selaya into the night, and as he turned the latch to leave, David rolled over and sat up. "Diogo?" But no one was with him. Selaya's sweet perfume hung in the air.

David pulled a chair near to the fire. Diogo was gone. Had he joined Selaya? He was now overcome with sobriety.

At the synagogue, David noticed gentiles, strangers, lurking in the shadows. And on another holiday drive with their mistresses, a dark carriage followed. Diogo and the others were unaware.

"Diogo," David asked, "how long have we tarried here in Portugal?"

"Coming up on a year."

*I should be gone already. I don't need these Conversos...* "A year. It is difficult to believe." David's thoughts returned to the beautiful Bilhah and Rome.

At the synagogue the following evening, in front of a large congregation, as David spoke his words to Diogo, he suddenly shrieked and fell prostrate to the ground, seemingly dumbstruck in pain. Diogo threw himself down to his knees at David's side and then put his ear to David's lips. David whispered to Diogo.

"Prince David is having a revelation!" Diogo shouted. He propped David up and then David murmured into his ear again. David snapped rigid, rolled his eyes back in his head, and sunk back to the floor. The congregation was in tumult, shouting, crying.

"Prince David says, 'Signal many nations to mobilize for war on the Turks!'"

The congregation noisily swarmed to the front of the synagogue. The lifeless David lay still on the floor.

"He's dead!" a lady cried.

David stirred. Diogo put his ear to David's lips. David whispered, his voice with an intensity that let Diogo know his master was fit. David was off script, he would have to improvise. He listened.

"I can't tell them that."

"Tell them what I told you."

"Prince David has had a vision! The Lord God calls Prince David to return to Rome!"

From a balcony on a stone tower overlooking the river, King John of Portugal stared out at a little ship sailing away from Lisbon. Jewish flags and banners flew from her masts.

"We think that Lisbon will be a less interesting place now that David Reuveni is gone, Selaya," said King John.

The Grand Inquisitor smiled and nodded. "Hmmm."

"Do you have anything new to report to us? What is this we overhear? What of this talk of Jewish conversions?"

"I have reports that two thousand or so Christians converted to Judaism during Reuveni's visit. Jews have come out of hiding. They and their converts have become increasingly zealous."

"Names? You have names?"

"Of course, Majesty."

"Restrain your Inquisitors no longer. We would have the Inquisition recommence. Cleanse the heretics from Portugal. The crown is not tolerant—the crown will no longer countenance these heresies. Our kindness was not rewarded by a suspension of the sanctions. So double the efforts of your Inquisitors. See to it that a few of these heretics are burned at the stake." John's black eyes burned a hole through his Grand Inquisitor. "Our intentions are clear on this?"

"Certainly, Majesty. How can God's kingdom be built on lies? Many Marranos also came out of hiding during Reuveni's stay."

King John returned his eyes to the little ship. "Let us also not neglect the Marranos, Selaya. The crown is generous. Repaid with contempt from the Marranos—Our benevolent forbearance—Perdition! We should have—Selaya, it is time for us to—We have also reconsidered this spurious policy of leniency toward the Marranos."

"Understood, Majesty."

"You have my leave."

The Grand Inquisitor smiled, bowed, and left the king's side.

John the Pious watched the little ship ride the ebbing tide, down-river to the sea, until it disappeared over the horizon.

# CHAPTER 20

The Turks thirsted to recover the Christian lands they once controlled on the shores of the Mediterranean Sea. Little was left in Europe that marked the conquest of the second caliphate in medieval times. A few structures in stood in España, and vestiges of Arabic grammar decorated the *língua portuguesa* and *español*. In many cities, the yellow star, a fashion born in Babylon, sullied its wearer as *negis*, the loathsome Jew. Only fifty years before, a Christian Romanian strongman, Vlad, had crossed the Danube to portion out death and destruction on Turks who held the provinces between Serbia and the Black Sea. Disguised as a Turkman, he infiltrated and destroyed Ottoman camps. He relished the act of impaling his enemies on poles.

In 1521, Suleiman the Magnificent sent forth his Ottoman army from Istanbul headed toward Hungary. His objective was to recover lands Islam lost to the Christians and establish a caliphate.

Although alerted to Suleiman's advance, the Hungarian nobles ignored their king's levy and call to colors. They convened a council of war, and by consensus, the military intelligencia of Hungary agreed that the capital city was secure. So Budapest was left unguarded.

Louis, the king of the Magyar Hungarians and Bohemia, led the main body of the army. His headquarters encamped near Budapest, but he positioned a full division to guard the passes in the Transylvanian Alps. Only a small force of Croatians supported Louis. The Ottoman army disguised their objective until it crossed the Balkan Mountains. They emerged at a location that put them closer to Budapest than either the Transylvanian army or the Croatians.

Louis beat a hasty retreat to Budapest. His army of thirty thousand was well-rested and a sufficient number to easily defend the capital from the Turks. They formed their divisions on an uneven plain spotted with swampy marshes, near the Danube River, at a place called Mohacs. In a strenuous march under a scorching sun, the Ottomans advanced fifty thousand men and 160 cannon without opposition. As the worn-out Turks arrived at the marshy fields of Mohacs, a vocal minority of generals encouraged Louis to mount an offensive. But chivalry demanded that Louis withhold his attack. His enemy was unprepared.

The Hungarian center guard was a mercenary infantry and artillery. Cavalry protected the flanks. The Hungarians routed Suleiman's first assault, and as a steady rain began to fall, they pressed forward. Several arrows launched from Hungarian bows penetrated Suleiman's cuirass, a piece of armor that covered his torso, front and back, from neck to waist. Seeing their king still mounted, shafts of flight arrows sprouting from his armor, the Ottomans rallied. Soon, reserves arrived, and the tide of battle turned.

The Hungarians took heavy casualties from the artillery and muskets of the Turks. Those who did not run died. King Louis fled the battlefield under cover of darkness. Thrown from his horse into a bog, and weighed down by his heavy armor and coat of mail, he drowned.

The battle lost at Mohacs ended Hungary's existence as a strong and independent country. Every son of a widow in Christendom believed the Ottoman Empire would become the greatest power in Europe. They imagined mosques erected in every capital city and prayers to Allah rising from minarets in every town square. French and Venetian ambassadors greeted Suleiman in Budapest to congratulate him on his great victory.

Suleiman pillaged the castle in Budapest but retreated to regroup soon afterward. He expected an attack from a Hungarian division stationed near the Alps. It never came.

The next summer, Suleiman regained Budapest and laid siege to Vienna. This, his most ambitious expedition, was doomed. The Austrians handed Suleiman his first defeat.

Suleiman turned his eye on Malta. He had unfinished business with its occupants, the Knights Hospitaller, formerly known as the Knights of Rhodes, a remnant of the Knights Templar, Islam's most ancient and bitter enemy.

Bourbon's staff surrounded him in his hilltop tent. The camps below were deserted. His aide de camp, a Spaniard, had been tasked with the duty of telling him the news. "The Spaniards break camp as we speak. The Germans are swarming to Rome."

Bourbon slammed his fist on the map table. "Out-gamed by the deceit of Francis and Charles," he said. Stripped of his dignity, his resolve was broken. "Let them go. Let them all go. Onward to Rome with the mutinous bastards."

The Spaniard choked back tears. "Excellency. It's the city of the Holy Church."

"The Pope has an alliance with England. Let King Henry defend Rome."

"Henry will never defend."

"Henry and England will defend. I'll wager my life on it."

"May God forgive us," the Spaniard said, crossing himself.

A vexed Bourbon turned away. *God has cheated me. I have reaped only shame from his service,* he told himself. *I will be damned to hell before I pray for forgiveness from him.*

Sap was rising in the trees, and powerful monarchs always seemed to get hot-blooded in the spring. Emperor Charles sent emissaries to Rome to press for an audience. He still wanted the Pope to crown him. Clement took many solemn walks.

"A papal coronation will give our king the added moral authority to quell the revolt of peasants in the German states," the emissaries argued. "It seems such a small thing."

But little things meant a lot. Clement took more private walks. *Perhaps if the citizens of Rome were more conscious of the empire's gluttonous appetite for conquest*, Clement thought.

A few literary men had written books that encouraged the Italian people to throw off the yoke of the Church, but the concept of freedom had little currency in Rome. Cynically, they believed that some strongman would eventually gain control, and he would probably spill a lot of Italian blood in the process. Freedom would be fleeting at best, even so, the Romans were growing distrustful of the Church.

Clement had two masters to serve, Church and family. The Church stood to lose if the empire became all-powerful.

And it was clear that no benefit would settle on Banco Medici if the empire enhanced its power. The Duke of Ferrara had defaulted on loans and the bank wanted to seize his estates that secured loans to the Duke of Ferrara. The emperor was standing in opposition.

Pope Clement stirred to action. If Charles wanted anything from the Church, then he had better prepare to pay, and to pay dearly. *What is good for famiglia de' Medici is good for the Church*, Clement reasoned.

So, secretly, agents for the Pope approached the Republic of Venice, the king of France, and the king of England. Clement's purpose was to form a holy league allied against the Empire. Henry, king of England, was designated its preserver and protector, and the Pope reduced the agreement to writing and sealed the pact with the issuance of a papal bull.

Rome was no place to keep secrets. Upon learning of the league, the exasperated ambassador that represented Charles took leave of Rome. His destination was Seville, in Spain, fifteen hundred miles to the west, where he would deliver his report to his monarch in person. He was chary of reducing his correspondence to writing and distrustful of other diplomats.

The ambassador made a pageant of his exodus. He mounted a great steed and departed Vatican City, led by his court-fool and followed by an entourage of twenty diplomats. The jester stood in his saddle and, urged on by the ambassador, bared the cheeks of his buttocks to the mobs of Romish citizens in the square. An angry crowd threatened to accost him for his vulgar affront, so he pissed in their direction, and gesturing with his genitals, he insinuated that he had carnal knowledge of the angry Roman mob. He displayed his contempt with a thousand more obscene monkey tricks on the way to the docks.

Word of his misdeeds dispersed quickly, and the insults managed to sway the opinion of the Roman citizenry far better than any proclamation the Pope could have issued. To a man, the subjects of the Eternal City saw with their own eyes how little the emperor cared for the Pope.

The ink was not dry on the treaty for the holy league when Clement next issued a brief that threatened the emperor with excommunication for the disrespect shown by his ambassador's fool. News traveled slowly. Before word of the papal bull, the ambassador, and brief for excommunication could reach Seville, the districts of Milan, Florence, and the Piedmont had declared their support for the Church and the holy league of Venice, France, and England. The Pope's generals mustered his army and pushed into Lombardy.

When his agents in Seville read him the Pope's threat of excommunication, the news shook Charles. It would be difficult to stay on as Christ's vicar if he were thrown out of the Church. He had barely recovered from the Pope's warning when military intelligence of the Church's victories in Lombardy barraged his court.

He responded by having his agents write a private letter to his brother. He instructed Ferdinand to lift the most severe of the sanctions on the rebellious peasants in the German states, sanctions that Ferdinand had been too spineless to impose. He no longer wanted to punish the peasants. Now he hoped to make common faith with those who were in protest, those Lutherans that the clerics were beginning to refer to as "Protestants." Charles also directed his brother to postpone the edict that had convicted and excommunicated Martin Luther.

Publicly, Charles charged the German ministers to join him, in a war either against the Turks or against Italy. "For the common good of Christendom," Charles told them. His plea was insincere, of course. He might as well have plead with them "for the good of Charles." But Charles thought he could end the revolt of the German peasants if he could convince the protestants that they had a common enemy. The identity of the enemy was of little consequence to the emperor.

His marching orders were in hand, but Ferdinand hesitated. He had kept the emperor's plans to punish the peasants a secret until now, and so he stood to gain nothing at all by announcing relaxation of secret sanctions. He was in over his youthful head.

In Ferdinand's most difficult hour, divine providence intervened on his behalf. It opened the door for him to graduate from brief-barer status, he would become a great man. News arrived of his brother-in-law's demise, drowned in a bog while fleeing Suleiman.

Succession would spawn a legal fight. Many nobles had flimsy claims on the twin crowns of Hungary and Bohemia, but no claim was better than Ferdinand's. He would show up in person to gather support for his right to Budapest and Prague and their empty thrones. Ferdinand, the Grand Master of the Order of the Golden Fleece, set forth from the Germanies like a bat out of Hades. It was God's will for him to muster an army and secure the thrones of Hungary and Bohemia for the rightful heir, the heir chosen by God, who by happy coincidence was himself. If Charles wanted a showdown with Luther, he could do the dirty work himself.

So in the next dispatch from Seville, the emperor addressed the Diet himself. His first draft told the assembly of nobles to raise an army that would defeat Luther and march on Italy. But even an emperor must cloak his intentions, disguise his goals. "Luther and the German protesters" was cut and replaced with "Lombardy and the Pope."

He still was not satisfied. "Announce to the army to prepare to march against the Turks," the emperor decreed. "Everyone will know which Turks are meant." And it was done. In those days, the emperor's word was law.

Who would the followers of Luther side with? On one side was the holy league: the Church, France, England, and Venice. On the other was their emperor, Charles. Charles was now an enemy of the Church. Was the emperor aligned with Luther? Was Charles, once so passionate to kill Luther, now his champion?

It was enough to know that Charles was the emperor who stood against the Church. Charles was a reformer. That's not what Charles intended, but no one in Germany would believe otherwise.

Erelong the armies of the Pope marched into Lombardy on the high roads. According to the intelligence reports of their spies, they could anticipate a showdown with the armies of the Empire at Milan. The battle never materialized. Their scouts never reckoned that the starving, ragged peasants, landsknechts, and Spanish regulars, traveling south on the low roads, were an angry, mutinous legion. They spilled out of Lombardy as if a colossal, unnoticed flood and poured forth into the top of Italy's boot. The Pope's army simply marched past them on their advance to Milan.

# CHAPTER 21

The hasty departure from Lisbon denied David an opportunity to send a message ahead to his friends in Rome. But a crowd of curious Jews formed to investigate a little caravel, flying Jewish flags, pennants, and Benvenida's banner as it made its way upstream toward the docks on the Tiber. Realizing David's identity, the Jewish people mobbed him as he stepped from the gangplank and onto the stone-covered landing. The air filled with hosannas, cries of praise, greetings, laughter, and hand clapping.

The crowd grew in enthusiasm and soon lofted David on shoulders as they would a Caesar returning from conquest. The rejoicing surged as news of David's arrival scattered and additional Jews joined the throng at the landing. Prince Reuveni. The man who had crushed the Portuguese Inquisition under his heel, the Redeemer, come to ransom the Jews. The Messiah.

Finally, David squirmed to ground level and shouted to Diogo, "See to our parcels and follow when you can." The multitude swept David away in the direction of Sant'Angelo.

Diogo shook his head as he watched the mob carry David away. "I am going to enjoy my stay in Rome this time," he told the riverboat captain.

David rented commodious rooms in Sant'Angelo, the rione that quartered the largest part of Rome's Jewish citizens. He and Diogo took up residence in an apartment that was up a flight of stairs. It looked over a courtyard. David's room was large and airy. Two different pairs of floor-to-ceiling doors opened inward to the room and onto small balconies over the street. Fit for an aristocrat.

David delighted in the cushy bed, which eased, for a time at least, severe back pains that confined him to his berth on his sea voyage. Diogo's room was smaller, but his bed offered comfort.

"Better than sleeping in a hallway," said Diogo, remembering his lodging in the days of his acting career.

The rooms offered no facilities for the preparation of meals, but food was offered by street vendors at most hours of the day, and also from inns. Invitations stood open for David to dine at the best tables of Sant'Angelo.

While David was in Lisbon, Samuel Abravanel had returned to Florence with his household. David began to search for Bilhah.

David now solicited an opportunity to speak in the Roman synagogue, to tell the story that so reliably shelled coins from purses. Language would not be a barrier and he was eager to test his own presentation techniques after his schooling by the masterful Diogo in Portugal.

At a gathering in the synagogue, David told the Jews, "Then the people of Israel and Judah shall join together, saying, 'Come, let us be united to the Lord.' The Lord God says: 'I am raising up an army of great nations from the north, and I will bring them against the Turks, and they shall be utterly destroyed. In those days, no sin shall be found in Israel or in Judah, for I will pardon the remnant I preserve.'"

Diogo circulated in the excited crowd, holding out a vessel for offerings and gratuities, reciting his lines. "For the cause of the Lord, the Crusade, for the Anointed One, Ransom Israel, Emmanuel."

But he quickly grew bored, and soon he was droning his lines with indifference.

Afterward, David asked Diogo, "Well, how did I do?"

"The Romans are just as generous as the Portuguese."

"Great. Wonderful. But the presentation. How well did I do?"

"It was all right, I suppose. I do not know. Really, I was almost asleep."

David clenched his jaw so tightly that he thought he might break a tooth. "I won't tolerate any disrespect from you, Marrano."

Diogo shrugged.

David found that Bilhah now had private rooms in Sant'Angelo. Abravanel's home had been in a neighboring rione. He visited her often and offered to help her find employment. Together they enjoyed dining at inns, followed by cozy and romantic evenings in her rooms.

Bilhah supported herself on a pension that Benvenida had provided for her. She was the first to tell him, "We don't think so highly of that disciple of yours. He and his kind."

"Diogo? He is wonderful. What do you mean, his kind?"

"They could have fled. Like my grandparents. Like all the others. They didn't have to convert," she replied. "People like that are beneath contempt. He is one of them. The renegades. The tornadizos."

"You should reserve judgment," David said. *Poor Marrano, despised by the Portuguese and hated by the Jews.*

David's confidence in his abilities grew. He boldly tested a "gathering" theme at the synagogue, teaching, "The Lord God says, 'Don't be afraid, for I am with you. I will gather you from east and west, from north and south. I will bring my sons and daughters back to Israel from the farthest corners of the earth. All who claim me as their God will come, for I have made them for my glory.'"

Again, Diogo foraged in the crowd, passing a vessel for offerings, without passion, almost yawning with each repetition, repeating as if it were a mantra: "For the cause of the Lord, the Crusade, for the Anointed One, Ransom Israel, Emmanuel."

On a sunny afternoon, David and Bilhah shared a carriage ride through the ruins of Rome, poking their noses in abandoned grottos, accompanied by Diogo and his lady of the day. David loved to entertain the others with little showman tricks.

While Diogo and the girls lounged on the ground, David juggled apricots. Both ladies thrilled in his antics, and they also seemed to delight in Diogo, his good looks and charm. Rolling across the grass, Diogo gripped Bilhah's ankle and pulled her to his side on the ground.

Bilhah seemed to forget the "tornizado" slur and even lost interest in the juggling for the moment.

The little man was quick to fume in anger. He performed a forward roll and then stood on his head. The girls laughed and clapped.

Diogo sneered.

David jumped forward and walked on his hands. Diogo, not to be outdone, snatched one of David's shoes and organized a game of keep-away. "Don't let him have it," Diogo told them.

He tossed the shoe to Bilhah, and when the little man came after her to snatch it away, she tossed the shoe to Diogo's lady. David did not have a chance. The shoe flew over his head from Diogo to the girls and back, and as it did, the girls laughed at David's futile efforts to retrieve it.

"Give it to me. Give it back, I said! Give it to me."

As David grew too weary to chase the shoe, Diogo simply held the shoe at his shoulder level. David jumped repeatedly to retrieve it, and with each jump, Diogo snatched it away above the little man's reach. The girls exploded in mirth. David's anger grew each time Diogo pulled the shoe away.

"I'm not going to ask again," David said. "I won't be a fool."

Diogo persisted in ignoring the request of his master.

"Give it to me," David demanded, and this time, when Diogo failed to do his bidding, the master rolled his hand into a ball. Adopting a strong stance, he set his feet shoulder-width apart, left foot leading, and pivoting off the ball of his right foot as if he were grinding a cockroach into the soil, he aimed his fist at a pair of targets that hung just inside Diogo's codpiece. Propelling his clenched hand forward with the pivot, he delivered a straight right punch into the unguarded groin of his disciple. The clash of fist to codpiece resounded in the arcades of broken marble and echoed in the grottoes as if it were a clap of thunder.

Diogo buckled and fell to the ground. All the air exhausted from his lungs. Clutching his crotch, he flopped on the ground as if in an epileptic seizure. The shoe had also fallen from the heavens and was lying at his side. David sat himself down beside the agonized manservant and fitted the prize shoe back onto his foot. Bilhah and Diogo's mistress chirruped, unaware of anything they could do to assist the fallen manservant.

Diogo worked to regain his feet. His larynx opened at last with a creaking that sounded like the rusted hinges of a sarcophagus. "David..."

"Does that make you feel tall? To make me look small?" David stood and put out his hand to Diogo's hip and pushed. The powerless Diogo fell sideways on the ground as if he were a fallen statue, and writhing in pain on the grass, he gulped for air like a landed carp.

Diogo's suffering at the hand of his master lingered several days. "My cods are the size of oranges," Diogo said, lying on his side in his apartment.

"My chastisement catches your attention." David's face distorted in an ugly grin as he imagined the throes of pain surging up from Diogo's sphincter and the nausea that was consuming his disciple's gut. "I suppose you are angry at the severity."

"I will even the score."

"I saw this same torture on your face at the synagogue," the master said, opening a bottle of wine. "I don't know what's come over you in Rome. As soon as you leave your bed, you begin to look for excuses to spend time away from the Jews. At the meetings in the synagogue, you make faces. You look as if you're being tortured."

"Rome is worse than torture. 'Tornadizo,' they call me. I am the most famous villain in Rome. This role of disciple has me shackled. It's worse than a part in the chorus."

"Every role has its own obligations."

"In Portugal, I spoke the words. It was I. I spelled out God's will. I fetched up their rapture."

David took a long guzzle of wine from the bottle. "You forget my role."

"They put themselves in my hands. I could have stopped their breath if I wanted."

"I am master. You are servant."

"If you think I'm your lackey, you are mistaken."

"I'm making a killing. Do you need lines written on paper? Just play your role."

"With every coin that drops into the vessel, I will recall your violation."

"It can't be that bad."

"You would have me sell tickets to charade. And nothing to show for it." Diogo wretched, and David handed him a chamber pot. "These things are going to change," Diogo said, and as he said it, he doubled over again with a wave of nausea.

A week later, David spoke to a gathering of Jews in the street. "The Lord God says, 'For your sakes I will send an invading army against the Turks, that will walk in unscathed. The boasts of the Turks will turn to cries of fear. I am the Lord, your Holy One, Israel's Creator and King, who opens a path right through the sea.'"

Working the crowd for offerings, David noticed that Diogo lightly touched the hand of an adolescent girl, the daughter of a merchant named da Pisa. *What is he up to now?*

But he continued, "The mighty army of Egypt, with all its chariots and horses, now lays beneath the waves, dead, their lives snuffed out like candlewicks. But that is nothing compared to what I am going to do."

Diogo touched her wrist more lightly than a baby's breath. He pursed his lips at her, hinting at a kiss. After David finished speaking, the girl implored her father to invite the holy men to dinner. "Prince David," the father said, "I would consider it great honor if you would dine with us."

He had promised the evening to Bilhah, but David bowed to da Pisa and accepted his invitation.

At the da Pisa house, the family table was covered with food. David sat beside da Pisa's mother-in-law. Da Pisa's daughter and Diogo hid in an alcove, enjoying an embrace, watching.

"Prince David, you must tell me again. Where is your home?" the old lady asked.

"Arabia," David replied. *Why did I agree to do this?*

"What?" The old dear was as deaf as a stone.

"Arabia," David shouted. *Diogo brought this on me. He is like a wild horse. Uncontrollable.*

"And what is the country like?"

"Sandy." Nothing registered on the face of da Pisa's mother-in-law. "Sandy!" *Damn Christian. He can hurt me more than I can hurt him.*

"Tell me about your mother."

"She's dead!" *I am dead. How could I be so stupid? A Christian for a disciple? What was I thinking?*

"Are you married?"

David shook his head. *Diogo would never convert to Judaism.*

"How is your health? My poor husband, God rest his soul...It was so sudden."

"I'm sure it was. I'm sure it was!"

"Are you regular?"

"What?"

"Do you start your stream easily?"

David's brow stitched with anger.

Returning home, David summoned Diogo to his room. The little man's face flushed with wrath. "I've taken just about all I can take from you."

"It was retribution for your offense to my cods." A smirk crept across Diogo's face. "It was just fun to see your face bleached with fear."

David's anger raged. "The only fear I have is that you will give these chuckleheads a reason to look into my story."

"I am teasing you, David. I was curious to see how little it takes to get an invitation from da Pisa."

"My story is watertight. Foolproof. And my manservant is pulling pranks like a fool. These lunkheads will figure it out if you tell them. Have you thought about what these Jews would do if they discover the truth?" David asked. "Surely you don't still believe that this lying is a matter of no consequence."

"No, I suppose not, but I'm not losing sleep over it either. These shopkeepers and moneylenders would not hesitate to defraud a peasant right out of his stockings. Or another Jew. Or a Marrano."

David was losing sleep. "We are cheating them out of their money, you stupid tornadizo."

"Always with the name-calling. Listen, David, one butcher with his thumb on the scale could cheat far more than you and me. The Jews are rich. They will never miss the paltry sums you are getting. So, I'm not going to have a bout of conscience over you lying about *detrito* these Jews won't even miss."

With nothing better to do as David's disciple, Diogo reconsidered his role. This manservant character was going nowhere. So he improvised. He became a student. He took Hebrew lessons from the young rabbis. He was quick to learn to read and write the language, and soon he was able to practice by discussing scripture in the tongue of the patriarchs.

The rabbis introduced him to the Tanakh, the books of the Bible the Christians called the Old Testament, books his own Christian religious training had largely overlooked. And he read the Talmud, a religious legal codebook that controlled practically every daily activity of Jewish life.

Nothing soothed the apostle like an evening's seclusion with a bottle of wine. Sometimes he brooded. His success in Rome had thus far satisfied his desires. No one investigated his story. What more could he want? He had a warm bed, warm food, and wine, plenty of wine, and a plump and willing lady friend. His station was secure, owing to the generous amount of silver and gold he had tucked safely away in the Roman branch of Abravanel's bank. Beyond that, he had a measure of what anyone would account to a man as importance, and it was his greatness that helped him mask his lies.

Diogo threatened it all, everything; every ducat that he had struggled to obtain was at jeopardy. He shuddered, worrying over his financial losses if the Jews discovered his ruse. But he was a dead man if the Christians found him out.

*Diogo craves praise,* the little man thought. He dreamed up a hundred schemes for dealing with his manservant. *Every meeting is laden with the risk of detection. Diogo.* He detested the thoughts that kept tumbling over in his mind. *His little jest with da Pisa's daughter. That is just the sort of erratic behavior that could easily lay bare the enterprise. The time is overdue for reigning in this wild horse. Once and for all.*

*But how? I cannot coerce him. I cannot dismiss him. He can hurt me more than I can hurt him. His damnable Christianity is the problem. He just does not respect the Jews. If I had only hired a Jew as disciple. If only Diogo was a Jew. If Diogo would only convert to Judaism. Convert? But no, he would never do that.*

David lifted the bottle only high enough for the liquid to trickle into his mouth. He rolled a swallow of wine around his mouth.

*Convert. He might convert if he thought it would get him back on the stage. His clowning around will surely diminish after he figures out he has the threat of the Inquisition over his head. Like me.*

David finished the bottle of wine. Could he convince Diogo to convert to Judaism? *I have convinced people of far more outrageous ideas than that.*

After teaching at the synagogue, David and Diogo returned to David's room to count the day's take.

"Nice take," David said. "Very satisfactory. Yes."

Diogo was unresponsive. David continued after a moment. "I had a lovely talk today with Rabbi Daniel."

Again, Diogo was silent.

"He expresses great lamentation for your Christian faith. He's mentioned it repeatedly," said David.

"David, Rabbi Daniel has a very plain daughter."

"Laugh, Harlequin. I wanted only to point out..."

"Spit it out."

"I'm saying that the gratuities might be somewhat larger..."

Diogo's countenance darkened. "Larger? What do I care? I earn the same whether or not the gifts are generous. What does that benefit me?"

"Diogo, I know these people. I only had reference to..."

"Just say what you are saying. Christ."

"I'm saying that you should consider"—and his voice dropped to a whisper that seemed to shout—"converting."

"Converting?!" Diogo exploded. "Have you thought about what

you just said? I thought you were a big expert on heresy. I would be a heretic if I converted to Judaism."

Diogo understood more than the master had anticipated, but David's voice remained calm. "Who would know? You could change your name. What you need to think about is your dramatic skills. They are going to waste. You know it, and I know it. I am suggesting that there might be a couple of ducats in it for you—"

"A couple of ducats. Ha. I wouldn't risk my life for a few—I mean, I would be risking my life for—What do you mean, wasting my dramatic skills?" Diogo stopped talking and started thinking.

"There's a statue in the piazza that can act better than you."

Diogo believed David. His skills were stiff, rusty. His job was the best he had ever had. "I guess that when you say 'a couple of ducats' that 'a couple of ducats' just serves as an illustration—you're talking about a sum that is a little more weighty, I suppose, than a couple of ducats?"

"Something more could be worked out," David said. After a long silence, David continued, "The circumcision isn't really all that bad."

# CHAPTER 22

In the following week, Diogo attended to his duties with care and spent his free time in quiet contemplation. He and David shared little.

David spoke often at the synagogue. He added to his balances at Abravanel's bank every week, but not as fast as he wanted. He was also giving large sums to Bilhah to purchase an inn. She wanted to open a brothel, but the law forbade landlords from renting rooms for prostitution. And she was hinting about taking a journey to Sicily. He hoped to raise the Jews to yet another orgy of ecstasy.

David was in his best form. "The Rock of Israel said to me, 'One shall come who shall be just, one who rules in the fear of God. And he shall be as the light of the morning, as a cloudless sunrise, as the tender grass springing out of the earth, as sunshine after the rain.'"

As Diogo took up the collection, he suddenly jolted as if struck by lightning. He shouted out, "Lord God Almighty. The rock of my salvation." His body slumped to the floor, and he dropped the offering vessel. Coins spilled everywhere. He trembled as if he were having a fit, totally out of control. He slobbered and mumbled.

The congregation let out a collective gasp. A rabbi scurried, and elbowing David aside, he arrived first at Diogo's side. David wobbled, then stumbled to the floor.

The rabbi fell to his knees and put his ear to Diogo's lips and listened. "Diogo has a vision of the Lord God."

A rich man collapsed to the floor, his hands gripped his belly. "My bowels," he shouted. "My bowels spoke the name of God."

A young woman, heavy with child, screamed out, "My child shrieks in my womb." Lying back on her bench, she cried out again, "'Messiah,' the child says. 'Messiah.'"

Again, the rabbi listened, his ear at Diogo's lips. "Quiet, please." His intensity grew, then: "Diogo wants to convert to Judaism."

The congregation cheered, grabbed one another's hands, and jumping up and down, danced in a circle, singing songs of Zion in this foreign land, and shouting praises to the Lord.

David sat on the floor with his head in his hands. Watching the spectacle of Diogo play out in front of him, he remembered himself abandoned on the muddy road, hidden in the dark forest, powerless, with nothing in his hand but his pizzle.

"David, oh, Prince David," a rabbi told David later, "Diogo's conversion pleases me so. I have always wanted to see someone convert."

*His conversion is supposed to put me in control, not him,* David thought. *This is not the way I would have played it, but he's put his neck in my snare now. My plans will not be waylaid.*

Without telling David first, Diogo cleaved his foreskin *a cappella*, unaccompanied by a moyel. As soon as he finished the deed, he lost consciousness. When a charwoman discovered his lifeless body, a shout of alarm went out. A physician rushed to his side to attend his recovery.

David and several rabbis looked in on the young disciple. The sour stench of perspiration and gore hung in the room. Diogo was lying on a bed. He looked like a sacrificial lamb on an altar, naked except for a sheet that covered him across the waist and groin. Blood splattered his bedding. Sweat poured from his forehead. He looked as if he were sweating blood, and his arms stretched wide. He stared at the ceiling, glassy-eyed.

"Is everything all right, Diogo?" David wished Diogo was dead. "I prophesized that your blood would go unspilled, do you remember?"

Diogo's voice quivered weakly. "I remember. I have envisioned Jerusalem. Jerusalem, the prophets—and Torah."

David smiled gleefully. "My brother. My brother."

"Abraham. Isaac. Jacob. Moses. All in shining raiment." Diogo's voice began to regather strength.

"Your vision will be a great blessing to me and the flock, my brother. But rest. Be calm," David's voice insisted. "The pain will subside."

"The Temple. Mount Zion."

"Yes, brother," David demanded. Then to the physician, the little man suggested, "Perhaps Diogo's mouth should be bound closed to avoid injury."

"All is revealed to me."

David climbed up on Diogo's bed and sitting astride his chest, tried to hold him down. Diogo writhed and shouted as if to wake the angels in heaven, "My name is Solomon Molko!"

After Diogo's conversion, his behavior grew even more erratic. It seemed to David as if his servant had become a different person. His name change helped mask his heresy. He defied David's orders daily, daring him, even more than before. David decided to allow Molko's role to evolve into one of a disciple.

But he had to send regrets to a rabbi who offered a lucrative engagement on short notice. Molko had not shown up for work and David fumed. *Diogo can deny everything, if worst comes to worst. I will never be on an equal footing with this reckless monster, the one I created— unless. I must implicate Diogo, or Molko, or whatever he calls himself now, in the hoax alongside me.*

As dusk fell, a whistling Molko, now wearing a yellow *bareta*, turned into the passageway that lead to David's courtyard. The master accosted him as soon as he entered.

"Where were you today? I had to send Rabbi Moshe my regrets. I cannot preach without a disciple. What were you thinking, anyway? Where were you?"

"I was ministering to the lame and blind at the market. Listen, David. Listen to this. Three more souls converted today."

"Stupid tornadizos."

"Tomorrow we plan to visit the lazzarettos."

"Lazzarettos." David spat. "Stay away from lepers if you want to have anything to do with me. What are you thinking? And what about me? Have you forgotten me? I need a disciple to function. I am preaching my ass off with no disciple. Look, I cannot do business with this kind of distraction. This reflects poorly on me, really, really poorly. Have you thought about that?"

Molko smiled and gazed into a heavenly otherworld. "I had the Lord God's work to take care of." Molko drew a purse from his belt and spilled a few coins out on the bed.

David's eyes bulged at the sight of the money. He sprung to the side of the bed. "Perhaps I have been too hasty in my rebuke." Then, greedily: "How much do you have there?"

"Not so quick there, David. And when did my role become disciple?"

David drew back. He could be magnanimous. "Go ahead. Take your share," he said. "Take a couple of extra florins for yourself."

"A couple of florins? Only a couple?"

"Yes," David said. "I have been trying to think of a way to show my gratitude."

"Some gratitude, a piddling couple of florins?"

David stared at Molko. He smiled. "Well, I guess you caught me with my guard down. I have been meaning to talk to you about partnership. I have been—"

"So, now it's partnership?"

"Certainly. Not share and share alike, mind you. We can work out the details."

"So, the fitness of this partnership is in the details. I see," Molko said. "Well, then, let's get down to the details. Let's see what you have in your purse there, little man."

"Your odd behavior is beginning to put a strain on our partnership. A line must be drawn." David stopped, then adopted a stern expression. "Because of me, the Inquisition has so far taken little notice of your conversion, Diogo."

"Molko. It is Molko. Solomon Molko. Or had you not heard? If I remember right, it was you who mentioned conversion in the first place. It appears that your concerns are no longer my concerns." The disciple picked up a mirror from David's dressing table and examined himself closely.

"Well, that may be true. And looking back, the idea of your conversion may have been a little clumsy." David scratched his head. "So far, my little enterprise hasn't even raised an eyebrow with the Christians. To them, I was just cheating Jews. And you, you alone, you are the only Christian I have converted. Jews can't be heretics, just Christians. You are now officially a heretic." This was David's trump card. The room was deathly silent for a long moment.

"You converted one, I will convert them all." Molko beat his chest with a fist.

"Oh, don't get me wrong. I agree with you. Indeed, I think the Christians would be quite surprised by the number of your converts," David said. "I draw less notice because I am less theatrical, Diogo."

David walked in silence around the room, each footstep deliberate. He took the looking glass and walked away, but his eyes fixed on the image of Molko. "What do you think these extremists would do if they found out your mother was a prostitute?"

David's knowledge of the impurity of Molko's birth first startled and then angered his disciple. His teeth gritted into a snarl. His complexion burned red. "This conversation is over. There's no profit in talking with you." Molko snatched up the coins and his purse, and as he stormed from the room, he cried out, "You don't know what you are talking about."

David kicked himself. He should not have provoked the actor to that degree. Now Molko might do something crazy. *Nothing more will I risk to gain the upper hand over him. I need to be rid of him, once and for all, finally.*

*If I ever see that bastard again, I am calling the law,* David thought, feeling the bone handle of the dagger in his belt. *He is lucky he did not try something. I would have killed him.*

David rendered an anonymous complaint to the constabulary. And as he predicted, the Roman authorities took notice of Molko's conversion and his ministry.

The citizens of Rome heard daily rumors concerning the mutinous army of the emperor that was bearing down on Rome, yet David continued in his role as emissary from the tribe of Reuben, including lavishing his lady friend with the wealth of his station. One day the proprietor of a shop bearing the sign *"CELLINI, GOLDSMITH"* received the benefit of David's patronage. A crowd of onlookers gathered, some adoring, and some jealous, as the man assisted Bilhah's exit and David behind her. The artisan had the look of a streetfighter, a burly, rough-and-tough Italian tradesman, but the threshold was tall and his best customer was unsteady on her platform shoes.

A golden Star of David locket was cradled between Bilhah's ample breasts. It hung from a heavy gilded chain.

"A masterpiece. Maestro, I'll recommend you to the Pope," David told the goldsmith.

Bilhah feigned nonchalance as she pulled back her yellow scarf from her lovely décolletage. The worshipful Jews who were approaching David also saw her golden locket when they reached out to touch the hem of his garment. Her countenance beamed.

A week later, David received word that Molko wanted to meet him at sunset near the wharves on the Tiber. He found Molko hidden in an alcove. David approached slowly, each step measured. He imagined his own throat slit to the gullet. However, to his relief, Molko cowered behind a post. Shrinking low, to be lower than David.

"David, my old patron. My old benefactor, dear friend. Could you spare a few ducats for your servant, Solomon Molko?"

David's voice betrayed no emotion. "I hear a voice in my head. The voice is saying, 'David, your concerns are no longer my concerns.'"

"David, be serious. This is a sober matter, brother."

"Brother! Brother? Ha. Why not go convert a few Christians; then your purse will swell. Oh. And here is a good idea. If you want to be so famous, why not heal all the blind people, so they can watch the conversions too. Ha-ha. And do it out in the piazza, so plenty of Inquisitors can see. Right out in the open."

"David, the Inquisitors have been asking questions. I fear that the Lord God has sent the Angel of Death to destroy my life. Please, David, just a few ducats."

"You won't need money where you're going. People wearing shrouds don't need purses."

"I'll be out of your life forever. For the love of God, David, do something."

"I'll do something. I will buy your passage. To Palestine, on the first ship."

David dealt out a few paltry coins, and as Molko reached out, repeating "Palestine, yes," the master allowed the coins to spill through his stubby fingers and onto the roadway below.

Molko dove to his knees to gather in the coins. Groveling in the dust, the beggar neither saw nor guessed that his patron had concealed a heavy cudgel under his cape, so he did not anticipate the blow that arose and came squarely to rest on the back of his head.

"May your roadway widen, you bastard. You won't stand between me and the fire again," David said. He kicked aside the unconscious man at his feet so that he could pick up the spilled coins.

# CHAPTER 23

David's preoccupation with protecting himself from the Molko scandal now matched his compulsion to seek refuge. Twice daily, he hazarded a departure from the haven of his rooms to take nourishment at an inn. He listened to the daily gossip of Bourbon's army in the North. The inn's patrons were hopeful that the Pope's army would turn them away.

Every chatterer at the long table considered himself to be the world's foremost expert. "Luther doesn't have a purgatory to make him rich." "Without money, Luther will never amount to a pile of cow dung." "They are beyond the point of mutiny." "Bourbon's insolvency is well known. He cannot restrain the army any longer. They raid the countryside at will."

*They know nothing, these idiots*, David told himself. He stood in front of the inn's hearth as if he were in the bimah of the synagogue. "But the Lord God is still in his holy temple," he said. "He still rules from heaven. He closely watches everything that happens here on earth. He puts the righteous and the wicked to the test. He hates those loving violence. He will rain down fire and brimstone on the wicked and scorch them with his burning wind." It was as if David were whistling past a graveyard.

*Perhaps I should journey to Venice,* he thought. He dropped the idea as if it were a burning ember. *Portugal? Out of the question.* No, it was easiest for a little man to disappear in the hurly-burly of Rome. The Eternal City was always in a tumult, always in some commotion.

The ragtag, mutinous army of the emperor army was indeed making its way to Rome. The ranks filled with new recruits, more peasants from the German states, supporters of Luther. Like the mercenaries, the peasants were hungry, poorly clothed, and ill-shod. Their hearts seethed with wrath, but their bodies and brains were untrained. The fury that led the landsknechts to march was for lack of payment for services rendered. The Lutherans motives were purer. Their anger and resentment was born in their sure and certain knowledge that the Church, through false doctrines, had purloined every ounce of treasure from them, their ancestors, their sons and daughters, and their countrymen and homeland. If the Church had its way, the peasants would be back in the press. The Lutherans would have none of it. Whole villages of peasants found their way into the ranks of the advancing landsknechts, armed with nothing but hand tools, shovels, rakes, and scythes.

The Austrian-born Charles declined to halt their advance.

Like the mercenaries, the Spaniards were starving and unpaid. But the insult contained in the plenary indulgence issued by the Pope drove their impulses. Moors. Indeed. Until the Pope crowned their king as emperor and thus paid the price for calling them such a cruel and offensive epithet, anger would grip the Spaniards. Moors! Both the trained infantrymen and the peasant rabble were rabid, and now, having slipped in behind the Pope's armies, they took the high roads southward. As had been the case fifteen hundred years before, all roads led the mutineers to Rome. Bourbon, his brigadiers and lieutenants could only follow.

Clement, convinced that the armies of France and England would rush to defend the Holy See, refused to listen to his generals when they warned him of the threat, even as the shouts of the mutinous armies echoed out of the north from beyond the Alps, even as Luther's words resonated their prayers, spurring them onwards. "The emperor's forces are triumphing in Italy. The Pope is visited from every quarter. His destruction draweth near. His hour and his end are come."

Near Florence, when the foot-sore mob was still a week's march away from Rome, Bourbon intervened to discuss terms of a truce with the generals of the Pope's legion army. The Pope's generals had belatedly come to their senses, turned, and were approaching the ragtag army from the west. Word of a possible agreement circulated throughout Bourbon's armies and an even more frightful tumult broke out. A division of Spanish regulars stormed and pillaged the general's tent. Bourbon and his lieutenants fled like frightened deer. The Imperial Spanish army rallied the landsknechts and peasants, egging them onward with shouts. They cried out the only German words they knew: "*Lanz! Lanz! Gelt! Gelt!*" "Lance! Lance! Gold! Gold!" Perfect nonsense. Pure insanity. The shouts had the desired effect. To the last man, the Spanish and Germans demanded that blood be spilled. They demanded a war. They demanded their pay.

In the road before them stood one man, one of the German leaders, Fruendesburg, the captain of the mercenaries, grizzled with age, his body covered with the scars of battles too numerous to count. Fruendesburg challenged the mob's defiance of the truce and demanded that they drop their weapons. Before he could draw his broadsword, his pikemen presented lances at his throat. The old warrior staggered back. His body trembled as if struck by St. Vitus dance. He fell senseless on a drum, paralyzed. A terrified lieutenant put his frightened ear to Fruendesburg's lips. No one could hear the old man's words, but the lieutenant lied, telling the mutineers that Fruendesburg had gasped, "Forward, God himself will bring us to our mark."

Hearing that, the landsknechts shouted as one. "Forward!" And leaving Fruendesburg on the road, surrounded by his aides, the armies resumed their advance on Rome. The old man was unable to go further. Soon his life spirit began its journey to some mythic place, seeking to restore his soul to a state of grace.

Bourbon continued to follow behind the mutineers. As they swarmed farther south, a great mob of Italian peasants and freemen streamed north, toward Rome, out of Naples. News had reached Naples and this second mob hoped to join the assault. They hated the Pope as much as the Germans. And like the German peasants, they were armed with nothing but farming tools.

On the eastern shore of the Tiber River, inside the walls of Rome, several thousand men, all capable of bearing arms, paraded their bravery in the streets. They dragged their long swords behind them and prowled the avenues, eager for any fight with another Roman that would promise gain. Frequent quarrels and brawls broke out among them. They had little thought of defending Rome and no interest whatsoever in shielding the Pope. Their fondest hope was for Charles to take Rome and remake it as his capital city.

On the morning of May 5, the roads leading Bourbon's mutinous armies to Rome converged at the Tiber River and veered south, following the west bank of the stream to the north side of Rome. Beyond a westward bend in the river, a bridge, the Ponte Milvio, invited the armies to cross to the eastern bank of the river and the main body of the city. At this same bridge, twelve hundred years earlier, a vision came to Constantine of the cross in the sky that told him "conquer with this sign." Bourbon urged the armies to avoid the bridge and continue southward along the west bank of the Tiber.

Erelong, Bourbon's host gathered under the walls that surrounded the rione of Borgo that bordered Vatican hill. The skeleton of the unfinished Basilica of St. Peter outlined the afternoon sky. Bourbon led his troops, following the walls, in a westward loop through the outlying fields and vineyards that were beyond the wall around the Vatican hill. The army followed, under the wall, beyond the place where it turned back east, reconnoitering the walls that surrounded Vatican Hill.

As evening approached, the army had completed its campaign. They were dead-ended now, again finding the western bank of the Tiber, under the southern wall that surrounded the Holy City. The mob of peasants from Naples stumbled upon them here. Nowhere had anyone seen a fortification that was more substantial than mud-brick walls, twenty-five feet in height. The barrier was uniformly weak and undefended. No one place offered a better opening for breaching the wall than another. Had it not been for a shortage of ladders, the armies would have assaulted the wall that evening. The mutineers built campfires and laid their heads on the ground to sleep.

A thick fog concealed the army on the following morning. The air seeping over the wall was thick with the smell of rich foodstuffs. Growling stomachs awoke the men.

> Soldiers break tents in haste at dawn
> Warriors roll heavy coats after the sun.
> A fighter drinks steaming, bitter swill
> A horse snorts vapor, keen to run.
>
> A pikeman fixes his stare beyond the horizon
> A sentry's hurrah hails a fireball in the sky.
> The leader heralds the call to arms
> His sergeant shouts the battlecry.
>
> Smoke drifts to heaven from a stubbed out fire
> Soldiers repent sins, coldly, in vain.

The starving mutineers assembled at the Porta San Spirito, the Gate of the Holy Ghost, southwest of the Vatican City near the Tiber River. The Spaniards took a position on one side of the gate. The Germans stationed themselves on the other side.

The Spaniards pushed a tall ladder up against the wall, and Bourbon, wearing his light armor, took the lead. He easily scrambled to the top rung. Seeing their brave general at the front of the assault, no soldier worth his salt could doubt the outcome. Bourbon called out for the others to follow and quickly, the ladders raised and filled with soldiers eager to spill the blood of their fellow man.

Fewer than five hundred Roman citizens congregated inside the Gate of the Holy Ghost to defend the Vatican City from Bourbon's army. Most of them were students at Collegio Capranica, which stood just inside the gate.

As Bourbon reached the ridge of the wall, he drew his broadsword and, with both hands, swung it wide over his head. He pointed its tip at the bony carcass of the unfinished St. Peter's Basilica, less than a half a mile away. "Forward, men!" he shouted in German. "For Charles and the empire!" His war cry carried on the dank mist. His voice rang out like the blast of a trumpet and fevered the rabble behind him.

At that same moment, from inside the wall, the goldsmith, Cellini, unleashed a bolt from a crossbow. It sliced through the fog, straight to its target, where its point ripped through Bourbon's thin iron breastplate and plunged deep into his chest. The young warlord sagged to his knees and, falling backward, tumbled down the pitiful, crumbling wall of the Vatican and into the snarl of flatfooted soldiers who were bracing the foot of his ladder. The traitor to his kin and country, his motives suspected by everyone, friend and foeman alike, having never set foot inside the Eternal City, was dead before his body hit the ground.

Far from shocking his army to immobility, a shout erupted from the invaders. The hazy mist could not hide their bloodlust. A German mercenary, grasping his two-handed sword, cleared the wall. "God above is marching before us!" he cried out, and with that, a swarm of Germans piled over the low brick wall. With a mighty heave, several soldiers lifted away the bar that held the gates fast. The gate sprang open, and the rest of the army poured through.

The assault force, with death and destruction before them, overran the students who had rallied to defend the Holy See. Cellini and those few other defenders turned tail and scampered away like scared rabbits.

Hearing news of the breach, the Pope, as others before him had done, fled to the Castel Sant'Angelo. The castle was a half-mile due east of the Vatican hill and connected to the apartments of the Pope and his cardinals by a narrow covered bridge. Built fourteen hundred years earlier as the mausoleum of Hadrian, the castle was now a virtually impregnable fortress. Under one arm, Clement carried parchment books and scrolls. His lungs screamed out for more air, and as he stopped to breathe, he could see below the colonnade the swarming masses of undisciplined attackers slaughtering any man standing in defense. Every street and pathway filled with blood.

Running again, the Pope's robes billowed behind him like wings of an angel. A unit of the Swiss Guard, permanently stationed at the Vatican, protected his retreat. They detained the onrushing Germans and Spaniards only long enough for the Pope to secure himself in Castel Sant'Angleo. In another minute, the marauders dispatched every last man of the Pope's guard to meet his maker.

In no time, the Germans and Spanish overtook the administrative buildings on Vatican Hill. They stormed and routed the rione of Borgo and from inside the walls, put every defender to the sword.

The assaulting force offered a peace on condition of the Church paying three hundred thousand crowns, but the Pope, still convinced that the holy league of French, English, and Papal armies would deliver him, refused every proposition. By midafternoon, the mob, lacking leaders, restrained their lust no longer. German peasants herded the Pope's entourage into a square below the Vatican hill and threw the clerics to their knees. Here, they made the Pope's minders shout at the top of their lungs, "Luther is Pope! Luther is Pope!" The Spaniards had no interest in seeing Luther become Pope. They shouted, "Heresy!" at the coterie of clerics and laid into them with swords. The clerics went to slaughter as if they were pigs.

Together, the mutinous army, the German peasants, and the riff-raff that had joined them from Naples crossed the Tiber and brought their assault to the main body of the city. By sunset, they mastered every district of Rome.

Once the marauders gained complete control, no commanders rose out of the ranks to organize them into an army. Seeing no effort to arrange either a war or a peace, the greedy wretches, who had for months lived on meager rations, were poorly fed, poorly shod, and who sought nothing but pay for past services rendered, fell upon the city that had for centuries squeezed Christendom as if it were a basket of ripe grapes. They abandoned any pretense of military discipline and set themselves to pillaging the city.

The Eternal City was fat on the treasure it had extorted from believers by the issuance of indulgences. Churches, palaces, convents, private houses, basilicas, banks, and tombs—the marauders pillaged every place. Inside the apartments of the Pope, the marauders ripped down tapestries, threw them on the floor, and loaded them with chalices and candlesticks. The golden ring on the finger of the corpse of Pope Julius II now adorned the bloodstained finger of a German peasant.

Like packs of wolves, the Spaniards displayed great skill in scenting out treasures in the most ingenious of Roman hiding places. Men from Naples committed the worse outrages on the women. Every rione and every street echoed the piteous shrieks of the Roman wives and daughters. Neapolitans dragged nuns away to satiate their carnal desires.

The marauders pilfered every chalice, pyxe, and silver remonstrance that they found in the churches. They clothed their servants and camp boys in sacerdotal garments. The piazzas became gambling houses, and the *Campo de Fiori* (field of flowers) became a boar's den of stolen pleasures for the mutineers, where soldiers brought gilded vessels they had stolen and bags full of gold and silver coins they had plundered. They staked their booty on the throw of the dice, and when they lost, they left to search out more.

The Germans paraded priests on asses throughout the city and forced bishops to pay ransoms. No sooner had they received their gold than the Germans turned the bishops over to the Spaniards, who made them pay a second time.

The Germans gorged themselves on food and drink. They staged bawdy theaters to mock the papal court and the relics that the Romans found most holy. One drunken *landsknecht* wrapped himself in the Pope's robe and tossed the pontiff's triple crown in the air. It landed upon his own head. Others gathered around him, wrapped in the long red robes of cardinals. They urinated into their red hats and then staged a parade. Draped in red, they rode asses to Clement's place of refuge, the Castel Sant'Angelo. Clement hid from their taunts behind his barricade. The walls of the castle held.

Below the castle walls, the soldier-cardinals lifted their robes to expose their genitals and kissed the feet of the counterfeit pontiff as he drank to the health of Clement. The kneeling cardinals pledged to be pious and careful not to excite future wars. When the pretender announced his intention to resign the papacy, a spontaneous conclave was organized. All the cardinals cast their vote for Luther, and their shouts reached for the heavens. "Luther is pope! Luther is pope!" the shout went out again. Never before had the election of a pope been unanimous.

Still smarting from the epithet *"Moors,"* nothing could restrain the wrath of the Spaniards. The resourceful Spanish Catholics put Church clerics to death with horrible cruelties designed to milk the last ounce of treasure from the priests and prelates. They did not spare rank, sex, or age.

It was not until the pillage of Rome had lasted ten days, and a booty of ten million golden crowns collected, that peace again came to the riones of the city. The mutinous army of Bourbon had exhausted its capacity to commit the seven deadly sins for even one more day. Eight thousand innocents had met the sword, but still the accounts of the German mercenaries were unsettled.

Luther said, "I would not have Rome burnt. It would be a monstrous deed."

Another reformer, Melancthon, had other fears. "Tremble for the libraries," he said. "We know how hateful books are to Mars."

Besieged in the Castel Sant'Angelo, under the threat that his attackers would blast the castle to high heaven with gunpowder, Clement relented. He renounced every alliance against Emperor Charles and the Holy Roman Empire. He bound himself to remain a prisoner until he had paid the mutinous army a ransom of four hundred thousand ducats.

The mob departed the Eternal City after two weeks, lured by rich cities in the south that were fat with treasure and ripe for the picking.

Against the wishes of the reformers, and in a triumph of God over the will of man, Rome had fallen under harsh judgment. The emperor who sought to persecute Luther on behalf of the Pope instead brought ruin on the Pope. Such is the nature of the Lord's will.

Every sanctuary of the Holy See had been defiled, except for the Sistine Chapel, where the putrefying body of the once constable of France, the hapless Charles de Bourbon, lay in state. The altar was unadorned, nevertheless, the chamber was the seat of Christendom's highest honor and dignity. The nock of a crossbow's bolt pointed straight out of his chest to the elaborate frescos in the vaulted ceiling. Shrouded in light armor, the corpse awaited a Christian burial.

The Jews cautiously came out of hiding as the mercenary rabble departed southward from Rome. The Jewish refugees found only what was left by the army of the Holy Roman Empire, who had gorged themselves on the spoils of war. No booty had gone unplundered, no stockpile unpillaged, no virgin undebauched. The marauders had taken apart even the poorest neighborhoods.

As they emerged from their homes in the rione of Sant'Angelo, the Jews met furious, noisy mobs of tattered Romans. "Kill the heathen bastards! The Jews have brought this on! It's their fault!" the voices shouted. The Romans citizens barricaded the streets and lanes of the rione Sant'Angelo with the wreckage left by the marauding Germans and Spanish. They tipped over wagons, wedging them sideways in the roadways and footpaths. On top, they threw barrels, stones that had fallen from burned-out buildings, and sticks of broken furniture. Thus the Romans confined the Jews to the rione of Sant'Angelo.

The rabbis agreed with David's assessment: the Sack of Rome was the judgment of the angel of the Lord on Rome. The Almighty had spared a remnant of the House of Israel, he told them. Their yearning for a liberator only grew, and David did nothing to deny the whispers that he was the Messiah. He continued to speak in the synagogue, all the while imploring the Jews to believe that all that had transpired was as he had foreseen. "I have not prophesized against the Germans or Spanish," he told them. "It is the Turk who is the true and unending enemy of the Jews."

# CHAPTER 24

Molko awoke on a hard surface. Stars flashed in his eyes, and his head seemed as if it would cleave open from pain. A bell pealed in his ears, and as he struggled to stand, the floor beneath his feet swayed from side to side. Nausea washed over him. He was aboard a ship, and the sun was rising. Thick iron shackles, bolted to the deck, gripped his ankles.

The ship had no captain and no helmsman. "David Reuveni, I'll kill you," he shouted at the misty horizon. The vessel's cargo was of the human variety. His shouts aroused other men, like him shackled to the deck, and soon, forty voices were shouting into the expansive beyond of the great sea.

Merchants in the cities, from time to time, swept the lanes and alleyways near the docks, clearing the city of demon-possessed souls. Some of them were the few that had the good fortune to have survived an exorcism, others were moonstruck mortals, madmen, piteous, irascible beggars vexed with distractions of the mind, delusions, and false beliefs, women who heard voices and maenads who experienced humors, those given to manias, and natural born idiots of every variety. This little ship was loaded to the gunwales with perhaps forty such fools, all in chains. All the captives had been set adrift for the betterment of the city, some deceived with a promise of passage to Paradise. Their voyage was intended to deliver them to the halls of the Leviathan.

The ship was old, slow, and pudgy. It had a single, square sail set, but it luffed against its mast. Roman citizens had towed the bark to sea and set it adrift. Beside Diogo, another lost soul slipped his bonds, having scraped his flesh to the bone. Once unbound, he ran screaming to the gunwale and threw himself overboard. Molko beat apart his chains with the bloody irons of his berth mate, slipped his own bonds, and took the ship's helm. He was able to steer the ship, but he lacked the skills to pilot a course. Maps were useless, but he knew the fools on board with him would obey his command if he pretended to be a captain. Winds were light. He barked orders at his shipmates, set a course to the east, where he knew he would find land.

The ship was without food or water. Molko remembered the words that Sophocles had written for the chorus in *Antigone:*

> Wonders are many on earth, and the greatest of these
> Is man, who rides the ocean and takes his way
> Through the deeps,
> Through wind-swept valleys of perilous seas
> That surge and sway.
> He is master of ageless Earth, to his own will bending
> The immortal mother of gods by the sweat of his brow,
> As year succeeds to year, with toil unending
> Of mule and plough.

*The earth would be a better place if I were its master,* Molko thought. *The day of Reuveni is past. Every man will know my name. Reuveni prophesied that my blood will go unspilled. I will then, by the heavens, bend the immortal mother of gods.*

A fool atop the ship's mast was first to spot the cone of a mountain on the eastern horizon, and Molko steered toward it. He had hoped to scuttle the craft on a sandy shore, but the peak of the mountain was a landmark that he identified as Naples, a city with a large port. He had every reason to suppose that Naples had its share of fools already, and a shipment from Rome would be unwelcome. "The Lord God has heard our prayer," he told his shipmates. "He has given us this fair city to be our own. We will rule there as popes."

The harbor was unguarded. The fools were excited about ascending to their individual papal thrones and shouted to the men working the docks, even as the ship glided into port and smashed head-on into a wooden wharf.

In the madness of splintering timbers, shouting madmen, and Neapolitan dockhands, Molko disappeared.

A week later, he found himself reprising the role of deckhand. Past the heel on Italy's boot, on the eastern shore, the Ionian Sea narrowed into the Adriatic Sea past the Bay of Taranto. This ship's captain had filled his hold with ceramics. Winds were favorable, and the captain set a course to sail the ship across the mouth of the Adriatic Sea and to the coast of Greece.

"Godspeed, my captain," Molko muttered as the little ship set course east. Italy's shore sank below the horizon at the ship's stern. Molko was off to a place where he could re-create himself, find a new role, bend the immortal mother of gods, and start his life anew.

The little ship was close to being unseaworthy, and the captain did not take this crossing lightly. The ship rode good winds but was out of sight of land for a day and a night.

Sighting Dalmatia's coast under the rising sun, the captain turned southeastward and kept his craft far offshore while still in sight of land.

By sailing east, the captain avoided Dalmatia, a district on the treacherous eastern Balkan shore of the Adriatic Sea. Small islands peopled by bloodthirsty Uskok pirates littered Dalmatia's coast, driven there by the Turks.

They were Christian Serbs and Croats, scattered but undefeated, that raided and killed as many of the Muslim invaders as possible. Austria, happy to have an ally to buffer the Turks, promised the Uskoks a military subsidy and allowed them to settle in the rugged coastal islands of Dalmatia.

The Austrians always found an excuse to renege on the subsidy, so the unyielding Uskoks turned to piracy. They attacked their prey in oar-driven longboats and could easily run circles around the Turkish merchantmen. The pirates surrounded their intended victim, usually attacking from the windward, boarding with grappling hooks, armed with short, broad sabers. If threatened, they fled into shallows and easily disappeared in creeks and inlets. No ship flying Turkish flags was safe. Venice exacted tolls for escorting Turkish ships past the Uskok raiders.

Outlaws and cutthroats from every corner of the Christian west wandered to Dalmatia. Their numbers grew, so too their hunger for plunder. No longer did they target just the Turks, they turned on their Christian brothers from Venice. From the Austrian point of view, the freebooters did the Lord's work. The Turks were at bay in the Adriatic, and the treasury did not have to spend a single wooden ducat.

The little bark rode the wind around the southern tip of Greece and up the eastern Peloponnesian shore and on to Athens, where they took on fresh water but found no buyers for their ceramics. The captain next dropped anchor in a harbor in northern Greece, at a place called Salonika. Molko reckoned his journey from Rome had taken forty days.

Each day brought more troublesome news to the worriers at the inn where David took meals. A division of soldiers loyal to Charles stood off the Castel Sant'Angelo in siege, in effect, holding the Pope as prisoner. With the sack of Rome, the Roman Catholic Church was in shambles, and incarcerated, the Pope had lost control over all the papal states. Every province on the Italian peninsula was now under the thumb of Charles, the emperor of the Holy Roman Empire.

Clement ranted that Charles could have stemmed the attack of the mercenaries and suppressed the atrocities. Charles vociferously denied it. The citizens of Rome never believed him. He could have easily paid the wages of the angry mercenaries, that much was clear to every man, woman, and child, and had he done so, he would have saved Rome. And neither did he occupy and rebuild Rome, such was his disdain.

On a chilly evening, David warmed himself alone by the fire in his parlor room, enjoying a bottle of wine. More and more, David drank alone in his room. The wine offered surcease from his back pain and gave him sleep. He worried constantly. He did not talk about the crusade. The Jews had been ravaged by the rabble and now were confined in the dense quarter called Sant'Angelo. *It is not surprising that the people do not worry about the Turks,* David thought. *The Turks are the furthest thing from their minds.*

David laid his head on the back of the couch. Perhaps his exhortations at the synagogue needed less fire and brimstone. He closed his eyelids and tried to concentrate. The wine helped his attention wander to the greatest hero of the children of Israel, King David. He visualized ancient passages from the Torah and prophets as if he could read them from the inside of his closed eyelids, scriptures he had learned as a boy in the Hebrew language.

David did not want to go into hiding like King David, but decided that in his future, he would adopt a lower profile, become less visible, for a time at least. *Perhaps I should preach a message of peace to the Jews, until things settle down.* The Jews stood to gain from a restoration of peace—peace and prosperity was to their advantage, certainly. He had nothing to gain in antagonizing the Hun German bastards and neither did his flock.

*I will temper my message for a time. That cannot hurt anything.* The wine relaxed him further, and he thought again about the lie, that he was an emissary, remembering the religious fervor of the Roman

Jews. Who could say that the passionate religious revival had been anything other than good for the Jews? It made no difference to David if Huns ruled Rome. All other things equal, it was probably better for the Jews to be the subjects of an emperor sitting on a throne six hundred miles away than it was to be the subjects of a unfettered Christian Pope sitting across the Tiber. His confinement in the rione of Sant'Angelo could not last forever. The Romans would come to their senses with these curfews. David thought the world had taken leave of its senses. Surely, things would return to normal.

In the months following the sack of Rome, Charles's forces seized control of Castel Sant'Angelo and held him there as a prisoner. Clement suffered several prolonged illnesses during the period of his confinement. On three occasions, priests prepared to deliver last rites to the pontiff.

Romans gossiped that Clement had aged by twenty years during his six-month confinement. He grew a full beard as a sign of mourning, a clear violation of canon law, which required priests to be clean-shaven. After buying off some Imperial officers, and disguised as a peddler, he escaped to hide at a villa in the country.

Still, the Pope had no safe haven and was incapable of coming to the defense of his family. Enemies of the de' Medici family seized on Rome's collapse and expelled the Pope's family from the birthplace of the Renaissance and reinstalled a republic. Broken and ill, an object of ridicule for the citizens of Rome because of his illegitimate birth, Clement had no alternative other than to make peace with Emperor Charles. "It is better to be the emperor's groom than a sport of the people," the pontiff said.

The articles of peace provided three major terms. In the first part, the Pope recognized and crowned Charles as emperor of the Holy Roman Empire and agreed that the coronation would take place in Rome. In the second part, the emperor appointed the Pope's illegitimate son, Alessandro, to a newly created duchy, which elevated the nineteen-year-old bastard son to the post of Duke of Florence. And in the third part, the emperor gave his seven-year-old daughter in marriage to Alessandro, who the Florentines called *il Moro*, as the mother of *Il Duca* Alessandro was a black slave in the de' Medici household.

Alessandro was immensely unpopular for his profligate spending and wenching, so Clement found no safe haven in Florence, his hometown. After signing the articles of peace, the Pope returned to Vatican Hill.

*Illegitimate, David thought. Illegitimate Allesandro. Ha. As if they cared. Diogo was illegitimate. Their Pope was illegitimate. Their Messiah was illegitimate.*

The Roman citizens sorrowed for Rome, trashed at the hand of a ragtag gang of Lutherans. And where was their protector, Henry?

Henry and the English aristocrats were afraid the Lutherans heresy would pollute their own ranks. Everyone knew it. Italy was lost, the English bishops were saved.

Salonika had long been a major port and trading hub. It was more Macedonian than Greek. The Republic of Venice once controlled Salonika; they called it Thessalonica, but the district had been lost to the Turks a hundred years before. The Turkish Sultan, Murad II, had brutally sacked the city and pillaged the countryside. Fearing death at the hands of the Turks, most of the Greek and Macedonian citizens fled into the countryside, and the city had fallen into decline.

Only a generation before, four thousand Muslims and six thousand Greek Orthodox Catholics occupied Salonika. The Greek Orthodox were led by Patriarchs, so Salonika did not have a single soul that owed a duty to a Pope, certainly not the Roman Pope. And not a single Jew lived in Salonika. But then, after their expulsion from Spain and Portugal, nearly twenty thousand Sephardic Jews made their way east, immigrating to Greece. On invitation from the Turks, most of them settled in Salonika.

The city was half the size of Rome, but the population of Jews was ten times greater. Salonika's population tripled in a generation, and all of the newcomers were Jews. The strategy of the Turks worked as if by magic. The Greek Orthodox Catholics no longer dominated the city. Only two thousand Jews lived in far-off Jerusalem, their population decimated in the Christian crusades. Now more Jews lived in Salonika than any place in the world.

The Jews in Salonika dressed like Turks, setting themselves apart by wearing a yarmulke.

If Molko wanted to recreate the miracles that he had worked in Portugal, he could not hope to find a more fertile territory than Salonika. In Spain or Portugal, unsanctioned ideas were punishable in the flames of the *auto-da-fé*, but in Salonika they were spoken in public. Religious beliefs whispered in Lisbon were shouted from Salonika's rooftops. The Jews were fervent with a longing for the Messiah and a regathering in Palestine. Molko jumped ship.

Smelling a free meal, Molko wheedled his way into a wedding feast. As the groom concluded his Talmudic discourse, Molko stepped forward to announce the wedding presents. And as the bride was escorted to the bridal chair for her veiling, he recited verse, some bawdy, some poignantly romantic, some playful. The wedding party alternately convulsed in laughter and choked with tears. Molko had no shortage of female partners eager to hold his hand at the ritual dance that ended the ceremony.

No longer under the thumb of the brainsick Jew haters in Spain and Portugal, in Salonika, the yearnings for a homeland of the Jews had become vocal, unrepressed, and full-throated. At the wedding, he met other young men, intellectually endowed, like himself. They spoke openly about their visions and offered to interpret Molko's dreams. He had heard mention of this mystic, occult, nontraditional style of approaching God, but as a Christian in Portugal, he had never been interested enough or had the time to investigate the movement. Kabbalah they called it. This fashion of worship of the Almighty had no place in the time-honored halakha (Jewish law) or the Talmud. The conservative rabbis in Rome shunned Kabbalah.

His new friends invited him to attend a yeshiva sponsored by a renowned Jew named Joseph Taytazak. So holy was Taytazak that for forty years, he never slept in a bed, but on a box, with his feet on the ground. He made an exception for nights of the Sabbath. Followers rumored that Taytazak had created an artificial man of clay, a golem that came to life when he wrote the name of God on a piece of paper and put it in the golem's mouth.

As far away as Damascus and Jerusalem, rabbis in the Judaic faith held Taytazak in the utmost esteem. He was devoted to Kabbalah.

Molko accepted an appointment to the yeshiva, which included room and board, and again he adopted the role of a student. He did not enjoy his studies in halakha, but he worked hard in the Talmud and quickly outpaced his classmates in the rabbinic discussions. He immersed himself in the mysticism of the Kabbalah. He stood at the head of his peers in his ability to interpret dreams. He looked forward to his study. It was becoming abundantly clear that he would be able to use Kabbalah to predict the future, perform miracles, and communicate with God and the angels. David Reuveni was in his past. Kabbalah would use him to bend the immortal mother of the gods.

Kabbalah means "to receive," to receive revelations, hidden meanings of scriptures that are knowable only by the holiest of Jews. Taytazak taught that God emanated aspects of his being that performed the work of creation, not God himself. With each descending emanation—and the number of emanations was ten—the thing given off became further away from God, as if each emanation was a lesser god—with the final emanations taking the form of angels.

Taytazak had no interest in the plain meaning of scripture. He used numerology to find hidden meanings, which of course were inaccessible to the unsanctified.

To support the yeshiva, the students made amulets. First, they wrote a talisman, a scroll of powerful words which sought a blessing from Taytazak. They inserted the talisman inside a necklace—the amulet. Health, protection, fertility, prosperity, no dream was impossible for the owner of a Rabbi Taytazak amulet.

The students also prepared tefillin, little leather boxes that observant Jews bound to the head and arm to help them commit both brain and brawn to the fulfillment of prayer. Inside the leather boxes, the students inserted four miniature parchment scrolls, each unique and written in a special style of writing.

Taytazak also told of a voice—a *maggid*—divine in origin, which spoke to scholars. His own *maggid* came to him in the form of automatic writing. The ongoing debate in the yeshiva was the nature of his out-of-body *maggid*. Was it, as Taytazak insisted, a voice of the divine? Or was it an angelic personification of the Mishnah, the ritual laws? A distinction worthy of academic debates, the students argued the finer points for endless hours.

While at the yeshiva, and hand-in-hand with his improving talent for dream interpretation, Molko found that he was remembering more of his own dreams. He challenged Taytazak and his opinions on the mysteries of creation, the most concealed concept of Kabbalah. He objected when the master insisted on inserting magic squares inside the amulets.

Unlike Taytazak, Molko had no desire to adopt the life of an ascetic. He fasted and bathed in cold water, but he shunned the complete self-denial and self-immolation practiced by his patron. His lust for fame was strong; his role as student sharpened his desire to return to center stage. Molko found lusty, needful young women in

Salonika who starved for the budding student's brand of one-on-one spiritual awakening.

Early on, Taytazak was at the point of expelling Molko from the yeshiva. No matter how headstrong the student was, he should not have spoken in opposition to the master's opinions on such critical matters as the magic squares and the mysteries of creation. That was enough to put Molko on thin ice. But then the master became enthralled with him when the student unexpectedly posed a question, "Rabbi, might you become the Messiah?"

The master answered a crisp "no," but flattered by the question, he changed his mind about his most brazen acolyte. It might have been wiser to have balked, or perhaps told his students that he would consider the question for a week, a month, a year. But the finality of the master's answer opened a wide door for the student. Thereafter, when Molko revealed and interpreted his own dreams to the others, he might identify the personality in the dreams as someone on a higher plane than himself and intertwine the interpretation with metaphors, symbols, allegories, and undisguised references. The protagonist of Molko's dreams was the Messiah. He began preaching on street corners and synagogues.

He pored over the most mystical texts, those which claimed to have the most ancient authorship as the claim of antiquity was the feature that appealed most to the Jewish mythical tradition. Molko's gifts, he discovered, came in the past from two angels, Aza and Azaz'el, who had fallen from heaven.

Molko published a portion of his sermons under the title *Derashot*. He undertook wanderings into the countryside, preaching to any who would hear, and achieved a great reputation. He liked roasted hare, wines, and women, and as an itinerant preacher, he got more of his favorite things than he could handle.

He offered to marry Taytazak's daughter, and in an attempt to fashion himself as an aesthetic celebrity, he promised her father that he would avoid sexual intercourse with her. Taytazak refused. Rumors circulated that the young wanderer had taken a wife of whoredom and shunned sexual relations with her, but those rumors were unfounded.

He began to develop unusual behaviors, sinking into deep depressions and long periods of isolation, followed by frenzied study, restlessness, and ecstasy. He worked on the Sabbath, ate non-kosher food, and spoke the name of God.

A wealthy wool merchant came crying to Molko. "I've been married seven years. Still, no children," he sobbed. "The physicians have been no help at all." Molko asked for the merchant's name, for his mother's name, and for a series of private audiences with the barren wife. After a month, Molko proclaimed his revelation. The wealthy merchant had not strapped his tefillin to his head in the manner ritual prescribed.

The rabbi's acolytes opened the tefillin at Taytazak's shop. They were startled to find that someone had inserted the parchments into the tefillin in an improper sequence. The wool merchant's usage of the tefillin had been a complete waste of time. Molko announced that a month later the merchant's wife would be pregnant, and it was so.

On another day, a farmer fell to his knees and kissed Molko's hand. "Nothing is going right. My crops are either burned to ash in the sun or washed away by floods. I cannot sleep. My teeth I'm losing, one by one."

Molko walked around the farmer, three times in a circle. "An evil eye," he announced. "You've been cursed by an evil eye for fourteen years."

The pitiful farmer broke into tears. "What am I to do?"

Molko led the farmer to Taytazak's shop and wrote a talisman in his own special writing. "Bring me water," he told the farmer, and when the man returned, he dipped the talisman in the cup. "Now drink." The farmer did as Molko instructed him and then fell into a deep sleep. That fall, he harvested a bountiful crop.

Molko erased from his memory the Christian image of Messiah that had burdened his thinking from his days at his mother's breast. He no longer conceived of the Messiah as the Son of God who came-and-will-come to establish an earthly throne. To Molko, the Messiah would be a leader who would unfold knowledge of the God of Israel across the world and unite humanity as one. He would be as pure and holy as a consecrated temple or an anointed sword. The Messiah would be a man, naturally born of the union of a man and woman. Molko embraced the supernatural and occult, but he found no conflict in rejecting the repugnant notion that a Messiah could be born of a virgin. *How could I have been so deluded to believe that?* he asked himself.

The Messiah would be a warrior and a leader. He would gather the Jews back to the land of Israel and in the land of the patriarchs; he would gather stones to repair that which had been torn down. He would build the Third Temple. He would usher in an era of world peace, an end to all hatred, oppression, suffering, and disease. Quoting the prophet, Molko told himself, "God will be king over all the world. On that day, God will be One and his name will be One."

Unlike the Messiah, God was above flesh and was not bound to the earth. God alone was to be worshiped, not a being of his creation, be he angel, saint, or...or even the Messiah. He was not sure. Perhaps one should worship the Messiah. It was a matter that was premature to debate. The rabbis would welcome a disputation on that issue once the Messiah announced his arrival.

Molko told those who would listen, "I wondered greatly that the time of miracles did not arrive. Then a dream came to me where a voice shouted, 'A son has been born. He will humble the great dragon. He, the true Messiah, will sit upon My throne.'"

After three years of study, Molko declared himself the Messiah. He stated publicly that a prophetic vision revealed to him that the messianic kingdom would come in 1540.

From Salonika, Molko traveled to Constantinople, to Damascus, and from there, on to Jerusalem. He bent the immortal mother of gods. Everywhere he traveled, he proclaimed the good news. His audiences were poor and downtrodden, in stark contrast to the images his mind conjured up concerning the Christians in the west, those back in Spain and Portugal. "The Marranos are as rich as lords now," he told the others. A dream revealed all to him.

He hinted to his followers that he would travel to Babylon, but his eyes looked into the setting sun, westward to a place of whoredom that sat on seven hills. He saw in the sky the vision of a whore he would not shun, arrayed in purple and scarlet, decked with gold and precious stones and pearls. With her right hand, she stroked a large reptile with strong jaws while in her left she held a golden cup, filled to overflowing with abominations and the filth of her fornication with the kings of Christendom, over which she reigned.

# CHAPTER 25

The Roman citizens gossiped about everything in the months and years following the sack of Rome. Earthquakes engulfing Carinthia, the tower of St. Mark in Venice split into four parts, ominous signs in the aspect of the quartiles of Saturn and Jupiter. No rumor went unrepeated, no bad news went untold.

All the Jews in the Eternal City now lived in the crowed rione Sant'Angelo, the smallest of the city's districts, and the Christians locked the rione down by curfew at dusk. The Roman authorities accosted any Jew found outside Sant'Angelo after dark. By law, the front of each house was required to display the number of Jewish occupants. A sign might say, *"5 Jews Live Here."* The western border of the rione was the Tiber River, which flooded the low, flat Jewish quarter at least once a year.

Benvenida Abravanel had set aside a sum of money so that David could receive a small pension that permitted him to pick up his stipend at the offices of one of Abravanel's agents once a month. The mansion house Abravanel owned was outside the Jewish quarter, and he had sold it for a pittance to a Christian bishop.

The steady income from his pension permitted David to slow down. Rubbing the muscles deep in his lower back, he told the rabbis, "My constitution insists."

He forwallowed in bed until the noontime noises of the street wakened him. His body had to summon all its energy to roll out of bed to take nourishment. Five years of nightly drinking had left him drained of vitality. His mood was melancholic, and he did not know why. He rarely felt aroused by sexual desire; most days he would prefer a good bowel movement. Every morning, as he sat on the side of his bed in his undershirt, he cursed the sunlight. He could not remember whether he had vomited the night before. He could not remember anything. His head pounded. His eyes had headaches.

He hoped he would never drink again and looked forward to getting drunk.

It was evening and David sat on a riser before an empty synagogue.

An elderly rabbi occupied a seat in the front row. "This oppression can't continue," the rabbi mumbled, shaking his head.

"Times will get better," David answered.

"When gentiles experience misfortune, the Jews suffer catastrophe," the rabbi said.

"It is written."

"The people hunger now for the Kabbalah," the rabbi said, gathering himself to stand.

"Kabbalah?"

"Ancient writings. Very mystic. Esoteric. Occult."

"I've never heard of it," David said, his head turning to the empty seats. "Maybe the people didn't know I'd be speaking tonight..."

"How could it be that a man from Arabia knows nothing of Kabbalah?" the rabbi asked.

"Perhaps I heard Simon Meshulam speak of it. The crusade is the only thing I know about."

Noises intruded from beyond the great hall of the synagogue. The rabbi shuffled off to investigate. David's station was secure. He had nothing to fear. Yet he was often mournful, beaten down by apprehension and dread. His closet offered no surcease. He withdrew a fabric mask from his bodice and then tiptoed out the hall in the opposite direction.

Standing in the dark courtyard outside the synagogue, David gripped the collar of his cloak high as if to disguise his face. In spite of the chilliness of the autumn evening, he let several open hacks pass by before hailing one with an enclosed cab. Looking twice in every direction, he stepped out of the entryway and boarded. After directing the driver to a house in a dark corner of the Jewish quarter, he looked back over his shoulder. He had not been observed.

The driver stopped the carriage outside a brothel. David pulled the mask over his face. It was a simple black sheath, with eyeholes and a cord to tie around his head.

The brothel was warm and illuminated by hundreds of candles flickering in lamps and reflecting from chandeliers.

"Prince David, nice to see you this evening," a departing patron said as David arrived. The other regular patrons easily recognized him. But the madam, Bilhah, his dear lady friend, willingly accommodated his customary desire with a knowing wink. Her customer wanted to be unseen, and she was happy to assist him in continuing the charade.

"And it seems we have an unknown visitor this evening," she announced in a loud voice.

"I have need to watch," David whispered to her. "Let me not be seen."

"Nothing here is untrue. We uncover for you things that others have hidden."

"Yes. This is what I desire."

She ushered him to a dim upper room filled with chairs. Several rowdy patrons faced a black fabric screen hung on a wall. Attendants snuffed out candles in the dim room, and a brightly lit adjoining chamber appeared through the now translucent screen.

A large bed served as the only piece of furniture in the adjoining room. Gaudy red walls exhibited ribald paintings of plump naked women with men, centaurs, animals and other women. Garish draperies festooned the windows.

David sat subdued. As he and the other onlookers watched, a succession of couples entered the lighted room and performed lewd carnal acts.

While the other spectators laughed or cheered, David stared out of the darkened room without lust. David had an undersized sense of right and wrong. Lechery was not his weakness. The lascivious scenes unfolding before his eyes caused him to cringe. It was not the debauchery he craved—it was the hiding—hiding, while at the same time uncovering. Uncovering something hidden. Masking and exposing, cloaking and undressing. The contradiction was reassuring. It helped quiet the nagging doubts.

After the conclusion of the performance, David politely skulked out of the darkened room and to the parlor on the first floor of the brothel. Furtive glances over his shoulder perfected his feeling of solace. The hiding and watching gave him tranquility, not release. But as always, he felt shame. In the parlor, Bilhah comforted David.

"I'm an idiot," he said, tears welling in his eyes. "I hate myself."

"It's harmless entertainment," she cooed.

"Rome weighs on me. My spirit needs renewal. I need the country."

"With me? May I go with you?"

"Yes. Some other place. Away from this place."

It was a Friday afternoon and getting late. David and Bilhah hired an open carriage and driver and spent the day in a peaceful glade far outside the city. They rode over a bumpy road below a rock-strewn hillside. The little man slumbered in the arms of his gentle lady, but he awoke when the carriage driver shouted, "Clear the way, fools!"

In the road ahead, a group of Jews, more women than men, straggled single-file across their path and uphill. And behind him, several other lines of walkers were scattered along the roadway, all heading uphill, merging with others into longer lines. Their destination seemed to be upward to a rock outcropping underneath the rim of the hill, where a large group of people had gathered.

"Where are these people going?" David asked, but the walkers smiled at him and continued walking uphill. "Stop the carriage, driver."

David and Bilhah got out of the carriage and fell into line with the others, walking uphill. Some event was drawing the Jews to the ridge.

At the outcropping, the people had bunched into a crowd. Women outnumbered men five to one. Inside the crowd, surrounded by swooning young women, a man dressed like a Turk preached to the swelling crowd. He wore knee-high shiny black leather boots. Over all was a blousy red tunic and trousers, and from under his turban, hair hung in long black curls. He walked toward the sunset, and speaking as if to the setting sun, he sang, "Come, my beloved; come, my bride." Then, turning to the followers, he told them, "Come, let us go out to greet the presence of the Sabbath, the presence of the queen."

A bearded face looked back at David, but the costume could not disguise the identity of the man.

"Diogo Pires," David shouted. The preacher was Solomon Molko. David did not know whether to be mad or not. Molko turned his head and nodded to acknowledge David's presence. Then, with a grin, he continued, "Come, let us go." He led the crowd of his followers into the west. They struggled to keep pace, almost skipping behind the man who was the object of their adoration. When he stopped, they held hands in a circle and danced.

"Friday evening is the time of the union of the queen presence of God with the king presence of God," he told them. "The Sabbath is God's wedding celebration."

One young woman giggled nervously. David easily read her thoughts. She imagined her person in a bedroom. The room was dark and unlit. It was night. She was reclined on a bed, and the preacher was kissing her modestly.

"I am a complete human being," his voice was saying. "I am husband of the Torah, master of the house. All Torah's secrets she has revealed to me, withholding nothing, concealing nothing. I have become aware, pursuing Torah to become her lover."

Several young women swooned and fainted. Now the crowd pushed lame and blind people forward. As they grabbed to touch the hem of Molko's garments, he said, "I once heard a chaste man bemoan the fact that sexual union is pleasurable."

Another young woman fell to her knees, looking up at the preacher with pleading eyes. David read her thoughts. The setting in her fantasy was much the same, set in a darkened bedchamber. Mostly naked, she dreamed of the preacher's strong embrace; his full, warm lips kissed her bosom. The powerful force of the preacher's desire was too strong to hide. In the dream, he laid the young woman back on a bed, and she was incapable of refusing him.

"He preferred that there be no physical pleasure at all, so that he could unite with his wife solely to fulfill the command of his creator: 'Be fruitful and multiply.' But our rabbis, may their memory be a blessing, tell us, 'One should hallow oneself during sexual union.' Sexual holiness is a secret, wondrous and awesome. The holiness derives precisely from feeling the pleasure."

*This is better than the peep show at the brothel*, David told himself. He removed his *bareta*, dropped in a few coins, and began circulating amid the congregation, pressing them for contributions. "For the glory of the Almighty," he told them.

David sent Bilhah home with the carriage. He wanted her safe in the quarter after curfew. He stayed on, hopeful to have a talk to his old manservant. As he waited, he stirred the contents of his *bareta* with his finger. *Puny*, he thought. Mostly the giving was small coins, inexpensive rings, and handwritten notes.

"David Reuveni, my old mentor." Molko was smiling.

"Diogo Pires. Son of a whore," David said. His hand gripped the handle of the dagger in his belt. "What are you doing here?"

"The Lord God restored me to Rome."

"When do you return to Palestine?"

"Palestine? You booked a ticket to the bottom of the sea. But as you foresaw, my blood would not be spilled. I'm here to establish my ministry."

David handed the offering to Diogo and asked, "You risk your life for this trifling sum?"

"You put the Inquisition after me," Molko said, his tone factual, not angry.

David sneered. "You wanted fame."

"Your vengeance is harsh. Christianity is a yoke you lifted from my shoulders."

"The Lutherans sacked Rome. The Pope crowned Charles Emperor."

"The crazy man was already emperor."

"The church paid him four hundred thousand ducats."

David read Diogo's thoughts. *What I could do with that much money*, his one-time disciple was thinking, but his mouth said, "Crazy, yes. But pious."

"Pope Clement. The bastard de' Medici. They've walled up the old neighborhood." The little man emphasized the indignity of the wall by slapping his right hand onto the bicep brachii of his left arm, and making an uppercut gesture with his left fisted arm, the universal gesture of disdain for the anus of one's fellow man.

"And what's become of England? The protector?"

"Mark my word. In no time, Henry will have his own church. No Lutherans. No Roman Pope."

"Perhaps, but I have more urgent matters to deal with. The Lord God led my exodus to Rome to reconcile with my transgressions. I have been drinking up knowledge. I have found the Kabbalah. I fasted and prayed long hours aboard ship, standing at the rail, looking into the wine-dark sea. I asked, 'Lord, am I to reconcile with all the people I have done evil to?' But then I thought, all of my make believe has only brought about an outcome of good for his people."

"Make believe. My, my." *This fool is every bit as self-delusional as before, if not more so,* David thought. With a chuckle, he added, "Make believe as the will of God. Interesting concept."

"Exactly. After I learned the secrets of Kabbalah...well, I realized there is nothing that I have taken that I have not returned a hundredfold."

"Deceit has earned God's blessing. It's becoming clear."

"Right. It was then that the Messiah weighed heavy on my mind. What kind of man would he be? Brave, a warrior king. Not one of these simpering monastic recluses."

"You are so correct. He'd have to be a man's man, virile, vigorous."

"Precisely."

"And tall. With curly black hair."

"Yes. I had insight."

"Oh, another revelation?"

"Some brave soul was needed to step forward and accept God's anointing."

David's second sight looked into Diogo's thoughts. Instead, the images that appeared to him were from his own mind. He saw his former manservant chained to a wall, insane, barking as if he were a dog, frothing at the mouth.

"Messiah is a prize for someone holy enough, raw and savage and fearless enough. So if one were simply brave enough to take up the mantle, then the Messiah would become. By faith anointed. I decided that I would be the Lord God's instrument."

"You schmuck."

"God called me to Rome. I will gather the exiles and restore his kingdom. Jerusalem will be reclaimed. I will form a nation that will last forever. I am the anointed. God has allowed me to become the Messiah."

David sat on the ground and buried his face in his hands. "The Christians will kill you for saying these words."

"Times have changed."

"Not that much. They would pour molten lead in my ears if they knew I heard this."

"People are more sophisticated."

"Maybe so. I haven't been getting out."

"The Church is powerless. You should be rich."

The master had no intention of taking criticism of any sort from his one-time servant. *This fool is still as dimwitted as a goose. He's no match for me.* "Look around you," he snapped back. "Where is my treasure? It's you—" David paused. He thrust his finger at Diogo. "It's you who has the gift..."

"I do?"

"...of second sight. You predicted an earthquake in Portugal."

"I don't, uh..."

"And a flood on the Tiber."

"I must have forgotten. Yes, I remember now. Well...my *maggid is* one of prophetic dreams!"

David shook his head in disbelief at Molko's gullibility. *Still a pushover*, he told himself.

David slept on the ground with a rock for a pillow and walked to Rome the following morning. He had not seen the sun in the eastern sky for years.

Returning home, he took pen to paper and wrote a scathing letter that questioned Molko's authenticity. He paid a printer to set type and ordered five hundred copies.

David examined the letter, now printed like a broadsheet, searching for errors. "Yes," he said. "This will do nicely. He'll wish he never left Palestine."

David gave a few coins to some urchins in the street who distributed the broadsheet to every corner of Sant'Angelo.

# CHAPTER 26

David moderated his message now. He denounced the Turks, to be sure, but perfunctorily. Themes of either peace or God's judgment on Rome dominated his messages. The fervor the Jews once held for a crusade against the Turks was in a downward spiral. The number of people who attended his speechmaking at the synagogue diminished, so he often met his followers in homes. He crafted his message to cater to the wealthier Jews, the doctors, lawyers, and mathematicians, so he continued to gather in modest financial rewards. Together with his pension, he was able to make ends meet and build on the funds credited to him at Abravanel's bank.

Before a small but well-dressed congregation, David's message also spoke to the affinity of the individual to his Maker, the intimate, the personal relationship. He stressed messages such as these: "The godly shall be rewarded here on earth." "The good man can look forward to happiness." "He who tills his ground shall have prosperity." "Only a fool idles away his time."

The wealthy merchants in the congregation rolled out their lower lips and nodded in agreement. "It is possible to give away and become richer," he urged them. "It is possible to hold on too tightly and lose everything. Yes, the liberal man shall be rich. By watering others, he waters himself." David's disciple Benjamin passed a collection vessel, and as always, he returned with contributions.

The little emissary had nothing to gain in antagonizing Molko further. His erstwhile manservant could still lay bare the truth of the crusade hoax. If the authorities cursed the servant, they would surely damn the master.

David dreamed frequently that a man without a face was demanding that he denounce Molko. *I would have killed him myself if I had a chance,* he told his tormentor. Even in the dream, he could hardly condemn his once-loyal retainer.

David shunned the light of day. Often, when he woke in the middle of the night fretting over Molko, he dressed and left his rooms to skulk the dark, empty streets, stopping at intervals to rub the pains that afflicted his back.

*It is not a matter of the money,* David told himself. He carried a grudge against Molko, his case aggravated by the usurpation, the violation, the breach of trust. *That bastard has appropriated my Messiah ploy for himself. My own recruit. I was Messiah when he was still hiding from his creditors. The audacity.* If Molko's followers only knew what he knew. *Son of a whore. Messiah, indeed.*

Jews wrapped fish in David's broadsheets. Haunted by Molko's presence in Rome, David began a diary. In it, he wrote obsessively about the crusade and imagined fanciful ways that he could help the Jews loosen the suffocating bonds placed on them by the Christians, bonds of velvet, crafted from textiles supplied by the merchant class of outcasts.

Many needy Jews drifted toward Molko's flamboyant ministry. He preached to the poor and ill. His focus centered on the underprivileged masses of the Jewish community, and the crowds thronging his messages devoured his words in orgies of religious fervor. His sermons taught a far different message than those of his erstwhile master, David Reuveni. He spoke of matters so abstruse and perplexing that it was difficult for his disciples to interpret his message, so of course, his followers revered him even more for his holiness. As Rome slowly rebuilt itself, arising from the ashes and rubble, a cult of veneration expanded around Molko. His esteem increased. Even the Catholics revered his supernatural gifts. Any overture David might make would certainly arouse the suspicion of his one-time servant. Molko must trust someone.

The monarch of England and his handsome queen had not produced a male heir who survived into adulthood, and Henry, onetime champion on the jousting lawns, now often found himself saddled to an overstuffed chair, battling gout. Chronic pain plagued every step, his joints swollen and sore. Incurable lesions festered on his shins, and his girth was expanding out of control. Catherine's twenty-year coverture with the robust king had produced six children, five of them in the grave, and his only living issue, a daughter, having been betrothed to the emperor and jilted, at ten now, had yet to find a husband. Henry needed a son to secure the throne for the House of Tudor.

The Tudor family's roots had grown out of an illicit liaison between the widow of Henry V and her clerk of the wardrobe, a Welshman. Two passions united by a torn seam. Henry VII's own claim to the English throne derived from his mother but through an illegitimate line. Only forty-five years earlier, Henry VII had wrested England's throne from the last Plantagenet king, Richard III. The War of the Roses ended when Henry number seven bedded Elizabeth of York.

The eighth Henry's anguish was palpable; his first marriage, to his brother's widow, was blighted in the eyes of God. Just the sight of Catherine was repugnant to Henry. He closed his eyes in dread of the fires of hell. His loins ached with desire for a young girl at court, Anne Boleyn, whose older sister, a decade earlier, had been one of good King Harry's most gifted and enthusiastic consorts.

The Tudors had overcome a mountain of turmoil. Surely, the great God in heaven had not chosen to maneuver the Tudor dynasty into a bog. Henry had left it to Wolsey to secure a divorce from Queen Catherine. An annulment. It was such a small thing, and the sulfurous Cardinal Wolsey had failed. The most powerful Cardinal in the Church. He had no excuse for failing to deliver. Why could he not?

His ministers feigned piety. "The Church gave dispensation for Henry to marry his brother's widow. How can it be annulled now?" the bishops asked. Henry was hoist on his own words. He had clouded the issues with the spirited defense of marriage so eloquently put forward in his best-selling anti-Luther book, *Defence of the Seven Sacraments.*

Perhaps the annulment would have been more accessible had Henry captured Paris. Was the Pope wanting to punish Henry, the defender of the faith, for his truancy when the Pope was in needed of an army to fend off the mutinous Lutherans and Spaniards? No one knew. The stand taken by the inscrutable Pope was that the Church had no choice.

At court, the English noblemen fumed with rage at the Tudor king. The treasury was drained after years of wars and lavish spending. Now, Henry demanded even greater tribute from the lords.

Henry would have blamed his dilemma on the Jews, but Edward Longshanks had banished them from England two hundred years previously. The only solution was for Henry to point the finger at Wolsey. It was all his doing. The cardinal must be replaced.

"Bring the cloven footed deceiver to me," Henry demanded, as he signed a warrant directing his officers to arrest Wolsey on charges of treason. The publicity surrounding Wolsey's trial promised to occupy the nobles and clergy for months to come, and divert attention away from the crown. But Wolsey had one final trick up his sleeve. On the way to London, in the custody of the king's guard, the disgraced cardinal took a fever and died.

Henry seized the reins of his government. Now the English clergy had no Wolsey to protect their cushy sinecures from the erratic wishes of the lustful, egotistical, and increasingly harsh king of England. Without a Wolsey to mince the king's avarice, no man's station was safe. All property in England was forfeit. The king was tired of the internecine infighting between factions of the nobles, he was tired of the clergy, he was tired of trying to sire a child with his brother's widow, tired of the French, the peasants, the weather...He was just tired. Someone would pay. Wolsey's death was a down payment.

Since Rome continued to refuse Henry's pleas for annulment, in desperation, the king set every lawyer in London to the task of researching ancient sources and texts. "Compile a brief," he demanded, and the king's word was law. Henry was convinced that relief hid itself in the Hebrew statutes—the levirate marriage law must provide for exceptions; out of necessity a back door must open. How could it be that the brother's-widow-as-wife rule that he had prayed for, the exemption that had permitted him to marry Catherine of Aragon in the first place, how could such an openhearted law have no escape clause? But the rule was ironclad, blackletter law. Even the Jewish scholars he consulted told him "no."

"It is my desire," the good king roared. "Damn the ancient law." Henry set his quill to parchment to draft his own brief.

"In law," Henry's document concluded, "spiritual supremacy rests with the monarch. The Pope has no legal authority." With the product of his own hand as absolute authority, Henry demanded a hundred-thousand-pound tribute from the English clergy, a just penalty, he argued, because the clergy had diminished the crown by what he described as unreasonable and uncharitable usurpations and exactions. The guilty parties were the Pope in general and the English clergy in particular, and payment in full was the condition precedent to a royal pardon. He also demanded that the clergy recognize him as their sole protector and supreme head.

Wolsey's years of profligate spending had rendered the clergy insolvent, too. The coffers of the monasteries were empty and unable to meet the king's demand. The churchmen had little choice. They recognized Henry as supreme head of the Church of England and surrendered legislative independence and canon law to the authority of the monarch. By removing then the Statute in Restraint of Appeals, the bishops ceded authority to the Archbishops of Canterbury and York. Thomas Cranmer, Wolsey's replacement, issued Henry's annulment and paved the way for the royal union with Anne Boleyn. Their ceremony took place in secret. Even as the couple repeated their vows, the seed of a noble daughter, Princess Elizabeth, was growing in the young queen's belly.

Hearing news of the clandestine nuptials, the Pope excommunicated Henry and Cranmer. For a time, the new queen was sheltered from the news for fear it would cause her to miscarry.

As Henry's final acts of defiance, he signed the Act of First Fruits and Tenths. This transferred the taxes on income from the Pope to the English Crown. And the Peter's Pence Act gave relief to landowners from the annual tax of one penny, which they formerly had paid to the Pope. Then did the vengeance of the king rain down on the monks.

The Pope's council of advisers pleaded with him daily. "The Church can ill afford enemies. The Holy See must befriend every leader of every group from every religious or political persuasion." Impotent to withstand the pressure of their constant urging, Pope Clement commanded an audience with the one man in Rome who was popular, Solomon Molko.

Molko strode down the long corridor of the Vatican Palace. Each side of the stark hall housed a few eager suitors. In fact, most of Europe's fortune seekers now occupied the lobbies of other sovereigns. The Church was too poor to make a man rich. All the chairs and tapestries that had once bedecked the marble chamber were gone. Ugly, gouging scars remained where gems once carbuncled the cornices.

Molko ignored the now-familiar disparaging glares of the other suitors. Inside tall doors protected by Swiss Guardsmen, Molko stepped to the foot of the papal throne, didn't kneel, as bold as brass.

"Greetings, Solomon Molko," the Pope said. Molko nodded acknowledgment, and the Pope continued. "The priests report that your name is on the lips of every Christian and that there is a new enthusiasm in religious observances in the synagogue. These sermons you have preached concerning Judgment Day..."

"The Day of the Lord, Eminence," Molko interrupted.

"Day of the Lord, certainly. Thank you for that correction. Well. Ahem. We have heard reports on these sermons, and, ahem, indeed..." The Pope's words deadened into an unintelligible mumble. When again his words became less slurred, he concluded, "Interesting to say the least. Your pastoral care of the poor and blind Jews has been an inspiration to all citizens of Rome, Solomon Molko."

"I am unable to do less, Holy Father." Molko bowed his head in acknowledgment.

"Yes. Well, as you know, we have learned that on occasion there have been misdeeds perpetrated on the Jews. Let me start by saying that the zeal of agents of the Inquisition has at times..." Again, the Pope's words thickened to a maunder. Then, regathering, straightening in his throne, he said, "And let there be no mistake. Our comments are not intended to be critical. Our confidence in the objectives of the Inquisition is not diluted. The Inquisition can't be blamed for the overzealous actions of a few."

All the members of the court nodded in sequence as the gaze of the Pope turned around the room. "In any event, we have decided that there should be no interference by the Inquisition on your worthy efforts, efforts which...comfort...Gods chosen people, who he has elected to disperse here in Rome."

"Your majesty." Molko swept his right arm high over his head and slowly down across his waist as he bent forward. Smiling, he never allowed his eyes to leave the pontiff.

"So, therefore and hereby, for service to the court of St. Peter, and to the Jewish citizens of the papal states, by these presents"—a papal secretary handed Molko a document—"be it known by all men that Solomon Molko and his followers are exempt to indictment by the Inquisition of the Holy Church of Rome."

Molko bowed again. "Thank you, Eminence."

"Thank you very much for your service, Solomon Molko," said the Pope. His lip twisted his careworn face in disgust just as if had he found dog feces under his slipper.

That evening, David sought to sport with Bilhah. They rolled on a couch and tussled. Her room smelled of crushed rose petals. "Ooh, David, did I tell you?" Bilhah asked. "I saw Solomon Molko yesterday in the market. He is so-ooo handsome. More handsome than ever."

"Forget about him," he told her.

"He was so stylish."

"That son of a whore hasn't heard the last of David Reuveni."

David leaned toward Bilhah, holding a wine bottle in his out-stretched arm, and tipped it forward. Bilhah put her hands under her ample bosom and leaned forward to the lip of the bottle. The wine welled up and pooled in her cleavage.

"I thought you hated the tornadizos," David said. "Let's talk about something else."

David put his face to Bilhah's breast and lapped up the wine. She threw her head back and laughed, then rolled David backward, holding him down.

"He looks so dashing. He was wearing a red knee-length tunic. It was so gallant. He wears tall black boots. You could see your face in them."

"I'm not that short. Could we please just talk about something else?"

Bilhah began tickling him. "And a wide leather belt and a sword. And a turban. Oh, David, he looks so rakish."

"He's standing awfully close to the fire, Bilhah," David said. "I can't stand the smell of burning flesh."

Bilhah was suddenly astride her little admirer. "If you smell flesh burning, its mine. I cannot quit thinking about him. I'm obsessed with him." Bilhah laughed again.

"I've heard enough about him." David remembered how his rage had once manifested itself on Molko's testicles. *I should have castrated the bastard when I had the chance.*

He pushed Bilhah aside. The urgency of his interest in the frolic had waned. Rising from the couch, he dressed silently. Bilhah wept.

He returned to his own lodging. He crawled into his wardrobe and drank more wine, determined to contrive a plan to rid himself of Molko once and for all.

*I wonder what he is hiding.* He could not investigate by himself. Any overture he might make would certainly arouse suspicion. He decided he must engage operatives to attend Molko's meetings, to spy on his organization, then to report back to him. Maybe they could infiltrate his inner circle.

The first reports David received pleased him, revealing that Molko was constantly angry over weak financial support for his ministry. Even with his information, David told his spies, "I'm paying you for more than this. Everyone knows he cannot handle money. He can't control his desires."

The rabbis spoke to David in hushed tones, sharing their own concerns. In the mundane matters of operating the councils and courts that dealt with civil matters between Jews, Molko's followers were increasingly unyielding. Kabbalists only supported Kabbalists, and their beliefs were beginning to influence the Jews in ways that were contrary to the interests of the rabbis. They acted with one will, for the interest of the Kabbalists and against the interests of the rabbis. The orthodox rabbis called them "the cabal," and needed near unanimous support from the conservative Jews to maintain their positions.

Kabbalists taught and recruited every day. Molko suggested that the cabal form a committee to send out patrols, an armed militia, to weed out the thieves and cutpurses in Sant'Angelo, and otherwise subdue crime in the rione. Of course, Molko headed the law enforcement force he organized. Erelong his outreach installed a Kabbalist judge in a Jewish court that settled disputes between the Jews. With Molko's support, promotions made him chief judge of the court that removed children from negligent parents and turned them over to foster homes. The orphans went exclusively to homes that had reverence for occult practices. The cabal sought to wrest control of the synagogue from the rabbis as Roman law did not allow two places of worship for the Jews. The rabbis had no intention of surrendering leadership to Molko.

Soon, David's spies drew a patchy picture of life inside the cabal. Kabbalistic adherents were making amulets and tefillin under Molko's direction. "He treats his disciples like peasants." "He storms up and down all the time." "All of them are afraid of his rages." "He's angry at his disciples if his cup so much as runs dry."

David was gratified but wanted more. "You call yourselves detectives? Uncover something worth my while."

A few weeks later, an urgent knock rousted David from sleep. He crossed the room and one by one freed the four latches securing the entry. Opening the door a crack, he peered through and recognized one of his operatives. "What the hell do you want? It's the middle of the night."

"It's midday. Let me in."

The spy needed a few moments to adjust his eyes to the unlit room, its draped windows turning away the sunlight. An aroma of sweetish wine permeated the air.

"I have something you can sink your teeth into, Prince David. He's telling his followers with whom they can have carnal pleasure." The spy unfolded a convoluted story that revealed how it was that Molko arranged the romantic pairings of his young followers.

"He just made sort of a stirring motion with his finger and said, 'It's the will of the Lord.'"

"It sounds to me like Molko ruined an afternoon's dalliance for you." The darkness concealed the blush on the spy's face. David found his purse and withdrew a couple of florins. "This is more like what I want. Bring me more." He pressed the coins in the hand of the detective.

David sought out a printer and gave him a text that David had scrawled in his own hand. "Print me five hundred copies," he told the printer. "No, a thousand."

The printer looked over the text of the broadsheet. It denounced the ribald nature of Molko's sexual domain. He accused Molko of consorting with prostitutes. To avoid hypocrisy, David said that the profession was "necessary but undesirable." He also alleged that the cabal was working to establish plural marriage.

That night, under mysterious circumstances, the printing press burned to the ground.

The spies returned with more gossip to appease David. His craving for scandal about Molko was insatiable.

"He's having his way with his women followers," one reported as David shelled out more coins. "It makes no difference if they are unmarried or not." An additional coin fell into the spy's hand, who earned another bonus when he reported, "He's having two at a time." And another for "Some of the young men know one another in the

Italian way." He earned a month's pay for reporting, "He binds them in cords. They bind him as well."

Much of what the spies reported was true. Despite that, Molko's cabal had a pact with the Church and his ministry widened. The cabal's income multiplied, its needs grew, and its success opened new doors for Molko's followers in trade and industry. Molko moved into banking. His plan was to accept deposits from the faithful, hold it in common, and lend it out at interest. Lending was risky, but the profits could be substantial. And he had a militia to help hold down crime and collect past-due loans.

"The voice of the great Almighty Lord told me to establish a bank," Molko told his adherents. "Like Aaron's rod, it will swallow up all the other banks and flourish to the ends of the earth and survive when all others shall be laid in ruins."

The opening of the banking house temporarily boosted trade in the rione of Sant'Angelo, but the borrowers had little in the way of collateral to pledge to repayment of their loans. The older Jews contributed less to the bank's capital than anticipated, but the letters of credit and bank notes the bank issued were widely circulated, even those notes that were denominated in sums that exceeded the capital of the bank.

Molko borrowed heavily from the bank to minister to the needy. His prestige was at risk because he was the bank's largest borrower. The threat of a bank failure was palpable; it hung over Molko's head as if it were a sword suspended on a strand of hair.

The smallish amount of treasure in the Kabbalist bank's strongbox would never be able to save the bank from a sudden surge of demands to settle accounts. If the depositors all asked for their money at once, the bank would be swarmed with angry creditors armed with threats and warrants, even a bank as strong as the Banco de' Medici.

Fearing the worst, Molko sent word to the cabal that all believers should default on any obligation to their exiting bankers, who, more likely than not, were either the Banco de' Medici or Samuel Abravanel.

David recorded these things in his diary while sitting at the secretary in his dark parlor. As he poured himself more wine, he contemplated his lies. *Things would have been different if I had stayed in Portugal,* he thought. *Or if I had never have come to Rome in the first place.*

*No one has ever appreciated just how much my story has benefited the Jews. A stubborn, ungrateful, thankless lot. And look at how many of the ninnies are falling under Molko's influence. He is just raping all of them.* He leaned back in his chair. *I never would believe it if I had not seen it with my own eyes.*

# CHAPTER 27

The years had ministered unkindly to Pope Clement VII. His visual aspect mirrored that of the Church. Now sickly and frail, with tired bleary, woebegone eyes, he had broken with the priestly tradition. Now he wore a long, brushy beard that gave him the appearance of a Jewish patriarch. England was lost. The Church was now little more than a vassal state of the Holy Roman Empire. The outlook for improving the Church's position was bleak. The Pope needed to convince the emperor to put down the Lutheran protesters, and at the same time, persuade him to abandon his plans for a general council of all the Church.

The most recent general council had ended just seven months before Martin Luther nailed his ninety-five theses to the door of the Castle Church in Wittenberg. It adopted progressive positions. It permitted the Church to open pawnshops, laid down rules for God to follow on the immortality of the soul, provided that local bishops had to authorize the printing of any book, and levied a tax to fund a final crusade to reclaim the Holy Land from the Turks. All laudable goals to be sure, but another council, one led by the emperor, whose motives the Pope feared, would surely walk back most of those advances and further weaken the Church. The emperor was on record of opposing any tax that benefited the Church.

Often Clement's thoughts slipped away to dwell on better days, seeking the germ of an idea that might return the Church to its former glory. Perhaps he could head off another general council if he could put together another crusade. His mind returned repeatedly to ponder the campaign he had discussed so many years ago with the little dwarf. It must have been an eternity ago. The Pope had never lost his sincere belief in the viability of a holy war, and if he did nothing, he stood to lose the revenue from the war tax.

"What was his name again?" the Pope asked.

"Whose name is that, Eminence?"

"That little man. You know, the Hebrew prince."

"Reuveni, majesty. David Reuveni." The attending priest had answered the same question the day before and on many days before that.

"Yes, yes. Of course, David Reuveni. Tribe of Reuben. This David Reuveni, is he here in Rome?"

A clutch of black-robed priests entered the gate of the rione of Sant'Angelo. The Jewish citizens recognized these hooded clerics as men of high station as lower ranking monks always wore brown. One carried a leather pouch that hung from a strap over his shoulder. Their feet unseen under long robes, the group seemed to float across the crushed rubble pathways that spread like capillaries through the Jewish quarter. Their route led unerringly to the door of the house where Molko and his disciples resided.

"Solomon Molko, come out," one priest shouted, pounding on the door, and soon they stood face to face with the man who would be the Messiah, the erstwhile theater showman who would redeem the Jews from oppression.

The priest with the pouch had a sheaf of documents that, hand over hand, made their way to Molko. Reading the paperwork, he laughed without joy.

"What is it, rabbi?" his assistants asked.

"The Pope wants an audience," he said, and reading further, excitement rose in his voice. "David Reuveni is commanded to attend along with me. He wants to send us together to the court of Emperor Charles..."

"With Reuveni? Never."

"...as emissaries of the Church."

"The little man is against us, master."

Molko was silent. His eyes were afire, darting back and forth. He could not think fast enough. *The Empire. Money. The Empire would advance money, enough money...to put the bank back on its feet! Yes! I can do this.* Molko let out a whoop and then said, "Yes, yes, yes, yes, yes. Ratisbon. As an emissary of the Pope. Thank you Lord God. Praise be to the Lord." He rolled the paperwork, shook it over his head, and danced a jig.

"Is everything all right, master?"

Still dancing, Molko answered, "Better than in my wildest dreams. Has any one of you ever been to the Germanies?"

His disciples shook their heads "no."

"The next time someone asks you that question, you'll have to answer yes. Begin preparing for a long journey."

The disciples stared while their master continued to dance in ecstasy.

David hid in his wardrobe when he saw below, in the street, black-robed couriers give a sheaf of papers to his disciple. He had been drinking wine, watching people from his balcony. The heavy door of the closet muffled Benjamin's voice, but as he listened to the words, he fought back a mordant taste in his mouth.

His stomach heaved when he read the papers. He fought to contain its contents. "Oh, Benjamin. Oh, Benjamin. This is not good."

"Is there something...?"

"Oh, Benjamin. This is dreadful."

"Master?"

"It's the Pope. He wants an audience."

"Wonderful."

"Not wonderful," David said. "Benjamin, the Pope wants a report on the crusade."

"When? How soon?"

"Soon. Too soon." David dropped his head in his hands. He wished the crusade idea would die a natural death.

On the appointed day, David and Molko met in the outer hall of the Vatican Palace. David shunned Molko's warm greeting. He crossed his arms on his chest and stuck out his chin. "I'm going to do anything I can to get out of this, so don't act surprised," David told Molko.

"David, this is my wedding feast. Nothing will keep me from going to Ratisbon," Molko said.

David inhaled shallowly. His brow snarled at his former manservant.

Together, David and Molko strode past the normal crowd of impatient and contemptuous suitors, up the staircase and into the court of St. Peter.

The Pope looked awful to David, his face and eyes sunken. David waited his turn, turban in hand. The little man did not need his mind-reading talents. The Pope's days on earth were numbered. Molko paced.

Oil dripped onto the pontiff's beard. He was eating stewed mushrooms while another supplicant stated his case, a Christian stonecutter, a boyhood friend of the Pope, a well-known Florentine named Michelangelo. It seemed that the Pope needed other grand gestures to punctuate his pontificate, to create a splendid legacy, and David could sense the urgency in his voice. "Just accept the commission," he told the artist. Spearing another oily mushroom on a two-pronged fork, he pleaded, "We are friends."

"I am no longer your friend. Four years ago, you laid siege to Florence, and I had to hide in the tombs that I built for your cousins."

"Let bygones be bygones, old friend," Clement answered. He inserted another mushroom in his mouth. "The wall behind the altar of the Sistine Chapel cries out to be decorated. To complement your frescos on the ceiling. Is that so much to ask?"

Michelangelo resisted, unrolling parchments. "Have you even looked at these?" On rolls of parchment, the obstinate stonecutter had composed a ferocious tableau of terror and anguish that he called "The Last Judgment."

"You'll have to do better. An altarpiece like that would shock decency."

"And what's wrong with it?"

"It's full of nudes."

"I'll accept the commission, but I won't tolerate your interference. I'm not a house painter," he shouted, his voice twisted in exasperation. The stonecutter rolled his parchments and, tucking them under his arm, stormed from the chamber.

A priest took up a station close to Pope Clement and, bowing deeply, announced with august volume, "Holy Father, David Reuveni, prince of the tribe of Reuben, and Solomon Molko, a Jew." Pope Clement cupped a hand behind his ear and strained forward.

David bent with respect. "Greetings, Holy Father," he said.

Molko refused to genuflect. "Praise the Lord, our God! All the days that I have been bound to this world, I have been bound in a single bond with the Blessed Holy One. That is why now his desire is upon me. He and his holy entourage have come to hear, in joy concealed, words and praise for the Holy Ancient One, concealed of all concealed."

The Pope said, "Welcome, Prince David, and welcome to you, Solomon Molko. Come with me. Let's take a walk."

The Pope's head hung stiffly. He stooped forward in discomfort and leaned on a cane. His slippers shuffled across the marble floor, through a door that led from the court to a wide, long terrace. The Pope used this concourse to impress his visitors with the construction work that was underway on and around the Vatican palace. Workers labored everywhere to rebuild structures in the Vatican compound damaged during the sack of Rome. But the skeletal structure of the Cathedral of St. Peter still stood starkly exposed, nothing more than a naked, crumbling frame. The ever-present papal entourage scuffed along behind the Pope and David.

Molko strutted from one end of the porch to the other as if inspecting his dominion. His left hand rested on the haft of his sword. David, beside himself in anxiety, tried to hold his tongue. But he could contain his curiosity no longer. "What is it, Holy Father, that importunes today's command to your humble servants? How can we serve you, Holy Father?" Pain stabbed deep into his back as David bowed low again.

The Pope nodded acknowledgment of David's bow but continued walking forward. "We have eagerly awaited your report on a crusade against the Turks. The Turkish threat is even worse now than before. Again and again have we envisioned this crusade. Discussions engender more discussions. Tell us, Prince Reuveni, where do we stand? How soon can we mount this campaign?"

"Eminence, this enterprise requires a considerable sum of money. And planning. The expedition lacks funds. More time is needed to detail strategies."

"Yes, yes, indeed. But the planning is profitless until we know which kings will join the alliance. Whether Venice will join the alliance. Whether Charles will join."

"But, Eminence, there are certain extremely delicate matters still pending, relating to the supply of weapons from King John of Portugal. And the money. King John's decision on his contribution abides... Well, Eminence, he has his expeditions to India, and Africa, and, and..."

The Pope stopped walking, as did all the entourage. He turned to David, who shivered in his icy glare.

Molko broke in. "It is revealed before the Holy Ancient One that I have not acted for my own honor nor for the honor of my family, but rather so I will not enter his palace in shame. I see that the Blessed Holy One and all these righteous ones approve. I see all of them rejoicing in this, my wedding celebration. All of them are invited, in that world, to my wedding celebration. Happy is my portion."

The Pope listened to Molko, hanging hopefully on every word spoken, expecting some good sense to emerge from his chaos of senseless diatribe. Then turning to David, he said bluntly, "The Church can't wait forever on King John. Portugal is more interested in this slave trade than he is a Holy Crusade against the infidels. And if the emperor doesn't find his rudder, he'll have a Martin Luther in every province of his empire."

The meaning of the pontiff's words were clear to David. *The Pope wants to level Charles's wrath on the Turks.* "The strength of the Turks is great, Holiness," David warned.

"It is our most earnest wish and desire that you fellows, Solomon Molko and David Reuveni, prince of the Tribe of Reuben, would travel to the city of Ratisbon, to the court of Emperor Charles the Fifth. It is also my earnest wish and desire that at Ratisbon, you and Molko offer Charles, emperor of the Holy Roman Empire, an alliance. This alliance would be an alliance of the Church, Portugal, the Holy Roman Empire, and perhaps even Venice. The alliance will be against the Turks."

The Pope turned and continued walking.

"The crusade will be joined in a rear action by King Joseph, king of the tribe of Reuben in Arabia," he went on. "The objective of the alliance is to make war on the filthy infidel Turks, to drive them across the Bosporus and back into Turkey. We will slay them all the way to the gates of Jerusalem, if providence allows!"

"But, your grace," David whined, "after all, Charles..." David rolled his eyes. "This is the same king who sacked Rome a mere five years ago!"

Molko broke in. "You are wise, Eminence, but not with a known wisdom. You understand, Your Grace, but not with known understanding. This just cause will prevail, just by making known your power and strength to human beings, showing them how the world is conducted by justice and compassion, according to human action."

The Pope had no idea what Molko meant, other than that his words spoke in support of the campaign to Ratisbon. "There you have it, David Reuveni. What say you now? Or do you have additional excuses for delay?"

David, now at hazard of raising the Pope's suspicions, measured his remaining options. He had none. He gathered himself to the fullness of his gnomish height and said, "Blessed be the name of God forever and ever, for he alone has all wisdom and power. World events are under his control. He removes kings and sets others on their thrones. He gives wise men their wisdom, and scholars their intelligence. He reveals profound mysteries beyond man's understanding. He knows all hidden things, for he is light, and darkness is no obstacle to him." With his eyes lifted to the heavens, he shouted, "I thank and praise you, O God of my fathers, for you have given me wisdom and glowing health, and now, even this understanding of the Pope's vision, and the comprehension of what it means."

Pope Clement smiled widely when David looked into his eyes. *He does not care a whit if the Turk is defeated or not. He only wants Charles weakened.*

Molko wondered to himself about the days ahead when he would sit on the throne; would he seat David on his right hand or the Pope? "This is the meaning of the verse 'Moses hid his face, for he was in awe.'" Molko said. "Through his experience of awe, Moses attained the hiding of his face, that is, he perceived no independent self. Everything was part of divinity."

David's body froze in abject fear. *What threat is worse,* David asked himself, *Molko's delusional ranting or the Pope seeking vengeance?* David retreated, tugging at Molko's robe, hoping to get the self-proclaimed Messiah to follow.

"We will see to a guard to escort you to Ratisbon," the Pope shouted. His voice sounded almost merry. "Return when you have good news, and Godspeed to you, Solomon Molko and David Reuveni, the Lord be with you."

On the night before the scheduled departure, David sat on the edge of the bed, Bilhah gently snoring beside him. *Powerless.* He could not tell the Jews the truth. He could not tell the Pope the truth. David tried to remember the first lie. Treviso. That is where he said it first. It got him out of trouble, but he would never have gone to Venice had he told the truth. And he would never have gone to Rome. Or Portugal. All the lies had obliged him to go to some other place. Worse than that, it was always a fool who told him where he had to go. *I am like a puppet, and the lies are strings held by fools.*

Without wine, sleep defied David. He would never tell Bilhah the truth. He was afraid, afraid his shame would be too great a burden to bear. *Perhaps it would have better if I disappeared.* Lies had stolen his dreams, his hopes, and his desires. Even his desire for Bilhah.

He slipped silently from the edge of the bed to the floor and collected his robes and turban. The golden locket he had bought for Bilhah was lying on top of a jewelry chest. He put it in his purse. In the moment he closed the latch on Bilhah's door, more than anything, David feared she would wake, she would know his shame, and he would have to tell her goodbye.

David's ankles wobbled as his feet hit the uneven paving stones. He brooded over the folly of this actor, and his body was weak with fatigue.

*Is he so lost in delusion that he forgets the deception? Yes. The swaggering fool has been swallowed up by his role. I know what he would say. Wasn't it God's will that Eve deceive Adam? Jacob deceived Esau* and Laban, Rachel deceived Jacob, and Tamar deceived Judah. God sanctions trickery. God deceives, he mocks us.

And his followers...where is the outrage? His selfishness, his familiarity with the ways of the world. They celebrate in his sin. And his wrongdoings cannot hold a candle to the intrigues of the nobles.

Molko would no more deny Ratisbon than he would sit on a mountaintop to watch his flesh putrefy. Not Molko. No, his role takes him to Ratisbon. In his own deluded mind, he is the man of God, God's warrior, God's sword. Solomon Molko, the Messiah. He is powerless to stay in Rome. And I am trapped in his web.

# CHAPTER 28

A wealthy Jewish liveryman gave David a gentle mare, a saddle, and a rein for the trip to Ratisbon. The emissary loaded a few necessities in a pack, mounted his horse, and departed, wearing his finest robe and a white scarf wrapped around his head. Before him, Benjamin carried the golden flag that David had received from Benvenida so many years ago. A large crowd of Jews followed him on foot. The men sang songs of praise while the women cried tears of grief.

At the gates of the rione of Sant'Angelo, Molko arrived with an even larger entourage. He sat astride a magnificent ash-colored horse, looking splendid in a red turban, tunic, and tall polished leather boots. His sword glistened in the morning sun. His followers sang songs of joy. Before him, Molko carried a flag inscribed with Hebrew characters that meant "Who among the mighty is like unto God?" Molko smiled as if he had never been happier.

The two columns merged without a nod of recognition between the men who would save mankind.

A guard of fifteen Swiss Guardsmen, all in their gaudy uniforms and mounted on horseback, provided David and Molko an escort. At the front of their column, at the tips of their lances, the leading horsemen carried flags, pendants, and banners. As the column of travelers departed Rome on the road to Florence, followers of each spiritual leader strayed behind, shouting songs and prayers.

The first few days of the journey retraced the trip that had brought David from Venice to Rome. The road traveled north from Rome to Florence, then up over the spine of the Apennines and back down to Bologna. From Bologna, a road led away north again to Verona and the wide Po valley. Across the river, the road, still pushing north, began a long climb through the pine-covered Alps, through the Brenner Pass, the ancient Roman roadway rutted by centuries of heavy wagonloads.

At daily intervals, the way wound past tall rock fortifications perched on either side of the narrow passes. *Nowhere to run.* The occupants of the castles exacted stiff tolls from travelers for maintenance and upkeep of the roads, but they told harrowing tales of the bands of marauding thieves just around the next bend. *Swindlers,* David thought. *Everyone has a scheme.*

The pass guided the travelers out of the Italian states and into Austria, higher still into the mountains, and the provincial capital city of Hall. For the first time in years, David dined on sauerkraut in the little hamlet of Innsbruck, where a bridge crossed the Inn River. In Austria, neither he nor Molko slept in the same house as the Christians in their company. Across the mountains, the road led down the north Alpine slope to Munich.

The road followed rivers north to the Kingdom of Bayern. Finally, at the confluence of the Regen and the Danube Rivers, the travelers would arrive at their destination, the city of Ratisbon.

Many Ratisbon merchants frequented the synagogue when they had business in Rome. David knew them all. It was a rich and busy river town with a long history of trade with the Middle East and India. It was the Danube that provided a commercial artery to the merchants of Ratisbon. Downriver to the east and south, the river shouldered heavy loads of iron ingots smelted in Bayern, carrying them to Budapest, Belgrade, and much farther, past Bucharest to the Black Sea. In earlier times, the merchants from the Danube accessed the Mediterranean Sea through the Straits of Bosporus. But now the Turks held a stranglehold on the straits and the city of Constantinople, which the Turks had renamed "Istanbul."

Of importance to the Church, Ratisbon served as the seat of several loose parliamentary bodies of princes, provinces, cities, and strongmen, collectively the formed a legislature known as the Imperial Diet of the Holy Roman Empire. Ratisbon was three weeks of hard overland travel north from Rome.

Bottled up on the Danube, unable to trade, the traders from Ratisbon seethed with anger at the Turks. They longed for the free trading days of their grandfathers, eager to restore profitable exchange with the rich ports of the Middle East and India.

Molko's spirits soared, despite the rigors of the journey.

David worried that Molko had stirred up a death-dealing wind that was carrying him north. His former manservant seemed indifferent to the danger of the mission, so David intrigued for a way to temper his behavior, at least long enough for David to escape. He nudged his mare forward in the column until he was at the front, riding side by side with Molko, who rode in the saddle as if he were posing for a sculpture.

"We should talk."

Molko could contain himself no longer and prattled, "I'm having an epiphany, David."

"What?"

"An epiphany. An epiphany enables one to sense creation not as something completed, but as constantly becoming, evolving, ascending."

David said, "I've heard all I want to hear about epiphanies. Can I discuss something that concerns me?"

"This transports you from a place where there is nothing new to a place where there is nothing old, where everything renews itself, where heaven and earth rejoice as at the moment of Creation."

"Yes. I see. Please, let's talk about something important."

"God contemplated the good deeds of the righteous which were yet to be created, and this act of thinking was enough to actualize the thought."

"Diogo, please."

"It's Solomon, David. Remember, David? My mentor? My teacher? My brother? You crusaded for my conversion. You have forgotten?"

"My greatest transgression." David shook his head from side to side, and paused. "You know, when I look into your eyes, I don't like what I see. Have you ever considered the risk we are taking on this mission?"

"Risk? Look at this magnificent guard we have."

"I was referring to our audience with the emperor."

"Do you know how eagerly I have been anticipating this audience? This journey will bring all of the German Jews to my spiritual leadership. And then Austria, and then Hungary, and then Poland. There are more Jews in Poland than there are Poles. And they are all praying for the Messiah, longing for my coming."

"Spare me."

"You have such an aversion to the truth, David!"

"The only aversion I have is to the smell of my flesh burning. Diogo, I'm afraid for the first time in a long time that I'm standing a little too close to the fire."

"Fear not the flame, David," he said. "Come unto me. You fill my heart with bitter laments. Become one of my disciples. Put aside this concern of your flesh."

David stared at Molko as if he were unhinged. "Maybe when we are in hell, I will let you stand between me and the fire."

Molko coughed up a dull laugh. "Trust me, David."

"Trust you? What do you think you know about this emperor we are going to see?"

"What is there to know?" Molko glared at David and then softened. "All right. What is it I should know about the emperor?"

"He's young. Just over thirty. He's younger than you."

"All right."

"He's been a king for more than half of his life."

"Is that it?"

"No. He cannot read. He can't write." David spoke more quickly. His volume rose. "During Lent, he whips himself until he bleeds," his voice shrilled.

Molko shrugged indifference but seemed now to take a small interest. "I'll admonish him about the whipping. I don't condone that kind of behavior among my disciples."

"His family is crazy. His mother is a lunatic," David shouted at Molko as if he were deaf.

"I will cast out her demons."

"*You're* crazy. This mission is crazy. Something terrible is going to happen to us."

"Now you have the gift of prophecy?" Molko asked.

"That's it. No more. I am not talking to you any more, Diogo, Molko, or whatever your name is. I don't want to talk to someone who is trying to get me killed."

"David, the Lord won't be satisfied if we just redeem the Jews in Rome. Every Jew in Germany is praying to live just long enough to see the Messiah."

"Then they don't need me. And if you had spent a little more time listening to what I had to say, and less time dramatizing—"

"Dramatizing? Listen, David, I have immersed myself in this role, and it is because I have lived a life of holiness that the Lord God created me as Messiah. I can still remember that you told my destiny when we first met. My blood will go unspilled."

In utter frustration, David said, "Just listen, friend. When we get to Ratisbon, think about keeping your mouth shut. Be silent for once. Just because you and a bunch of ignorant Jews—"

"That's fine with me. That is an excellent idea. In fact, I had thought it undignified for me, the Prince of Peace, to hold a council of war. David, did you know *Solomon* means 'Peaceful?'"

David pounded the saddle horn with his fists and yelled obscenities until he was dizzy. Leaning forward to steady himself, he allowed his reins to fall slack. *Stop walking*, his mind said to the mare. She clopped on.

"Peaceful. Prince of Peace. What do you think of that?" Molko asked.

Beyond Munich a day's travel, the entourage arrived at the Regen River, where a ferry raft afforded travelers a safe crossing over the torrent. A rope that spanned the river secured the raft. As the captain of the guard paid the ferryman, the entourage dismounted. Molko and half the column walked their horses onto the wide, flat wooden raft and then tied the reins of the horses to a rail that divided the raft lengthwise. David hung back, preferring to traverse the river alone. Molko stood, gripping the outer rail of the raft facing the opposite shore. He was wide-eyed, a grin brightened his face as the ferry, pulled by a huge draft horse from the other side, floated out across the river.

As his mare drank from the cool, flowing water, David sat on the bank to rest his aching back. "Poor deluded bastard," David said to no one. "He's going to get us killed."

"Who? The Messiah?" The colorful captain of the Swiss Guard stood behind David. "He's here to save us!" The captain laughed heartily at his own biting wit.

*Muttonheads like this captain are easy marks.* David decided to attempt an escape. The woods were deep. He could find a place of refuge. *Perhaps a bribe. It's desperate but worth a try*, David thought.

"He's going to get me killed, and that's what I'm worried about."

"No. They will not kill you. Why, the Jews even say that you are the Messiah. We Christians do not kill Messiahs. We leave that up to the Jews!" The captain laughed, unaccustomed to his own display of mental agility.

"Listen, Captain. I am not the Messiah. I've never told anyone that I was."

"You are telling me that you're not Jesus reborn?"

"No, I am not. Absolutely not."

"You could be right, then."

"I could be right about what?"

"They might kill you." The captain had himself in stitches now.

"Thanks."

"What is your story then, if you're not Messiah?"

"My brother is a king in Arabia who wants to make an alliance with Emperor Charles." Pausing to exchange a meaningful glance with the captain, he added, "My brother is very generous with his friends."

The captain shrugged. "I'd never trust a Jew. So you are wasting your time if you want to bribe me. I would be just as happy to ride into Ratisbon with your head on a pike. So, watch now that you do not drop back. Like you did this morning."

David dropped his head into his hands. He had done it again. He had lied. Not only had he lied again, he had lied to an ignorant goon. An ignorant Christian goon. And for what?

David spoke to the gentle mare and stroked her forehead. *If I get out of this, I am going back to Rome, and Bilhah. I will just live with Bilhah, that is what I will do. I will probably have to tell her the truth. No, I will tell her the truth. She loves me. She will love me in spite of my shame...I hope she will love me in spite of this. Or maybe not. She might not love me anymore. Why would she? We will not be able to afford—What will I do for an income? The speaking in the synagogues, that is over. Maybe I can start juggling again. I will go back to juggling. I will make enough money juggling in Rome to keep a home for Bilhah and me. Then I will never need to lie to another person again.*

David looked down into the purling water, and hoping not to see his own reflection, hid his face. *What am I doing now, he asked himself, lying to a horse?* He knew it was impossible for him to support Bilhah in Rome by juggling. David's sorrowful eyes rose away from the river. Molko and the others had arrived on the opposite bank.

"What a fool," David said aloud. *Diogo has completely deluded himself.*

# CHAPTER 29

Upon arrival in Ratisbon, the band of travelers pushed straightaway to the castle of the emperor. They passed the city's cathedral, its walls decorated with *Judensau* carvings, each more monstrous and grotesque than the last.

Still dusty from the road but armed with letters from the Pope, the two intrepid crusaders marched side by side, heedless of the sinister glare of other suitors. This was the court of the emperor of the Holy Roman Empire, the king of Spain, the king of the Netherlands, Sicily, Sardinia, Burgundy, the man who was considered to be the monarch over half the non-Christian world.

Past the outer court, ushers led David and Molko down a long, splendidly appointed corridor and directly into the court of young Charles the Fifth. A horde of landgraves, margraves, nobles, strongmen, and emissaries flanked the room.

"I'll do the talking," David told Molko.

The emperor's throne stood at the end opposite the entrance. Behind him, and on either side of the court, to the rear of the nobles and emissaries, hung low balconies crowded with stout, decorated courtesans and fancy women. David's eye caught the eye of one of the plump ladies above and behind Emperor Charles. She smiled. David smiled back.

An aide announced, "Your Highness, Emissaries from the Holy See." The vast hall reverberated his declaration.

David stepped forward, intent on making his appearance at the court forgettable. He said, "Oh my Great Lord, unto you I complain of my weakness, of my helplessness, and my lowliness before men. O most merciful of the merciful, you are Lord of the weak. No foe can stand against you. No far off stranger can ill-treat those that seek to serve you. Your Majesty, gracious greetings. I am David Reuveni, the son of King Solomon, may the memory of the righteous be for a blessing, and my brother is King Joseph, who is older than I, and who sits on the throne of his kingdom beyond the wilderness of Arabia. My brother rules over thirty myriads of the tribe of Gad and of the tribe of Reuben and of the half-tribe of Manasseh. I have journeyed from before the king, my brother, his counselors, and his seventy elders. And this is Solomon Molko, whom I attend. He and I are here on an urgent mission at the request of Clement the Seventh, the Holy Father of the Church of Rome." David bowed again, this time too deeply. An unpropitious pain stabbed his back and dropped him to one knee. He struggled to stand again in the presence of the monarch. He reminded himself that his story was flawless.

Molko still declined to bow or to make any show of respect.

"I don't understand, sir," said the Emperor. "Tell us who you are again."

"As I said, your majesty, I am David Reuveni, prince of the Tribe of Reuben, brother of King Joseph of the Tribe of Reuben, one of the twelve tribes of Israel." The plump lady behind the emperor smiled and winked.

David continued, "Solomon Molko and I have traveled, at great peril, Your Majesty, to Ratisbon, to your court, Great Emperor, on a mission to discuss an alliance with the Holy Roman Empire, the Church, Portugal, and possibly Venice, as well. The alliance will be against the Turks. This crusade was authorized, I am told, by the Fifth Lateran Council, and will be joined in a rear action by King

Joseph, king of the tribe of Reuben in Arabia. The objective of the alliance is to make war on the filthy infidel Turks, to drive them back to Turkey—to utterly destroy them. We also have prophecy from the Lord God."

Charles's face twisted quizzically. "I've never heard of this tribe of Reuben. Where does this tribe of Reuben reside? What land does it occupy?"

"Arabia, Your Majesty. Arabia. The tribe of Reuben is a tribe of Israel, Majesty. The people here call Reuben a lost tribe, one of the lost tribes of Israel, Majesty. We occupy the lands beyond the River Sambayton."

"And what is this again about your mission?"

"I am on a diplomatic mission from my brother, King Joseph ibn Reuveni, your Majesty. King Joseph is the King of the Tribe of Reuben. I, a prince of the Tribe of Reuben, have been in consultation with Andrea Gritti, the Doge of Venice. I have conferred with King John of Portugal. And I have given counsel to Pope Clement at the Court of Saint Peter. My mission is to forge an alliance. The Holy Father has sent Solomon Molko and me to engage the Holy Roman Empire in the enterprise."

"Enterprise? What enterprise?"

"Why, a Crusade against the filthy infidel Turks, Your Majesty. What the Holy Father seeks is an alliance of the Church and the Holy Roman Empire. Against the Turks."

"You are a Jew, then..."

"I am a Hebrew, Majesty, but not a Jew. I am a prince of the Tribe of Reuben."

"And you have the gift of prophecy?"

Gathering himself, David held forward both arms. Bending his head down, he closed his eyes and took an acrid draught of air. "Ahem. The Lord God says, 'I am against you, Turk, as I was against the mighty mountain Babylon. I am against you, Turk, destroyer of the earth. You shall be desolate forever. Signal many nations to mobilize for war on the Turk. Appoint a leader. Bring a multitude of horses. Bring against her the armies of the kings and the armies of all the countries they rule. I will bring the Turks like lambs to be slaughtered.'" And noticing the leopard skin robe draped over the emperor's shoulder, David quickly added, "'Slaughtered by a leopard. Heaven and earth shall rejoice, for out of the north shall come destroying armies, pouncing like a leopard on the armies of the Turk.' So says the Lord God."

"Very nice. Very nice indeed. You have pleased us immensely." Charles rubbed his lips and turned to Molko. Noticing his Arab dress, Charles asked him, "What are you? Are you a Mohammadan?"

"I am Solomon Molko, Your Majesty. A Jew."

Charles's eyes twinkled. "More. More. Tell me more."

*Good. The fool is saying nothing.* David scoured the hall, trying to move just his eyes, not his whole head. He was afraid he would tremble if he moved more, afraid that others could see his fear. *I wish I could be invisible.* The plump lady above and behind the emperor was still watching his every move, smiling. He motioned a little wave in her direction, which she returned girlishly, giggling.

"The Holy Father enlisted my assistance, Majesty," Molko was talking. David elbowed him in the hip. "I am here to offer guidance to the Holy Roman Emperor in the composition of this alliance."

"Why you? Why did the Holy Father send you, Jew?"

"Shut up, fool," David whispered. He winked at the nice plump lady, who giggled again, her eyes flickered from behind a fan.

Molko adopted his most theatrical tones. "Majesty, I was born a peasant, a Christian Jew. I was converted to Judaism five years ago, and the Lord's will was revealed to me."

"What was revealed?"

"It was revealed to me that I was the Messiah."

David startled as if he had been shot. He snapped to rigid attention. Involuntarily, he closed his eyes. When he was a child, he thought if he held them shut tightly enough, he also would be unseen.

Disappear. Now he could only wish that the word *"Messiah"* was on a string so he could reel it back into Molko's mouth.

"Messiah, eh? An exalted station for one so low."

"The greater you are, Majesty, the more you need to search for yourself. Your deep soul hides itself from consciousness. So you need to increase aloneness, elevation of thinking, penetration of thought, liberation of mind, until finally your soul reveals itself to you. The light of peace and a fierce boldness manifest in you. The splendor of compassion and the glory of love shine through you. All these band together in your spirit and you become holy."

Charles's expression was blank. "And I become holy. Becoming holy, me. Strange choice of a word, *becoming*."

Molko shrugged.

"What would you think," the emperor asked, "if I told you that news has come to my court that informs me Pope Clement has become dead from eating mushrooms?"

Everyone at court gasped, they knew it must be true. The little man, a messenger from Arabia, from the Pope, from kings, now knew that he was emissary to no one, he had no protector. A great hush gripped the hall.

The silence was shattered when David screamed "Eaaagh!" as the top of his lungs, and shouting, "My lord," threw himself prostrate on the cold stone floor.

"This changes nothing," Molko said. He stuck out his chest and shoved his fists into his hips. The hall was quiet again.

Then Charles raised a nonchalant finger in the direction of the escorts flanking David and Molko. "Guards, we are wearied by these two heretics. Bind them. Have them delivered with all swiftness to the Lord Inquisitor. See that each is given a chance to disavow his story. Particularly, give this Molko fellow every opportunity to disavow his so-called conversion."

Guards grabbed David as others seized Molko. David's heart pounded. A discordant clangor tolled in his ears, hammering his brain with each beat of his heart. Cold, wet flesh blenched on his back. His face burned.

"If they fail to renounce these heresies, burn them at the stake. But if they renounce, show mercy. Have them beheaded."

But Molko was still fully absorbed in his role of Messiah. In his former role, as Diogo, he would have feared the consequence of losing control of events. But as the Messiah, he was confident. The chance to uproot the Jewish people from exile and lead them to Palestine was at hand. With no fear, he spoke to the emperor with indignation. "Majesty! Would you have the Messiah's blood on your hands? Would you desecrate the savior of mankind? I am the Messiah, and this little wretch," gesturing with a tilt of his head to David, "is God's mighty warrior."

Charles, unmoved, shook his head.

Molko struggled against the grip of the men holding his arms but still directed his remarks to the emperor. "Emperor Charles, this is beneath your dignity. I beseech you, Majesty, for David Reuveni, for the sake of this Holy Crusade." Molko gestured toward David. For the first time in his life, he offered an appeal for a fellow man. "Bind my flesh but release this little one, the most noble of God's warriors."

"Away with the little one, guard."

The selfless Molko could not be quieted. "Great Emperor. Majesty. Charles. I implore you. I beg..."

David's eyes searched the room, frantic to discover an escape. A hiding place. A tunnel. He found nothing but the eyes of the plump lady in the balcony, her face horribly wrenched.

"Let us have another moment with the Messiah," the emperor commanded.

Soldiers dragged David, kicking and screaming, toward the door. Suddenly, the chamber was alive with the screech of a cat in heat. It came from the lungs of the pudgy lady on the balcony. Her shrill yowls pierced every ear and seemed to confound Charles. He gestured for the guards holding David to wait and then shouted at

Molko over the shrieks. "Do you repudiate this conversion, heretic?"

With great composure, Molko said, "Your Grace, Your Majesty, there is no question of repudiating my conversion. The real question—"

"Take him away too." Charles turned back, his attention still distracted by the lady in the balcony whose agitation grew ever the more conspicuous. She plopped on the floor, arms and legs flailing akimbo, hazarding the welfare of the blue-blooded ladies situated in her vicinity in the balcony of the emperor's court. Charles said brightly "Come, Mother. Let us see what these nice people have prepared for your dinner."

David had never converted; he had nothing to renounce. Charles did not believe his claim to be a Hebrew prince. And if Charles did not believe, then none of the landgraves, margraves, nobles, strongmen, emissaries or guards at the Imperial court believed either.

The echo of an Inquisitor penetrated into David's dungeon cell. David knew Molko would never deny his entitlement to the mantle of the Messiah.

"Do you repudiate your conversion?" the voice of the Inquisitor asked.

Silence.

"Renounce this claim."

Silence.

"Renounce it."

Silence.

"Renounce."

Nausea pumped in David's gut, and retching, he spun dizzily, crashing his head into the wall, falling agreeably into unconsciousness.

Rustling sounds echoed into David's perception, causing him to awaken. He found himself lying on a soft couch, his back screaming at him in pain. From what must have been an adjoining room, a hesitant voice spoke, "Molko failed to repudiate his conversion, Majesty.

You may be gratified to know, however, that he generously offered to sacrifice himself to save mankind."

"Sacrifice himself to save mankind? Hmmm," said the voice of the emperor. "Perhaps we should reconsider. The Church abhors the spilling of blood." The emperor paused, then said emphatically "Have it recorded that the Crown is tormented by Molko's unselfish offer to redeem mankind. Publish it. I decree that his name be spoken in every corner of my realm."

David sat up and looked around the room. He pinched himself. The moment of silence ended, broken by a burst of laughter from the monarch, followed promptly by loud guffaws from his army of flatterers.

David arose painfully from the couch and stumbled out of the chamber and onto a balcony overlooking a square in the middle of the castle. In the courtyard, surrounded by a crowd of grubby thrill seekers, Molko stood tied to a tall pole in the middle of a pile of firewood. Still in a stupor, and bent over from his afflicted back, David watched transfixed as cowled executioners threw torches into the wood at the foot of the *auto-da-fé*. Diogo's blood would indeed go unspilled.

As flames engulfed the Messiah's body, tears welled up in the corners of David's eyes, jarring him from his trance. He swabbed at his eyes with the tail end of his turban. *What is this?* he asked his damp eyes. *Perhaps a cinder.*

A soft hand seized David by the wrist and led him away from the balcony.

"We will play now," said Joan the Mad, Charles's mother, the plump lady from the balcony of the emperor's court. She was as happy as she could be. Joan tossed a wooden ball across the room, and it crashed into the corridor. "Get it, little man. Go get it now."

David searched her eyes. She returned a stare, vacuous, blank. He was unable to read her thoughts. She was a blank slate. *She is not mad,* David told himself. *She is a complete imbecile.*

His eyes searched the chamber and its furnishings. Dry beds with heavy blankets. A cozy fire. A tray of sausages steamed on a sideboard. His gaze returned to Joan. Joan the Mad...Joan the Redeemer. David had been rescued from a fiery grave by an imbecile.

She was undeniably plump.

*Everything I ever wanted. It is mine. It is mine without shame. I have nothing to fear. They will never make me lie again.* David straightened his posture, as if he had just stepped out of a dark closet, walking away from fear, having chosen dignity and honor. For the first time in years, his back pain was gone. He knew that his crippling infirmity would never punish him again.

Joan's orbs opened wide. Her lips tightened, and she snorted, signaling her impatience. "Go get it now, I said."

Free of pain, David scampered to retrieve the ball.

# ACKNOWLEDGMENTS

This book's purpose is to entertain. The standard of its scholarship is low. I am not a historian. I did not rigorously investigate the events it describes. However, I am happy to acknowledge that I liberally consulted *History of the Reformation of the Sixteenth Century*, by J. H. Merle D'Aubigne, D. D. (1846). In addition, I relied heavily on an article, "Ancient Tactics Tested," by Eric Niderost, for a wonderful and helpful description of the Battle of Marignano, *Jews, God and History*, by Max I. Dimont, (Signet, May 1964), and *Medieval Warfare*, by Terence Wise, (Osprey Publishing Ltd., 1976).

Dennis Maley

www.ingramcontent.com/pod-product-compliance
Lightning Source LLC
Chambersburg PA
CBHW030352120726
47901CB00007B/1996